PRAISE

"I spent the entire 18 years of my life in the U.S. House and Senate attempting to find the answers about what happened to our POWs from WWII, the Cold War, Korea and Viet Nam. I have spoken to witnesses who told me personally, and testified under oath, that they were privy to information regarding POWs being transferred from Viet Nam to the Eastern Bloc and some even sent to Cuba. Although Mr. West has written a fictional account, unfortunately, the plot is based upon truth. Our government knowingly left men to die in the Gulags, and God knows where else, after they fought for their country. *The Thin Wall* is a gripping account which highlights one of the saddest and most disgraceful chapters in American history."

— Senator Bob Smith [R-NH, 1990-2002]

"In a very real sense . . . *The Thin Wall* exposes bits of truth and reality about the suppressed saga of un-repatriated American Prisoners of War (POWs)——ordeals that took place not just in the 1960s, but throughout the 1900s from the end of the Great War well past the end of the Vietnam era."

— William (Chip) Beck
Commander, USNR (retired)
Ex-POW Special Investigator

"*The Thin Wall* is an intelligent, richly atmospheric, character-driven portrayal of the Soviet occupation of Czechoslovakia in 1968, brought to vivid immediacy through the conflict between an intriguingly cultured, yet conniving KGB colonel and the people of a small village who courageously (and sometimes timidly) try to resist oppression."

— Ron Terpening, author of *Cloud Cover*

"Be prepared for a roller coaster ride through a moving, thoughtful story with a credibly surprising ending."

— Ron Argo, author of *The Year of the Monkey*

"In *The Thin Wall*, R. Cyril West raises one of the most important issues of our time——the fate of prisoners of war left behind in enemy hands. This happened in Vietnam, Korea and after World War II when the Soviets took Allied prisoners into the Gulag. Normally this is a depressing tale but West brings it to life."

— Nigel Cawthorne, author of *The Bamboo Cage*

"Using the backdrop of Soviet-occupied Czechoslovakia in 1968, *The Thin Wall* paints a vivid picture of communist tyranny in a local village. It also exposes the clandestine activities of a Russian operative, which gives us insight as to what might've happened to American POWs who never came home."

— Jim Escalle, author of *Unforgotten Hero*

"As the wife of a serviceman who has been listed as Missing In Action since 1968 during the Vietnam War, I have learned just how far our government will go. Even though *The Thin Wall* is fiction, many of the references made to the POW/MIA issue are real: men were moved to Russia, they were detained many years after the Vietnam War and our country denies knowingly leaving any live serviceman behind."

— Barbara Birchim, author of *Is Anybody Listening?*

"*The Thin Wall* is a fictional account that reads as truth and exposes the reality and untold personal agonies of the Cold War. As a child I was safe and ignorant of these realities, an inactive bystander and observer. The media reported the Cold War——*The Thin Wall* lives it. A compelling personal level portrayal revealing not just fear and struggle, but revealing the unreported destinies of American POW's who were never returned home. During a 21-year Army career I became more aware of the non-return of American POW's and learned that what we know to be true and what governments acknowledge to be true are two very different facts——*The Thin Wall* sheds light on these facts."

— Warren Martin, author of *Forgotten Soldiers*
Master Sergeant, US Army Special Forces (retired)

R. CYRIL WEST

THE THIN WALL

MOLON LABE™ BOOKS
Portland, Ore.

Forward written by William (Chip) Beck, and used in this edition with permission.

First Edition, Liberty

West, R. Cyril
The Thin Wall: a novel

ISBN 978-0-9895396-0-9 (acid-free paper)
1. Cold War—fiction 2. POW/MIA—fiction. 3. Conspiracy—fiction. 4. Czechoslovakia: Prague Spring—fiction 5. Politics

Library of Congress Control Number: 2013911323

Printed in the United States of America.
Author's website: www.rcyrilwest.com

In honor of those who served.

In memory of those who never came home.

For families seeking truth.

Czechoslovakia 1918-1993

This map will help readers acquaint themselves with the Socialist Republic of Czechoslovakia, a landlocked country in Central Europe that existed from 1918 to 1993. After World War II, the country was ruled by pro-Moscow communists and was a key member in the Warsaw Pact.

Czechoslovakia's borders served as the frontline between East and West during the period known as the Cold War.

Czechoslovakia was comprised of three regions, each with its own cultural and historical identity: Bohemia, Moravia, and Slovakia. The country dissolved peacefully in 1993, when Bohemia and Moravia united to become the Czech Republic, and Slovakia split away to become the Slovak Republic.

Most of *The Thin Wall* takes place in Bohemia, a region once known as the Kingdom of Bohemia, which thrived from 1198–1918. The village of Mersk, located near the Austrian border, is a fictional setting. Certain geographical markers have been fabricated to enhance the story.

In some instances (for ease of reading) American terms have been used instead of the European equivalence.

CAST OF CHARACTERS

Ayna Sahhat: Cellist in village quartet

Grigori Dal: Soviet KGB colonel

Milan Husak: Physician and war hero

Bedrich: Village idiot

Emil Kepler: Owner of marionette theatre

Evzen: Husband of Verushka

Father Sudek: Priest

Frank Stevens: CIA operative

Irena: Librarian

Jiri Sahhat: Teenage son of Ayna Sahhat

Josef Novak: Village baker

Gurko: Soviet sergeant major

Horbachsky: Ukrainian private in Soviet Army

Mazur: Ukrainian private in Soviet Army

Nadezda Sahhat: Mother of Ayna Sahhat

Oflan Jakubek: Violist in village quartet

Ota Janus: Schoolteacher

Pavel: Mayor's chauffeur

Philip Jagr: Proprietor of music shop in Liben

Potapov: Ukrainian private in Soviet Army

Russell Johnston: American prisoner of war

Sascha Boyd: Violinist in village quartet

Tad Kriz: Violinist in village quartet

Verushka: Wife of Evzen

Zdenek Seifert: Mayor

HISTORICAL FIGURES

Alexander Dubček: First Secretary of the Czech Communist Party (b. 1921-1992)

Bedrich Smetana: Celebrated composer (b. 1824-1884)

Leonid Brezhnev: President of the Soviet Union (b. 1906-1982)

Ludvík Svoboda: President of Czechoslovakia (b. 1895-1979)

FOREWORD

In what seems like only yesterday, but in reality was almost 30 years ago (1984), I helped a *Time Magazine* crew emerge from the tattered ruins of West Beirut, which during the previous night had fallen from Christian government control into the hands of the Muslim Amal and Druze militias. A few weeks later, the *Time* Bureau Chief and I coincidentally sat together flying from Cyprus to London.

During the flight, I mentioned that I wanted to write stories about my six years in the Indochina War (Vietnam, Laos, Cambodia), but I was not sure whether to write fiction or non-fiction. The older and experienced editor, who had excellent instincts and sources, surmised that I was an intelligence officer, but had the courtesy not to press the issue directly. He was a friend of John Le Carré and knew that career spooks had interesting stories to tell, but that they have restrictions on what they can say and how.

His advice to me at the time resonated and stuck with me all these years. "If you write non-fiction," he said, "you can tell the facts. If you write fiction, you can tell the truth."

In a very real sense, that is what R. Cyril West has done with his novel, *The Thin Wall.* The story exposes bits of truth and reality about the suppressed saga of un-repatriated American Prisoners of War (POWs)—ordeals that took place not just in the 1960s, but throughout the 1900s from the end of the Great War well past the end of the Vietnam era.

Scattered among the fictional characters that populate R. Cyril West's story—which covers real historical events of the 1960s that I remembered as a young Naval Officer——are people that I recognize as real types of operatives and knew about from my last years in the Navy as a POW Special Investigator in the mid-1990s.

If anyone doubts that Americans were held long past the end of the separate wars in which they fought, and detained secretly by the Soviets and their allies in a 50-60 year span of the 20th century, then the long-term deception operations by the NKVD, GRU, KGB, and SVR is still alive and working today. From 1918 until at least 1979, approximately nine thousand American Soldiers, Sailors, Marines, and Airmen were transported clandestinely from prison camps of the Murmansk Peninsula, Korea, Europe, and Indochina and buried deep in the Gulag Archipelago along with 35 million other Russians and foreign soldiers.

Sometimes telling the immense story about the nine thousand un-repatriated POWs, as I have done with Congressional Committees, Veterans, POW families, and Rolling Thunder, boggles the minds of ordinary citizens and politicians. Relating what happened to many by the telling of one vulnerable prisoner——Gunnery Sergeant Johnston——as R. Cyril West does, can open eyes to a broader *truth*.

As I write this foreword for my friend Rob, it is Memorial Day, 2013. What readers should remember is that POWs like the one in *The Thin Wall* were active duty U.S. military personnel until the days when they died, forgotten by a grateful nation, abandoned by the military, yet surviving for years, even decades after the conflicts in which they served had ended for their compatriots on the Home Front. To me, these men are the unsung heroes and non-cataloged veterans of the 20th Century. Their individual stories and collective saga has not been adequately told, properly exposed, or duly recognized by any American administration.

As you read *The Thin Wall*, think about that. This may be a work of fiction, but it contains far more than just an element of truth in its telling. To honor these lost heroes, America needs to complete the mission by first accepting the truth about them, then exposing it.

William (Chip) Beck
Commander, USNR (retired)
Arlington, Virginia
27 May 2013

THE THIN WALL

~ Liberty Edition ~

Prologue: Shock

LENIN WAKE UP, BREZHNEV HAS GONE MAD!

God has mercifully ordered that the human brain works slowly;
first the blow, hours afterwards the bruise.

WALTER DE LA MARE

By noon the people of Mersk were in a panic.

Several men with a Czechoslovak flag stumbled from the village tavern and marched down the street. "Russians go home," they shouted, "Hands off Czechoslovakia!" They drank mugs of *Budvar* and threw angry fists in the air. Invasion had come. They had watched it on the tavern's black and white television. Tens of thousands of foreign troops were pouring into their homeland. Tanks. Machine guns. Grenades. Who would have thought it possible? When they reached the flower shop, a drunk, savagely murderous voice cried hoarsely, "Brezhnev is a war criminal!"

At the bus stop in front of the marionette theatre they paused to sing the national anthem with a street musician and his black accordion. It was quite a performance. The accordionist, who was in his seventies, swayed on the heels of his feet and squeezed the lungs of his wheezing instrument without missing a key. And the men, swaying arm in arm, sang high above the red-tiled rooftops with rumbling voices. Their faces were pitched to the sky, rapt in hymn, "And this is that beautiful land, the Czech land, my home . . ." They might have made a fortune that day, but no one was throwing coins.

While they savored their performance, a barista left the coffee house. "Secretary Dubček has been arrested," he said, terror in his voice. "Russian soldiers stormed the Central Committee building and put him in handcuffs."

"Dubček?"

"Along with Comrades Cernik and Kriegel."

Now tears filled their troubled eyes.

A tall fellow with a deep growl reminded them that they had survived the Habsburg rule and the Thousand-Year Reich. They would survive this. "Keep singing, comrades." And they did. This time a patriotic tune from the army.

They kept their heads up and walked on.

They passed a barbershop with its polished mirrors, the historic eight-room inn, and a butcher shop that smelled like sausage.

On this street the two-story row houses were painted in yellows and blues. It was the main road leading into the heart of the village, lined with street lamps and tall birch trees. Someone tossed a warm loaf of bread from an upstairs window. Another person threw a fist and spat, "push them back to Moscow!"

Door by door people joined them, man and woman, old and young, and the impromptu parade gained strength like a slow moving hurricane. Soon the sound of clacking heels had grown to fifty citizens. Yet there were no banners or drums to march to, only handholding and solidarity. By the time the procession reached the marketplace it was white hot with voices declaring their allegiance to President Ludvík Svboda——hero and victim of the Stalinist purges.

In the church, a block away at the square, citizens sat shoulder to shoulder in the summer heat, fanning themselves with prayer sheets and hats. It was 21 August, 1968. There was much to be said this day about the Russians. But who dared speak first? The butcher, the banker, the blind veteran?

From their dropped jaws came a sense of shock, as though a respected member of the neighborhood had been murdered. Maybe this was worse. They had woken up to catastrophic news: hours earlier, at the stroke of midnight, Russian agents had seized Prague's Ruzyne airport and cleared the way for Soviet planes to land. Indeed, everyone was stunned.

"The Kremlin lies," the blind veteran finally said to the white-haired priest. "They promised peace two months ago. Now this." A look of strain and hatred came to his face. He was standing against a stone wall, surrounded by people pouring into the church.

"We have many questions," Father Sudek said calmly, hovering at the pulpit. "I know how you must feel. But have faith. Time has a way of sorting these things out . . ."

The parishioners were restless. They did have many questions. Most went unanswered. They cried out against the Soviet Union, damning Stalin, cursing Brezhnev, and some even blamed members of the Czech government, calling them "collaborators" for what had happened.

AYNA SAHHAT was aware of the fuss. She lived in a narrow row house along the square. On the streets below her window, she saw the drunks with the flag and the angry mob gathered on the cobble. Only twice in her lifetime had the people been this upset: when she was a baby during the German occupation from 1938 to 1945 and ten years ago when vandals desecrated their ancestors at the cemetery.

Now the Russians. *Had they really taken over the airport?*

Ayna was afraid of them. Always had been. The butchers who ran the Soviet Union held a shadowy hand in their lives——a hand that sometimes felt more like a fist. Russian agents lurked in the halls of the Castle, in the press, at the university, on the streets. How many Czechs had they arrested over the years? How many people were sent to the Gulags? How many lives ruined?

Ayna dreaded the answers.

This was all too real.

She zipped up her natty bell-bottom jeans, pulled her hair into a ponytail, and set off.

She left the house, headed toward the square across the street. There was a group of young men and women her age, many of them former high school classmates, huddled near a row of parked cars. They were listening to the grim news from Radio Prague and peering at her through a sheathe of cigarette smoke.

Someone made a joke, "Look, it's Ayna-the-gypsy. Maybe she will save us from the Russian invaders." Some laughed.

She was numb to the familiar jeers. But the memories of their teasing had stayed with her like a clump of mud on her shoe. They knew better. She was not Romani. Or Arabian. Or even Asian. She was a mix of her mother's Czech and her father's Azeri blood. She was, as most people in town agreed, unique. If anything, she was proud of her bloodline. She was a descendant of the 19th century poet Khurshidbanu Natavan, the hereditary princess of Karabakh. In Ayna's mind, this made her a princess, too. Even if it meant a princess without a country.

She stood with her chin up and a strand of black hair falling over her eyes. As they gossiped, calling her a Gypsy, a foreigner, and a terrible musician, her teenage years flashed into her mind and she recalled all the sleepless nights when she had stayed up late reading books on Soviet Azerbaijan, where her father was born. The people were different there, in the *Land of Fire*. She loved them. The local women, like many of the girls standing in front of her, whispered that she belonged in Baku; they insisted she was a child of the East, a Muslim.

She worked up a smile. A child of the East? Was that so wrong? The women were ignorant, she thought. No matter how hard they tried, there was no tearing her apart. She had seen a painting of the princess-poet Natavan. Her grandmother always said she looked just like her. Beautiful.

Ayna made no reply, rather walked away from the childish insults and stepped tentatively toward the church. She felt a vague sense of angst. It was tempting to race home and lock the door. And why not? Her presence was always frowned upon: for being the daughter of a Muslim, and for other reasons, personal matters that she refused to admit were true. Life was much, much safer at home. She took another step toward St. Nepomuk's high double-doors, then started to trot.

If anyone, Father Sudek would have answers. He would know what to do . . .

A crowd blocked the entrance to the church. She pushed past the bodies. "Did you hear the Soviet jets?" she asked the street musician. The MiGs had been roaring in the gray sullen sky all morning long.

"Can you believe what has happened?" Without waiting for an answer, she jostled her way into the two-hundred-year-old building, made the sign of the cross, then skirted along a side aisle, whispering a friendly hello to the veteran as she passed.

All eyes were on Father Sudek. "My friends," he was saying, "the reports on the radio are true. At midnight last night, in an unprovoked act of violence, the army of the Soviet Union invaded our country."

There were mutterings, boos, and hisses.

She pinched her slender frame into a pew next to the brawny Josef Novak.

"We have had decent relations with the Russians for many years," Josef said. His forehead was sweating and there was pastry flour powdered on his muttonchops. "How could this happen?"

"There have been wars since the days of Tiberius and the crucifixion," the priest explained. "War is the evil of man. It's senseless to kill. Why would a man want to harm another man? I can't answer this question. What I do know, is that wars have one thing in common——wars always come to an end."

"Amen," someone said.

"If anything, we must stand for peace."

"Except there are Russian tanks in Prague." Ayna said. "Tanks in Pilsen. Tanks in Ostrava. Tanks in Liberec."

"Unfortunately, this is true."

"And Russian soldiers have taken hold of Wenceslas Square," she added.

Father Sudek clasped his hands piously. "Our mayor is stuck in Prague. He has seen the chaos firsthand. The situation, he says, is 'tense.' A citizen was shot outside of the Central Committee building."

Ayna had a flash of her teenage son. He was still sleeping, unaware of the invasion. She felt her stomach sink. "On the radio, they say our generals refuse to fight the invaders. Is this true?"

"Yes, Ayna."

"But why?"

The priest stepped away from the pulpit. "The president, having the best interest of Czechoslovakia in mind, has ordered the army to stay confined to the barracks. Why, you ask? It's simple. To prevent our troops from being slaughtered."

Sascha Boyd, a student at the university in Prague, stood and pumped a fist. His fiery red hair made him easy to spot in the pews. "Confined to the barracks?" he said. "That sounds more like submission. And submission, for those blind to the reality we face, doesn't pay."

Father Sudek sighed. "We have been overwhelmed. The Soviet Army is joined by soldiers from Poland, Hungary, Bulgaria, and East Germany. It's pointless to fight them."

"Then foreigners simply waltzed into our country," Sascha said. "And to whose melody do they march? Russia's Tchaikovsky? Poland's Chopin? Germany's Strauss? How is this defending the homeland?"

"Technically speaking, Richard Strauss was West German," someone blurted. "Born in Munich."

There were grumblings.

Ayna felt sweat dripping down her chest and fanned herself with a prayer sheet. The mood of the people was getting uglier by the second. With trembling fingers, she moved the strand of hair from her eyes and looked at the bewildered faces: farmers, shopkeepers, the librarian, the locksmith, the barber. Would they stand together? Or bow to the Russians?

"The Kremlin has deceived us," Josef said, banging his fist on the back of the pew. Ayna leaned away and gave him room to vent. "For years they promised peace. 'Comrades and fellow citizens,' they said, 'we swear to guard the interests of the workers. Long live the Democratic Socialist Czechoslovakia.' All lies."

"This is Prague's war," someone bellowed. "Josef, you and Sascha are only asking for trouble."

People shuffled in the pews.

Father Sudek replied, "We must carry on peacefully with our lives. If confronted by the foreign soldiers, turn your cheek the other way.

Humility. This is our best weapon."

"Here. Here." voices concurred.

"In any event," Father Sudek went on, speaking over Sascha's disruption as he exited the church in a fluster, "Mayor Zdenek Seifert assures me the Russian troops can't possibly occupy our land for any significant length of time."

Ayna said, "They have come to squash the reforms. What of free speech? We have worked hard for these liberties. The Russians will take over the press. They will turn it into a machine of lies. Just like the old days."

People murmured with a mix of dread and disbelief. Many worried the government was in shambles. Most nodded eagerly each time the priest called for restraint.

Father Sudek raised a hand. "I promise you, sooner or later the invaders will take their machine guns and go home. We endured Hitler's occupation twenty-five years ago. It was only a matter of time before the Germans retreated with their tails between their legs."

"But those were intolerable years," Josef reminded the priest. "The Nazis were madmen. They forced people into labor camps, into the coal mines, into the tank factories. Before retreating to Berlin, they took our art and burned our fields."

People shook their heads and shuddered with the awful memories.

"Yes, Josef. I remember, too."

The church, with its high-coffered ceiling and stone floor, reverberated with the sound of troubled voices, each person shouting over the next.

Ayna sat with her head buried in her hands, her eyes closed, trying to make sense of their words. The last time she felt this scared was two years ago, when the secret police ransacked the homes of several neighbors and arrested the manager of the cinema house for tax evasion. She had come here for answers, not for bickering among neighbors. She grunted with frustration. The discussion had degenerated into an upheaval between the handful of people who wanted to fight the Russians and the rest of them who were angry but believed it was best not to provoke the soldiers.

Josef placed a comforting hand on her shoulder. "Don't be afraid. You are safe here in the mountains."

"I hope you are right." Ayna's voice wavered with emotion. "Nevertheless, I'm worried for my family. For Jiri."

"Your son will be safe."

"But will the Russians come here?"

"To Mersk? No."

"How can you be certain?"

"Because there's nothing in our harmless village except for this squabbling parish, a few misled communists, and some chickens."

"When you put it like that, it's hard to disagree with you."

"Consider us fortunate."

"Oh, how so?"

"Terror doesn't strike twice. The Germans dealt us a heavy blow during the war. It couldn't possibly happen again." He looked at her calmly. "It's the law of nature."

"I have a sick feeling in my stomach."

"Besides," Josef went on, "we have always been productive citizens. Sow the fields. Sell the goods. Train more workers. Even in my bakery, everything runs like clockwork. What could the Russians possibly want with us?"

First Act: Fear

AND THEY CAME . . .

Fear is pain arising from the anticipation of evil.

ARISTOTLE

Colonel Grigori Dal had left Moscow on a four-engine turboprop AN-12 transport during the first hours of the invasion, landing at the airport in Prague shortly after agents secured the terminal. With four soldiers under his command, including three prison guards from the Ukraine's Odessa Military District and a hardened Russian sergeant, he climbed into a GAZ utility truck and led his team in secrecy out from the city. There was only light traffic as they entered the agricultural countryside. News of tanks in Prague kept most Czechs locked inside their homes.

"I know this country like the back of my hand," he told Sergeant Major Dmitry Gurko, who drove the truck. "After the war, as a newly commissioned officer, I helped lead the effort to expel the ethnic Germans from the rural towns, first putting them in internment camps, later sending them to East Germany."

"It remains among your finest achievements," Gurko said.

"Given the Nazi atrocities, I forced them to walk past the bodies of Jews, victims of starvation at the hands of SS troops. Like many comrades, I was disturbed, then angered by what we found upon liberating this country. I wanted them to see for themselves what the Thousand Year Reich had done."

"For this, and for your medals, you have earned the respect of our men."

An eight-wheeled BTR-60 armored personnel carrier made of welded steel and capable of carrying up to sixteen fully equipped soldiers stuck close behind them. It was occupied by the three Ukrainians, Privates Mazur, Potapov, and Horbachsky. They had been handpicked for the mission, plucked from the prison system, where they were responsible for securing the most notorious inmates in the U.S.S.R., including Brezhnev's sworn enemies.

"The Ukrainian guards hold the key to our success," Dal said gravely. "We must ride them hard in the coming weeks. They are skilled with handling political prisoners and military criminals, but inexperienced with the sensitivities associated with keeping common civilians in order."

"I will be on them," Gurko said. "Like flies on shit."

By sunrise the two military vehicles had exited the main road and driven into an orchard, arriving at an 18th century château at the base of the rugged Drahanska Highlands. It was home to the influential Lugosi family and the doorway to the largest prostitution ring in Central Europe.

Dal looked at his watch: 8:35 a.m. In five minutes the Ukrainian soldiers would fan out and eliminate enemy targets outside the château. He left the truck, walked across the gravel driveway and entered the mansion. A guard wearing a double-breasted suit greeted him at the foyer.

"Get your boss," Dal said impatiently. "We have little time to waste."

After the guard hurried away, Dal grabbed his cigarettes and struck a wooden matchstick. The photographs on the wall made him feel nostalgic. They showcased an impressive Who's Who of Moravian politics since the 1930s: former presidents, Party secretaries, army brass, prominent mayors, and ministers. The family ties to Czech communist officials ran deep.

Yet many photos were recent additions to the wall and unfamiliar to him. He rubbed the back of his neck. What had happened to the photographs of the brave men who once stood side by side with Joseph Stalin? Much had changed since the death of his friend Ernst Lugosi, the family patriarch who had succumbed to cancer over the winter. The heroic wartime images of the old man had been taken down and replaced by assorted snapshots of his oldest son, Andres Lugosi, the so-called "boss" and new Moravian crime czar.

Pathetic, he thought. The photos showed boys, not men, wearing expensive designer clothes, a collection of their fast German sports cars, and wild parties fueled by decadence and drug abuse. The 1960s had ushered in too much social change in the Western countries——changes creeping closer and closer to home. The photographs spoke of a spoiled rock & roll generation, of a youth movement lacking respect.

"Ah, look at this," he whispered, shaking his head at a staged photo-op between Andres Lugosi and the German Socialist Unity secretary. Dal dropped his cigarette butt onto the plush carpeting and ground it with his boot. The photo was a complete mockery, meant to impress, to somehow solidify the young Lugosi's sudden rise to the family helm.

He heard the door handle click and glanced over his shoulder. Sergeant Gurko stepped into the foyer with an army duffel bag slung over his shoulder. "The men are on the move," Gurko said. "The perimeter will be secured in a matter of minutes."

Dal nodded. "They will enjoy shooting the new PB pistols. Their silencers are an assassin's best friend."

"They spoke fondly of the weapons."

"From what I understand, a skilled shooter can get off thirty rounds a minute with a PB."

"Impressive. However they won't need that many bullets. The château is weakly defended."

"Excellent."

"But there is an unforeseen twist."

"What do you mean?"

"Lugosi's guards are mostly teenage boys."

"Teenagers?" Dal asked with surprise.

"Sixteen years old."

"Hmm."

"Seventeen at most."

"Hmm."

"While I was pissing in the garden," Gurko explained, "I saw them. They were smoking cigarettes near the garage. You'd be hardpressed to find an ounce of discipline among them."

Dal had made secret arrangements with the local police to have most of Lugosi's security team arrested in the days leading up to the invasion, leaving only a handful of guards to protect the grounds. He had no idea teenagers would be involved in the day's mess and felt somewhat remorseful. "Easy pickings," he said, thinking *what must be done, must be done.* "Anyway, comrade, you didn't piss on the roses in the garden, did you?"

"The roses? No. Why do you ask?"

"Because I helped Ernst Lugosi plant those rose bushes many years ago. They are Galicia, a species of rose first cultivated by the Greeks after the Battle of Corinth in 146 BC. I have always appreciated the ancients for their accomplishments, particularly in the arts. Those stunning roses are dear to my heart. Before we leave the château, I want to snap a few photographs to show my wife."

"I assure you, comrade colonel, I didn't urinate on the roses."

The Moravian guard returned and interrupted their conversation. "Andres Lugosi has finished his swim," he said. "He is ready to make the deal with you for the prisoner of war."

"Excellent." Dal cracked his knuckles. "Then the rumor is true, you have our *man*?"

"Yes. We have him. We have the American."

The guard led them down a grand hallway, past a series of Habsburg busts and baroque paintings, to an indoor pool room that reeked of chlorine. He motioned for them to enter, then stood with a taunting stance at the door, his jacket open to expose the CZ-52 pistol at his hip.

"Security is lax," Dal told Gurko. "The elder Lugosi must be turning over in his grave." The loaded Makarov pistol in his chest holster felt snug against his rapidly beating heart. The guard had overlooked a pat down. Then again, he supposed they had some rationale for trust. He was like an uncle to Andres Lugosi.

"As you say, 'easy pickings.'"

They proceeded along the rectangular pool. Plastic cups, a beach ball, and a woman's bra floated in the shallow end of the water. A

Silesian groundskeeper was straining the debris with a net. A master gardener, Dal appreciated how the Silesian had cared for the rose bushes along the exterior of the château for the last ten years.

"There was a party last night," Gurko said, pointing to a cluster of vomit chunks in the water. "I imagine a party with many pretty women."

"Shame we were not invited. I love a party."

"Me too. Especially a party with hookers."

Dal gazed out the wall of French windows. A series of red brick steps led to a lush lawn, flower beds, and a Japanese fish pond. He recalled his last visit with Ernst Lugosi, after the cancer had been diagnosed, and remembered how they had discussed caring for the prized koi. It was his dying wish that his sons care for the fish after he passed.

"Well, well, well, look who's here . . ." Andres Lugosi's voice shot into his head with a jolt. Dal looked over his shoulder and watched Lugosi enter the pool room with three thugs, each armed with a World War II-era Mosin-Nagant carbine. "You must be wondering what happened to the fish?"

"The koi are gone?"

"Dead . . ." Lugosi declared, plopping his bony frame in a rattan chair, then depositing a briefcase on the table next to him. He was a gaunt man, thinned by a nagging heroin addiction, with greased hair swept back over his ears. "The fish were annoying. Always wanting more food. Always demanding more and more of my time."

"How unfortunate," Dal sneered. "Concerning the koi, your father had hoped—"

"To hell with my father. And his damn fish. Like a woman, the little fish bastards could never be satisfied."

Dal attempted to meet Lugosi eye to eye, but the young crime boss was intimidated and glanced at the floor. "Speaking of women, how is your lovely mother?"

"She is at the spa in Romania."

"Ah, the spa is a relaxing place this time of year . . ." Dal pulled off his gloves, finger by finger. "May she be blessed with good health.

To this day she is the loveliest woman I have ever seen in a wedding gown. Now then, Andres, let's stop pretending we like each other. We have business to discuss. I have a busy schedule to keep." He nodded at Gurko to proceed.

Stepping forward, the stocky sergeant placed the duffel bag on the table and unzipped it, revealing forty bricks of heroin. "Direct from Turkey," Gurko said. "Made by the hardworking peasants of the Afyon-Karahisar Province."

"We have kept our part of the arrangement," Dal injected, lighting a cigarette. "With more drugs to come. How about you?"

Lugosi reached into the briefcase, pulled out a brown manila folder, and dropped the file onto the table. "As promised, here are the documents——the Devil Dog dossier."

The KGB had been in pursuit of the sensitive documents for nearly two years. The CIA, too. The paper trail was proof that a grave injustice had been committed against the Americans. The pages, nearly two-hundred of them, identified nine United States Marines who had been captured in Vietnam, and detailed how they were interrogated by Soviet GRU agents, then smuggled out of Indochina. The Kremlin, of course, denied accusations from U.S. senators that the Soviets were embedded with the Viet Cong, sending them weapons, helping them detain prisoners, conducting interrogations. *They are lies,* the Soviet foreign minister told the press. *We are not involved in the American conflict.*

Only a handful in Moscow knew the truth: that the POW's were secretly extracted from North Vietnam, taken to an airport in Laos, flown to Prague, and ultimately sent to Siberia via the railroad. The files identified everyone who had been involved in the scandal since June 1966, when the first Marine was captured. The dossier should have been destroyed long ago, but the carelessness of the progressive Czechoslovak Communist Party and its blatant defiance of Premier Brezhnev ensured their existence in a Prague vault, where secrets thrived. The KGB, taking advantage of the midnight invasion, had simply moved to clean up the mess left behind by Soviet military intelligence.

"Recovering the dossier is impressive work," Dal said with harsh eyes. He flipped through the pages of information on the POWs: names, ranks, abduction dates, internment areas. All shamelessly documented with official government seals and signatures.

Lugosi said, "The documents show that the Devil Dog Marines were sent to labor camps, where Soviet Army doctors performed mind control experiments on them."

"Research," Dal corrected him. "Scientific investigation in the name of the people. For the good of all."

"The people? No. This is a serious violation of the Geneva Convention. I should've demanded more than a bag full of schmeck."

Lugosi's cocky attitude annoyed Dal. "Speaking of which, where is he? Where is the American POW? There is no deal without him."

"Relax, comrade." Lugosi snapped his fingers. "We negotiated for his release in the nick of time. Moments before your army crossed the border."

A minute later, a guard escorted a shirtless carrot top in fatigue trousers into the pool room. The Marine——Dal knew his name was Russell Edward Johnston, from Houston——had a scraggly beard and his ribs protruded grotesquely from his skin. Memories of the Holocaust returned to Dal's mind; the American's skeletal condition reminded him of the Jews he had helped to liberate in Terezín.

"And yet, you have abused him," Dal said with disappointment, looking at the POW's black eye and the cigarette burns on his arm. "Considering everything he has been through in recent months, why?"

"Entertainment." Lugosi grinned. "Hollywood style. You know, like in the American movies. John Wayne. Steve McQueen. Humphrey Bogart. My party guests had never seen a man beaten in real life. Hell, he is only a Yankee. Do you want the bastard or not?"

Dal was furious. Then again, what did he expect from the foolhardy Lugosi? "The Kremlin will be pleased by your effort," he lied, biting his lip.

Eight of the nine Marines were officially accounted for. Their bodies had been disposed of in unmarked graves across Siberia. Only Gunnery Sergeant Johnston remained alive. He was the last of the cohort, living proof of the abductions. After a final scan, Dal handed the dossier to Gurko.

"I have read the dossier," Lugosi said. "It's damming evidence."

"Oh?"

"Johnston was captured last year in Vietnam."

"Tell me. What do you know?"

"Like many American prisoners, the Viet Cong kept him in a bamboo cage, moving him from camp to camp, hiding him from his rescuers. Then came you Soviets. The interrogations. The long trip by foot to Laos. After he arrived in Prague, with orders to send him to Moscow, the army instead imprisoned him in the D Complex south of the city."

"Impressive. You have done your homework."

"International kidnapping is big money these days. American Marines demand top dollar. Where can I get more?"

"I have no idea," Dal said, annoyed with Lugosi's sarcasm. "I am only the KGB bone collector. What do I know of kidnappings?"

Dal knew that thousands of American servicemen were taken from German prisoner of war camps after World War II and sent to the Soviet Union. Many of them with Russian, Ukrainian, and Jewish names were still alive in the Gulags. There were also military personnel captured from Korea. But none of this was any of Lugosi's business.

A guard moved near Gurko and peeked at the heroin inside the duffel bag before pacing along the pool.

Lugosi said, "You should be careful in Moravia. The secret police have been asking questions. Once you leave the château, I consider our business done. I won't bail you out of any trouble."

Dal's eyebrows shot up. "I am in a very dangerous profession, comrade. Heartbreaking, at times. In fact four of my closest colleagues have been assassinated in recent years. They were seasoned veterans. And good family men. It was unfortunate for their careers to have ended so tragically. Anyway, I assure you, we will be careful to avoid the secret police." Dal looked directly into Lugosi's eyes. "Careful even in our dealings with a miniscule crime boss like you." As though reaching coolly in his jacket for a cigarette, he pulled the Makarov pistol from the holster and pumped a bullet into Lugosi's heart. It had been years since he killed and was amazed at how easy it was to pull the trigger. But firing at close range made the job messy and blood splattered on his hand, staining his wedding ring.

The next moments were a blur.

A guard near the door fumbled with his handgun when the Ukrainian soldiers stormed inside the pool room. The rapid gunfire caught the daydreaming thugs by surprise and the soldiers gunned them down in a matter of seconds. Their bodies were thrown into the pool, along with the Silesian groundskeeper, who had been forced to his knees and shot execution style.

"Put the American POW in the troop carrier," Dal said. "Time to move. This place will soon be swarming with the police. Nevertheless, I need ten minutes. I must snap some photos of the rose garden. I have spoken fondly of the flowers over the years. It will make my wife happy to see how they have flourished."

By 1:00 p.m., Lugosi's assassination was little more than a footnote in Moravian history. They were on the highway, heading west. Dal had paid a heavy bribe to the local police chief, asking for time, time to make the kill, time to disappear before the police cars showed up. Now driving on the road, he worked diligently to clean the specks of dried blood from beneath his fingernails.

Even with the day's success and with the clean getaway, he felt troubled. The groundskeeper's execution, he thought with a pang of regret. Had it been necessary? His wife would disapprove. Violence turned her stomach. It was why he kept secrets from the woman. But the groundskeeper's death was inescapable. He had witnessed the shootings; he had overheard the conversation concerning the POW; and he would have reported on them.

Dal embraced his decision. He learned long ago that masking his emotions only led to pent-up grief, which ultimately opened the door to hesitation and second-guessing——both toxins of his profession. Unlike most of his colleagues at the Lubyanka, he never pretended that killing innocent civilians was an acceptable practice; rather, it was a necessary evil, a harsh reality of his dangerous line of work. He believed it was important to distinguish the difference between *acceptable* and *necessary*. One word was a term used by savages, the other by professionals. He grieved inwardly, and within the hour had moved on, never thinking of the groundskeeper's death again.

Poor Czechoslovakia.

It had been a day of national tragedy. At last report, over 100,000 foreign soldiers occupied the country, with more troops pouring in. At least very few Czechs had been killed, Ayna thought, remaining hopeful for a peaceful outcome. She slipped off her clogs and put them in the bedroom closet. Most of the townspeople in Mersk were glued to their radios. A few, like Evzen, leaned out the window every half-hour and shouted to people on the street, "The hospital in Frantisek reports four dead today" and "The Academy of Sciences is occupied."

While her mother and Jiri slept, Ayna picked up a transistor radio from the dresser and tuned the dial, searching for her favorite music station. She needed music. During the day, she listened mostly to rock & roll, to Czech bands, and sometimes to British bands. She loved feeling the steady bang of drums, and electric guitars, and voices shouting out against oppression. The energetic pulse of a rock band was thrilling and often freed her mind from undue stress. At night, before going to sleep, she preferred the soothing sounds of classical music. The classics touched her soul.

But where was the music tonight?

Gone. She only found news on the radio. Grim. Depressing. Awful news. The music had been stolen from the people with the rage of a Russian grenade. An angry DJ was yelling into a microphone, *more protests in the cities, more shootings on the streets, more arrests in the government halls.*

She switched off the radio and buried it in a drawer.

She shuddered. Reports of students clashing with soldiers in Prague ushered back memories of her grade school years. That time long ago when she had fallen asleep with a wad of chewing gum in her mouth, only to wake up in horror and discover her bangs were in a sticky mess. Rather than using olive oil to thin away the gum, her mother grabbed scissors and simply lopped off the bangs.

Then came the taunting. *You look like a boy*, and *You're the ugliest girl in Mersk*, and *Gypsy*.

Even at twenty-eight-years-old, it was impossible to escape the cruel voices of her childhood, the years of political indoctrination when she pretended to read and love Karl Marx. The blonde schoolgirls had ridiculed her for many things: her Muslim roots, her Asian-looking black hair, her Persian-looking thick eyebrows.

Ayna stood at the bedroom mirror and undid her ponytail, letting the hair fall over her face. *What has happened to you?* She leaned into her pale reflection. Her eyes were puffy and when she looked again, she saw dark rings. After going into the bathroom and washing her face with a warm washcloth, she felt a little better.

Nearly 24 hours had elapsed since the midnight invasion and she was unable to pull herself together. Her grief ran deep. Beyond the threat of Russian tanks. Or fearing for Jiri's safety. It was also the stillness of the house. The subtle creaking of wood that reminded her how she longed for something more, something always out of reach. In fact her life felt incomplete. She was lonely in the mountains. More than anything, she wanted to be around modern people. People who went to trendy cafés and appreciated the arts. People who read literature that did not glorify the socialist state.

Was it asking too much?

Probably.

She owned five Italian marionettes: a king, a queen, a court jester, and two peasants. The wooden characters had been crafted in the 18th century by an artist in Milan. They were a gift from her grandfather, the famed Bohemian manipulator who had built the local marionette theatre during his lifetime. If she sold them, she could afford a few months in Prague. Until the invasion put things on hold, she had been planning to do just that, taking Jiri to bunk with a friend who lived near the opera house. No one in particular would care if she left Mersk.

She heard an outcry on the street and went to the open window. Men were stumbling from the café, the cheapest place to buy a beer on a Tuesday night. They were arguing again, unable to decide who was worse, the Germans or the Russians? It was the angriest they had sounded since the Warsaw Pact tanks crossed the border.

"Keep quiet," she hollered. "Some of us are trying to sleep."

"Join us," the jeweler shouted back. "Brothers. Sisters. Join us. This protest is for our freedom."

The men were mad at the local communists for raising their taxes. They were irate at the politicians in Prague for collectivizing the farms. They called the generals *cowards* for hiding in the barracks. Eventually a scuffle broke out and someone tossed a chair through the café's window.

"Now you've done it," she said. The shattering window prompted lights to turn on inside homes along the street. "You've woken up the entire village."

Faces gazed up to her bedroom window with hungry eyes, undressing her for god knows what, the millionth time?

"We're raising an army," the butcher said. "We're going to fight the Russians."

The banker shook his finger. "You should be protesting, young woman, not sleeping. How can you close your eyes at a time like this?"

The revelers stood arm in arm, many of them disenchanted communists, ashamed they had been duped by the false promises of the 1950s, shouting, "Death to the Soviets" and "Long live Czechoslovakia."

She paused, considering the invitation to join them, the absurdity of it all. Their courageous words were meaningless. Love for country? They meant well, but were drunk to the reality: the Russians had machine guns, the people had pitchforks.

Ayna slipped on a sleeping gown and climbed into bed. She pulled a patchwork blanket over her shoulders and rested her head on the pillow. Close your eyes and forget the hatred. *You're safe here.*

The bedroom was her sanctuary: grandmother's rocking chair, the feather pillows, the Italian marionettes, a prized Rogeri cello, the sheet music scattered across the floor.

She was imagining her fingers on the long neck of her cello, working the *First String Quartet From My Life*, when she dreamed of the handsome face of her ex-fiancé Peter Lanik. Peter had been a paratrooper in the army. His rebellious panache and love for the arts always lit up her face. Once, she had been told, he defied the army sergeants by jumping from an airplane while reading poetry and drinking wine from a canteen. He got ninety days in a military prison for that. His sudden death in a car accident last year had sent her into a tailspin.

She rolled into the pillow and closed her eyes. She pictured dancing with Peter in a grassy field and imagined romantic music, *The Swan Lake Ballet*. She missed him.

Before falling asleep, with the last of the patriotic drunks fading into the shadow of the night, a solitary voice cried out, "If the Russians come to Mersk, we will kill them."

The GAZ truck weaved in and out of traffic, slowing for a disabled tank and the congestion near Stranecka Zhor. "How many have you assassinated?" Gurko asked, steering in the rain.

"With the death of Andres Lugosi," Dal replied after some reflection, "three."

"Three? I might've guessed many, many more."

"I have never had much need for killing." Dal gazed blankly out the passenger window. A whirl of smoke blasted from the tank's engine. "Of course, the body count was high during the Great Patriotic War. Since then, I have been content with letting other men pull the trigger. How about you?"

"In the army's interrogation unit, I must admit to dozens," Gurko confessed, acne scars stretching across his grinning face. "Dozens killed."

"May your ghosts haunt you. I, on the other hand, have a clear conscience."

Gurko snorted. "You have received the Gold Star for an act of heroism at Stalingrad . . . the Order of Aleksandr Nevskiy for courage in defense of the Motherland . . . yet you downplay your achievements and choose to play the part of the commonplace man."

"It's true," Dal said. "Had things turned out differently for me, I could have lived my life as a peasant farmer. Perfectly content with my role in society."

"I doubt that."

"Bah." Dal dismissed the sergeant's comments with a wave of his hand. "Drive, comrade. You make me nervous when your eyes are not on the road."

Now that he had recovered the Devil Dog dossier, Dal planned to protect it for a minimum of four weeks——long enough for a purge at the Lubyanka and for agents to eliminate those closest to the heart of the crime. Until the dossier could be returned to Moscow, the documents were safe in his possession.

"The KGB has a remarkable fascination with safeguarding some of its more outlandish secrets," Dal said. "Do you know we have Hitler's teeth stored away in a concrete vault?"

"His teeth?"

"And part of his skull where the bullet pierced. It's true. I have seen the Führer's burnt remains in person. They were found outside his command bunker, along with Eva Braun's, then quietly flown to Moscow."

"I have heard this rumor."

"It's no rumor."

"I believe you."

"Ah, we KGB romantics hold onto our accomplishments as though they are sacred trophies, so we can boast amongst our comrades, 'Here is more proof of Soviet superiority.'"

"You question our superiority?"

"No. I am only making conversation, comrade."

"Good. You had me concerned for a moment."

Dal knew how KGB egos worked. Devil Dog would become a showpiece. A privileged few would flaunt the documents as proof of what the Soviet Union was capable of accomplishing against the imperialists. He dismissed this type of bravado. Once he handed the dossier over to agents in Prague, it would cease to be of any interest to him.

"The next few weeks will be the most crucial," Dal went on. "Keeping the American prisoner of war behind closed doors, out of public view, will not be easy. We cannot allow the police an opportunity to catch wind of him. In the wrong hands, Russell Johnston could give testimony of what happened during the last eighteen months. He could point out the faces of his captors, and possibly remember names. If somehow he could escape and make his way back to the West. I shudder to think . . ."

"The American will be guarded with vigilance, both night and day," Gurko insisted. "I've been stern with our men——in particular with the muscular Private Mazur. I've promised him voluptuous women and vodka for the American's security over the coming weeks."

"And Private Potapov?"

"He is very disciplined."

"What about Horbachsky?"

"He is lazy. But I will keep my eye on him."

"Excellent. I am depending on your management skills. I will have many distractions in the coming weeks. I do not have time to supervise the Ukrainians."

"I assure you, comrade colonel. It's impossible for anything to go wrong. Most of all, impossible for the prisoner to escape."

Dal leaned back in his seat. He was tired of talking, yet unable to sleep. He looked out the window. The road to Bohemia snaked along the Vah River, through the fertile lowland until it rose into the Bohemian-Moravian heights, where it reached a plateau. Along the way, they passed through successive checkpoints and around Russian tanks with identifying white stripes on their armor. They drove in the rain, in darkness. Silence was good company for the better part of the night.

The drive gave him time to think. What had he gotten himself into? How would this end? He was overcome by shame. He had betrayed the Soviet Union. The Kremlin had ordered him to take Johnston into the Moravian Forest and execute him. *Bury the Marine in an unmarked grave far from the nearest public road*, his chief had said. However a splinter group in the Lubyanka had recruited him with an alternate plan——*foolproof*, they insisted.

"When this is done," Dal said, "we will be rewarded handsomely for our part in smuggling the American to East Germany."

"I'm looking forward to the big payoff."

"What will you do with your share of the money?"

"I will get drunk and spend it on the prettiest hookers in Moscow."

Dal reached for his filterless Belomorkanal cigarettes. The Russian smokes were brawny, the strongest available in Eastern Europe. He caught a glimpse of the sergeant's tired eyes in the headlights of an oncoming car. Like him, the man was committed to this mission, which ultimately would send the POW to Cuba——a prized trophy for Castro.

A few moments passed, and he wondered: why did you get involved in this mess?

For financial gains, he reminded himself. For the betterment of his family. It was worth the risk. *Foolproof, remember?*

Ayna had fond memories of the boarded-up cinema house. It was where she had gone on her first date, had her first kiss, saw her first tearjerker, and taken Jiri to countless children's films. Sadly, the theatre had not shown a film for several years; not since the manager went to jail for tax evasion. Another good reason, she believed, for moving to Prague. She was looking at a faded movie poster, the war film *Diamonds of the Night*, when a roar of jets in the sky made her skin crawl.

"Those are MiG-21s," Jiri said, pointing at the airplanes. "The supersonic Mikoyan-Gurevich."

"Mikoyan who?" Ayna asked.

"Gurevich."

"Russian?"

"Yes. And fast as lightning."

Her thirteen-year-old son's knowledge of the Soviet Air Force was disturbing. He should be focused on mathematics, not war. "Where did you learn about the Russian airplanes?"

"I've seen photographs in the magazines at school."

Ayna shielded her eyes from the morning sun and searched for the aircraft. Three long white vapor lines stretched across the heavens. But where were the MiGs? Perhaps they were too fast for her eyes. Or flying too high. Or had some magical shield that made them invisible. The planes flew over the valley twice a day, climbing to incredible heights like rockets launched toward the moon. The jeweler had mentioned it was how the sky might look during a nuclear war, except with dozens more contrails and missiles instead of jets soaring in the atmosphere. It was a creepy and horrifying conversation. Russians. Americans. Missiles. Warheads. The fear of nuclear war was always on her mind.

"There's too much violence in the world," Ayna said. "People are cruel and vicious——especially the Russians."

"Didn't the Russians liberate us from the Nazis?"

"Maybe so. But that's beside the point."

She felt her heart sink. Jiri was growing fast these days, two inches since Christmas. His questions to her questions, and his misinformed opinions about many topics, drove her nuts. There were times during Jiri's formative years when she wished she'd had a husband. The boy needed a father figure. Especially now. Against her protest, he had shaved his head and was spending more and more time playing football on the streets. To make matters worse, he was chumming with older boys who smoked cigarettes and ditched school.

She grabbed his arm and hurried him past several women dressed in head scarves and dirty work boots. They threw her a stern look of disapproval, an unspoken remark, *You're a terrible influence on the sons in the village.* Many of the sons these women alluded to——some were married men——had attempted to get her in bed, and failed. In retaliation, they spread rumors that she was promiscuous and had slept with the entire presidium. Obvious lies, she thought, squeezing Jiri's hand. Lies that somehow survived to this day. Ironically, it was their daughters who were sleeping around, going to nearby towns and getting drunk with the local boys, and having abortions. Not her.

She and Jiri passed a row of houses, the town hall, a flower shop, and the bakery. The café, where the night revelers had drunk themselves into oblivion, had a boarded-up window, though was opening for business.

They turned a corner. They passed what used to be the village toy store, now an empty space seeking a renter. At the street level, there was an inescapable gloom in Mersk. Many of the buildings were vacant, reminders of harsh times that began a decade ago. To compensate for the doldrums, Mayor Zdenek Seifert had instituted a policy of painting the storefronts. He had insisted that shopkeepers maintain flower baskets on street corners. This created a façade that times were improving. He had even made arrangements for oompah bands to play in the square on Friday nights, although few young people showed up.

While Ayna loathed her backwoods community, calling it *feudal* and *unenlightened*, it broke her heart seeing families struggle to pay the bills. Most of the citizens meant well, regardless of their pessimistic outlook on life. They deserved some sort of happiness. If nothing else, she wanted Jiri to live a joyful life, to get an education, to attend the university. But what kind of future was there for anyone in Mersk? *Not much.*

People, many of them her former school mates, had left in recent years. The desperate ones. Jumping on buses. Hitching rides. Whatever it took to get away. Many fled in search for work at the coal mines in Moravia. The Ministry of Labour had made promises to them, better pay, better housing, and better vodka. But mining, she cautioned Jiri, was a terrible way of life. Now and then a former citizen would come home, often very ill and with a cough, having lost body weight, and, importantly, a zest for life. Then some never came home at all. She had overheard the mayor and several Party members mention an ore called uranium, though never asked why it was dangerous to humans. She always believed men were better served by staying in the army, not picking rocks in a dark cave. Sure, the pay was good, but the risks too high. No family had ever gained any substantial wealth or status by committing to the mining industry.

Ayna stopped at the ice cream parlor door and said, "Tell me what your teachers are saying about the Soviet occupation."

"Nothing much . . ."

"They must say something?"

"Well, to start with, they don't call it an occupation."

"Oh? What do they call it?"

"A 'liberation,'" he said. "The teachers say our good politicians invited the Soviet and Warsaw Pact armies here to help fight the bad politicians." Jiri frowned, insecure. "Mama, why are you asking so many questions?"

"I'm your mother. I must know whether or not your teachers are telling you the truth."

Jiri grew silent, staring at his feet. Then, as though admitting a secret, he blurted, "Okay, well, since you asked, don't be mad, but it's Mr. Janus. He says the foreign soldiers are actually very 'friendly.'"

"Friendly? Mr. Janus said this?" Ayna raised her voice. "And you believe him?"

"Sort of."

His name was seldom mentioned, because it always invoked Ayna's rage. Nevertheless she remembered Mr. Janus well. He had been her schoolteacher, too. No one knew more about Karl Marx than Mr. Janus. After school, he liked to discuss politics with the drunks at the tavern, where he pried into people's personal lives, asking questions about family and friends——secretly keeping track of the citizens who were anti-communists. Aside from teaching, he worked at the Party Secretariat office in Pilsen.

Ayna ranted, "I hate him. I hate your teacher Mr. Janus. Do you know this? He's a bad man."

"I know. I know. You've told me . . ."

"He's a despicable schoolteacher. And a vile human being."

"Why do you hate him so much?"

She looked at Jiri and sighed. His question struck at the core of her misery. Years ago, during the dreadful days of high school, the worst days of her life, Ota Janus had given her poor marks in government studies. Not because she sympathized with Trotsky over Stalin, rather because she showed little interest in Marxism or the class struggle. Ayna was more enchanted by the melodies of Mozart and Dvorak than uniting with the world's workers. It must have been the hundredth time he had inquired about her hatred for Mr. Janus. But what could she possibly say to make him understand? She loathed the schoolteacher for more than his pro-Moscow propaganda or the bad grades he doled out to those who were unsupportive of Karl Marx's principles. There was something else. Something she refused to discuss——especially with her son. She could never tell him the truth about Mr. Janus. Never.

Trouble. Already. Dal had made a phone call to the desk in Prague, to a group monitoring Zdenek Seifert, only to receive bad news: the mayor was stuck in the city. A student rally and traffic jams were keeping him hunkered down at the university. For things to play out as planned, Dal needed him in Mersk with his fellow citizens. He considered his options and decided to stay at a quaint roadside hotel for a few days until the politician could return home and address the concerns of his electorate.

First, he ordered the handful of frightened hotel guests to vacate the premises, then he barricaded the entrance to the parking lot with the BTR armored personnel carrier. This allowed the team to carry on with the mission in complete seclusion——guarding the POW.

"It hass been a long road," Dal said, speaking to Johnston, who sat in a wooden chair, secured by leg irons and handcuffs. "I know there is more fight in you. I can see it in your eyes. However I do not intend to harm you like your previous captors did. I am a decent man. If you cooperate, and do not attempt to escape, life will turn out much better for you."

Johnston maintained his code of silence, glaring at the soldiers in the room.

Dal offered him a glass of water before leaving him alone. Already the burn marks on his skin were healing. He directed his men to work in shifts, keeping an eye on Johnston, monitoring the parking lot for intruders, driving to the nearest town to get provisions. The days passed. Three days at the hotel felt like a month. Exhausted from living in close quarters with men who smelled like pigs, and tired of the local food, he was more than happy to leave the hotel and be on the highway again.

They left the hotel on a sunny morning and drove in scant traffic. Dal had his head buried in the pages of Tolstoy's short masterpiece *The Death of Ivan Ilyich*, the only book he had packed prior to leaving Moscow. After an hour and a half of reading, he closed the novella and motioned with his hand for Gurko to pull the truck over to the side of the road.

"What is it?" the sergeant asked, pressing his foot on the brakes.

"Are we close to Mersk?"

"Yes. The village is just down the road."

"Excellent. There has been a slight change of plans." The armored personnel carrier, its gun turret pointing toward the mountain peaks, stopped in a whirl of smoke behind them, the engine roaring.

"What do you mean change of plans?" Gurko spoke above the clamor. "We're already behind schedule."

"At this point, the schedule is insignificant." Dal grabbed a camera from his bag, then motioned with his eyes toward the BTR-60. "I am more concerned about the health of the POW. It gets hot inside the troop compartment. Make sure the American has plenty of water. We do not want him to have a heat stroke."

"Of course, comrade. The American is our million dollar man." Gurko wore a blank face. "So——what are you up to?"

"Reading Tolstoy has me thinking about life and death. When it is all said and done, what do we leave behind? Accomplishments? Awards? A place in the history books? What is it worth when a man is not recognized for simply being a decent, compassionate human being? Mmm. People often live for themselves. We are selfish this way."

"Oh?"

"I need time to reflect. You and the Ukrainians . . . come join me in an hour. In Mersk."

"You will enter the village alone?"

"Yes. Much like a tourist exploring a strange country for the first time." Dal put the camera strap around his neck. "See, moments ago, I had an epiphany. I realized we must not startle these people with our military might. No doubt they already live in fear of us. In the end, politics aside, we are brothers."

Gurko's forehead wrinkled. "But we planned to strike quickly."

"This change of direction will test the team's ability to improvise. If the men cannot improvise, this mission will end in failure."

Dal left his weapon in the truck and walked toward a narrow bridge. He did not expect Gurko to understand the rationale behind his thinking. He wanted to assess small town life in the Bohemian Forest as a solitary man. Entering the community alone and without weapons would soften the blow and give the citizens fair warning before the military vehicles stormed the streets. In the way the great Tolstoy had written about kindness and sympathy, Dal wanted to show some humility and not startle the locals. Then, because it was his orders to do so, he would seize their town.

He crossed over the bridge and walked past large haystacks, a water well, and a derelict Cistercian monastery. He snapped photographs of plants and flowers. He was thinking of his wife's love of nature and botany. She would enjoy it here in the mountains. This was her kind of place.

For show, he wore his khaki officer uniform trimmed in royal blue and adorned with service medals, including his Gold Star identifying him as a *Hero of the Soviet Union*.

The Church of Nepomuk was founded as a chapel in 1735, before reconstruction began eighty-two years later to expand the nave. It held four hundred people and was divided by a wide center aisle. Elevated above the streets by a series of steps, the white building had a gabled roof and a bell tower with skylight windows. According to the librarian, the tower was the tallest manmade structure in the mountains, completed in 1914, just days before the Archduke Franz Ferdinand was assassinated.

Ayna was not much of a history buff, but she remembered the construction dates of the buildings in town: the town hall, 1751; the bakery building, 1789; her home, 1848; the marionette theatre, 1890; the hardware store, 1910; and the grocery store, 1922.

At 12:10 p.m., she entered the square and sat cross-legged on the cobble with her diary. Of all the historic buildings in town, the church was the pride and grace of Mersk. There was a time, maybe ten, fifteen years ago, when couples came here from as far away as Brno to have their weddings. They flooded the streets with their passion and their romance, with their flashing cameras and their bright smiles. They were happy times. But it was before the economy collapsed. Before the inn closed. Before many of the town's restaurants shut down. And before many of Ayna's neighbors, who for better or worse, had left for the mines. These days, very few people visited Mersk. Most travelers simply passed through the town without stopping, on their way to Black Lake in Šumava.

She grabbed a pencil from her purse. It was four days into the occupation and she had decided to take a lunch break from her job at the marionette theatre. For some relaxation, but mostly to get her mind off the Soviet Army, she wanted to sketch the church's stone bell tower, added in 1850 and home to a single bell molded by a prominent master in Pasov, Germany.

She put the lead tip to the blank page of her diary and drew several diagonal lines. In minutes, the tower began to take shape. She added the windows, the bell, and the tiled roof with its bulbous cupola and iron cross. "Absolutely. Positively. Wonderful," she whispered, pausing to reflect on her work. It actually resembled a giant caterpillar. She added eyes and a headband to the caterpillar-like tower, with a flower poking from behind an ear. Finally, she drew a woman straddling the caterpillar's back and wrote the words MY GREAT ESCAPE FROM MERSK in block print. It was nothing less than a work of genius, she decided with a grin. A magnum opus.

Walking over and squatting beside her, Sascha said, "What the heck is that?"

Ayna gazed up from the diary. "A caterpillar. Can't you tell?" She showed him the drawing.

"It looks more like the bell tower."

"Silly me. I forgot you have no imagination."

"That's why you love me."

"I don't love you," Ayna said.

"You will. Someday. When we get married."

"Oh, stop."

"It's true."

"Don't make me gag."

Shrugging away the banter, he handed her a sheet of anti-communist statements, printed at an underground shop in a nearby town. No one was more upset over the invasion than Sascha. "This explains everything that has happened since the communists took over in 1948. It all starts with censorship. They have rewritten our history books."

"That's nothing new."

"No. But the Americans liberated Western Bohemia from Nazi oppression," he added. "Not communist factory workers like Mr. Janus always claimed."

"You've seen more proof?"

"Film footage. At the university. It shows American soldiers in Bohemia. A monument has even been erected in Pilzen in honor of America's General Patton."

"My mother never mentions the Americans. She won't talk about the war. You know, because of what happened to my father."

These political conversations with Sascha were typically one-sided. He spoke and as usual she pretended to listen. There was nothing more boring than discussing politics, though she had a strong sense of what was good for the people, and, in what was most often the case, what was bad for them. She longed for the lifestyle in cities such as Paris and London, where people were free to live their lives as they wish, without the communists watching them. She had very little in common with Sascha, except for sharing a passion for classical music. He was among the most talented violinists in Bohemia. Like Peter, he was also anti-authority. Unlike Peter, she felt no physical attraction to him.

"Much of the history we learned as children isn't entirely accurate," Sascha said. "It's more of a stretching of the truth, and in some instances, flat-out lies. I have learned a lot at the university this past year. Especially concerning the atrocities." He explained how in the 1950s the Russians had carted away hundreds of Czechs to Siberia, men accused of false crimes and forced to make confessions after having their genitals electrocuted.

She was numb to his description of abductions and human torture. Few things shocked her these days.

Just then, a pre-World War II Škoda Rapid with rusted fenders and several dents pulled into a parking space. The driver, who was blasting rock music from an 8-track stereo, beat a set of drumsticks against the dashboard. In the back seat, a couple of girls drank vodka and called Sascha's name.

Ayna closed the diary. "You'd better go."

"There's a roadblock on the road leading to Ceske Budejovice," Sascha said. "We're going there to protest. Come with us."

"Can't. Have to keep an eye on Jiri."

The girls whistled anxiously, telling him to hurry. "Keep your chin up. Everything will turn out okay. Jiri is safe. Nothing bad will happen to him."

"What if the Russians come here?"

Sascha shrugged. "Why would they?"

"They're looking for people who have spoken out against the communists."

"I'm not worried," he insisted. "The days of arresting people over differing opinions are behind us. Things have changed for the better. Besides the president is in negotiations to restore the peace and secure the drawback of troops from our soil."

"I'll believe it when I see it."

"Remember what Mayor Seifert said? 'Our government,' he said, 'won't allow them' to take away our new freedoms. We have free speech now. We have fought hard for this."

Yesterday, like so many clinging to hope in town, Ayna had stood beside Sascha to listen to the mayor speak at the town hall. She left thinking he sounded more like a politician up for reelection than someone concerned about their safety. She didn't really trust the mayor. When he was young, he had been a member of the secret police. That was all she needed to know about his heart, who he was deep down inside. "I don't care what the mayor says. From what I can tell, the Russians have no plans to leave our country."

Sascha walked backwards toward the car. "Even if the soldiers do come here, what can they do? The days of throwing people into prison because of our opposing views are over."

"Goodbye then," she said, getting to her feet and brushing the dust off her dress. She was naive to how the government functioned, but was certain Sascha was wrong when it came to the Russians. Something told her the Russians could do anything they wanted. She watched him get into the car. Sascha was the most outspoken citizen in the community. If they came for anyone, they would come for him . . .

They were aware of him.

Dal heard their church bell clanging long before he reached Mersk. Someone had sent out a warning. Now he entered the village with the sound of panicked voices buzzing in his ear, "Russians. Russians. Russians."

Several cars sped down the road, leaving the village in a hurry, and he wondered, why must you go? I am here to protect your best interests.

He took a photograph of the bell tower rising above the rooftops. Lovely, he thought. Bohemian churches were exquisite this time of year, especially with the trees in full summer foliage.

On the narrow cobbled street leading into town, where houses clustered wall to wall, a woman with a baby stroller retreated into a doorway. "Good day," he said, before she rudely closed the door in his face. He felt toxic. Here and there, people fled the wet cobble for the safety of their stucco homes. Windows shut. Shutters closed. Doors locked. When he reached the village square, shopkeepers had already dead-bolted the doors and posted CLOSED signs in the windows.

Only a group of teenage boys playing football remained on the street. A tall kid attempted to score a goal between two trash cans, but kicked the ball too hard. The ball struck the fender of a parked car, ricocheted against a motorcycle, rolled down the street, and came to an abrupt stop against Dal's black boot. I wonder, he mused playfully, who among you is the most courageous? Who will retrieve the football from beneath my foot? After the boys huddled for a brief conversation, the shortest broke free and approached him.

"Hello," Dal said. His Czech was good. "I have been watching your game. You are an excellent football player."

"The best in the village," the boy agreed. His eyes were fixed on the hat's KGB Sword and Shield emblem. "I can score from fifteen yards."

"Fifteen?"

"Easy."

"I'm impressed. You must have a name?"

"My name is Jiri."

"That is a good name."

"Son of Ayna Sahhat."

"Well, Jiri, 'son of Ayna Sahhat,' while others hide from me, you stand here unafraid. You are the brave one." Dal's smile was calming. "I am a colonel in the Soviet KGB. More importantly, I am a huge football fan."

"Really?"

"I played for the army," Dal said. "Once, amid a zealous cheer, and with time running off the clock, I scored from midfield to win a game. Best of all, it was against the navy."

"Wow, that's good."

"I was heroically carried off the field on the shoulders of my teammates to the chant of Gri-gor-i . . . Gri-gor-i . . . Gri-gor-i . . ."

Maybe it was the ease of conversation, or how respectfully Dal spoke, but something gave Jiri a false sense of encouragement. When he went for the ball beneath his boot, Dal, with a flash of athleticism, lifted the football with his toe and dribbled it several times in the air. "See here," he said. "I have maintained my skills. I can still play." The boy's eyes widened. Dal caught the ball and handed it to him with a fatherly pat on the shoulder. "Go. Return to your comrades. Report to them what has happened. Say to them, 'Grigori Dal is your friend.' As proof, I will purchase uniforms for every player who wants to share in this special friendship. We will start our own football team and play against the kids from across the river."

"We don't like those boys," Jiri said with venom. "They're German."

"All the more motivation to defeat them."

"Can we wear red and white? Those are the colors of Bohemia."

"You can wear golden jerseys if it's your heart's desire."

He watched the boy leave to share the good news with his comrades. Dal had made a positive first impression. A seasoned political administrator, he understood how winning the hearts of women and children was the key to any civic triumph. He had spent the breadth of his KGB career in the Balkans as a political advisor and mastermind of civil obedience to many pro-Moscow communist leaders. Now he was embarking upon one of the greatest assignments of his career as the political administrator in Southern Bohemia.

He stood tall. He had looked forward to a post like this for many years. It was, in some ways, the brightest jewel in a crown of achievements stretching back to the 1940s when he first enlisted to fight in the Great Patriotic War. Nevertheless, even with the accolades, a dark cloud loomed over him, over every step he made that day and no doubt in the days to come. He felt pressure. He felt an unbearable heaviness. The feelings smothered his once proud and lively spirit. He had been ordered to put a bullet into the back of the POW's head. Simple, clearly understood orders. Yet several days into the operation, Johnston was still breathing——and there were no plans to kill him.

At precisely 3:13 p.m., he heard the roar of military vehicles and stepped aside. His soldiers were right on time. He threw a friendly farewell salute to the boys and climbed into the GAZ truck when it stopped next to him. With its Red Star on the doors, the truck spoke of Soviet strength and dominance.

"These Czechs love their football," Gurko said, observing the young players. "They're proud of their national team."

The armored personnel carrier rumbled behind them, reeking of gas and exhaust fumes. The boys pointed and jumped with excitement, impressed by the armor.

Dal asked, "Were you a decent football player, comrade?"

"I chose not to participate in team sports."

"Seriously, no sports?"

"I was a hunter."

"Ah, well, in any event, we will need uniforms for the young football players. Red and white."

"Consider it done."

"The local boys are brave. We need their friendship."

"Of course, comrade."

Dal looked into the clear sky. He appreciated the warm sun and how it felt on his face. The Bohemian rain had been relentless in the days leading up to their arrival, so the change in weather from cloudy to clear skies felt like an omen of good things to come.

"Some of the most important music in the history of civilization has poured from the souls of these Bohemians," Dal said. "Antonin Dvorak. Leos Janacek. Bedrich Smetana."

"I don't listen to music."

"How tragic."

"It's true."

"Sometimes I do not understand where your heart lies. Where is your emotion, comrade?"

"Emotion?" Gurko considered the question and shrugged.

Dal grunted. "Anyway, I am afraid we might have underestimated the people of this town." He knew the hostile eyes of at least a hundred adults were peeking between their curtains, watching every step he made. "Mersk is a remote community. Its isolation will help conceal the POW while we move forward with our day-to-day administrative duties. All the same, I sense this village is a cesspool of young and deviant behavior. Artists. Intellectuals. Musicians. I understand how their creative minds work."

"Oh?"

"If they are anything like the famous composer and national hero Bedrich Smetana, they could be trouble."

"Why do you say that?"

"Smetana was a master composer. He fought against all odds to become one of the foremost composers of the last century. He was highly motivated and driven to succeed. Unfortunately he was stricken with syphilis and became deaf. Still he continued to compose. It's true. *Má vlast* was written after his deafness had developed."

Gurko yawned. "I mean no disrespect, but I'm not following you. Music? What does that have to do with anything?"

"Comrade, if these people are half the man of the great Czech Bedrich Smetana, they will not easily be governed. They could pose a serious problem for us, especially over the coming weeks when we must hide the American from public view."

"Trust me," Gurko said. "I'm an old army sergeant. If they are unruly, I will smash them. Just like bugs."

After the bell stopped ringing, a squat oddball with thinning blond hair and almond-shaped eyes appeared from within the church. The toller, Dal assumed. The man, who seemed to be about fifty-years-old, paused on the steps and had a good look at them before hobbling away.

Dal turned to Gurko and spoke over the rumbling BTR-60. "You secretly visited Mersk twice in the weeks leading up to the invasion, scouting the inhabitants, identifying potential problems, and noting deviant personalities. In your advanced report, you failed to mention a word about this unusual citizen."

"He's only an imbecile. The village idiot."

"Hmm."

"Perfectly harmless."

"Perhaps."

"Coincidently, his name is also Bedrich."

Dal supposed it was a minor oversight, for retarded men were typically peaceful men, uninterested in stirring up trouble. He thumped the sergeant playfully on the shoulder, and said, "Let's go find the mayor. And then later, we will celebrate our day of triumph by drinking vodka."

AYNA SAW Bedrich cover his head with both hands when the Soviet truck and troop carrier buzzed by on either side of him. The roar of heavy armor sent him twisting to the pavement. She unlocked the deadbolt and raced from the marionette theatre to help.

"Lousy Russians," she said, thankful Bedrich was okay. "They're heartless, cruel, wicked people."

She was proud of Bedrich for ringing the church bell. The warning had given people time to lock their doors and hide. On the other hand, she was saddened that, at twenty-three-years-old, he was ignorant to the real danger they were in.

She walked him back to the theatre, straightening his untucked shirt along the way. Her boss, Emil Kepler, a pot-bellied man with a curled mustache, was waiting. He offered Bedrich a cup of water.

Just then, the phone rang. Emil answered. Ayna sensed something was wrong by his frown. After a brief conversation, he hung up the phone and turned to her with unblinking eyes.

"What is it?" she asked.

"My wife says Jiri isn't at school today."

"What?"

"She saw him playing football in the square."

"Football? Is she positive?"

"Yes. And then a few minutes ago, he approached one of the Russian soldiers——a big man with several medals on his uniform. Probably the boss."

Ayna could not believe it. She dashed out the door and found Jiri a short block away, in a long alley that ran to the street. He was with the older boys again, smoking cigarettes and kicking a football against the wall of the barbershop. Ditching school? She would put him on restriction this time. She would make him stay in his bedroom for a week. She pinched his ear and rushed him back to the theatre.

"Why are you ditching school?" she asked, closing and locking the door. "The principal will punish you."

"They closed the school for the day. And told us to go home."

"Closed it?"

"Something about Russians in town."

"Then you should've gone home."

"I was going to——eventually."

"Mrs. Kepler said you were talking to the Russians? Is this true?"

"Yes, but only because I wanted to get our football."

"Do you ever use your brain? I told you. Never talk to strangers."

"But the ball," he argued.

"You were being stupid."

"The colonel is a football player. He's going to get us uni—"

"Oh, stop this nonsense." Her voice quivered. "Haven't I taught you to recognize danger?"

TUCKED AWAY in the woods, the three-story villa reminded Dal of the Imperial Estates on the outskirts of St. Petersburg. The impressive home, with its arched windows and domed cupolas, was a short walking distance from town, located beyond an overgrown field, a creek, and a stone bridge.

The Soviet vehicles passed through an open wrought-iron gate and stopped in the crescent-shaped drive, beneath the shadow of a flapping Czechoslovak Socialist Republic flag. Dal gazed at the ivy crawling along a red brick wall. It reminded him of the ivy on his own house. Home, he thought, feeling a pang of homesickness. Since December he had spent a mere eight days with his family and was feeling even more isolated from them with the scent of autumn in the wind. He sighed, regretting recent decisions to fish with his comrades in the Georgian SSR, and to visit his mistress in Gori, when he should have gone home to be with his wife and children.

He left the truck and lit a cigarette. With its lush gardens and placid ponds, the villa had a reputation for being a favorite summer retreat among the nomenklatura. It was also the working residence of Mayor Zdenek Seifert, whose popular voice in the effort to humanize socialism was in question these days.

Dal walked toward the entrance, opened the door and stepped inside the villa. A heavy middle-aged man in round spectacles sat behind a long carriage typewriter. He had a double chin and greasy, thinning hair.

"Ota Janus," the man said with a pleasant tone. "Welcome to Mersk." His hair wrapped from his left ear to his right without the slightest crack of scalp showing.

"Dobryj dyen," Dal said, squeezing the cigarette between his finger and thumb.

Janus went on to say a good deal more, informing Dal that he wss not a member of the mayor's staff, rather was a schoolteacher and longtime comrade to Zdenek Seifert. "I'm lending a helping hand due to the unexpected strife in the country. With the school sending the pupils home for the day, I simply stopped by to chat and offer my assistance."

Dal had a long drag on his cigarette. Like many elitist, Zdenek Seifert had many luxuries, the largest residence in the area, expensive furniture, and even a vacation home in the north country. While most of the people lived meagerly, the mayor enjoyed a life of opulence.

Near a bookshelf, a lanky man appeared very frightened, and stuttered when introducing himself as "Pavel Bilak, the ma-ma-mayor's chauffeur."

Dal turned away from Pavel. "Listen closely," he said. "The villa has officially been sequestered by the Soviet Union." Janus was reading the eviction paperwork. "It will be my personal residence and office during the coming months. From here, I will oversee the political affairs of the villages from Frymburk to Kaplice. If anyone in the district has a grievance to make, it may be conducted by appointment. I will post the procedures. In the coming days, spread word of this to the people. Undoubtedly, they will have questions."

The local Communist Party met at the villa twice a month, rather than at the town hall. With voter fraud firmly in place, the mayor's decade long rule over the people had come to resemble an oligarchy. It was not unlike the mayors who had preceded him. The people voted, but the Party decided who would represent them, regardless of the official vote count. With a phone call, all future gatherings would come to a halt. As well, the town hall would be locked.

Janus spoke calmly. "I don't have the authority to surrender the villa to you. I'm a schoolteacher by profession. Not a member of the mayor's staff."

"Your position in the community is inconsequential," Dal said. "You can either surrender the villa peacefully or force me to take aggressive measures to secure the place." He brandished his Makarov while Potapov circled around the desk with his rifle.

"I assure you," Janus insisted, "I'm in good standing with the Party."

Dal recognized the teacher's name from prior mission briefings. According to records, Ota Janus was an astute scholar of Marx. He had taught the children well over the years, being instrumental in the Youth Union and serving on the textbook advisory council. He secretly reported to the district committee, exposing those in the community who spoke out against the Communist Party.

"I have heard of you," Dal said. "You should have tenure at the university during this stage of your career, not teaching social studies to peasant children in the country."

"I have always considered the early years most important to one's education," Janus said. "Perhaps nowhere is teaching more vital than in the countryside, where the words of Karl Marx are often misinterpreted. Besides, higher education is not what it once was."

"That is the truth," Dal agreed. "There are many agents of imperialism walking the halls of the university. Many befuddled comrades. Which brings me full circle back to the mayor. He has sided with politicians who wish to stamp this so-called 'human face' on socialism. It has become messy business."

"Mayor Seifert is confused with the direction of the struggle," Janus said. "It's an honest mistake, influenced by the politics of Prague. Anyway, I am loyal to Moscow. On behalf of the mayor, and the village, I will sign the paperwork to acknowledge that you have sequestered the villa. In the meantime, how can I help you, comrade?"

"Simple . . ." Dal aimed the pistol at Pavel. "You can start by telling me where I might find Zdenek Seifert."

Before Janus opened his mouth, Mayor Zdenek Seifert appeared at the stairwell balcony overlooking the foyer. He was a stout man, fiftyish, and wore a thick mustache. He said, "Please. There is no need for guns inside my residence."

Dal gave the mayor a swift once-over. "Arrest this criminal."

Zdenek Seifert's jaw dropped. "Criminal? On what charges?"

Dal pulled the KGB arrest warrant from a pocket, flashing it in the air while Potapov rushed the L-shaped stairs.

"On conspiracy charges," Dal said, "stemming from your crimes against the Party."

"Rubbish," Zdenek Seifert retorted. "Utter rubbish. I'm a communist."

The lean and muscled Potapov put the mayor in handcuffs and escorted him down the stairs.

"But you are no longer a communist in *good standing*. There is a difference. If only you had listened more astutely to your comrade, Ota Janus, perhaps this arrest would have been unnecessary."

"Insanity," the mayor barked.

"By orders of President Ludvík Svoboda, I have authority to seize control of the village and begin the restitution of socialist order."

"Svoboda? No. That's a lie."

Dal leaned menacingly into the mayor's face. "You should have thought twice before signing the *Two Thousand Words* memorandum."

The *Two Thousand Words* was a controversial document written by an intellectual and progressive member of the Czech Communist Party. The manifesto urged swift social democratization and freedom of expression, demanding the resignation of people who had misused their power. It had circulated amongst the Czech elite since June, gathering the signatures of scientists, farmers, artists, and intellectuals. Because it suggested methods of violence as a possible means to bring about change, the KGB interpreted the document as an attack on the communists in Moscow.

The mayor said, "The document favors the working class. It speaks of socialist humanitarianism."

"Humanitarianism? Bah. It is nothing but a regrettable political interlude."

"I would sign it again."

"Is that so?"

"Without hesitation."

"Then you are more misguided than I had previously thought."

"I merely desire my God-given freedom."

Dal shook his head. These Christian communists were a farce. To him, Marx and Christ went together like Stalin and Trotsky. He told Janus and Pavel to go home and spread word that the mayor had penned his name to a document of anarchy. As well, he had been kicked out of the Communist Party. Then turning to Potapov, he said, "Take Zdenek Seifert upstairs and lock him in a room. He is under house arrest. There will be no visitors. Not even his wife."

At 7:05 p.m., St. Nepomuk was bustling with townsfolk.

Ayna led Jiri into the church and sat with her mother in a pew behind Emil and Josef. She was in a state of disbelief. The invasion. The fighting in Prague. The fighting in Pilsen. The fighting everywhere. Now came news the mayor had been arrested. Why him? Wasn't he one of them?

"Who will they arrest next?" Sascha shouted. "Joseph? Oflan? I tell you: none of us are safe. We must stand up to the invaders before it is too late."

Father Sudek had called for an emergency meeting to address the unexpected arrival of Colonel Dal and his four soldiers, whom he referred to as "henchmen."

"What will they do to Zdenek Seifert," Irena asked.

"The mayor hasn't been harmed," Father Sudek said. "I assure you. His arrest is a simple misunderstanding. I will talk to the KGB colonel about releasing him. He must be a sensible man."

Father Sudek spoke for an hour, appealing for calm and insisting that self-control was still their best weapon against the invaders.

The people nodded their heads.

No one wanted violence.

During normal Sunday services, the pews were typically filled by citizens over fifty-years-old, the townspeople who were unafraid of the regime or the Communist Party's stance against religion. Tonight the pews were jammed with people of all ages. This encouraged Ayna. She kept her arm over Jiri, reminding him that everything was going to turn out okay. If Father Sudek was correct in his appraisal, then the soldiers were only passing through Bohemia. In a matter of days, they would release the mayor and vacate the villa.

She looked over her shoulder. The mayor's wife was sitting in a nearby pew. Ayna did not know the woman very well, mostly because the Seiferts typically socialized with well-to-do citizens in the big cities, not the small town people in Mersk. Like most politicians in the country, they lived a privileged life. While their special status was annoying, and she refused to look the mayor in the eyes, Mrs. Seifert had a kind face and she admired her sense of fashion, especially her taste for expensive shoes.

Morning, cold. Ayna returned to the church with her cello and a renewed love for the string quartet. With protesting and gunfire making headlines on the big city streets, music meant more to her now than ever. She was determined to keep the Russians from squashing her passion for the musical arts. They could have their machine guns, she would keep her cello.

Four music stands and chairs had been arranged in a semicircle next to an upright piano near the altar. Taking a seat, she overheard the members of the quartet arguing about Colonel Dal and the soldiers at the villa. Instead of preparing to rehearse for Smetana's *String Quartet No. 1 in E Minor*, the two irate violinists——Sascha Boyd and Tad Kriz——were focused on getting the priest to take a harsh stance against the aggressors.

"One man standing up to these wolves will lead to another man joining," Sascha said. "Mersk might have a small population, but other towns will come to our aid." His violin case was locked and the morning's sheet music was stuck behind a book that criticized the government's land seizure policies.

Father Sudek sat patiently at the piano. "Are you proposing we raise an army, Sascha? That we fight with our pitchforks?"

"Why not? Mine is sharpened."

"And what do you imagine this army of farmers would be capable of doing, eh? Flatten the tires of their armored cars?"

Tad slashed his bow in the air. "Better to fight these invaders with a pitchfork than to stand on the sidelines like cowards." He had a wisp of a scraggly beard, his sideburns speckled.

"For love of country," Sascha declared. "For Czechoslovakia. For Bohemia."

"Love of country?" The priest wore a look of disbelief. "Bah. What are the progressive thinkers teaching you at the university these days?"

"They talk about life without the Moscow communists, the good ol' days. Is that such a bad thing? We want socialism, not chains."

Father Sudek mumbled a little at this, in a reluctant and vaguely shocked sort of way. A self-proclaimed pacifist, he had quietly stood for Czech independence from the Austro-Hungarian Empire, had helped organize a network of safe houses during Hitler's occupation, and openly detested the communists. Yet even with these efforts to combat his enemies, he was set against drawing blood. He never endorsed violence as a means to an end. "Socialism, communism," he whispered. "Politics, always the dreadful politics. We are God's children."

Ayna was empathetic. The priest had spent eight years in prison after the communists took over and dispersed the churches, eventually closing St. Nepomuk in 1953. During that time, he was denied a Bible and forced to recite Marx at gunpoint before two-hundred students——men who were political prisoners themselves. After Mayor Seifert was able to secure his release from prison several years ago, he took a job as a bookkeeper at a farm, where he secretly held onto the dream of recovering his parish. On New Year's Day 1966, as the government's stance on religion began to soften, he led a peaceful revolt against the local Communist Party and took back his church. Zdenek Seifert, who regretted the atrocious life he had lived as a younger man serving in the secret police, had undergone a religious experience during the priest's incarceration and publically urged him on.

"We sacrifice our egos for the sake of the quartet," Sascha said. "What about for our freedom? Shouldn't it be worth that same sacrifice?"

Father Sudek scratched his head. "It's complicated. I just don't know."

"We discussed this at the secret town council meeting last night at the tavern. Many are prepared to die if this is what it takes to preserve our names and the good names of our fathers."

"Young man," Father Sudek said. "Less than twenty-four hours have passed since the Russians entered our village. We should give it time. As I have said all along, it's possible they will leave in a matter of days. Either way, we must think about this decision before we do something rash. Before we have regrets."

"I have no regrets," Sascha declared. "I say we stand together and fight these bastardly invaders."

Ayna had heard enough. "What's wrong with us? Are we a quartet or a presidium?" She straddled her cello. "In a few weeks, a prominent judge will sit in this very church and listen to us play. If he likes what he hears, we will be invited to participate in the national Smetana festival in Prague."

"Yes, we know this," Sascha said impatiently.

"Good. When you think of the Russians, when you get angry at what they have done to our country, remember Zdenek Seifert. He was to be the guest of honor at this recital. We must honor him, even in absentia. This is how I intend to fight back."

Father Sudek rose from the piano. "The mayor was a student of Smetana. He, of all people, would approve of moving forward with the recital as planned."

"But Smetana was a patriot," Sascha jeered. "He would never have sat back and done nothing about the invaders."

Oflan Jakubek, a chubby sixty-four-year-old violist in steel spectacles, wanted nothing more from life than to play his viola and recite poetry to his wife. He winked at Ayna before taking a sip from a silver flask. Like the priest, he had seen much war and violence in his day.

After a few minutes, they stopped squabbling and began to rehearse. But their timing was off. Sascha and Tad were pushing too heavily into their bows, unable to set aside their hatred for the Russians or their frustration with Father Sudek. She ignored their selfish behavior by focusing on her finger spacing. It seemed to ease her mind. An hour and a half later, the session ended with an uncomfortable silence. After the priest left, the men quickly put away their instruments and exited the church.

Ayna shut her cello case. Bickering, not music, thrummed in her head: *fight the Russians, don't fight the Russians.*

She heaved a sigh, before walking home with her head to the sidewalk, feeling regretful. Why did she even bother? Playing in the quartet came at a price——spending less time with Jiri. There were moments when she felt guilty over the endless hours of rehearsal, for abandoning him.

She fought through the frustration.

If anything, the recital was too important to be hijacked by politics, especially with all the chaos in the cities.

At night, Ayna prepared dinner, but ate very little. Her spirits were down. Worrying about Jiri's safety made her feel lethargic. She wanted to go to bed, bury herself in the sheets and close her eyes. Instead she made hot chocolate, then somehow mustered the strength to play dominoes with him in his bedroom.

"Your turn," she said, staring at a row of dominoes.

They sat on the floor, sipping their drinks and listening to music by the popular rock band Olympic. She ignored the clothes hanging from the open drawers, his muddy shoes near the bed and the awful smells. She would make him clean his room in the morning. Tonight she wanted things to be cheerful——even if it meant pretending to be happy.

Jiri was talking about his football team. "We're going to play the German boys from across the river," he said, organizing his domino pieces. "And whoop them good."

She was painting her toenails, not paying much attention while he boasted about his team. Before long she had lost three games and was yawning. "I'm through," she finally said, hugging him. "You win again. Good night. And remember, no matter what, I love you."

The next day, a crowd comprised predominately of men and teenage boys gathered outside the doors of St. Nepomuk, and spilled into the square. Some were reading the handwritten notice Gurko had posted the previous night:

IMPORTANT ANNOUNCEMENT TODAY
YOU MUST ATTEND OR FACE ARREST

"They're angered by our presence," Gurko said, driving the GAZ truck with the top down. Potapov was in the back with an AK.

Riding shotgun, Dal asked, "Was that bit about 'or face arrest' really necessary?"

"I just wanted to get my point across."

Dal grunted. "Ah, well, we should expect nothing less than anger from a people crushed by the fist of defeat." With a sense of amusement, he pointed to a bedsheet strung from the nearby cinema house. On it, someone had painted the words RUSSIANS GO HOME. An infuriated Ota Janus was pushing away several protestors as he ripped the sheet from the wall.

The schoolteacher's effort to defend the liberation pleased Dal. It reminded him of the battlefield heroics in Stalingrad, where in the thick of gunfire, brave soldiers had died attempting to fly Soviet colors on the streets. Later he would invite Janus to dinner and pick his brain on Marxist theory, gaining fresh insight into the struggle and learning more about the *Státní bezpečnost*—Czechoslovakia's plainclothes secret police, an organization that had a reputation for implementing a policy of terror against opponents of the regime.

Gurko said, "Other than Comrade Janus, the Czechs in this town don't see us as their liberators."

"It doesn't surprise me . . ." Dal scanned the faces in the crowd, some brave, some scared. A group of men standing near the row houses extended their middle fingers and mouthed, *go to hell!*

"I'm sure they plan to bitch," Gurko went on, "not listen."

"No need to fret," Dal insisted. "The mob is like a young Cabernet Sauvignon. Once uncorked, you cannot consume it right away. Mmm. You must allow it adequate time to breathe. I am not planning to reason with these people. Liberators or occupiers? It does not matter. These people need time to process what has happened. The key, comrade, is to keep our heads and allow them sufficient room to vent."

"Vent? They show no respect for the Soviet Union." The swarming crowd forced Gurko to drive at a crawl. "We should've clamped down on these people many years ago, like we did the Poles."

Dal glanced over his shoulder. "And you, private? Are you comfortable with unruly crowds?"

Potapov sat with a stony expression and gripped his rifle. "We have deadly work to do this morning, comrade colonel. I'm just eager to pull the trigger."

The villagers had surrounded the slow-moving truck by the time the priest approached. "The mayor is a pillar in the community," Father Sudek was saying, keeping pace on his cane. "His incarceration is unjust. Don't you see?"

From the onset, Dal had anticipated this confrontation with the holy man. "I understand your concerns. I really do. However I am currently preoccupied with official state business. Let's have a chat later this afternoon. I will gladly move you to the head of the line."

"The mayor is loved by everyone."

"His condition is out of my hands." Dal cleared his throat. "Move away from the vehicle."

"He has children."

"As do I," Dal admitted. He threw out their names as though naming excuses, "Anna, Marc, Pavel, and Konstantin, all waiting for me at our home in Stalingrad." He refused to call his childhood city Volgograd, its new name since 1961.

"Couldn't you make an exception? And release him?"

"This is difficult for me, Father. Consider for a moment that I might rather be at home with my wife and children, enjoying the family life." The priest seemed befuddled. "I, too, am a victim of the politics. We must be strong. The community is depending on our mutual strength in order to get through this difficult time."

When the vehicle stopped, Dal fitted his sunglasses, took hold of the windshield, and stood on the seat. It was his first opportunity to address the concerns of the townspeople. Undoubtedly, they had questions. He viewed the crowd for several moments before speaking to them with an authoritative tone. "Comrades of Mersk," he began, holding up his hands to quell the voices. "I have an important announcement . . ." He was comfortable in the spotlight and well-practiced with civil confrontations, having previously faced down student protests in Romania and in Bulgaria. Today's village square gathering, however, was on a much smaller scale. Today he was dealing with rural workers, people tied to agriculture, not the textbook, which made them less inquisitive of policy and law. Unlike students, farmhands did not have time to sit in the coffee houses to discuss politics and philosophy. They were oblivious to the pulse of what was happening in Prague, at the Castle, and in the presidium. With this knowledge, Dal had chosen to dress with pageantry, so everyone could appreciate his medals. His military accomplishments demanded respect.

"Comrades of Mersk," he said again, "upon invitation by your government, the Warsaw armies have come to the aid of the working class to defend years of socialist gains. We have heard your voices, the masses, the workers, the citizens who stand united. Your call for protection from corrupt ideas has been received with the gravest of concern in Moscow. I stand before you as proof. My name is Colonel Grigori Dal." The men responded with a mixture of thunderous boos and disruptive groans. Raising a hand to calm them, Dal resumed with confidence, "I have been assigned to this district as the new public administrator. As I believe transparency is the hallmark of trust, my credentials are posted at the villa. I encourage you to read them."

"Where is the mayor?" Emil asked.

Pavel raised a hand, and said, "Why has Ma-ma-mayor Seifert been im-im-imprisoned?"

Groans and angry accusations filled the air. There were concerns that Zdenek Seifert had been mistreated, or worse, beaten. Dal took their unfriendliness in good spirit and like a speedy tennis ball served over a net, he returned their anger in a sincere voice. "Your mayor has penned his name to a document of anarchy. For that reason, he has been charged with conspiracy and relieved of his official responsibilities."

"Anarchy?" Oflan said. "It can't be true."

Potapov had jumped from the truck. With his training in the martial arts, crowd control was his specialty. Prior to Dal plucking him from a military prison in Odessa, where he was considered one of the top guards, he had been the Division karate champion, having killed two men in the ring. With a tightened grip on his AK, he nudged people away from the vehicle.

"Listen to me," Dal said. "This is a serious situation. Moscow has been watching. There has been much discontent in Czechoslovakia. Jazz music? Rock and roll? Miniskirts?" The public horde became quiet, perhaps a reflection of their guilt. "This behavior has been frowned upon. Maybe none are culpable in Mersk, but in the cities, in Prague, in Pilsen, in Ostrava, the moral decay is rampant. As a precaution, until I am convinced the village is not a breeding ground for more anarchists, I have instituted Martial Law." He examined the sea of bewildered faces, many of them bemoaning his speech. "What does this mean, you people ask? It means a curfew is in force, from sunset to sunrise."

Josef shook a rolling pin above his head. He had arrived at the last minute, his long apron covered in sugar and jam. With his thick forearms, he had a bruising way of drawing attention to himself. "A curfew?" he said, standing next to Emil. "You must be kidding? I have important deliveries to make. I can't possibly work around your stinking curfew."

Dal held the official edict. "This validates my authority . . ." He gave the paperwork to Father Sudek, while Potapov shoved and bumped shoulders with the angry protestors, maintaining a safety zone around the truck. "I expect farmhands and shopkeepers to register for exempt status. This way production will not be hindered. You do not need me to lecture you on the importance of production. Cooperate, good citizens of Mersk. And this will make for an easy transition. However be warned: my men have orders to take any precaution necessary to protect themselves from enemies of the regime, as well as to implement my initiatives, which come with full support from the National Committee in Prague."

"Prague?" a lone voice cried out. "Don't you mean the politburo in Moscow? Your regime is a lie."

There was a flurry of groans.

When the mob became obnoxious and more hateful with their insults, Dal held up his hands to calm their hostility. It was Sascha Boyd who had spoken. He realized this, yet pretended ignorance, an attitude learned as an actor.

"Who speaks?" Dal asked. From the corner of his eye, he caught Potapov ready with the rifle.

Sascha stood tall. "You and your Stalinist pigs aren't welcome on these streets."

Dal looked at the redheaded Sascha. "Is that so?"

"If your goal is to establish a Soviet protectorate, I warn you, we will not follow in the fate of Lithuania, Latvia, and Estonia. I'd advise you to pack up and leave, before this protest becomes your Waterloo."

There was a long interlude while Dal stepped down from the truck and walked through the parting crowd. In the early days of the Hungarian uprising of 1956, he had entered a similar mob, equally boisterous in its cry against Soviet authority, and was sliced in the stomach by a radical wielding a knife. The wound required forty-eight stitches and was poorly sewn by a young Soviet doctor, leaving a horrendous scar like an animal had bitten him. Dal made the best of the near death experience, telling his children the teeth marks on his skin were where a great white shark had attacked him off the coast of Indonesia. They believed everything he told them, especially Konstantin, the youngest at twelve. Having survived the vicious stabbing in Budapest, he lived with a sense of untold destiny, accepting his importance in Russian military lore alongside other heroic soldiers such as Field Marshal Mikhail Kutuzov, who defeated Napoleon's Grande Armée during the French invasion of 1812. Like Kutuzov, he believed it was important to show strength when engaging the enemy, in particular when confronting a mob.

Dal stopped in front of Sascha, removed his sunglasses, and looked fiercely down on him. Even up close, the young man's facial features were strikingly similar to the American POW. Like brothers, he thought coldly. Could they have found a more suitable body double?

"What is your name?" Dal asked.

Sascha said, "Antonin fucking Dvorak. But that's *maestro* to you."

Several men laughed.

Dal welcomed the young man's confidence, relishing the chance to stir up his emotions. He thought of fencing, of saber play, and looked for an opportunity to score points against his ego. After the boom of a MiG jet flying overhead faded, Dal said, "You must be a student, no?"

"Charles University." Sascha was full of ludicrous pride. "I'm working on an advanced degree. Economics."

Dal considered his next move. He glanced at Janus, then to the priest, before he asked Sascha, "Do you respect my legal authority on behalf of the Czechoslovak government? It is a simple question, one which requires either a 'yes' or a 'no' answer."

"To hell with you. And your October Revolution." Sascha shook with adrenaline. His voice was choked up in the way angry men often get when they aren't in control of their emotions.

Dal leaned hard against him. "Obviously, you have little respect for socialism."

"Socialism? You know nothing about my politics . . ." Sascha heaved a chunk of mucus and spat on Dal's cheek.

A long, stunned silence fell.

Dal kept his cool, wiping away the glop with slow, deliberate movements. He recalled a play where he had portrayed a Bolshevik, and drew upon this early experience as an actor, which had been met with thunderous applause in the theatre. "Already you must have regrets over that poor decision to spit on my face," he said, recognizing the livid Czech was primed for a fight. He calmly took a pack from his breast pocket and lit a cigarette. "Where I come from, you would not stand a chance with your piss-poor attitude. Most military officers aren't as tolerant as I am."

Dal blew smoke into the young man's face. If anything, he needed Sascha Boyd to throw the first punch.

A FEW BLOCKS away, Ayna was walking to the marionette theatre when she encountered a group of young women——the very same girls she had despised since grade school. The rumors they once spread about her stuffing tissue in her bra and having multiple sexual diseases was printed on her mind in permanent marker. All these years later, she thought, they were still trite and immature.

Someone whispered, "Ayna's curse has brought the Russians to Mersk."

Another girl mentioned her father's Azerbaijani heritage, adding, "Her grandfathers are Muslims. What do you expect from someone who doesn't believe in the same God we do?"

Ayna shook her head. It was just like them to mention the curse and the Russians in the same breath. And then blame her distant relatives in the Azerbaijan SSR for the recent troubles in Mersk.

It was not any big secret that three of Ayna's boyfriends had died under unusual circumstances. Most recently, it had been Peter. Before him, it was her first love, Dana, drowned in a pond, then Strom, a bricklayer, kicked in the head by a horse. Their sudden deaths were heartbreaking; but the girls were heartless. They had never shown any compassion for her misfortunes, or for the dead men. Instead they used it like ammunition and flung the hate back into her face.

One of the girls commented on how "pretty" Ayna was, though another muttered, "Maybe these days she is pretty. But who cares? She is cursed. She will never find a man to love."

When Ayna was younger and had a shorter fuse, she often snapped and charged after them for making such vicious comments. Thanks to Josef's boxing lessons, she had learned to defend herself in grade school. All these years later, after the fist fighting and hair pulling had ceased, the mean-spirited whispers persisted.

She kept her head up and brushed past them. Ignoring a final, chasing insult, "face like a Muslim abortion." Further down the street, at the square, she heard people yelling and ran toward the disturbance.

"You don't know what you're doing," Nadezda said, reaching for Ayna's arm when she arrived at the fountain. "The KGB colonel is angry. Stay away from him."

Ayna ignored the warning and threaded her way through the rowdy mob. A few steps later, she found herself entering an open circle, and standing next to Dal. "What the hell," she said, when she got a look at him. He was blowing cigarette smoke into Sascha's face.

After a pause, Dal asked, "And you would be?"

His eyes were gray and wolf-like. Worse than anything else, he was checking her out with a seductive gesture. She wanted to stare him down, instead glanced away. "I'm one of the many who despise you," she finally said.

"Let's not get off on the wrong foot."

"Do you plan on staying long? In Mersk?"

"I know you must have many questions."

"When are you leaving?"

"When the work is done." After a pause, he added, "And we have much work to do."

Sascha moved in front of Ayna, and said to Dal, "This is between you and me. Leave her out of this quarrel."

"So . . ." Dal puffed his cigarette. "This must be your little sweetie?"

"She's my friend."

"Gypsy?"

"No."

"Your friend's a real catch."

Now she flung a look of scorn, closer yet to punching him. There was a heavy, sick feeling in her stomach along with a feeling that a fight was about to erupt. With her. With Sascha. With whomever the soldiers picked on next. Instead of defusing the conversation, she said, "You. Are. Rude."

Ignoring the comment, Dal leaned over and whispered into Sascha's ear.

She overheard words like "sex" and "whore" and "rousing good time." What a disgusting pig, she thought, clapping her hand over her mouth when Sascha suddenly, most unexpectedly, punched the colonel in the stomach.

Then someone yelled, "Fight."

Bystanders in the crowd began to push forward. Some of them were standing on their toes, trying for a better view. Others were throwing a fist in the air and hollering, "Punish him," and "Don't back down," and "For Czechoslovakia."

A feeling of elation surged through Ayna's veins. "Hit him hard," she said. "Knock his block off!"

Sascha lurched forward and took hold of the colonel's throat, choking him.

Could he win this fight? Would the people stand behind her best friend and push the foreign mongrels out of town? She watched with mixed emotions. It was dangerous for Sascha to confront the Soviets like this. Stupid, even. He was a star debater, not a warrior.

A second later, Potapov stepped forward and slammed the butt of his AK into Sascha's shoulder blades.

Sascha fell.

She rushed to his side, slightly panicked, aware that fighting had been a mistake. "It's useless," she insisted, trying to prevent him from standing up. "They have guns. You can't win."

He brushed her aside, scrambled to his feet and charged after Potapov. "Nazis," he was shouting, attempting to commandeer the rifle. But the Ukrainian was waiting for him and pulled the trigger. The deafening *ack, ack, ack, ack* of the assault rifle exploded and sent a shockwave rippling through her body.

She stood there. A few seconds of confusion took hold. A sense of where was she? And what had happened? It was followed by a full-throttled ringing in her ears. Had she been shot? No. She saw people screaming and crying but their voices were muffled. Then she looked at her feet and found Sascha lying on the ground, blood oozing from his chest. "Oh, Sascha," she said urgently, kneeling by his side. "Hang on. We will take you to the hospital. You won't die."

As people moved away from him, Dal staggered with a handgun above his head and fired several times into the air. "Stand down," he demanded. "I order you. Stand down."

People gave him room. Many ducked for cover or ran away.

She was cradling Sascha's head in her lap and Josef had his wrist, searching for a pulse. Tad crawled over next to her and attempted to stop the bleeding.

"He's dead," Josef said, weeping.

She looked into her friend's lifeless eyes. Josef must be lying. Dead? Josef doesn't know what he's talking about. *Sascha can't be dead.*

Father Sudek shook his head mournfully.

But it was true. Dreadfully true. She looked at the colonel. He was breathing deeply through an open mouth. "Why?" she asked. "How could you do this?"

Dal gave an unapologetic expression. "I did not start this fight," he said, turning to the crowd. "Nevertheless I warn you. Each and every one of you. Do not push me. The rest of your countrymen have capitulated in Prague. Why not you?"

"Murderers," she said.

Dal turned to the priest. "With you as witness, this anarchist assaulted one of my men. His death will be reported as an act of self-defense."

"Self-defense?" Father Sudek said doubtfully.

"Get control of your parish, Father. Next time, the blood will be on your hands, not mine."

"Yes but—"

"Tomorrow morning, after we file our official report concerning the day's tragic incident, this man's body will be returned to the church, at which time you may give him one of your proper Christian burials."

"But——"

"But nothing." While Dal spoke, his soldiers took Sascha's body from her grasp and like a sack of grain dropped it in the back of the truck.

After they drove away, she sat on the bloody cobble with her head down; her bloodshot eyes were dry and burning. She refused to shed more tears. What good would crying do now?

Father Sudek, Josef, Emil, and Tad stayed with her. She shunned them away. She did not need their sympathy. Her mind was like a broken record, replaying Sascha's words from the other day: *Even if the soldiers come here, what can they do?*

She felt a cramp in her side, as if a seed had taken root.

PRIOR TO PROVOKING the hotheaded Sascha, Dal had been firm with Potapov, instructing the sharpshooting private to aim for the redhead's heart. *Two, three bullets shot in rapid succession will kill him instantly*, he had explained. *Like flipping a light switch.*

Death without pain. It was the way civilized men preferred to kill. After all, Dal had some sense of humanity when it came to taking a life. He was a father as much as he was a soldier. What sort of monster enjoyed taking lives when pain was involved? Driving back to the villa, he asked, "Who was the feisty woman at the square?"

"The dark-haired beauty?"

"Yes."

"Ayna," Gurko said, stepping on the gas when chickens entered the road. "'Ayna the Terrible,' or so I have heard some people say."

"Terrible? She's exquisite."

"She's an outcast."

"She looks somewhat different from the typical Czech. I was thinking Gypsy."

"Trust me, comrade. You don't want anything to do with the woman. She isn't a real Czech. She is half Azerbaijani. They say she is what happens when a Christian and a Muslim fornicate. As such, she is cursed by her Mohammedan roots."

Dal looked stupidly at Gurko. "What do you mean——cursed?"

The parlor, with its wall of windows overlooking the garden, was the staging area for Sascha's body. As soon as Potapov left the room, Gurko peeled back the bloody shirt and examined the wounds. One bullet had penetrated the man's heart. Two bullets had pierced the abdomen. A fourth shot had ripped through his thigh. There was little blood.

"The POW and him," Dal said, "their likeness is not so similar now that Sascha is dead."

"This is what happens when the breath leaves the body."

"I see . . ." Dal bit his lip. "Except for the color of the hair, which is an exceptional shade of bright copper, I'd say we are in deep trouble trying to pass him off for the American."

Gurko raised an eyebrow. "You have reservations concerning our body double?"

"It is simply an observation."

The sergeant grabbed scissors and a razor and cropped Sascha's hair in a military cut, leaving a mat of red hair. The corpse would be carried into the forest and photographed near a makeshift grave. The photos and a detailed report would be delivered to fellow conspirators in the Lubyanka. They would lead a superficial investigation and validate the death certificate as GySgt Russell E. Johnston, United States Marine Corps.

"Fortunately, the American has moles on his face," Gurko said. "I can duplicate them with women's makeup."

"You make it sound so easy."

"It's usually the case."

"You trick photographers work like magicians."

"By sunrise his face will be fuller. There will be no difference between the Czech and the American. Trust me, comrade. They will look like identical twins once rigor mortis has set in. There will be little need for trick photography. To be safe, I will take the color photographs at dawn and be reprimanded for my sloppiness."

Dal nodded. "You are committed to the cause."

"Without question."

"Good."

"Yet might I say something, comrade?"

"What is it?"

"About your acting . . . while Sascha strangled you . . . how you grabbed your throat and gasped for breath."

"Impressed?"

"It was a bit of an exaggeration."

"Nonsense. You have never performed Shakespeare."

"I'm not an actor."

"William Shakespeare speaks to me of tragedy. To be convincing, tragedy must be larger than life. It must be of epic proportion, as though reaching out to the audience and plucking the life breath from their souls. Had I not overacted as you seem to suggest, and let the anarchist Sascha Boyd have his way with me, the people of Mersk would fail to remember that it was I, Colonel Grigori Dal, who was first assaulted by the hands of an angry student."

"Forgive me, comrade."

"Ah, no apologies are necessary. Do what you must do to the cadaver. Then take your photographs."

Everything was coming together. The Czech police had been bribed. Agents were prepared to take custody of the American prisoner of war. Soon funds would be transferred to Dal's anonymous Swiss Bank account. In five years, he intended to retire from the KGB and move his family to a villa along the green banks of the Volga River. He longed to eat good food and drink fine wine and spend his best years pursuing that elusive acting career.

Dal breathed a sigh of relief. He had a corpse and complete faith in the sergeant's photographic skills. He was one step closer to the good life on the Volga.

Who could stop him now?

Second Act: Conformity

COOPERATION IS PEACE

The opposite of courage in our society is not cowardice, it is conformity.

ROLLO MAY

When Milan Husak told his colleagues that he planned to keep working regardless of the invaders, he meant it. "I don't care how many guns the Russians point at me, I'm moving forward with our plans for a clinic in Mersk."

The invasion had entered its sixth day and Milan had spent every one of those days at the hospital, lending a hand as injured citizens swarmed the emergency room. On Monday morning he drove south.

He left his modest concrete apartment building shortly before sunrise, hoping to pass through the layers of Soviet checkpoints without an incident. As a representative of the ministry, he had special access to the roads during the city's curfew hours and intended to take advantage of this privilege, regardless of the tanks, the soldiers, and the machine gun nests positioned at key intersections across town.

He drove past a fire department, a grocery store, and a bank. He turned right at an avenue swarming with soldiers and sped toward the highway. There were only a handful of civilian vehicles on the roads at this early hour of the morning. The city streets, he began to notice, were patrolled in all directions by Soviet jeeps and armored vehicles. Little Nazis, he thought. They would not intimidate him. However his status as a low-level director at the ministry meant little to the Russians. They had randomly stopped him, demanding to know what he was up to, where he was going, and why his business was so urgent that it could not wait for the curfew hours to end. Yesterday, while driving to the hospital, soldiers had pulled him from his car at gunpoint to inspect the trunk for weapons, slamming him against the hood and putting a pistol to his head. *Counter-revolutionary*, they yelled, *confess your crimes!* The soldiers were only joking and afterward offered him a sip of vodka; but Milan was pissed.

When he reached the wooden barricades near the warehouses, he frowned at the Russian soldier who approached his Škoda sedan, unsure what to expect.

"There's a curfew," the soldier said, leaning into the window. "Don't you know?"

Milan found his identity card and handed it over. "I'm with the Ministry of Health."

"Is that supposed to impress me?"

"It means I have permission to be out during curfew. It's all right there. Have a peek."

"Yet another Czech with an excuse to defy the curfew." The soldier spoke as though addressing a criminal.

"Look here," Milan said, pushing the round spectacles up on his nose. "I'm late for an important meeting with one of your commanding officers. He won't like that I've been unnecessarily delayed."

The Russian gave a perfunctory scan of the medical journals and files in the back seat, then studied Milan's identification. "I don't like this. Not at all."

"Problem?"

"This photo doesn't look like you."

The photo ID showed Milan with a clean-shaven face, rather than today's goatee and peppered gray hair. "It's me," he said, noticing his hairline at forty-seven-years-old had begun to recede.

"Maybe so."

"Can't I just enter the highway? Be on my way?"

"No. I need approval."

Milan glanced at his watch while the soldier huddled with an officer near a military motorbike. In the Soviet system, everything flowed through a commander. Soldiers at the bottom of the ranks were trained to get approval before acting on their own initiative. Milan remembered a conversation he'd had a while back with a friend who claimed to have the secret to defeating the Red Army. *Just shoot the tank commanders. It's that simple. Shoot them. The tanks will drive in circles.*

A few minutes later, the soldier came back to the Škoda and retuned Milan's identification card. "It's your lucky day, doctor."

"Oh, how so?"

"You could be held for questioning."

"Questioning?" Milan snickered. "What the hell?"

"Instead we have decided to let you proceed for the sake of the public health."

"That's generous," Milan said, thinking: jerk.

"Cooperation is all we ask."

"Then give my regards to Comrade Brezhnev . . ."

Milan rolled up his window and drove onto the highway. With journals and hospital paperwork stacked on the passenger seats, a box of medical files in the footwell, and pens and miscellaneous receipts crammed into the glove compartment, his dinged up 1952 Škoda functioned much like a second office. He loved this black car. It cost little to maintain and rarely broke down. Its chrome grill, which gleamed in the sun, reminded him of an open shark's mouth. The Škoda was the perfect vehicle for a Czech on the go.

Like him.

Always on the go these days.

Working nonstop to establish a network of clinics in rural Bohemia.

He had spent the last few months sequestered in cramped rooms with public health committees and local organizations, trying to cut through the bureaucratic language and red tape that impeded clinicians. Progress was slow, but he had already laid the framework for the construction of several clinics. Mersk was one of eight communities on his list.

Farther along the highway, a farmer stood near the flipped open hood of a 1940s Praga farm truck, a wrench in his hand. The truck was painted green and had wood slats along the bed. Had there been time, Milan would have stopped and offered some help. As he passed the truck, the farmer tipped his hat and Milan threw a friendly hand.

Like all Czechs, the farmer carried on with his life in spite of the occupying armies. Even in defeat, the people remained proud. They would stomach the invaders. Throw rocks at them. Hurl Molotovs at their tanks. Then each night, when climbing into bed, they hoped and prayed the disputing governments would reach an agreement and the foreign armies withdraw.

He drove with a sense of déjà vu. That farmer. His hunter's hat with a jaybird feather. He reminded him of someone. *Who?*

THE LIBRARY SHELVES were lined with books: history, literature, poetry, essays and almanacs dating back to the 17th century. Translations in Russian screamed out to Dal. With its glass bookcases, the room reminded him of the rare book room at the university in Moscow, where he had spent many nights reading original manuscripts by Anton Chekhov and Aleksandr Kuprin.

Dal sat broodingly at an executive desk made of oak. He was skimming Milan's credentials, the wall of books behind him, a window and a row of file cabinets to his right. Aside from outlining his outstanding career at the ministry, the paperwork shed light on his Communist Party membership and his distinguished military record.

"I'm impressed by your soldier years," Dal said in a cryptic tone, easing himself back in the chair. "Hitler must have put a Kaiser-size bounty on you."

"We made things uncomfortable for his troops," Milan admitted.

"You fought with the Czech resistance?"

"The Council of the Three."

"Ah, an impressive group. You must feel at home here in Bohemia, with the peasantry?"

"I'm envious of them."

"Envious?"

"They're the heart of the country."

Dal flicked the ashes of his cigarette in the nearby ashtray. "Heart? I wonder how many of them support the political problems caused by Dubček and his ill-advised comrades?"

"I don't mean to disappoint you. The politicking and factional tussles at the Castle bore me to no end."

"But you are a communist, no?"

"I'm a doctor."

Dal smiled ruefully. Physicians sworn to their profession, not the Party, irritated him. He traced his finger on the paperwork. "You have been assigned to this district to work with children, is that correct?"

"Yes. The ministry is putting in a new clinic," Milan said. "Right here in Mersk."

"Oh?"

"At the abandoned police station."

"I see. Tell me more."

"The building reeks of mildew and its electrical system is shot to hell. But there is good news. Thanks to the mayor, the town council recently approved some needed renovations. The building has been gutted and two patient rooms have already been constructed."

This all sounded good on the surface. Crime was mostly non-existent in Mersk. People looked out for each other. Hence there was no need for the police. The old station, once home to drunks and petty thieves, had been closed due to the population decline of the 1950s. All the same, the last thing Dal wanted was a representative of the ministry——even a doctor turned health administrator——setting up office within earshot of the villa.

Dal asked, "Who made this decision?"

"Minister Precan."

Dal glanced to his sergeant with questioning eyes. "This is news to me," Gurko admitted. "The official report from the Lubyanka mentioned nothing of a clinic."

"A fire in Kamenny destroyed the building we originally planned to occupy," Milan explained. "We decided to relocate to another town rather than rebuild the clinic. Mersk was always our second choice."

Dal spent several minutes interrogating him, asking questions about the ministry and his associations. "Does the minister support stronger ties with Moscow? Do you stand with President Svoboda?

What do you think of Alexander Dubček's progressive policies?"

Milan's answers were benign, mumblings of, "I'm not sure," and "I suppose," and "They seem encouraging." He would not elaborate.

"The ship has been steered off course. You might want to pay attention. It affects everyone. Even you." Dal examined the physician with caution.

"Any further questions?"

"For the time being, no," Dal said disarmingly. He had seen Dr. Husak's type in hospitals across Eastern Europe. He reeked of self-protection. While he was devoted to health care policy, and quite possibly the hardest working doctor in the country, he avoided making political statements, in particular choosing sides on divisive issues. This was not surprising. Likely he feared being ostracized by his bosses or being reported on by a colleague. Did he want to blend in with the system and stay out of the limelight? Perhaps. However something struck Dal as unusual. Unlike most veterans he had met over the years, Milan spoke humbly of his war hero label and showed no interest in reliving the glory days. Dal found this peculiar. Veterans typically wore their merits with pride. Not Milan Husak. He shunned the accolades and praise for his heroics combating the Nazis. Any mention of the fighting tightened his lips. He was hiding something——maybe a past pain, a war horror.

"I have instituted Martial Law in Mersk," Dal went on, signing paperwork that allowed Milan access to Zdenek Seifert. "A bold move, I admit. Be that as it may, I support dialogue with the citizens, not confrontation. I am not against these people, you see. My plan is to maintain order. Your plan, turning the streets into a destination spot for the weary and sick, is not something that appeals to me. Is it possible to delay the clinic's opening, say, for a few weeks?"

"No," Milan said. "It's important we move forward as planned. Each passing day is another day a child goes without care. Over the years, the folks have had various excuses to stay away from the hospitals in the cities. This is unfortunate, considering there is no shortage of physicians to care for them."

"It does not concern me."

"I'm sure you'll agree. The people need this clinic."

"To me, it is an issue of timing. That is all."

"I'm certain Minister Pre—"

"Minister Precan is a questionable communist," Dal barked. "What does the misguided minister know? He has nothing in common with socialism. He is a political corpse, nothing more."

"I take my orders from him," Milan said.

Minister Klaus Precan's political career, and the careers of other progressives in the government halls, were numbered. Within weeks, administrators loyal to the true class struggle would be running the country, taking over for those who sought to soften government policies. "You appear to be biting off more than you can chew," Dal said, visible frustration rising in the lines of his face. "I must ask you. Keep matters low key at your clinic. These are precarious times in Czechoslovakia."

Dal stood. As a precaution, he asked the physician to limit his visits with Zdenek Seifert to thirty minutes before heading downstairs to conduct the business of the day. There was much work to be done. He had already locked the doors to the town hall and disbanded the citizen committee. Soon he would replace members with pro-Moscow sympathizers.

He sat at the reception desk and found his cigarettes. He wanted to prevent the doctor from opening the clinic; however rattling the ministry's attention was risky. They might send someone to investigate. He did not need Czech officials probing into his affairs.

The front door opened. "An irate farmer from Ceske Krumlov has arrived," Potapov said, stepping into the foyer. "He insists on speaking with you."

"What does he want?"

"He claims soldiers have stolen produce from his truck."

"Things like this happen during war."

"He demands justice, compensation to pay for the lost goods."

"Ah, these people live in the Dark Ages. First the doctor brings his bag of medicine to Mersk. Now this farmer cannot barter with our troops."

"What should I tell him?"

Dal grunted. "I will hear his side of the story. After all, it's my role as an administrator to listen to their complaints."

He went outside and stood on the porch. He was understaffed at the villa, thus incapable of meeting the community's petty and excessive needs. He needed a civilian clerk, someone to whom he could delegate civic matters to. His soldiers were trained in security, not administration. They lacked social skills and the ability to do more than one thing at a time. This had been his concern all along. Even so, faced with concealing the American prisoner of war, he decided to minimize the team——the fewer eyes the better.

Dal left the porch and approached the farmer, who removed his hunter's hat and placed it on the hood of the truck.

"Do we have a problem?" Dal asked.

"Yes," the farmer replied. "Your army. The troops are out of control."

ZDENEK SEIFERT was dressed in gray trousers and a matching jacket. He had splashed on aftershave and polished his shoes, ready for work but unable to leave the room. He greeted Milan with a firm handshake after Mazur closed and locked the door.

"They can't do this to you," Milan said. The television cord had been cut and the telephone line ripped from the wall, leaving the mayor without communication to the outside world. "This house arrest stinks to high heaven."

"I'm okay. Really."

"It's hardly legal."

They sat on the sofa near the stone fireplace.

"Oh, I saw this damn thing coming," Zdenek Seifert said. "First that neo-Stalinist Bratislava Declaration, then in May, those military exercises along our border by the Warsaw armies. I knew the Soviets wouldn't tolerate our recent reforms."

"I've been busy. It took me by surprise."

"The whole country has been busy——including the damn

presidium."

"I figured if Marshal Tito could break away from Soviet claws, why not us?"

"Let's be realistic. We wanted the impossible. And for the last seven months we had it——our freedom. Now it's gone."

"Moscow can't keep us in chains."

"Try telling Brezhnev that."

"Well, when it ends, like it did for Hitler and Stalin, the world will be reminded of the Nuremberg trials."

"You think?"

"Yes. Because they are protesting this occupation, you see. Everywhere. Even in America."

"America?"

"The world is watching."

"I hope so. I really hope so."

"And while we work for a resolution to this crisis, I'll do my best to keep Colonel Dal and his cronies from mistreating you."

"Fact is, my situation means little in the big picture. Even with Soviet troops occupying our country, today is a day to celebrate. Thanks to you, Mersk is finally getting a clinic."

They had met in the previous weeks and spoken several times by phone to discuss the clinic. The mayor was the chair of the local health care committee and the clinic's biggest advocate. He had personally taken charge of overseeing the renovations. During this time, Milan had grown attached to his raspy voice and childlike laughter, which had gone into hibernation since his arrest. "They won't even grant visitation rights with my wife," Zdenek Seifert complained. "What harm could there be in letting a man speak to his wife? I feel lost without her."

"I understand." Milan gave him an unmarked bottle of vitamins. "I've fooled the colonel into believing that you have diabetes."

"Oh?"

"Pretend these vitamin pills are for your condition."

"Diabetes, you say?"

"Yes. And make sure they see you take them."

"But why?"

"Pretending to have diabetes means I can visit you multiple times a week."

"Ah, you are a clever man."

"I'm only looking out for a fellow countryman. You'll be freed soon."

"Not if the colonel has his way. He's a Stalinist. He has it in for me. And for my progressive brothers."

"Don't fret. Things will work out for you."

"I'm not so sure."

"What do you mean?"

"They plan to send me to Siberia."

Milan opened his medical bag and grabbed the sphygmomanometer. He wrapped the cuff around the mayor's upper arm. "Siberia? Aren't you jumping to conclusions?"

"No." The tone of Zdenek Seifert's voice was serious. "The ticket is already stamped. I published several op-eds in the newspapers this spring. Each exposed the various weaknesses of the *Communist Manifesto*, in particular how the elimination of capital and competition has given birth to a stagnant society."

"You're not alone. Hundreds of other intellectuals have spoken out across the country."

"It's a pecking order. And I am at the top of the list."

Milan agreed with his principles on competition and admitted his love for a free market system, which raised the mayor's eyebrows. Milan opposed socialism, yet confessing this to Zdenek Seifert might break the important bond they had established. While the mayor was not a hardened communist, he embraced a system whereby most ownership of manufacturing and property was at the discretion of the government. His ideas of competition had little to do with capitalism. He simply wanted to return the most basic elements of power and decision making to the people, calling for, among other things, the decentralization of government-managed farms. The mayor confessed his progressive political agenda with a mix of pride and regret. When he was done speaking, Milan realized deportation was a real possibility but kept quiet.

Milan paused to reflect. He had lived his adult life detesting the communists and how they had made the people dependent upon government. The 1948 coup had paved the way for the poor housing conditions, the destruction of the economy, and the decay of the health care system. There had been a time not long ago when Czechoslovakia had had the most ambitious hospitals in Europe, when innovation led the way at the institutes in Prague. While the protection of health was guaranteed by the constitution, he felt little to be proud of these days. Shame, really. Stripping away incentive for profit had destroyed the quality of health care in the country.

"And then there is this question of the army," the mayor said. "To fight or not to fight?"

"The people have mixed feelings. When it's all said and done, no Czech wants slaughter."

"True. Nevertheless, I'd like to plant my fist on the face of his Excellency, the Soviet ambassador. Have you met him?"

"No. Can't say I have."

"Lucky you. He's a two-faced mongrel. You wouldn't like him."

"I'm sure I wouldn't." Milan put the medical instrument in his bag. He had completed the physical examination. "I'll see you soon. Keep your spirits up. We outnumber these jerks."

As he turned away, the mayor grabbed him by the arm. "Before you leave, I must tell you something . . ."

"Yes, what is it?"

"They're holding someone. Down the hall. In another room."

"Oh?"

"I overheard the soldiers interrogating him last night."

"Another prisoner?"

"So it seems. The walls are thick. I couldn't understand what they were saying. Could you find out who he is? I feel responsible."

"I'll see what I can do." Milan stood to go. "Don't forget, no more mints. You're supposed to have diabetes, remember?"

Milan knocked on the door and asked to be let out. Privates

Mazur and Horbachsky, who smelled like they had not showered in weeks, threw a combined scowl before suggesting he had been in the room for five minutes too long. After the door banged shut, and Mazur locked it, Milan took a step and unintentionally bumped shoulders with Horbachsky.

"Ease off," Milan said, refusing to be drawn in.

Horbachsky gripped Milan's arm, and said, "Time to go. Don't give me any trouble."

Milan made a dismissive sound. "Whatever."

Horbachsky released his grip, then nudged him down the hallway with a rifle. Milan stumbled forward. He had seen better days, been with better company. After another shove, he turned to the soldier and said, "Push me again . . . you will regret it, punk."

The Ukrainian eased up with his rifle and they proceeded down the stairs. Milan was serious. He would have punched him. He had met all three privates that morning, Mazur, Horbachsky, and Potapov. As well, he had been ordered to show his identification to the stocky Sergeant Gurko. Already, Milan's patience was wearing thin. Having witnessed the wounded people in the hospital, he was on the verge of snapping. Near the reception desk, he saw a large portrait of Leonid Brezhnev hanging on the wall and a Soviet flag folded on a shelf, signs the Russians were staying put.

"The boss wants to speak with you," Horbachsky said sternly, pointing to the door. "Go outside. Report to him."

"Yeah. Yeah. I hear you."

"And don't delay . . ." The Ukrainian hurried into a restroom, apparently in a rush to urinate.

Milan had a weird feeling about these soldiers. Holding the mayor in a bedroom rather than at a military guardhouse went against protocol. Making it worse, Colonel Dal's annoyed response to the clinic was troublesome. If his duty was to administer the social and political affairs of the region, then opening a clinic should have been met with enthusiasm. If for no other reason, it would give a boost to public morale, which was currently in the dumps.

He glanced through the windows on either side of the entrance door. Dal was in the driveway, speaking to someone who looked like the farmer he had seen earlier on the road. Milan sensed the colonel was berating the man and felt an unpleasant sinking sensation in his stomach.

He reached for the door handle, then stopped. He smelled something. The bitter smell of dead flesh? Instead of stepping outside, he turned abruptly and walked to an adjacent door, which was ajar. He pushed open the door and entered the parlor. Just curious. But not expecting to find a corpse in the middle of the room. It lay across a conference table, bathed within a shaft of light from the garden window.

What was a dead man doing here?

DAL HAD MADE a rash decision. Stepping outside to speak with the farmer was a mistake, a stupid one. What should have taken a minute or two had turned into a half-hour long conversation. Now he cursed himself for leaving the foyer unguarded. He returned to the villa and caught the doctor examining Sascha's body in the parlor.

"The smell," Milan said. "I couldn't help myself. Tell me. What happened to this poor man?"

"We had an unfortunate incident," Dal lied, clearing his throat. "A shooting." He began his made up version of the story, not wanting to reveal the truth, that Potapov had shot a civilian named Sascha Boyd. "This dead man on the table was one of my best soldiers. Yesterday, he was killed in a roadside ambush by hooligans."

"Butchered is more like it."

Dal pulled the sheet over Sascha's face. He knew the doctor would likely hear about the confrontation between him and Sascha, and the resulting death. Word traveled fast on the street. But with Sascha's shaved head and rigor mortis having its way, it would be difficult to question the body's real identity. Had he simply told him the truth, that he and his soldiers had killed an innocent civilian, it would have resulted in a much longer conversation, which he was trying to avoid. Dal could bribe the local police to look the other way, but Milan was from out of town, and if he learned the truth, that a resident had been murdered, he might take the news to the ministry. This would jeopardize the mission. To be safe, he would distract Milan, require that he attend a meeting at the villa during Sascha's funeral, thus preventing him from learning more about the shooting.

"These are unstable hours," Dal said. "Full of lawlessness and mayhem. Take your mayor, for example. He knew it was dangerous to speak out against the regime. Yet his voice was among the loudest."

"Our government has passed reforms. Stalinism is dead. We have free speech now."

"Alas," Dal said, "free speech is the root of societal decay. Among other ills, it stifles productivity."

"Stifles? That's a bit harsh, don't you think?"

"You disagree?"

"To me, free speech spurns creativity."

"Hmm." Dal raised an eyebrow. "Creativity is often misguided and spawns anarchy. It's true. Think of liberal intellectuals mingling in the coffee shops of Prague, huddled together to discuss philosophy, overanalyzing the words of Marx, as liberals often do, translating them to take on new meaning. This is where the spark of anarchism ignites. In part, it helps explain how your progressive public servants have gone astray."

"Like I said, I'm not political."

"For now, let's agree to disagree." Milan was watching him with distaste. "All things considered, I take it Zdenek Seifert's living conditions meet with your approval? He has been allowed sufficient comfort."

"I suppose. It could be worse."

"He gets out twice a day to stroll in the garden. He has his record collection. And his favorite books. I have even afforded him a good bottle of cognac."

Milan said, "What about visitation rights with his wife?"

"Coming. In due time."

"Good."

"You, as a Czechoslovakian, are witness that he is being treated with respect. Perhaps you will report this to the people?"

"If the opportunity presents itself. Sure."

"Wonderful."

"Which reminds me. Are you holding another prisoner?"

"Prisoner? I'm not sure I understand the question."

"Someone besides the mayor. Here at the villa."

Dal felt his stomach drop. "Why do you ask?"

"Zdenek Seifert overheard an interrogation last night."

Interrogation? Dal had simply asked the POW a few questions about his time in the Czech prison system, who he had met there and what they had discussed. The American's answers were the same, name, rank, serial number.

"Yes, in fact, we are holding a civilian prisoner. He is in a room down the hall from the mayor." Dal's mind added to the fabricated story with little effort, pretending that Johnston was the civilian prisoner. "We suspect he was part of the roadside ambush that killed the soldier you see lying on this table." It was just like creating fictional characters in a play. Easy to get away with, Dal thought. Especially since he would never allow Milan or Zdenek Seifert the opportunity to meet the American prisoner of war. If Dal said he was holding a civilian, not a POW, if he said the body on the table was that of a Soviet soldier, not Sascha, then Milan and the mayor had no choice but to believe him.

"I ask," Milan said, "because I serve everyone in town, Czech, Russian, and Ukrainian. Should you or any of your men require—"

"Thank you, doctor." Dal extended an arm toward the door. "It's time for you to leave. Good day."

HOW DOES *this happen?* One day Czechs are minding their own business, the next day, warmongering Russians are on the streets with automatic rifles, bossing people around at gunpoint and tossing them into jail. Goddamn Brezhnev and his henchmen. Milan was furious and wanted to punch something.

He walked to his car without saying another word, somehow keeping himself together. He was going to butt heads with the KGB colonel. Dal was an unsympathetic man——a conservative Party hardliner as Zdenek Seifert had warned. Milan planned to file a report with the ministry that afternoon, letting his bosses know of possible trouble to come.

His agitation intensified when he approached the Škoda and discovered the Czech flag no longer hung from the flagpole. The flag had been flapping in the wind when he arrived a little over an hour ago; someone had since taken it down. He began to reconsider the idea of a quick Soviet withdraw. How long did they really plan to stay, months, years? He reached for the car's door handle. Then froze. Someone had fingered his name in dust on the window. Or was it the name Mickey?

His heart skipped.

Who wrote this?

Milan turned to the guard at the gate. Him? He glanced over his shoulder to where Dal stood poised in the doorway, smoking a cigarette. Him?

He erased the word with his shirtsleeve, pitched his satchel on the seat and climbed in behind the wheel.

"You're imagining things," Milan told himself, driving over a stone bridge that led into town. The writing in dust had probably been there for several days and it read Milan. *Not Mickey.*

No one could possibly know what the name Mickey meant to him. That was years ago.

Or could someone?

Did someone?

DAL DECIDED to make an example of Horbachsky and had him tied to the flagpole and whipped for his insubordination. "Next time you leave a visitor unguarded," he roared, "you will be shot between the eyes." The dimwitted Ukrainian was a last minute addition to the team and had not been properly vetted. Like a bomb capable of premature detonation, Horbachsky was always a potential detriment to the operation.

Gurko applied the lashing with a satisfying grin, whipping the soldier's back multiple times with a frayed army belt.

Dal watched, his face cold, deadpan. When the punishment ended, the sergeant doused vodka over Horbachsky's bloody lacerations and curled his lip.

"No more," Horbachsky shouted painfully. "I promise to pay attention." His cry for mercy swept over the villa walls and flitted through the surrounding forest like a swarm of bats.

"Mercy? No, too late for that," Dal said. He instructed Gurko to leave the undisciplined private tied to the flagpole for the remainder of the day, before storming inside the villa.

They had problems now. Fucking problems. Allowing the doctor a view of Sascha's body was a serious blunder. Did Milan believe his made-up story? That the body in the parlor was a Soviet soldier? He felt a pang of doubt. The mayor's eavesdropping was likewise troublesome. Dal had originally planned to send Zdenek Seifert to Prague within a day or two, but complications had surfaced, the military police sending notice that they would not arrive to collect him until, at the earliest, the following week. From this point forward, the doctor and the mayor would conduct their medical examinations in the garden. Dr. Husak would never set foot inside the villa again.

Night fell.

Dal went to the library to be alone, to think. Aside from the day's comedy of errors, the mission had been successful: recovering Devil Dog, apprehending the prisoner of war, carrying out Sascha Boyd's murder. Even with all this behind him, he felt anxious about hiding the POW and needed to relax. Typically a good book calmed his nerves.

He poured himself a tall vodka and went to the bookshelf. He found a book by Fyodor Dostoyevsky, a Russian writer of human psychology and politics who had influenced German philosopher Friedrich Nietzsche. He sat at the desk and read for an hour, but his mind obsessed on the doctor's gruesome discovery of Sascha's body, so he closed the book and stared at the ceiling. He realized, too, that he had not sufficiently worked out Horbachsky's role on the team. He needed to address the problem. His brain went over a plan, finding errors and fixing them. Horbachsky would be assigned to the gate on a permanent basis——entrusted with simple tasks like signing-in visitors. Under no circumstances was he to guard the POW.

Feeling better, he slid out the desk drawer and poked at the pencils, paperclips, and coins in a wooden tray. He found a brass key in an envelope located beneath the tray. Would it unlock the file cabinet near the window, the only cabinet he had yet to open?

He stood from the desk and gave it a try.

The lock snapped open. He pulled out the steel drawer. Oh dear Lenin, he thought with a sobering grin. Since October 1938, he discovered all at once, when the German occupation began, the mayors had kept detailed records of the happenings in town. Here, as though spoon-fed to him, was the pulse of the citizenry, historical notes organized in files by family name, starting with Adamec and ending with Zitnik.

Dal began to snoop, one manila folder after another, his heart beating hard. There were documents claiming land ownership, notes on public fights, letters concerning adulterous affairs, and snippets of other scandalous rumors. Most importantly, he had found a list of those who had joined the Communist Party.

He grabbed a stack of folders——the names of the people he had recently met——and returned to the desk. What motivated them? How had they conducted their lives? Who among the villagers had the courage to oppose Dal's authority?

He smoked, prying deeper into their secrets. Only a loyal handful were real communists, most had joined the Party due to social pressure. In this tightly knit community, the farmers held the real balance of power, siding with Father Sudek on the most important issues of the day, an alignment which often influenced the mayor's governing decisions. Adding to their strength, only a few citizens had reported on each other. It was often the way things worked in the mountains. Townspeople stood together, protecting the centuries-old ties that bound relationships, good and bad. They bitched in their church. They argued at the town hall. They went to the mayor when a dispute was beyond reconciliation. But their discontent was rarely heard in Prague. It was not an eye-opening discovery, though important to note.

He drank the vodka and picked up another file. This one addressed the farmers' constant battle to produce more crops. Whether Stalingrad or Mersk, farmhands were always at war with the elements, drought, fungi, insects. He glossed over these pages with causal interest. The names of people arrested in the 1950s for illegal food hoarding shot up a red flag and he noted their identities on a pad of paper.

Next he read about a feud between neighbors and a conflict over the historical rights to a dairy farm, which resulted in a stabbing and a divorce.

And there was Pavel's brother, an outspoken member of the Writer's Union.

And the violist Oflan Jakubek, who had killed a man in a drunk driving accident.

He had a drink and felt the alcohol burn his throat. The thickest file, he soon discovered, was devoted to the cursed Ayna Sahhat, and the violent deaths of her three lovers. The men had lost their lives by a drowning, a head trauma, and a car accident. He leaned forward into the light of the desk lamp and turned a page. The curse she supposedly put on these men fascinated him. It spoke of sacrilege, of a centuries-old jinx, and of her Muslim grandfathers in Baku.

"Unfathomable," he whispered. "I must get to know you. Dear. Sweet. Ayna."

He examined the haunting black and white photos of the girl, his hand hovering over the glass of vodka. There was a sense of darkness to her face, of catastrophe.

Dal wondered, could she put a curse on him?

At midnight he mashed his cigarette in a porcelain ashtray on the desk, on the face of Charles IV, King of Bohemia and Holy Roman Emperor.

Sascha Boyd's body lay in an open casket, dressed in a white suit with his Stradivarius across his chest. Ayna refused to believe he was dead. For the last few weeks, the Smetana Festival had been the hot topic of conversation. *Our quartet is good enough to earn the approval of the judge,* Sascha had told her repeatedly. *He will like our quartet and invite us to Prague.* She heard his mother sniffing in a nearby pew and wanted to give the woman a hug. The family had come in from the farms for the funeral. Later, in the cemetery, she would speak with them in private, say her condolences, and remind them what a hero Sascha had been for standing up to the Russians.

"It was murder," Ayna shouted to the mourners. She was too angry for tears. "You witnessed it. Sascha was provoked into a fight."

"Sit," Evzen said. He was nearing ninety, hunched over his cane. "We're here to honor the departed, not hold court."

"I do honor him," she insisted.

"Have you no respect for Sascha?" Irena asked. She was a teacher turned librarian, an acquaintance of Ota Janus and former president of the local women's communist league. She had never approved of Ayna or the Sahhat family.

"Respect?" Ayna said. "I was Sascha's closest friend."

Because the Russians had shaved his head for no apparent reason, she offered it as proof of their barbarism and disrespect for the dead. No one understood her point of view. They wanted the trouble to end with Sascha's unfortunate death——no more questions. Appeasement, she thought irritably. She knew Irena had sent chocolates to the villa. Evzen, who was grinding on his dentures, had gone so far as to stand on the street and wave to the invaders that morning.

Catching her breath, Ayna scanned the congregation for a strong face, but found none. Only faces of fear and dread stared back. Even the strapping Josef Novak, arm wrestling champion of the village for the last eleven years, appeared timid.

How had they come to this?

In the aftermath of the shooting, the people of Mersk had raised a white flag, embracing a riding-out-the-storm mentality. They fought back by tactics of name calling and tearing down road signs. Passive resistance. This was the extent of their discontent. Ayna had heard their warnings for days: *don't approach the soldiers on the street, don't look them in the eye, don't challenge the colonel's authority.*

"A few nights ago, many of you groveled outside my bedroom window," she said, her hands in fists. The more they insisted she sit, the louder she spoke. "You cried out, 'long live Czechoslovakia.' Then what happened? A single Russian bullet sent you running with your tails between your legs."

Their silence was an admission of guilt. Most of them hung their heads like ostriches poking their heads into the sand. For once didn't they want to pluck someone's eyes out? Isn't that what their brothers and sisters were doing in the cities? When Jiri asked why the people were so angry, Ayna snapped at him, "Stop interrupting." And she regretted saying this even as the words left her mouth. Deep inside, she was hurt by their accusations that she was *cursed*, that she was an *outcast*, that she was a *Muslim*, but she did not expect him to understand.

Father Sudek stood at the pulpit. "Fighting fire with fire is never the solution to a problem. The Soviet Army is equipped with machine guns. They have plenty of ammunition. Don't give them an excuse to pull the trigger. It will end with unnecessary bloodshed if we don't cooperate."

"You are correct, Father," Evzen said. "Cooperation is peace. Look what happened to Sascha."

"They will eventually go home," the priest went on.

"They always do," Oflan agreed.

Ayna looked across the aisle at Tad——the once proud and

vigilant violinist——surprisingly defeated by Sascha's death. It appeared he, too, had thrown his convictions into the river. "And you?" she asked. "Was your friend's death an act of self-defense?"

"It's complicated," Tad said. His son and daughter clutched to his arms, cementing his body to the pew. "What would my children do without me?"

Ayna huffed with frustration.

Why did Sascha's death move her to resist the Russians, while it sent every other villager back into their ancient hiding holes?

Josef rose from his pew and bowed his head to the priest. "Father, we hear of resistance in Prague, in Pilzen, and in Liberec. Fourteen million Czechs are outraged. It's true, Sascha was too aggressive in the way he confronted the Russians. You are certainly right to oppose fighting fire with fire. Yet I wonder, isn't it possible for us to make some sort of a stand without raising a fist?"

Ayna said, "Words will get us nowhere, Josef."

The townspeople booed and hissed.

Verushka, a skeletal old woman in a headscarf, who had recently celebrated her 70th wedding anniversary to Evzen, leapt to her feet, shook a finger at Ayna, and said, "Who do you think you are?"

"Fools." Josef glared at the congregation. "Let the young woman speak."

Verushka spoke over him, "We used to burn girls like Ayna at the stake. Azerbaijani. Gypsy. Muslim."

Nadezda Sahhat stood with tight, bitter lips. "My daughter isn't a Muslim," she said, looking directly at Verushka.

"Your daughter bears the curse of her Muslim grandfathers." Verushka pointed her finger. "She has the Azeri blood. Those people pray to Mohammed."

Ayna restrained her frustrated mother by the arm. "Ignore them. It's not worth it."

But Nadezda would not back down, and said, "Have you forgotten? Ayna was baptized in this church. Leave her be."

Father Sudek raised his hand to hush the parish. "I have been assured by the Bishop that this occupation will be short-lived."

"Short-lived?" Josef blurted. "Really? What is acceptable to us these days? The army never left the barracks. Not a single bullet was fired at the Russians. How is this defending the homeland?"

"Didn't we previously discuss this?" Father Sudek said. "How to avoid a slaughter?"

Josef raised his voice. "Yes. But now comes word that even Polish soldiers are sleeping in Prague."

"You are half Polish," someone reminded the baker. "Maybe three-quarters Polish, for all we know."

The people were becoming bellicose, hateful, and racist.

Ayna placed her hands over her ears.

"The Russians will shoot you, Josef." Evzen threw a fist in the air. "If you make them mad, maybe they will come after me and Verushka, too."

"Ayna speaks the truth," Josef pleaded. "We've struggled for years to have these freedoms. I have been to Prague many times. I have seen firsthand how we have torn free from Soviet grasp. What of free speech?"

"My good friend," Father Sudek said. "We have known each other for many, many years. Again, I must remind you, fighting would result in more foolish bloodshed. Let the fallen body of Sascha serve as witness."

"Father, if you tell me to do nothing, if you tell me to be peaceful, if you say to me, 'Josef, today we are allowed to be angry, but we won't fight because it isn't worth dying for,' if this is what you tell me, Father, then, I will obey." The baker hesitated before taking a seat.

Father Sudek nodded. "This is what I tell you."

Ayna leaned into her mother, putting an arm over the sobbing woman's shoulders. She heard Emil whisper, "I'm sorry."

With tempers eased, Father Sudek held up a hand. "We must pray for Sascha. And for Zdenek Seifert's release. Tonight I will send a letter to the Bishop seeking advice. Until then, we should remain calm. Let us honor the fallen and read from David."

BEDRICH STOOD in the square with a dustpan and broom. What was it they had called him, a heathen? He had no idea what that word meant, but guessed it had something to do with the fact that he no longer attended church services, wedding ceremonies, or funerals. He had also stopped handing out prayer sheets at the door on Sundays and refused for some months to be an usher. After years of sporadic attendance, which included several stints as an altar boy, Father Sudek patted him on the back one day, and said, "You are adventurous. You have a hard time sitting still. At church. At the dinner table. Don't worry, the Lord will find you. You are the easiest of all the citizens to spot. You have a very large heart."

It was true. Bedrich was adventurous. He often spent nights alone at the derelict monastery, or walking in the countryside with the Holstein cows, or prowling on the rooftops. Once, in a nearby village, he had even pretended to be part of a construction work crew so he could sneak atop a roof with his Romanian Army binoculars to spy on a girl sunbathing in the nude. He loved girls, especially naked girls.

He gripped the broom handle and cast his eyes on the cobblestones. While the organist played, and the people remembered Sascha's life, he began to sweep the gutters and pick up cigarette butts and other trash near the fountain. He had already scooped a handful of rubbish into the dustpan when a screeching sound jolted through his ears. He shook his head, thinking the noise was buried inside his brain, the same way pond water got stuck in his ears when he swam. After another awful screech, he looked over his shoulder and spotted an iron monster, a creature with a red star painted on its skin, something the people called a *tank*.

NOW WHAT? Ayna thought, shifting in the pew as Father Sudek spoke about the upcoming recital and reminded them that he would not invite the Russians to attend. Alarmed by the clanging bell, she lurched to her feet, took Jiri by the hand and whisked him toward the doors. Voices trailed after her steps, "Where is the cursed Azeri going?" and "What right does she have to disrupt the funeral?" and "Muslim."

Father Sudek raised his voice in an effort to maintain calm over the mourners. "Sascha's light did not burn for very long," he was saying, "but his light was among the brightest we have ever seen." The people turned their heads and watched Ayna trample off. Josef stood and proceeded down the aisle, chased by Emil, and Oflan, and Pavel. The priest finally surrendered, hurrying into an exasperated "amen."

Her heart racing, Ayna pushed open the church doors and found a Soviet tank abandoned on the street. Its long gun barrel was pointed at the steeple. She could scream in frustration. *A tank in Mersk?* She closed her eyes. Maybe when she opened them she would discover these awful days of occupation had been a nightmare.

"Now they've done it," the banker said, speaking over her shoulder.

The mourners shuffled down the steps and surrounded the iron beast with curiosity.

The street musician was playing the somber *Blue Street Waltz* on his accordion. Predictably out of key, she detected. He needed a good lesson or two. She had told him this many, many times. He was lazy and had acquired a decade's worth of bad habits. It was why he played on the street by himself and not in a band.

By the time Father Sudek joined the crowd, the bell had stopped ringing and the people were turning to him for answers.

"Short-lived?" Ayna asked, thunder grumbling on the horizon. "Is that what you said?"

"There must be a logical explanation," Father Sudek replied.

"Nothing is logical about any of this."

Oflan whispered, "It's clearly a sign of the beast."

"Clearly," Emil agreed.

"Russians," Josef spat on the ground.

The boys had climbed onto the pear-shaped turret and were hanging from the cannon, caught up in a moment of fascination.

Evzen attempted to chase them down.

Father Sudek stood in anguish. "How could they park a tank in front of my church?"

Josef snorted, and said, "You might better ask, 'why have they pointed its gun at the steeple?' They closed the doors once. Who's to say they won't close them again?"

A few minutes later it started to drizzle. Josef snapped open his umbrella and kept the priest's head dry. The parishioners, chased by the musician, scurried back inside the church.

Emil said, "Do you really think they would close the doors again?"

Father Sudek's lips tightened.

Oflan took a sip from his flask. "As the good Father has said all along, this isn't our war. It's Prague's war. The progressives brought this disaster upon the people by throwing reforms too quickly into the face of the Kremlin."

"Regardless of who's at fault," Josef said, "this morning I witnessed Evzen waving to the soldiers. What's next, eh? Playing a game of Taroky on Friday night? Someone needs to have a talk with him."

Enough, Ayna thought. Enough of their idle grumblings. These were the men she respected most. Unfortunately they were more interested in playing the blame game than doing anything to address the problem. She shook her head. Their wheels were spinning in mud. If she were not so upset, she would have laughed at their grumblings, how they stood in the shadows while the Soviets gained a foothold over their lives with each passing day. She pulled the shawl over her head and walked away.

Father Sudek noticed her leaving, and asked, "Where are you going?"

"To do a man's work," she said without looking back.

"Man's work?"

"Yes. Someone must."

"But Ayna?"

Walking down the wet street, she brushed past Bedrich just as he attempted to give her the blossom of a crushed iris from his pocket. "Not now," she huffed. "Not now."

The walk gave her time to think. The colonel's speech about standing together and cooperating for the common good was bogus. What had he claimed? That the Russians were there to "protect" them? What message of solidarity was he sending by parking a tank in front of the church? Considering they were at a funeral for a man he was responsible for killing, it was nothing less than a slap to the face.

Then again, what did she expect?

She had, Ayna realized, been waiting to confront Dal ever since his soldier shot Sascha at the square. Did the colonel think he could get away with coldblooded murder? Now a tank? She tucked her chin and walked straight to the villa without stopping.

Horbachsky saw her coming and opened the gate with a twisted grin. "Hey sexy woman," he said. "Want to fool around?"

She stuck the palm of her hand against his chest and thumped him. "I demand to speak with your boss. If you don't take me to him this second, I will kick you in the balls."

Ayna marched into Dal's office and came to a standstill in front of his desk, rain drumming against the roof. She was drenched. Water dripped from her clothes and pooled on the floor. "I'm here," she said, "to make a grievance."

Dal looked up from a stack of paperwork and sniggered. "Aren't you aware? We have procedures in place for making grievances."

"I don't care about your procedures," she snapped. "I have something to say."

Dal leaned back in his desk chair. "Go on. What is it?"

"The tank. You. Your soldiers. Everything."

Dal's face showed no compassion, rather an arrogance that suggested he had more important things to do than listen to her complain. Worse, his cold mannerisms, the way he rolled his eyes and how he twirled a pencil between his fingers, reminded her of Ota

Janus.

"First you murder Sascha . . ." She squeezed the wet shawl in her hand. "Now this awful tank while we mourn his death. It's an insult."

"Insult? Please. You are being a bit melodramatic, don't you think? It's only a tank. A T-62 to be exact, designed by the OKB-520 design bureau some years ago. The tank is actually a remarkable creature. Light. Mobile. Its outer shell resembles the T-55." She glared at him while he scratched the mosquito bite on his neck. "Anyway, the timing is a matter of coincidence. If it bothers you so much, why not turn the other way? The rest of your clan has been cooperative thus far. I applaud them for meeting me halfway on the road to peace." He leaned forward in the squeaking seat and swatted a mosquito with a flyswatter.

"You have pointed the gun barrel toward our church," she said. "As though prepared to blow a hole through the steeple. Wasn't killing Sascha enough?"

"I appreciate your concern for the community. You have moxie, young lady. It's more than I can say for most people I have met in recent days. But listen, may I ask you a question? Why are Bohemian mosquitoes so damn big, eh? I have not seen insects this size since I was in Sri Lanka." He slapped his neck, then rolled the bloody mosquito guts between his fingers. "They seem to leave you alone. Why is that?"

His nonchalant attitude irritated Ayna. When he attempted to speak, she roared over him. "Have you not heard a single word I've said?"

"I know you are upset with what happened to your good friend." Dal reached for a pack of cigarettes in his jacket. "So you know, I have reprimanded the soldier who pulled the trigger. He will be investigated. If found guilty of wrongful death, he will do time in a military prison. Of course, this is of little consequence to you, no? I understand Sascha Boyd was dear to your heart."

He was attempting to divert the conversation. "I want you to move the tank," she persisted. "That's all."

"Move the tank?" Dal inhaled a breath of smoke and let it slip through his nostrils. "You think moving the tank is that simple?"

". . . it's all I ask."

He pushed himself up from the desk and circled Ayna like a hawk. "You are different than the rest of the women in town. Why is that?"

She smelled his awful tobacco breath. "I've come here to discuss the tank, nothing else."

"When I look at you, I see Paris, New York, Rome. Not fifteenth century. Not peasant." He breathed onto her neck. "Pretty smells. Western jeans. A cosmopolitan outlook on life. How is it you are so different from the rest of the citizens?"

". . . the tank."

Dal placed the dirty flyswatter on her shoulder and traced it across her neck, leaving a smear of insect blood. Ayna closed her eyes, mortified. If she had any concern for her life, she should run.

"Tell me. This curse you put on men. Does it date back to the time when you were sexually assaulted as a young girl?"

This struck a painful chord. "That's none of your business."

"They could not protect you from that in your church, could they?"

"The tank," she reminded him.

"They call you *l'enfant terrible of Bohemia*." Dal turned on his heels and went to retrieve a folder from a stack on the desk. He stubbed his cigarette in the ashtray. "It says so in your citizen documentation. It recalls the incident right here, and I quote from Mayor Astrom——mayor of Mersk during much of the 1950s——who writes, 'Ayna Sahhat is a promiscuous young girl. At fifteen, the Azeri child brings much disgrace and humiliation to the village. Neither Nadezda Sahhat nor Father Sudek can control her immoral liaisons with older men. As proof, on the morning of September 29, 1954, she accompanied Ota Janus to the ponds, where the charitable teacher intended to expand her knowledge of the indigenous wildlife in the area. On this particular day, the couple engaged in consensual sexual relations. A later investigation by the police revealed that she did not resist Janus, rather had teased him, inviting his hand to touch her breasts.'" Dal put down the file. "Though you claim rape. Why is that?"

Ayna looked resignedly at the floor beneath her feet. "I don't want to discuss this."

"I'm not saying you're a whore. I am simply reading what it says in the public records. Do I need to read the section titled 'who is Jiri's real father? Ota Janus or Dana Herd?'"

"No."

"But you were pregnant shortly thereafter?"

"My boyfriend was Jiri's father."

Dal pulled another cigarette from the pack on the desk, struck a match, then returned his attention to Ayna. "I have heard of this *curse of death* you put on men. It is intriguing to say the least. I wonder——could you put a curse on me?"

". . . the tank."

He moved to stand face-to-face with her, caressing her cheek with his hand. Like making a wrong turn into a bad neighborhood, she recognized the mistake of coming here and wanted to leave, except her feet remained nailed to the floor.

"I could lower the cannon," he said. "Or even move the tank."

"That would be a step in the right direction."

"But it would come at a price." He placed his hand on her waist, his fingers tracing along her curves.

She began to tremble and stepped away from him. "Don't ever touch me again," she said, the words stuck in her throat. "Or . . ."

He was not the least bit interested in moving the tank, or even listening to her speak. He had an agenda. There was a plan in his head, as there must be a Soviet master plan to rule the country, and he would not stray from it. The people of Mersk would come here in droves during the next few weeks and months and even years to complain, as they often did with the mayor, seeking ways to fulfill themselves. And he would pretend to listen by giving them just enough scraps of attention to please them or make them feel like he had somehow made a difference in their lives, all the while tightening the noose around their necks.

"Or what?" he asked.

Ayna tried finding the words. Something to put him in his place. Anything. Even a few simple words, like *leave us be*. Instead, her mouth tightened, followed by a heaving, anguished breath. Then she stormed out from the room.

DAL HAD NARROWED the list of troublemakers to a few men: the most likely to oppose him were the priest and the baker. Dr. Husak, who had left the villa only minutes before Ayna arrived, was also a man to keep an eye on. But Ayna? He had never considered the skinny Azeri woman a threat . . . until now.

He stood at the library window, hands tightly clenched behind him, and gazed down on the driveway. Ayna had already walked to the gate and was waiting for Horbachsky to open it. Her premeditated actions were alarming. She understood the risk of confronting him, nonetheless she had found the courage to speak her mind. He was aware of the red flags waving inside his head. She was the type of person who would be difficult to control with fear and with other tricks he had harnessed over the years to subdue the masses. He needed time to think about his next moves. Had he sent her away with a strong sense of authority? He suspected the answer was no. She was young, headstrong.

Dal lit a cigarette and watched her proceed in the direction of the stone bridge, toward the steeple and the village further down the road. And Bedrich was there, too. Hobbling behind her, his bum leg struggling to keep pace. They made an odd pair, he thought. *The Beauty and the Beast.* The imbecile's affection for Ayna puzzled him. The fool. Then again, could he blame the village idiot for having sexual fantasies? For trying? He blew smoke. No. He could not. Even imbeciles must crave women now and then. Even imbeciles.

At 8:40 p.m., Dal retrieved a file labeled *Sahhat*. For the next hour, he sat at the library desk with his cigarettes and read about the deadly events near the end of the war, which began on Christmas day 1944.

Here is Father Sudek standing before his congregation. Faces worn down from years of war and hardship are staring back at him. When will it end? When will we be free again? The question is on everyone's mind.

Jesus, he reminds them. Jesus is the only one who can give us unshakable peace during Hitler's unholy reign of terror.

Just then an unfamiliar Roma woman enters the church. She is about thirty, dressed in rags and work boots. She places a loaf of bread on the floor, makes a sign of the cross, and then turns and rushes outside.

Something doesn't add up.

Wait, where are you going? Father Sudek asks, chasing after her. He senses something. Sadness? Regret? Shame?

Already the parishioners are gossiping in the pews.

Dal flipped the page . . .

Come back, Father Sudek is shouting to the woman. We must talk. But she is gone. She has vanished in a blanket of falling snow, into the nothingness that has become war-torn Czechoslovakia. He turns and discovers a bassinet on the steps. Did she leave it on purpose? He has a sick feeling. He picks up the wicker cradle and carries it inside the nave.

Who was the woman? someone asks. Why did she leave a bassinet?

The bassinet is covered by a wool blanket. Father Sudek kneels in the center aisle and has a peek beneath it. Just as he feared. A baby. An abandoned baby. The odd-looking newborn is smiling back at him. He unbundles the baby boy and holds him above his head for all to see. On this Christmas day, he says, a child has been delivered to us. The choir has sung Bedrich Smetana's, "Ma hvezda," so the priest names him Bedrich.

The people are overjoyed.

They weep.

In the days that follow, rumors ripple across the village: Bedrich's mother is an outcast Roma, a member of the gypsy population, and his father is the hated deputy Reich Protector, a man solely responsible for the deaths of dozens.

By then the weeping has stopped.

By then there is fear.

Dal poured himself a drink. A Roma. A Nazi. Were Bedrich's parents a match made in hell? Like reading one of Chekov's masterful short stories, he turned the page with excitement, longing for answers. There was more, much more . . .

Days of nonstop searching follow. Where is the mother? Why did she abandon her baby? Is it really the Reich Protector's son? Finally the violinist Alasgar Sahhat tracks the mother down at a vegetable farm by the lake. She is a house slave serving the German officers at a nearby garrison. It's the lowliest of jobs. She carries the shame with her. In her eyes. In her heart. In the way she hangs her head. It's the kind of disgraceful job no one wants. But a task one must carry out to avoid punishment or death.

I had a secret affair with the Reich Protector, she admits. My husband is gone. Fighting in the war. Or maybe he is in a concentration camp. I don't know. But I was lonely. And very frightened. Then he entered my life.

I see, Alasgar says. Tell me more.

At first, he was nice to me. He gave me gifts. Perfume. Jewelry. Best of all, a job in the kitchen. It was more than I deserved for being a Roma. More than I could've hoped for.

But the baby. Why give him away?

Because, she says, a mystic has warned the Reich Protector of his own doom. That he will die a horrible death by shellfire if he doesn't find and slay his deformed son. She cries. She has been beaten in recent days. A bruise on her face has left the impression of a hand slap. I don't love my baby, she moans. Not like a mother should love her own child, but I don't want him to die either. The Reich Protector came here. I broke. Mersk, I told him. Go to Mersk.

Coldhearted, he thought. Although it made sense. Really, it did. She was simply trying to protect her baby.

Then it's Spring. 1945. A Friday. The Reich Protector arrives to the village with a squad of soldiers. Don't deny a father his own flesh and blood, he warns. We are in this fight against the evil Allies together. If you bring the baby to me, I will reward the entire village with a feast. German. Czech. We are like bloodbrothers. Come now. Let's put this little misunderstanding to rest. Let's feast.

But they don't listen to him. The people have already fallen in love with Bedrich. He has become their shining star during hours of darkness and despair. They are aware of the prophecy. That the Nazi plans to slaughter his son. So they pass him from farm to farm, house to house, keeping him from the German soldiers. For strength, they congregate in the church and pray that the Reich Protector will eventually go away.

Trouble. If they rebelled once, they could rebel again. Dal noted his concerns on a pad of paper. Since 1944, many of the influential townspeople had grown old and died. Nevertheless, many of the resilient citizens, like Josef, Emil, and Oflan were still living.

Instead of moving on, the irate Reich Protector returns the following

week. Where is my baby? he asks furiously. He orders his soldiers to
ransack the village. And the nearby farms. And arrest random
bystanders. He no longer speaks of a feast, rather instructs his soldiers
to beat several men. Still, he doesn't find Bedrich.

The next morning, the Nazi orders the citizens to assemble at the
square. His soldiers are holding the townspeople at gunpoint while he
paces back and forth. The lies, he bellows. The lies must end.

The villagers lower their heads and pretend ignorance, fearing the
punishment to come. How ruthless could he be? Would he kill someone?
Then suddenly the Nazi grabs Father Sudek by the neck and thrusts a
Lugar into his temple.

One last time——the baby?

Alasgar is standing next to Nadezda and their four-year-old
daughter, Ayna. He kisses Ayna, then places her in Nadezda's waiting
arms. Cover her eyes, he says. Don't let her see this.

He steps from the crowd and approaches the irate German officer. I
found your baby, he claims. It's true. But I gave the deformed child to
gypsies passing through the village. Now the gypsies are gone, traveling
like gypsies do.

Dal took a deep breath and leaned back in the chair, thinking of
how fearless Ayna had been today. Her father's courage lived in her
blood. As a clock struck, he mashed the stub of his cigarette in the
dirty Charles IV ashtray and returned his eyes to the final page of the
document.

Gypsies? The Reich Protector shakes his head in disbelief. More lies.
You have made a serious mistake by attempting to deceive me, he says.
He shoots Father Sudek in the leg, then grabs Alasgar by the hair and
drags him to the fountain.

Where is my baby?

Nadezda turns away, shielding Ayna from the violence.

The Reich Protector gives the defiant Alasgar six times to confess, shouting, no gypsies, no gypsies, no gypsies, no gypsies, no gypsies, no gypsies. He thrusts Alasgar's face into the water, holding it longer with each shout, until the sixth time, when bubbles swarm the water's surface and he lets go of the lifeless body.

A week later, the fighting erupts north of the lake. The two-day artillery barrage forces the citizens of Mersk to evacuate. When it's done, and sightings of the Americans begin to spread, the Reich Protector never again returns to their village.

. . . the people assume the mystic's prophecy has come true. That the tyrant was killed in battle.

Dal closed the file. A shadow loomed over Mersk. Not only Ayna's shadow, but that damn farmer who claimed the Soviets had done him wrong. He called for Gurko. "I want him checked out," he told the sergeant, standing at attention in front of the desk. "There are holes in his story."

"You doubt his produce was confiscated by our troops?"

"I'm not sure what I believe."

"What then?"

"A hunch."

"Do you care to elaborate?"

"Let me explain something . . ." Dal blew hot cigarette smoke through his nostrils. "As you know, I am well studied in the performing arts, both in literature and on the stage. Had it not been for my calling to Mother Russia, I would have been at the forefront of the Moscow theatre."

"You are considered a fine actor," Gurko said. "The most respected actor in all the Soviet Armed Forces."

Dal grinned proudly. He had performed in Moscow on several occasions, for Stalin, for Khrushchev, for Brezhnev. "The stage enhances the senses," he said. "It makes a man more aware of his surroundings. As actors, we look at other faces and attempt to find something we can mimic, like a subtle expression or quirky way of speaking. As such, I detected something peculiar with that farmer."

"Oh?"

"He appeared a little polished for my taste."

"I'm not following you."

"I keep remembering our conversation. Something about him was inauthentic. It has left me feeling suspicious. Maybe he was lying about troops stealing his food."

"Acting?"

"Yes."

"I wouldn't have noticed," Gurko admitted.

"More than once I caught his eyes searching the villa windows while we discussed the supposed injustice imposed on him."

"He must've been snooping."

"It's possible." Dal scratched his neck, one of many mosquito bites causing his skin to itch. "My instinct tells me this has the makings of State Security probing into our affairs."

"Maybe they sent someone to monitor us?"

"It would not surprise me. Therefore, I want more information on this farmer from Ceske Krumlov."

"I will look into it, comrade."

"We cannot take any chances."

"And if I discover he is a government agent?"

"Use your best judgment. Take advantage of the fact that blood will spill during these initial weeks of occupation. A roadside death here and there will not alarm the police. As long as we are holding the American prisoner of war in secrecy, we cannot afford to have eyes watching us." Dal took another drag of his cigarette. "Even if you are marginally convinced, you will know what to do."

"It will look like an accident."

Roadblocks aside, the drive in the midday traffic was mostly relaxing. Already he sensed the leaves were changing color. He loved the onset of autumn.

Milan rolled down the window and let in some air. He knew all about this part of the country. During the Middle Ages the people referred to Bohemia and the surrounding woods as "The Forest." The land, once home to kings and noble armies, in prosperous times and in war, encompassed most of their known world—essentially the edge of the universe. Even today the majestic mounds of woods rolled together from hilltop to hilltop like the deep green swells of an ancient ocean, endless it seemed to him, and when covered in snow made for the perfect holiday postcard.

He braked for traffic, a cement truck and several cars. On the radio, a DJ caught his ear, "Soviet oppressors, you have failed to bring us to our knees." The man ended his angry outburst by playing a bootlegged recording of the song *Revolution* by the outlawed British pop group, The Beatles.

Milan listened to a few more songs, all of them favorites of young people, and, as could be expected, frowned upon by the Party. They were followed by the DJ's courageous rants mocking Brezhnev's unibrow and taunting the KGB to find the secret broadcasting transmitter hidden inside his home. It was comical, depressing, hardhitting. Most of all, it lifted Milan's spirits knowing his countrymen refused to lie down.

Driving along the river, he passed an old mill with a water wheel, and a herder with his flock of goats. There was a boy leading a cow by a rope who looked over his shoulder and smiled. Again he spotted the green Ural truck parked in a muddy pullout. The farmer climbed from the cab as Milan waved to him. *Sweet Jesus, who did that man remind him of?*

Milan grabbed a newspaper and spread it across the steering wheel.

. . . on the other hand there was Prague.

. . . proud, bloody Prague.

The headlines shot off the page: hundreds of people had gathered at the National Museum to face down the Soviet troops. Students, standing arm in arm, formed human blockades, and some of them hurled Molotov cocktails at the tanks. The violence rocking the streets of the capital hadn't diminished one bit. The people were still protesting in swarms, fighting tooth and nail for their sovereignty.

Milan was turning the page when he took a curve too fast and felt the car sliding off the pavement. Just then he saw a woman walking in the way. He stomped on the brakes and cut the wheel sharply. Books, journals, and pencils hurled forward against the dashboard. The Škoda spun full circle in the grass, before coming to a stop. When he looked through the windshield, he saw her lying on the road, next to a cello case.

Oh my god, he thought. *I've killed her . . .*

DAL EXAMINED the mosquito bites on the POW's arms. "A trick I learned in Sri Lanka is to use your fingernail to press several times into the center of the bite, making a star shaped pattern. This helps alleviate the itching."

Johnston scratched the bite marks instead of pressing.

"Always uncooperative," Gurko said. "We say 'stand,' he sits. We say 'run,' he walks. You say 'press,' and he scratches. What is his problem?"

"What makes Americans irritating is their cocky attitude. Always wanting things done their way. It's also what makes them so formidable on the battlefield."

"They're nothing but arrogant imperialists."

"The American soldier is strong this way. Just look at their

General Patton. You must appreciate how this translates down the ranks, no?"

"I've never met a damn Yankee I liked."

Johnston was in leg irons. His ankle skin was cut and bruised from repeated attempts to escape.

"Interestingly," Dal said to Johnston, "from what I understand, male mosquitoes don't bite people, the females do. They need human blood to develop fertile eggs."

"It's a lost cause," Gurko injected. "You're wasting your breath. No sense in attempting conversation."

Dal helped the POW to a sitting position on the bed and offered him a cup of water, which he drank. He felt a sense of attachment to the prisoner. "I respect his silence," he said in Russian. "As a soldier, I admire how he has been a complete pain in the ass. When the time comes and he wants to talk, I will be available with listening ears. With answers."

"Except for his typical 'fuck you' and 'go to hell,' he is as mute as that damn village idiot."

"Let him curse. His insubordination is proof he gets stronger by the day."

"Yes, comrade."

"You know, the Vietnamese treated him like an animal. They almost starved him to death on a diet of fish guts and roaches. Remember, when it is all said and done, we are Russians. We are civilized."

Leaving the room, Dal said to Gurko, "In fourteen days, agents friendly to our cause will smuggle Johnston into East Germany. From there, a plane waits to fly him to Cuba. We will soon wash our hands of this mess. Until then, feed him lamb and dumplings, whatever it takes to fill his belly. He must be strong for the long trip to Havana. We promised Castro a healthy American prisoner of war for his belated birthday gift. Not a man who will simply keel over and die on the tarmac."

"Yes, comrade."

Dal rubbed his temples. "This damn headache will not go away." He felt nauseated most of the time, like suffering from a constant state of car sickness.

"The mosquito bite on your neck looks infected."

"It stings like hell."

"Maybe it's responsible for the headaches."

"Hmm."

"Maybe you should go to the hospital. Just in case."

"It's nothing," Dal said defensively.

"Except that it could cause you to—"

"Little things destroy men." Dal spoke over a grimace. "It's true. I have seen a soldier in shock express no pain after having his arm blown off by a grenade. I have seen a soldier with bullet holes in his chest look me in the eye and say 'comrade, send me to the front, the fight is not done.' Yet some men whine about ingrown toenails."

"Everyone has a pain threshold."

"In fact, Napoleon's defeat at Waterloo had much to do with his pain. Hemorrhoids."

"I had no idea."

"His hemorrhoids kept him from mounting his horse to survey the battlefield."

"You're making this up. Another one of your farfetched stories."

"No. I am telling you the truth, comrade. His ass gave him a world of hurt that day. In the end, his inability to manage pain doomed him." Dal tensed as another jolt spiked behind his eyes. "It will take more than a pesky insect to take me down."

"I'M SORRY," Milan said, kneeling at her side. "I wasn't paying attention to the road."

She sat on the pavement with her black summer dress pulled to her scratched knees. She looked confused and her skin was chalky.

"Everything happened so fast," she said.

"My stupid driving."

"I'm okay."

"Do you feel any pain?"

"No. Just lightheaded."

"I can help."

She pushed the hair away from her face. She noticed his leather satchel. "You're a doctor?"

"Yes."

"How fortunate."

"My name is Milan."

"Nice to meet you, Milan."

Her magnetic eyes sucked him in. He had never seen anyone so naturally pretty. A gypsy girl? he wanted to ask but didn't. All these thoughts came to him in a flash. He was flirting. He felt ashamed. What had they taught him in medical school? The patient first? Snapping back to medicine, he said, "Here, let me have a look."

"I'm fine," she insisted. "Just some ugly scratches."

"Most likely—"

"I jumped out of the way in the nick of time. However if you insist on making a fuss."

"We can't take this lightly."

She smiled. "I do like the attention."

Milan opened the satchel, grabbed a bottle of peroxide and disinfected the cuts. "We're lucky this is the extent of your injuries," he said, wrapping gauze around a knee.

She took a breath, which seemed to give her strength. "It looks worse than it feels."

Milan helped her stand. "Regardless, I hope this won't affect your cello playing."

"I play with my fingers, not my knees."

"You have a good sense of humor about this accident."

"Well, a little scrape on my knee pales in comparison to how I feel about the occupation troops. And the people they've hurt."

"Yes, damn them." Milan's mind flashed back to the hospital, to the bloodied citizens jammed into the emergency room, people in pain, lives destroyed.

"Anyway, I'm okay."

"At the very least, let me drive you home. Where are you headed?"

She was fidgeting with her hair, the way girls do when they are nervous. "Just down the road."

"Mersk?"

"Yes."

"I happen to be going that way myself."

"Oh?"

"Why not let me take you?"

"I suspect I'm much safer walking, don't you?"

"Good point."

"Besides I need the exercise."

He picked up the cello case. The handle was cracked. "Oops. Sorry."

"Not a problem. It's an old shell. Made cheaply."

"I'm sure it has sentimental value." He helped her with the shoulder strap. "Do you live in Mersk?"

"All my life."

"How wonderful."

"Such a bore, really."

"Well, a friend of mine has a music shop in Liben. I'll get you a replacement case."

"I better go," she said, the case resting against her hip, a hand on the strap.

Milan stood in the middle of the road while she walked away. "I mean it," he called after her. "I'll get you that case. It's the least I can do."

"Goodbye," she said.

"By the way, what's your name?"

AYNA WALKED with her head down and stayed clear of the road. The cool breeze seemed to have shifted a little, blowing in her face. When his car passed, she glanced through her hair, happy he had slowed to give her a second look. She felt compelled to shout her name but it was too late.

A few steps later, she saw a rabbit hop across the road and crawl up to a tree. What a cute little bunny, she thought happily. Politicians could learn a lot from rabbits. *For one thing, they don't start wars.*

She adjusted the strap on her shoulder and pressed on. She never minded lugging the heavy cello around town or on the country roads. By now, she was used to it. As for protecting her instrument, the cracked wooden case was of little value these days; it was actually a seventy-year-old relic from Budapest, purchased at a local secondhand store. The handle had been broken for many years. Indeed, it was in need of a ceremonious burial.

She stopped for a roar of cars. Someone called her name, followed by a cruel remark, "Witch!" Ayna was unable to make out the rest of their words, though could care less. She was still thinking about the doctor. Something about him. A moment. That instant when her heart had fluttered. And hearing his voice, *I hope this won't affect your cello playing.* She felt slightly ashamed for misleading him about the cracked handle.

After another car passed, Ayna realized Milan must be the new doctor in town. What had Josef called him? *Husak the war hero.* Lucky them. The village could use a hero right now.

STANDING WITH a colorful arrangement of marigolds and violets, Dal rang the doorbell and waited for a response. He wore civilian clothes and a thick coat of aftershave that hung like a wool jacket. It was 3:00 p.m. Moments ago, sitting at the café and chatting with the waiter, he had watched Ayna leave with her cello, on her way to music lessons on the outskirts of town.

"Good afternoon," he said when Ayna's mother opened the door. "You must be the divine Nadezda Sahhat, no?"

She was surprised. "Why do you ask?"

Dal politely removed his hat and introduced himself as the new district administrator. "I have heard nothing but good things about the Sahhat family, including the proud husband you lost during the war." When he called the man a "hero" for standing up to the Nazis, she put a hand to her mouth, her eyes glistening with tears. He had suspected mentioning the husband would evoke emotion; the flowers, handpicked in the fields east of the river, were meant to cement their budding friendship. "Please accept this lovely bouquet as a gesture of peace and goodwill between our nations."

"I don't understand," she said. Townspeople had gathered on the street. "Flowers. For me?"

Dal drew parallels between this encounter and a vagrant character he once portrayed in the theatre, a wily man who posed as a member of the nobility so he could have access to a wealthy family's home to rob them. Unlike that character, he was not after money today; rather, he wanted to gain the trust of the Sahhat family, which would ultimately lead to Ayna's hand.

"Flowers," he confirmed, placing the arrangement in her hands and wrapping her fingers around the wet stems. "For a beautiful lady on this warm and sunny day."

"You're too kind."

"The flowers are even kinder. They leave their fragrance in the hand that bestows them."

"Oh?"

"An ancient Chinese proverb."

"Lovely."

"In the Orient, I am told marigolds are the opium of a woman's heart." His mouth made a thin smile. He had a manner that seemed genuine and sincere.

"This feels wrong." Nadezda's voice began to tremble. "I can't accept these flowers. What would the people say?"

"I understand how you must feel." He looked into her taut face, the deep wrinkles around her mouth reminders of an unspoken sadness, of loneliness. "However from what I have been told, you are a pillar of this community. You, of all people, deserve these beautiful flowers."

Nadezda smelled the marigolds and the violets, then exhaled, a sign her walls were coming down. She had lived many years in solitude, without the company of a man. Dal knew this. He knew she could be vulnerable to his advances. If he could just keep the door open a little longer, he would reel her in, just like a fish falling for bait. He placed his palm on the door and budged it open another inch.

"It's been many years," she confessed, "since a man gave me flowers."

"They accentuate your lovely brown eyes."

Nadezda flushed with embarrassment. "So kind of you. I had no idea. I mean, don't take offense, but you're a Russian."

"Ah, when it comes to love, we Muscovites invented romance, not the Italians or the French."

Like an Indonesian Shadow Puppet, she seemed controlled by his unseen hands, by an irresistible desire to be cherished. He was skilled at propping up people's emotions this way. Knowing she had spent years in solitude without the company of a man, that her future was bleak, he turned on the charm.

"Come in," Nadezda said, somewhat hypnotically. "You're so kind. These flowers. What can I say?" By then, the wary onlookers were gathered in force. Someone whistled as she closed the door.

Dal took a step, a smile stretching across his face. "In the words of the great Tolstoy, 'Nothing can make our lives, or the lives of other people, more beautiful than perpetual kindness.'"

"I agree," she said. "Make yourself at home. I'll put the kettle on the stove." With her back to him, she picked up her purse from a nearby credenza, fished out a tube of lipstick and quickly applied a few strokes.

Dal walked into the modestly furnished living room. There was a tattered sofa, a rocking chair, and a china cabinet with a missing door. "I'm fighting for this town," he said. An oil painting of her dead husband hung shoulder-high above a small television, tinfoil wrapped around the antennae. The Turkic man's strong jaw and thick chevron mustache spoke of a hunter, his eyes watching him no matter where he stood in the room.

"Fighting for us? That's good." Nadezda disappeared around a corner, stepping into the kitchen.

"I remain optimistic for the future. You must not fret our presence. I may be Russian, but I'm a small town boy, not unlike you people in Mersk. It's true. I was raised by humble parents on a farm south of Stalingrad, in Kumsky."

"Never heard of Kumsky. Sounds nice."

The home smelled damp, the result of a leak in a corner of the ceiling where the plaster had peeled away. He knew the buildings in the Bohemian Forest took a beating from the rain and the snow. Like most structures in the Šumava Mountains, they were full of charm from the street view, but inside, in the attics, behind the walls, there was much maintenance to be done; many of the buildings, he suspected, were simply rotting away due to the economic downturn of recent years that prevented people from making needed repairs. He felt nauseated and tugged on his collar to get fresh air. Though the mosquito bite on his neck no longer bled, it had a bluish discoloration and he feared it was fungus-infected.

"Your government has made some poor decisions," he said. "Comrades Dubček and Svoboda are disillusioned public servants. They do not have your well-being or the best interests of the Czechoslovak Socialist Republic in mind."

"I don't read the newspapers," she admitted.

"Yes, of course," he concurred. According to records at the villa, she was illiterate. Nearly half of Mersk was ignorant, having no formal education beyond grade school. In the last hundred years, a handful at most had studied at the university. "Can't say I blame you for avoiding the newspapers. Except for *Pravda* and *Rude Pravo*, they are mostly sprinkled with lies."

"So I hear."

Dal took a moment to examine his cut lip in a mirror near a window, the result of the scuffle with the anarchist Sascha Boyd. He wore the wound like a medal of honor, proof of his unwavering commitment to Mother Russia. "I am thinking of the unfortunate incident the other day. The young man . . . Sascha."

"The boy had an ego the size of Siberia." The kettle gave out a sharp whistle. "He should've known better than to spit in your face. Shame. These kids today have no self-control."

There were many photographs in the room, mostly of her husband and Jiri. But of Ayna? His eyes searched, eventually finding a black and white photo of her on a shelf near a vase with plastic flowers. He picked up the photo of Ayna straddling her cello. Lovely. He glanced over a shoulder toward the stairs and began to wonder what the young woman's bedroom looked like, what her sheets smelled like.

"Ayna has your beautiful eyes." Dal set aside the frame. "Deep, like an ocean of mystery."

With this flattery, Nadezda emerged from the kitchen with a teapot and tray of ginger cookies. She deposited the items on the table and took a seat. "My eyes, you say?"

"Yes."

"Thank you. I appreciate the compliment. Were you offended by how she confronted you at the villa?"

"No. Though I admit, her fire caught me off guard."

"Don't take it personally. Like Sascha, she is young and thinks she has all the answers to the world's problems."

"I might have been a bit harsh."

"An apology isn't necessary."

"She asked that I move the tank," he said, joining her at the table.

"Oh?"

"It was bold of her. I was impressed by her courage. In fact, I have sent a request to Prague. I requested permission to withdraw the tank. Is she home?" He knew Ayna was gone for a few hours. "I would like to inform her of this exciting development."

"She's at her cello lessons. I'll share the good news when she returns."

"I would appreciate that."

They sipped the spicy tea without speaking. The silence was awkward, although necessary. She needed time to come down from the emotional high and accept the reality that she was sitting at the table with a Russian, a man who had given her flowers.

"My husband . . ." The words died when they passed through her lips.

Dal shook a cigarette from a package. He lit it while looking at his hostess with compassion. "I know. The village journal describes his horrible drowning at the hands of the Nazis." He blew a stream of smoke toward the ceiling. "I was moved by what I read, how he heroically stood up to the Reich Protector to save the imbecile's life. How could the Germans be so cruel, eh? How could they drown a decent man in cold blood?"

"It's painful to remember that day."

"I understand."

"He was a warrior . . ." There was a vacant expression on her worn face, and her eyes had a faraway look in them. "That's how those people are in the East. The men aren't afraid to stand up for their beliefs, even if it means sacrificing their lives."

"I am familiar with their impressive warrior mentality."

"Don't misunderstand me, he was also gentle and made me feel like a woman."

Dal suspected it had been years since she last opened her heart to the memories, instead choosing to shut the door on that chapter of her life, suppressing the pain, maybe even harboring some guilt for the drowning. He wondered if his wife loved him this way. If Grigori Dal died today, would his Olga think fondly of him in the years to come?

"Your husband Alasgar was an accomplished violinist, no?" Dal pushed the conversation toward reverence.

"The most talented violinist in Bohemia," she said. "He charmed me with Pachelbel, with Ravel, and with his Dvorak. I could listen to him play for hours."

"Did he play in the symphony?"

"In Baku."

"Wonderful."

She was simple, so typically country. Her reflections of a lost love had a numbing effect on him. He leaned back in the chair and sipped his tea. The sweet aroma reminded him of the lazy tea lounges of

East Java, where he often vacationed with his family. While she spoke, his attention began to drift and he recalled a Kenyan economist he had befriended some years ago at a hotel in Bali. The man, who was married to a white woman from America, had offered to take him on safari. The couple had had a baby together——born in Nairobi——and schooled by the mullahs of Jakarta. Though older, Nadezda reminded him of the man's wife. Maybe it was the interracial aspect of the marriage, that their children were the offspring of Muslims. Something.

"I haven't spoken of my dear husband for many years," Nadezda said, sipping her tea without looking at him.

"Oh, I suppose you must have longed for companionship. I admire how you have lived your life devoted to a single love. I'm truly humbled by your presence."

"How is it you know me so well?"

"We are simply sharing this moment in the way people often reflect and search for meaning in life."

Nadezda thanked him for being a good listener. When he asked about Ayna's sadness for having never known her father, she explained, "It's been difficult. As you know, a father's love can't be replaced. Worse, I confess, I've been a disciplinarian. I'm hard on her at times. When I see her face . . . I see his face . . . and I'm reminded of the pain." She heaved a deep breath. "I know, I know, it's not fair."

"You are blessed with family, your daughter, your grandson. There is much to look forward to in the coming years."

"I hope so."

"Nadezda . . . you must question why I am here?"

"It has crossed my mind."

He took a long drag on his cigarette. "If the truth be known, I'm afraid for things to come," he said. "At some point, once socialist order has been restored in the mountains, I will move to an office in Ceske Budejovice. After I am gone, different soldiers will come here. This has me concerned."

"Different?"

"The East Germans." It was a lie. He knew much of the German Army had already pulled back to their borders.

Nadezda snapped, "We don't like the Germans, colonel. They've left a bad taste in our mouths. To this day, many mourn the deaths of their loved ones at the hands of the Nazis. If you must send someone, why not send the Bulgarians?"

"Like the decision to move the tank from your church, it's not in my power to control what happens or when. You see, I am a little man following the orders of a much bigger machine. However as long as I oversee the affairs of the mountains and river valley, I will look out for the workers of Mersk, in particular the good people like you." Dal blew smoke through his nostrils. "Your beautiful daughter, well, to be honest with you, she will attract the eye of many lusting officers."

"The Germans are pigs."

"They are fierce aggressors. Responsible for two world wars."

"And savages," Nadezda added.

She was right. *Savages.* Though it was not necessarily a negative way to describe the proud German people. They came from strength, he recognized, not weakness. "I can protect this home. I can keep the soldiers away from your front door. Away from your daughter."

"How do you mean?"

"Ah, maybe this was a bad idea." Dal mashed his cigarette in the ashtray. "My apologies. I have crossed the line."

She placed her hand on his hand. "What's on your mind?"

Dal faked a sigh. "Nadezda, I confess. I am quite taken with your daughter. In particular with her courage to confront me. Unfortunately, courage alone cannot save her from the possible danger to come."

"Danger?"

"From the Germans." His friendly face masked his lust for Ayna.

"Oh, what are you getting at?"

"With your blessing, I would like to take your daughter on a picnic. I want to explain things . . . explain how I can help your family during these dangerous times. Help Jiri."

While Nadezda stirred sugar into her teacup, he listened to the roar of the armored troop carrier's engine on the street and knew his soldiers had dropped cardboard boxes in the square. Inside the boxes were red and white football uniforms, the colors of Bohemia, just what her grandson had requested. Dal waited for her to respond, all the while imagining the boys tearing jubilantly through the boxes.

"Other than protecting Bedrich from the Nazis, we have always been a cooperative family," she said. "Even when the communists closed our church, we did nothing to stop them. What is good for the peace is good for the Sahhat family."

"Then it is simply a matter of siding with those who mean you well. The savage Germans might not be so, well, they might not be so sensitive as I am."

THE SQUARE was a bustling marketplace by the time Ayna walked back to the village. Farmers, about twenty of them from the cooperative, sold their eggs, cheese, fruits and vegetables from flatbed trucks. Heaped out on the stones were green watermelons and bags of rice. She stepped among a bleating of sheep and goats, careful of the cello, and purchased some berries from a friendly farmer who had been her father's fishing buddy.

It seemed strange not working today, or yesterday, or the day before that. She had taken time off to prepare for the recital. Emil had insisted she have a few days to herself. *It would do some good.* Of course, she jumped on the offer to rehearse and not sell tickets at the theatre or control one of the marionettes during a show. Emil was one of the few people who supported her farfetched dream to play in the Prague Symphony Orchestra. He even paid for the cello lessons.

Ayna crossed the street and started for the library. She had a book on hold, *The Life of Richard Wagner.* She had ordered the biography a month ago from the library in Pilsen and could not wait to get her hands on it. She stopped at the town hall, noticing the doors were locked with heavy chains. Why did Colonel Dal do this? A sign in bold letters read: NO MEETINGS UNTIL FURTHER NOTICE. She glowered. What would the Russians close next? The library? She found a watering can and watered a flower basket hanging from a nearby streetlamp. Against the backdrop of war, the beautiful petals, yellows, purples, pinks, were a reminder of happier times. With all the violence in the country, and the sudden discovery of these chains, their pleasant smells were a welcome gift to her senses.

But happier times? Could she actually pinpoint a time when she had been happy? With Peter, of course. Yes, Peter. And, Jiri made her happy, but that was different.

She walked in the middle of the narrow street, beneath the clear sky. The sadness she had felt in recent weeks, the slowing of her heart and the depression that came with it, had grown less in recent days. Then it dawned on her, something to be happy for: the Soviet MiGs had been silent for the last 24 hours.

"How is the quartet?" a middle-aged woman asked. She was hanging laundry over a balcony. "I hear you have found a replacement for Sascha's violin."

"Yes. A high school student. She's brilliant."

"Sascha would approve."

"I know."

"Keep practicing. You know what they say. Practice makes perfect."

"It does, Mrs. Nemec," Ayna replied. "All things considered, we are more than ready for the judge."

"Tell your mother we must have tea. And celebrate."

"I will."

From a block away, she heard the street musician pushing on his accordion, then something else——boys shouting? She gripped the shoulder strap and pressed on. At the hardware store, she turned into an alley and found Bedrich on his knees, wearing a dunce cap on his head. With horror, she saw Jiri and his friends pointing their fingers and laughing at him.

"Jiri," she yelled, "what do you think you're doing?" She took him by the arm and led him to the halfwit. The rest of the boys trampled off.

"Sorry," Jiri said.

She shot her son a disgusted look. "That's no excuse."

"I won't do it again."

She tore the dunce cap from Bedrich's head and threw it in the street. "You're safe," she informed Bedrich. "The boys are gone."

She made Jiri say sorry three times.

Bedrich gave a crooked smile. If he had the sense to stand up for himself and punch someone in the nose, it would likely put an end to the perpetual harassment. But even as Jiri apologized for being a bully, Bedrich seemed more concerned for the safety of a white mouse inside the cage he was holding. When he hobbled away, she noticed the boys had taped a piece of paper to his back——RETARD.

"If you tease him again, I'll . . ."

Like a lobster, she pinched Jiri's ear and led him briskly down the street, past women who commented "he deserves a spanking" and "hooligan."

She turned at the bank building, and then crossed the street by the clinic, circling back to her home. Her frustration intensified when she arrived at the front door and saw the people huddled next to the Soviet truck. She knew right away something was wrong. How many had gathered, ten? Fifteen?

"What's going on here?" she asked, wanting them to go away.

"Your mother is fraternizing with the enemy," Verushka said, nose turned up. "I saw the whole thing. She accepted a bouquet of flowers from him."

"We would expect nothing less from your family," someone added.

"Leave," Ayna demanded, letting go of Jiri's ear. He held a jersey, number 9. "Mind your own business."

Throwing a palm to silence their insults, she burst inside the home and set aside the cello.

An irate Evzen shouted, "Collaborators," as she closed the door and sighed. Collaborators? The accusation was simply untrue.

She shut her eyes and counted to five, the way she did when she stubbed her toe or slammed a window on her finger. She leaned, put all her weight against the door and tried to ignore Verushka and company who were still breathing the hateful fires of yesteryear.

"What's wrong?" Jiri asked.

"Nothing." *No time to explain.*

She came alive with the sound of the colonel's voice. Why was he in her home? Had he come to make an arrest? Her heart was like a war drum, beating, beating, beating, calling her to battle.

"Go to the bakery," she told Jiri. "Find Josef. Stay with him until I come get you. And don't talk to any soldiers along the way."

"I won't."

"Be careful," she said. "And remember my instructions. Don't talk to them. Ever." She pushed him out the door, past the hecklers, though not past the life-long reminders that she didn't belong in Mersk.

Turning her attention upstairs, Ayna heard her mother say something about the marionettes. And Dal replied, "Lovely."

Now the irritation hit hard.

She placed a hand on the banister. *Were they actually in her bedroom?*

She took a deep breath and pulled herself together. As she climbed the stairs, her mind relived that awful moment at the villa, when he groped at her waist and breathed onto her neck. She thought about his arrogance, his smug confidence. The colonel was accustomed to getting what, *and who*, he wanted. She should have slapped him in the face.

At the top of the stairs, she smelled his blue cheese scented aftershave and quickly walked to her bedroom.

"You're home early," Nadezda said with surprise, as if caught red-handed.

"My lesson was canceled." Her mother had gone without makeup since the town's Christmas party. So why the lipstick today? She must be flirting with the KGB mongrel. Ayna felt disgusted. Her mother had done more than raise a white flag, she had courted the enemy——perhaps collaboration was next.

"Too bad it was canceled."

"Why are you in my bedroom? It's off-limits to you."

"I was just showing the colonel around our home."

Dal breathed cigarette smoke over the pages of her diary. "Hello," he said, closing the cover.

"And why are you reading my diary?" Ayna snatched the book from his hands. She was more angry than embarrassed by what he might have read.

Dal examined her from head to toe, pausing on the bandage wrapped around her knee. "You are an impressive writer. Your inner voice is reminiscent of the poetic Marina Tsvetaeva."

"And you would be a literary critic?" Ayna heard the cynicism in her voice, a good mimic of her mother's. One of the few genes she had passed along.

"Accept it as a compliment." He pointed to her record collection, an album by The Beatles. "On the other hand, you have peculiar taste in music for a classically trained cellist."

"First of all, I'm not classically trained. I'm self-taught. I appreciate all types of music: classical, folk, pop, rock. I like to keep an open mind."

"Well, I am out of touch with this western fad called rock & roll. The politburo frowns upon its existence. Between the loud drums and the obnoxious electric guitars, it hurts one's head." The colonel thought he was being funny, maybe even charming. "Personally, I have always preferred the breathtaking cannons of Tchaikovsky's *War of 1812*."

She glared at him, not wishing to have a conversation, before restacking her albums. "And secondly: don't touch my personal belongings ever again. Your hands are filthy."

"Please. Give me a chance," he insisted.

"Why should I?"

"I have good news."

"And that would be?"

"I have requested permission to have the tank pulled back to the fields near Ceske Krumlov."

"Oh? When will this happen?" Ayna remained stiff.

"It must go through the proper channels. The typical paperwork must be processed. Procedures, you know. How long it will take? A few days? A week? Remain hopeful, Ayna."

"I'm not that stupid."

The people outside her home had justification to hiss. Her mother had crossed the line. Socializing with the KGB was wrong. While she did not directly blame the colonel for Sascha's death, Ayna believed he had provoked her friend into a fight. And that made him an accessory to a murder.

"This is my home," Ayna said. "You aren't welcome here, regardless of what my mother has led you to believe."

"She has given us her blessing." It sounded more like a warning.

"Blessing?"

"To take you on a picnic."

"You can't be serious." Ayna was horrified. A picnic? With him?

"I know a beautiful spot along the river. You would enjoy the view. We might sit and talk about the tank. And about other concerns you have."

"No. Never." Ayna shook her head, throwing her mother a sharp eye.

"He means well," Nadezda insisted.

"You've gone mad."

"It's complicated. The Germans are coming to Mersk."

"I would sooner drown myself in the river than spend time with him." Ayna noticed her underwear drawer was cracked open and closed it.

"Most of this abhorrent pop music you listen to," Dal said, gazing at the record, "has been banned by the Communist Party."

"Banned?"

"Yes."

"What a joke."

"It's no laughing matter." The blood was rushing to his face. "I would strongly advise you to get rid of this counter-revolutionary paraphernalia. Should word get out—"

"Unless we have official Party business to discuss or unless you intend to arrest me . . ." She taunted him by holding out her wrists, which shocked Nadezda. "I would like you to leave my home at once."

Dal's lips tightened. He put on his hat and gave a polite nod. "Good day, ladies," he said and strode down the stairs.

Emotions overwhelmed Ayna. Terror. Panic. Rage. Resentment. "How could you, mother? How could you let the KGB into our home?"

"It was tea," Nadezda said. "A simple conversation. I was worried you had made enemies."

"We all have enemies."

"I wanted to make some peace."

"There you go again."

"You've created a mess. Someone must throw some water on your fire."

"Stop being such a conformist."

"You shouldn't have gone to the villa this morning. Do you understand what you've done?"

"I made a stand for Jiri."

"Why? Because of a tank?"

"The tank represents enslavement," Ayna said. "Today a tank. Tomorrow chains."

"You and your rhetoric."

"I also went there to honor Sascha, something no one else seems interested in doing."

"Then your reasons are doubly wrong."

"How can you say that?"

"It was Sascha's choice to assault the soldier. The Russians were only defending themselves."

"Ridiculous. You think like everyone else."

"That boy should've known better than to provoke a fight." Nadezda pointed a finger. "He was always a hothead. And stupid if you ask me. All this foolhardy talk against Moscow? All those secret meetings at the tavern. Well, they weren't so secret. It finally caught up with him."

"Now I've heard everything."

"This is a problem for the president, not for a country girl like you."

"The president got us into this mess."

"Regardless, we must be smarter than the soldiers or more violence will come." Nadezda was flustered. "If you push them, they will arrest you, then Jiri will become an orphan, too."

This hit hard. Ayna walked to the bed and sat with her head buried in her hands. There was no denying her mother's grim warning about Jiri's safety. "You're giving me a headache. Go away. I want to be alone."

"Father Sudek has spoken with the police. They have cleared the Russians from any wrongdoing. There will be no investigation into Sascha's death." Nadezda wore a long face. "This is how we live. Sascha should've known better."

"Leave," Ayna said again. "I need some time to myself."

Although it would be many weeks before the examination rooms officially met with the ministry's standards, and before a patient table and other necessary medical equipment arrived, Milan decided to break with regulations and opened the doors to the clinic the next morning. He posted a sign in the clinic's window:

VACCINATIONS TODAY

By 11:00 a.m., the lobby was jammed with people from all across the valley. A table occupied the center of the room, along with two folding metal chairs. Milan sat in one chair; the other chair was reserved for patients, most of them children. He had already given thirty-two vaccine injections for whooping cough and the line snaking out the door was growing longer.

"They've come in from the villages," Josef said, standing beside the table with a jar of black licorice. "Most of these folks have gone years without seeing a doctor. Whether it's too long a bus ride to the hospital or another bad excuse, some have chosen to live with an illness."

"Those days are officially over," Milan said. "Better times are ahead of us, brother."

There was a buzz of excitement in the room. Milan had hoped the decision to open the clinic would provide an encouraging jolt to the gloomy and openly frustrated public morale. Judging by all the cheerful faces standing in line, it seemed to have worked. He rubbed a swab of alcohol on a six-year-old girl's shoulder, poked the needle into her skin, then placed a bandage over the prick mark.

Josef gazed at the people standing in line and sighed. "This could go on all day."

"I imagine so."

"Do you have time to see them all?"

"I'm going nowhere, Josef. Not until the work is done."

"Well then, what can I get you? To keep you comfortable?"

Milan wiped a bead of sweat from his forehead. "A cool breeze would help." Even with open windows, the clinic was stifling hot and reeked of sweat and body odor.

After telling Bedrich to get a floor fan from the bakery, Josef said, "Father Sudek was right about you."

"Oh?"

"He says you're an unselfish man."

"Lies. Don't believe him."

"And humble."

"Please. Enough. You're embarrassing me."

"Okay. But there's something I've been meaning to ask . . ."

"What is it?"

Josef raised an eyebrow. "Why dedicate your life to the sick? Your hours are so long. It seems an underappreciated job."

Milan flinched. He always hated that often asked question: *why did you become a doctor?* How could he explain what had happened that snowy day in 1944 when he led a team of resistance soldiers to derail a Nazi freight train?

The plan had been to blow the tracks and heave a satchel of grenades into the targeted freight car.

The objective was to annihilate its cargo of radio communications gear.

. . . then run like hell.

On paper, it was a routine mission. The intelligence seemed reliable and the weather, even with eight inches of snowfall, worked to their advantage. They were seasoned warriors. All of them. When someone fell, another fighter stepped in. They had ambushed several freight trains and supply trucks during 1943 and 1944. Three weeks earlier, in fact, they had attacked a convoy on the road near Pilsen and killed several German soldiers.

Yet none of their work seemed as crucial to victory as destroying the cargo on that particular train. The Nazis had their backs to the wall. They were a major blow or two from defeat.

For the mission, Milan had packed the satchel with nine grenades. It was more than enough to destroy the equipment. Later, on the way to the ambush zone, he joked about slipping in an extra grenade for good luck.

Except he was unlucky.

The train's communications gear had been swapped, he learned the next morning, with twelve Roma orphans on their way to an internment camp in Poland.

Dead.

All of them.

Dead because there was an unexpected snow flurry and bullets zipping above his head.

Dead because he had shot the lock off the door and thrown the grenades into the railcar without looking.

Dead because when things are routine you don't expect the unexpected.

And that high-pitched scream? The voice that sounded like a little girl? He bowed his head and stared at the concrete floor.

"It's just the way things worked out for me," Milan finally said, a lump in his throat. "Now, which child is next?"

DAL WAS DRIVING past the square, on his way to Ceske Budejovice for a meeting with district Party leaders, when he witnessed the long line of people snaking around the block. "Unbelievable," he said to himself, abruptly parking the GAZ truck on the street near the café. "I gave the doctor specific instructions to keep things orderly. 'Do not move too quickly,' I told him. And he responds by drawing crowds? By inciting a raging mob outside the clinic?"

He mopped the perspiration from his face with a handkerchief before climbing from the truck with his black baton.

MILAN HEARD a disruptive noise and looked abruptly toward the door. It was Colonel Dal. The colonel was storming into the clinic like a man possessed, roaring at the women and children standing in the way. *Now what?* He set aside a needle and stood between Josef and Oflan. Thinking trouble, he asked, "What brings you to the clinic, comrade? Vaccination?"

"No."

"What then?"

"I am irritated." Dal squeezed his baton. "Why, you ask? Because my quiet Bohemian village is no longer quiet."

"Well, I never actually asked *why you're irritated.* But since you mention it, what seems to be the problem?"

"Take a look out the window."

"Oh, something wrong?"

"It looks like the gypsy carnival has come to town."

"I don't understand?"

Dal pointed toward the large window near the entrance. It had a broad view of the square, the trees lining the street, the cars, the people. "The square has become a parking lot," he said. "Your patients are obstructing traffic."

"I can explain."

"There could not possibly be a good explanation."

"This is a proud day for you, comrade." Milan savored the cynicism in his voice. He emphasized the word comrade as though speaking to a commanding officer. "We are fighting Bordetella pertussis this afternoon, otherwise known as whooping cough."

The colonel gazed at Josef and Oflan, then over his shoulder to the families standing in line, and back to Milan. "Why didn't you inform me of this public event?"

"It slipped my mind."

"That is no excuse."

"I don't know what to say. I have a clinic to run."

"This is severe. Every mother and child in the Bohemian Forest has come to town."

"For a good reason." Milan meant it. "I'm amazed. After all these years, the children are finally receiving quality treatment."

Dal swatted his baton against the desk. "Is this your idea of keeping things low key?"

Milan was taken aback. "Like any Czech, I'm simply carrying on with my work."

Dal turned to the families in the room. "Everyone must go home," he said. "If you are not a resident of Mersk, you have precisely ten minutes to leave town. Or else be arrested."

Mothers began to grab their children and flee.

"You have no authority to close the clinic," Milan insisted. "Your military jurisdiction, which isn't legal anyway, doesn't include compromising the public health." He reminded Dal how the Soviets had claimed to arrive as a liberating force, not an occupying army, and mentioned the names of important government officials who supported the clinic. He cited health laws put in place for the public good, emphasizing the need for them. By the time Milan finished speaking, the colonel wore a frown, disinterested in laws and unimpressed with his name dropping.

Dal said, "I let you have your way with this clinic because I trusted you would move slowly, that you would keep me informed every step of the way." He leaned menacingly into Milan. "On the contrary, your mob interferes with my ability to manage the affairs of Mersk."

"That's a bit of an exaggeration, don't you think?"

"I cannot have a rabble on my hands."

Josef injected, "A rabble? People are in desperate need of the doctor's good services."

Milan placed a hand on Josef's shoulder and spoke with a calm voice. "These families mean no trouble to your security nor do they intend to interfere with any Warsaw Pact operations. I assure you—"

"From this point forward, lines are forbidden in Mersk. Any line. Here. At the bakery. At the grocery store. Everywhere. I will not tolerate them." Dal stepped away from Milan and kicked the table. Needles, swabs and vials of medicine flew in the air. "All visits to this clinic must be made by appointment."

"That's ridiculous." Milan shook his head, looking at the medical paraphernalia scattered across the floor.

"I suggest you schedule them wisely."

"Have you lost your mind? The ministry—"

"The ministry is in turmoil," Dal said. "Exactly who do you think will be running the affairs of your country by this time next week?"

"I have children to care for, colonel. You're interfering with official directives from the Ministry of Health." Milan brushed against Dal, who was taller than him. "Until my superiors tell me otherwise, this clinic will operate as any clinic in Czechoslovakia operates."

"I am putting you on notice, Doctor Husak. Compromising my mission would be a very serious mistake."

Milan wanted to fire away an insult, instead he bit his lip, and with a deadpan voice said, "These doors are to remain open for any visitor —scheduled or not. Furthermore, I will visit Zdenek Seifert tomorrow to administer his insulin. If you have a problem with this or with my clinic, then I suggest you contact Minister Precan at once."

Milan thought back to the 1950s, to the progress made on eradicating malaria, which had been mostly eliminated from Czechoslovakia by the early 1960s. He recalled other mosquito-borne viruses, like the Tahyna virus, a disease that had been isolated in a Slovakian village ten years ago, causing patients to suffer from acute fevers, vomiting, headaches, and neurological infections. He was also familiar with the deadly West Nile virus, which had yet to be reported in Czechoslovakia, although was endemic to many neighboring countries. There was always concern the disease would eventually reach Bohemia.

And he had grounds to be concerned. He worried the heavy summer rains had created the perfect breeding environments for the mosquitoes, which thrived in wet areas across the valley. It was possible some of the flying insects were carrying deadly diseases, including malaria, dengue fever, yellow fever, and the West Nile virus.

Right away, he saw what looked like an infection on the colonel's neck. It would explain his flu-like symptoms and delusional state of mind. He remembered a serious case from three years ago when a man from Hodonin had suffered an inflammation of the brain after being bitten by a mosquito. Even though such cases were rare, the infected man had experienced a high fever and suffered from hallucinations until he eventually leaped to his death from a hotel balcony.

And Dal's health? Milan was so infuriated by his unrealistic demands to meet with patients by "appointment only" that he neglected to offer an examination——which would have been the right thing to do. In the meantime, the colonel had stormed away from the clinic and driven out of town.

"Once again, the KGB meddles in our affairs," Oflan said.

"The soldiers have crossed the line," Josef agreed. "This is a Czech clinic."

Oflan sat on a chair. His eyes were downcast, shoulders slumped. "What can we do? Father Sudek prevents us from defending ourselves."

"I'd like to clobber him," Milan said. "Except that would get us nowhere. He would arrest me, then use the arrest as an excuse to close the clinic."

"Resisting the impulse to fight was a good decision," Oflan said, wiping the sweat from his forehead. "Father Sudek would approve. Picking and choosing one's battles is always important."

"However we must spread the word," Milan went on. "That all are welcome at this clinic. We can't live in fear of these mongrels."

"Perhaps we could shut off the water to the villa," Josef said. "That would inconvenience them. Possibly force them to move on."

Milan grunted. "And where do you think they would go? They would move to your home. Or maybe to Oflan's home. They won't leave Mersk. Trust me. They're here until they receive orders to leave."

"I'm ashamed." Josef was gathering the needles from the floor.

"Ashamed of the army for allowing this to happen."

"We are in agreement, O'brother." Oflan nodded eagerly. "As usual, in utter agreement."

The men discussed the army's unwillingness to defend the homeland. They were unsure who to blame. They agreed it was an act of betrayal. Meanwhile something outside the window caught Milan's attention——the beautiful cellist he had almost killed.

"That woman . . ." Milan watched her walk through the square. She wore a black dress. "Who is she?"

Josef joined Milan at the window. "She is someone who would stand up to the Russians."

"She already has," Oflan said. "Apparently, the doctor has yet to meet our gutsy Ayna Sahhat."

Hearing Ayna's name for the first time excited him. He removed his physician's coat and left the clinic without saying another word.

. . . and he ran after her, across the square. His eyes were locked onto her swaying hips as he chased her stride down the sidewalk. She turned one corner, then another. It was not until he had reached the cemetery behind the church that he realized he was being tugged by the pull of gravity.

People stood in the way, greeting him. "Hello? How's it going, doctor?"

He looked straight ahead rather than meet their eyes, brushing them aside. They treated him like a celebrity, wanting to glom onto his war hero label, thinking that somehow he might protect them if and when the Russians came knocking on their front door. But it was a foolish way of thinking. Just foolish. He wanted to tell them this but didn't.

She glanced over her shoulder as if physically aware of his presence. "Excuse me," he shouted to her, waving a hand. "Can I have a word with you?"

She ignored him.

Two boys playing football in the street nearly tripped him when chasing an errant pass. One of the boys fell at his feet. "Sorry, sir."

"Careful," Milan said, lifting the kid. When he looked up, he had lost sight of her. He started into a trot, hoping to catch up, only to find that she had vanished.

He went on, hurrying to the next block, and the next, looking up and down the street. He stood on the pavement with his hands on his hips. He was breathing hard. Vanished? Or did she intentionally ditch him? He took grim inventory of the passing strangers. A man entered the bookshop. A small grocery store was filled with shoppers. Children left the schoolhouse.

Then a car screamed by. "Get off the road," the driver shouted, laying into the horn. "What's wrong with you?"

Milan paid no attention to the hotheaded driver. Instead his eyes were impenetrable and constant, focused on the storefronts, the schoolhouse, the sidewalk, the road.

Where was she?

Third Act: Shame

MYTH AND REALITY

A man that flies from his fear may find that he has only taken a short cut to meet it.

J.R.R. TOLKIEN

Dal at the café patio with a *Rude Pravo* newspaper—the official paper of the Communist Party of Czechoslovakia. The front page reported on a factory shutdown and clashes on the streets. More bad news for the country, but better news than had been published in previous days, when the sirens in Prague sounded, and a demonstration at the railroad station resulted in a woman's death.

His eyes drifted to an article at the bottom of the page, an appeal from the Central Committee urging citizen responsibility and trust:

These are grave moments in our history, comrades.
Long live Dubček!

During the early hours of the invasion, Alexander Dubček, along with several high-ranking Party members, had been arrested in the name of the "revolutionary government." Now came word he would be released and carry on as first secretary, thanks to the negotiations by President Svoboda's delegation in Moscow. The government, according to the article, had sworn to protect socialism in Czechoslovakia. This marked the first step in working toward a Soviet drawdown from Czech territory. It was true, Dal thought. The bulk of the troops would eventually withdraw, but the pro-Moscow mindset was here to stay. The invasion had not been about a long-term occupation of Czech land, rather an occupation of the mind, and with it the course of socialism. He sneered at the final words of the appeal:

We are with you. Be with us.

He folded the paper when a waiter approached and served him a cup of black tea and a slice of toast. "Spasiba," Dal said. "The service here is exceptional."

"We try to please," the waiter said, sliding a small jar of blueberry jam next to Dal's hand.

The waiter's long bistro apron was spotless, his hair and nails impeccably groomed. The café was the nicest restaurant in town and the workers took pride in their appearances, holding on to a much grander past. Life in Mersk, from the lonely street musician to the sparsely attended marionette theatre, was eerily surreal. With so many abandoned buildings in the village, the streets felt like a ghost town. Yet here endured a gem of a restaurant, of five-star caliber, where the food and the service stood second to none in the country.

"Have you worked at this café for many years?"

"Ten."

"Excellent. This place must have been packed during its heyday."

"Even Comrade Gottwald ate at these tables during the final years of his life."

"Wonderful." Dal spoke cheerfully. "You are a loyal worker."

"I like to think so."

This was his morning routine, dressing in civilian clothes, eating at the local café, making idle conversation with the friendly waiter. After breakfast, he enjoyed visiting the quaint bookshop a few blocks away and perusing the works of Plato and Aristotle. Though most of the citizens were standoffish or avoided him, some people, like the impassive waiter and the intellectual bookshop clerk, were willing to chat.

While farmers unloaded fresh produce for the local market, the imbecile appeared from behind their work trucks and entered the square. Dal tucked a napkin into his collar and spread jam on his toast. "You simpleminded fool," he whispered, thinking of Bedrich. "We share something in common. So few comrades in the mountains." He scrutinized the retarded man's youthful smile and the carefree way in which he threw handfuls of seeds to the cooing pigeons. It reminded him of an eight-year-old boy.

Dal had a bite of toast. The morning sunshine felt good and he was enjoying the time to himself. He needed restful moments like this. He was looking forward to the day when the Soviet military had fully secured the country and he could slip away to the spa for some rest and relaxation. It would do him some good.

Just then, Horbachsky approached the table. He was holding a metal bucket. "The hardware store employees were reluctant to help," the Ukrainian private said.

Dal set aside his toast. "You didn't steal that bucket, did you?"

"I paid for it with the crowns you gave me."

"Good." Dal had a drink of water. "Putting money into the local economy is a good thing. These people have seen better times."

"Maybe so, but I don't understand the currency exchange. I think they might've shortchanged me."

"Oh? Where is the change?"

"They took it."

"All of it?"

"Yes."

"Dear Lenin, why are you such a moron?" Dal wiped jam from the corner of his mouth with the napkin. "I have little patience today. Get to work, private. You have already wasted enough of my time."

"Yes, comrade colonel."

When Horbachsky crossed the street, Dal dropped a lump of sugar into his teacup and watched the gangly soldier approach the imbecile.

"You there," Horbachsky said to Bedrich, flashing a pornographic magazine. "Do you like girls? Help me drain the water from this fountain and I will let you look at the naked lady pictures inside this magazine."

Bedrich's eyes lit up. He took the bucket and stepped shin-deep into the fountain. Heaving a grunt, he scooped a pail of water, never pausing to break. Meanwhile Horbachsky stepped aside, distracted by a couple of flirtatious girls who had stopped to peek at his gun. He bummed a cigarette from them, and chatted.

Thirty minutes later, Father Sudek limped into the square on his cane. Dal glanced up from the paper. He was struck by how quickly the priest walked. The Nazi bullet trapped in his leg had slowed him very little over the years.

"Bedrich, what in God's kingdom are you doing?" the priest asked.

"What do you think, eh?" Horbachsky towered over Father Sudek. "He is emptying the fountain."

"Emptying it. Why?"

"The colonel has a surprise for you people."

"This is unnecessary."

"I'm only following orders."

"That doesn't make it right."

"If you have a problem, talk to Colonel Dal."

Dal sipped his tea and nodded approvingly at the priest.

"We don't need your help," Father Sudek said to Horbachsky. He pulled Bedrich by the arm. "The street cleaner will take care of the muck water in due time."

Horbachsky inspected the nearly dry basin with a grin. "Too late. Job's already done."

Bedrich groped Horbachsky's army jacket, trying to grab the magazine. Instead of letting him look at the pictures, the private pushed him away and returned rapidly to the café.

"I was clear," Dal said to Horbachsky, "from the onset of this mission. Pornographic materials are strictly forbidden."

"I forgot, comrade colonel."

"And furthermore, why tease the imbecile?"

"I don't understand?"

Dal shook his head. "You promised him the magazine, private. Are you not a man of your word?"

"But—"

"Give it to me." Dal yanked the magazine from the soldier's jacket.

"Comrade colonel, the village idiot can't read."

"Read?"

"He has no brain, comrade."

"Do you actually think he wants to read the articles?" Dal smacked Horbachsky across the head with the pages.

"But—"

"You put him to work on my behalf. You promised the poor man the magazine for a job well done. He desires a naked woman as much as anyone. Don't make promises in my name if you cannot keep them." He had distaste in his mouth for Horbachsky. The private had no reason to display arrogance; he had accomplished nothing noteworthy in his brief military career.

"Yes, Comrade colonel."

Dal walked to the square and delivered the magazine to the overjoyed imbecile, patting him on the shoulder. "You are a productive worker. I will report back to the presidium on how you have joined the trust of pro-Moscow communists." Encouraging Bedrich and other young members of society to engage in open sex and pornography went against the old moral virtues of the church, thus diverting them from their religion, from the source of their strength.

The fountain dry, Dal returned to the GAZ, put the truck in gear and drove away, leaving Horbachsky standing alone on the street with the bucket.

At 7:00 a.m., Milan stopped in Lisov for coffee with an old friend. A member of an exclusive gun club, the retired doctor had invited him to join a wild boar hunt in the north, at a lodge built by Duke Schönburg-Waldenburg in 1876. Even though the invasion had put the outing on hold, Milan looked forward to spending time with the members, to a break from the long hours of medicine, and from the hassles of the occupation troops. Shooting a rifle, those rare opportunities he actually had these days, often relieved his stress. He had just left the man's home when he saw the Praga truck parked in a vacant lot near a petrol station. It was the same green truck he had seen in the previous days.

He stomped on the brakes and got out of the car. Another coincidence? Or was the secret police watching him? He walked briskly toward the truck. He was fuming, wanting answers. But his anger was replaced by confusion, by that familiar sense of déjà vu. He recognized the man climbing from the truck. "Frank Stevens?" Milan said in English. "Is that really you?"

"Yes," Frank said with an American accent. He tipped his hunter's hat. "It's been a long time. How are you, Mickey?"

Milan "Mickey" Husak was born in the village of Humsova, near the German border in 1921. Shortly thereafter, his parents immigrated to America, settling in Chicago, where he eventually acquired the name Mickey from his classmates. While his mother and father never lost their distinct Czech accent, and always dressed decades behind the fashion, Mickey was as American as the kid next door, right down to his knickers and striped T-shirts.

He was young then, Milan remembered. And patriotic.

In 1941, Milan was a biology major at the University of Illinois when the Japanese bombed Pearl Harbor. Like everyone, the surprise attack shocked, then angered him. The next day when America entered the war, he put his education on hold, joined the army and several months later shipped off to England to train for the war in Europe. His parents——he had last seen them waving goodbye from a terminal at O'Hare airport——were proud of his fighting spirit. They always spoke of how good life was in America, and other than missing their relatives in Czechoslovakia, they had raised him to understand that the United States was a land of opportunity and, as the anthem declared, *land of the free.*

It was Frank who had found him in the English town of Dorset and recruited him into the OSS. Frank who had trained him in the art of deception. Frank who had taught him how to kill with a single hand.

In February 1943, in preparation for its liberation, and because Milan spoke Czech, he parachuted into German occupied Bohemia to serve with the resistance. After landing in a barren wheat field, he donned his civvies, buried his gear in the snow, and then reached his rendezvous point within an hour. He had passed his first test by avoiding capture.

Now what? he remembered thinking. Even with his military training, Milan felt lost and unprepared for combat. He was only twenty-two-years-old. Nothing in life could have possibly prepared him for this, for the killing that lay ahead.

The following day, he took to the streets, joining the handful of British soldiers already embedded into the fabric of society with their forged identities. He did his best to blend in, without drawing attention to himself. Frank had forewarned him, *you must never reveal your American roots. You're Czech. Born and raised in Humsova.*

Milan understood.

The Germans shot allied soldiers who aided partisans——no questions asked.

Spring 1943. Milan had snuffed out his first German, a young officer in charge of a local communications depot. Now he was a wanted man, living a meager day-to-day existence, constantly on the run and looking over his shoulder for enemies. He slept in barn lofts, in hidden attic spaces, in slum apartments. He kept a loaded pistol near his hand and an ear alert to any unexpected sounds lurking in the night. You never knew who the informants were; the Nazis had their spies, too.

But most missions were not very dangerous. He spent the majority of his time in disguise, reporting on troop movements and photographing military facilities. Walking among the people, the crowded downtown Prague streets, he had perfected the art of trailing German officers and learning how to identify them by the way they stepped and by their body language. He memorized their favorite restaurants, the places they went to for sausage and a beer. He noted which brothels they frequented and the ladies they preferred. Some of the prostitutes were informants, luring valuable information from their partners. Everyone, it seemed, had a hand in helping push back the Germans, from prostitutes to the clergy, to the average person on the street.

He delivered the information to Frank, who kept a low profile, yet always seemed to be around when Milan needed him. When orders came to engage the enemy in combat——the missions he looked forward to most——he led a team of fighters in ambushes against convoys and other military targets.

He soon found himself on the Nazi's most wanted list, his face plastered on posters from Prague to Brno. It was quite an accomplishment for a science-minded kid from Chicago. Just a few years earlier he had been a whiz with a Bunsen burner and centrifuge, never having fired a weapon. By August, he was kicking Nazi ass. He was proud of his notoriety, though careful to keep overconfidence from seeping into his blood. He had seen the graves of those who fell due to overt cockiness and delusions of invincibility. In the end, his work helped pave the way for George S. Patton, Jr.'s Third U.S. Army, which liberated Western Czechoslovakia in May, 1945.

But no matter how much information he gathered, or how much

mayhem he stirred up with his resistance soldiers, Milan lived with an unshakable remorse for the unintended deaths of the Roma orphans. Not a single day went by that he wasn't reminded of the tragedy:

Children on the streets.

Children at the park.

Children in his nightmares.

In the days immediately following the war, while people celebrated at the Old Town Square and embraced their families, Milan slumped into a state of drunkenness and withdrew to the isolation of his cold apartment. He had no friends in the Prague ghetto. Not a girl. Not a drinking buddy. Not even a damn dog.

So-called "war hero" turned loner, he had been contemplating suicide for weeks, slipping from one drinking binge to another, sleeping with prostitutes, playing dice with sketchy gamblers, his hair grown out and looking like a disheveled bum. He planned to step in front of a moving bus or more symbolically a speeding train when his money ran out. It was only a matter of days. A few more rolls of the dice. A run of bad luck.

Then Frank found him lying in an alley with a bloody nose. He had been mugged and left for dead. Frank helped him to his feet and took him to a nearby café and bought him a meal. *I have an idea,* he said. *Might sound crazy. But would you consider staying in Czechoslovakia for a few years?*

Frank, like a football coach motivating his players before a big game, explained how the Soviets had no intention on withdrawing from the territory they liberated during the war, especially from Czechoslovakia. Stalin was breathing down the backs of democratic countries and planned to rule Eastern Europe with an iron fist. Half of Europe would soon be in chains. America, Frank made the case, must have agents in place with open eyes and listening ears. *The free world needs you, Milan.*

And there was more to the plan. Of course, there was always more. Things were never that simple with Frank. He had designs for Milan to attend medical school. *It'll do you some good*, he insisted. After all, Milan had a strong background in science. *Why not try medicine?* Frank's team had already forged the paperwork, which included an undergraduate degree in biology from Austria.

He slept on the offer and the next day found Frank on the hill at Letenske Sady Park, sitting on a bench overlooking the streets of Prague. *I'll do it,* he said. Going to medical school made sense. It gave him an opportunity to make amends with the past. If he could help the children of Czechoslovakia, perhaps it would shed some light on his lair of darkness. Forgiveness. He needed forgiveness. And the spying thing? He would give it his best shot.

But the last time he chatted with Frank was in the winter of 1948, three years into medical school and a week after the communists had taken over the country in a bloodless coup. At that time, Czechoslovakia was in complete disarray. Frank had arranged for a private meeting with him at the museum. *Sorry, Mickey, your parents were killed in an auto accident.* The devastating news hit like a brick. Milan had no siblings or relatives in the U.S. He was suddenly alone. There was, for the first time, no incentive to go home.

Soon thereafter the Iron Curtain was drawn and foreign agents rounded up, imprisoned, shot, or kicked out of the country. Milan had done very little intelligence gathering, reporting mostly on the bickering at his Party meetings and on a faculty member who was a Nazi sympathizer. Although he survived with his secret identity intact, the American intelligence community never contacted him again. As the years passed, soon to become decades, Milan assumed he had been forgotten and settled in, calling Pilsen home. Then sometime in the early 1960s, the exact time or moment having escaped him, Milan realized he was no longer an American citizen. He was, once again, Czechoslovakian.

"I haven't been called 'Mickey' in years," Milan said, numb with nostalgia.

"It's been two decades . . ." Frank patted him on the back. "Oh, how time flies."

"Hard to believe."

"I know what you mean. How are you?"

"The country has been besieged by Russians. Other than that, not bad."

"It's good to see you."

They exchanged memories rapidly, summarizing the previous decades in less than half an hour, talking about old friends in the U.S., and career milestones. Milan explained how he had started off at a hospital, only to find himself in an administrative role with the ministry, these days serving as a liaison to the hospital in Ceske Budejovice.

But Frank, he sensed, already knew about his life, his career, and the clinic in Mersk. Like a master chess player, he was in a constant state of tactical maneuvering, always one step ahead of everyone. He was the kind of guy you wanted to have a beer with; at the same time, the kind of guy you never wanted to pick up the tab. You didn't want to owe anything to someone like Frank Stevens.

"You've more than made up for what happened to those kids," Frank said heartlessly. "Hell, I'd say 'mission accomplished.' Well done, brother."

Milan shook his head. "Haven't changed, have you? You'd sell your mother's soul if it made for good business."

"Like I've always said, 'The fight for freedom must come first.' Besides, she would understand."

"Jesus Christ."

They walked to the truck. Frank grabbed a newspaper from the seat. It was the sports section from the *Chicago Tribune*. "Thought you'd like to catch up with the Cubs."

"It's been years . . ."

Milan took the paper with a thrill. His mind raced back to the summer of 1941, months before America was drawn into the war, when the nation was still reeling from Lou Gehrig's *Luckiest Man on The Face of the Earth* speech. While Europe faced off against the menace of Hitler, he and his college buddies had their own challenges, mainly sneaking past the ticket collectors at Wrigley Field.

Frank said, "Mickey, we kept the damn Krauts running in circles, didn't we?"

"The bastards. Every last one of them."

"You know, this Soviet-led invasion has stirred up old memories."

"For me, too."

"I've been thinking of you lately."

"Oh . . .?"

"Do you ever think about Chicago?"

"Now and then."

"Do you regret staying behind in Czechoslovakia?"

"No," Milan said. "It was exciting when Berlin fell. I was proud of our effort to defeat the Germans. Proud of the U.S. Army."

"That makes two of us."

"Then you forged my undergrad records, making it easy for me to get into medical school. Plus you gave me Czech papers."

"Easy enough to do."

"I wanted to stay. I wanted to help the children. You didn't have to twist my arm." This unexpected encounter reeked of agency work. Frank wasn't the type for small talk. "So, what are you doing here?"

"Good question." Frank grinned sheepishly. "I'm still a government agent. Been in the country for three weeks now."

"And . . .?"

"There was this farmer. Guy about my age. He was traveling in the north just prior to the invasion when he had a massive heart attack."

"So you assumed his identity, his name, and driving his truck?"

"Hell, even his damn hat." Frank tugged on the brim of the hunter's hat on his head. "Strange. We even share the same hat size. Guess it was meant to be."

Milan's jaw dropped. "How could you?"

"His family," Frank went on, ignoring the question, "doesn't know about the death yet."

"That's cold."

"Like you say, it's business. Anyway, my man in Prague has

doctored everything. I'm in good hands. But with Warsaw soldiers combing the countryside, things have been tricky getting around. My time is limited. Sooner or later the farmer's family is going to catch wind of his disappearance and report it to the police. I don't know, maybe I have a few days. I've about blown my cover trying to attract your attention."

"What's this have to do with me?"

"An American's life is at stake." Frank grabbed a file from the truck and showed him a black and white military photo. "This man: Gunnery Sergeant Russell E. Johnston."

Milan took the photo. "He looks familiar. That face. Tell me."

"He was on his second tour. Just three months from leaving 'Nam when it happened. Johnston. And two other Marines. They were on patrol when they came under heavy fire and were separated from their platoon. Despite heavy search and rescue efforts, we just couldn't find them. That Vietnamese jungle. It's a damn labyrinth."

"I can only imagine how hard you tried."

"But Johnston, from what I heard, took care of his men. They survived three days in the Que Son Valley before finally being captured by the Viet Cong."

"Gunnies are good men, Frank."

"But that's not all . . ." Frank plowed ahead with his agenda. "A few months after being captured, Johnston and his two Marine buddies were interrogated by Caucasians in a jungle camp."

"Soviets?"

"That's what it looks like."

"How do you know?"

"The Viet Cong released one of our boys. A levelheaded airman. Says he saw Johnston. Says he saw two other Marines. They were being questioned by who we believe were Soviet GRU agents disguised as Russian reporters."

"Sounds sloppy."

"It's war, not science."

"The Soviets would've been more discrete."

"Mistakes happen." Frank paused while a couple of cars drove away from the petrol station. "From what we know, prior to the arrival of the GRU, the Viet Cong pulled Johnston and his Marine buddies from their bamboo cages and housed them in a remote hootch. Apparently, they wanted to prevent them from having contact with fellow prisoners during and after the visit with the interrogators."

"Hmm . . ."

"The next day, the three Marines were marched away from the camp. They never returned."

"I don't know," Milan said. "A story like this has a way of taking on a life of its own, becoming more fabrication than truth by the time it's been told several times."

"The GRU," Frank pressed on, "had worked a deal. They provided guns and ammunitions to a warlord in the Quảng Nam province. In return, the Marines were handed over to them."

"Abducted?"

"Yes. Moscow wanted the Marines. Wanted them for an army program we've only recently learned about."

"What program?"

"Captured U.S. soldiers and airmen are being analyzed by Soviet psychologists. Then, when the Reds are done screwing with their heads, they become human guinea pigs in medical experiments."

"You serious? I have a hard time believing that, Frank."

"It's true."

"And Johnston? How can you be certain he was abducted? Maybe he's still in Vietnam."

"Eyewitness accounts put the Marines in Laos shortly after they left the jungle camp. Johnston has an unmistakable tattoo on his back, *Don't Tread on Me*. It runs shoulder to shoulder. Locals working for the CIA reported seeing a man with this tattoo in Vientiane. We can confirm Czech AN-12 cargo planes flying in and out of the Laos capitol during this specific time frame. Everything adds up."

"Damn."

"But get this, Mickey. He's here. In Czechoslovakia."

"What do you mean?"

"It's true. And at this very moment, he's imprisoned at the villa. Your villa. In Mersk."

"Mersk?"

"Yes."

Milan recognized the face and the red hair in the photograph. It looked like the body he had stumbled upon in the parlor. Dal had said the dead man was a soldier, one of his *best men*. But that was a lie, Milan realized, a cover-up of the man's real identity——a United States Marine.

"Oh, brother, you're too late."

"What do you mean?"

"Your gunny. He's dead." Milan returned the photo, his gut aching for the loss of the gunnery sergeant. "Sorry for the bad news. I saw his body. He was shot in the chest. Three times."

"You sure it was him?"

"Yes. The red hair."

"That's not enough evidence."

"Not every day you see a redhead in Bohemia."

Frank scratched his scalp. "I've been in this grind for a long time. Dead? No. Can't be. I know better."

"His face was swollen. Rigor mortis had set in. What can I say?"

Milan had been overjoyed to see his former commanding officer. Now he wanted to get back in his car and leave. If the police caught him speaking to Frank, an interrogation would bring up the past. They would learn everything. And they would send him to prison for his clandestine activities. Or maybe they would simply execute him for committing an act of treason. Still, he was overcome with anger for the abduction of the gunnery sergeant and could not walk away without learning more. After a bus passed, he said, "If true, this would be a serious problem for Moscow."

"Not just for the Soviets——for both sides."

"What do you mean?"

"To be honest, there are people in Washington who want to pull the plug on this operation. Damn career bureaucrats. Pencil pushers. You know. The type who avoided the war. Some of them think it's best to prevent POWs from reaching the nightly news. Especially abducted POWs."

"That can't be true."

"I'm not making this up."

"That's un-American."

"It would make your head spin if you knew the details."

"But why? Why would they pull the plug?"

"Reports of American soldiers held in secret Soviet Bloc prisons would blemish political records. Think about it. It would muddy legacies and reelection campaigns. Questions would surface, 'How did this happen? How many are there? What are you going to do to bring our boys home?' The public doesn't have the stomach for this."

"Unbelievable." Milan shook his head.

"I'm not suggesting the administration or anyone else in congress intentionally wants to leave our boys behind. It's more of a *turn your head the other way* kind of thing. No one wants to dig deeper into this mess. Because they're afraid of what they might find. So they don't. They don't want the headache. To them, it's best to pretend it never happened."

Milan groaned. "If they don't know about it . . . then they can't be blamed for it. Is that what you're saying?"

"Exactly."

"Jesus."

"If I ever verify the name of anyone involved. Trust me. The son of a bitch is going to get it from me."

"Good, Frank."

"Anyway, I'm not here on official agency business concerning the missing Marines. It's only a group of us veterans in Langley taking matters into our own hands. A side job. We just want to do the right thing and save them."

"God bless you, Frank. You're a good American."

Frank shrugged off the compliment. "Officially, I'm here to monitor Warsaw troop movements."

"You better be careful."

"I'm not worried." Frank rubbed the back of his neck. "I have the necessary assets in place to save my butt. In the meantime, if you could look around the villa for—"

Milan held up his hand. "Are you asking me to spy for you?"

"If Johnston is alive, my people can intervene before he leaves the country. We have collaborators in the Czech Army willing to help and—"

"And he's dead." Milan looked directly into Frank's eyes. "I saw his body."

"I have reliable intelligence. As recently as yesterday. It suggests KGB operatives are mobilizing as we speak. They plan to slip Johnston into East Germany. Trust me. He's alive. I have no doubt about it."

Milan groaned. "Don't get me wrong. It's been great seeing you again, but a lot has changed in twenty years. I'm Czech now."

"Some of our spooks have gone longer without contact."

"Spook?" Milan rubbed his forehead. "Oh, you've got this wrong. Our contract expired years ago, soon after the communists took over, when I was abandoned by you people. I haven't heard a word from anyone in your intelligence agency. Not a single word. Not since I last saw you in '48 at the museum."

"You must have known we'd contact you someday?"

"It crossed my mind," Milan said. "But two decades later? No. I've moved on. This is my home. Had you come here fifteen, even ten years ago."

"Okay." Frank sighed. "Fair enough. I'm not here to coerce you. Just thought I'd give it a shot."

"You deceptive son of a bitch. I suppose you had the clinic burned down in Kamenny."

"Why do you say that?"

"It was public information that the clinic would be moved to Mersk instead of rebuilding in Kamenny. Destroying the clinic conveniently put me close to your Russian dirtbags."

"Mickey, c'mon . . ."

"How could you think I would just drop everything?"

"It's not so unusual for things to play out like this. Business is business."

"You shouldn't have come here." Milan pulled the keys from his pocket and started briskly for the car.

"Listen. I can get you back to the States."

"I'm not interested."

Frank handed him a piece of paper with a phone number scribbled on it. "This number is your ticket out of this decade's old nightmare. Pick up the phone. Dial the number."

"Who says it's a nightmare?"

Frank placed a hand on his shoulder. "Give it some thought, Mickey. My people can get you safely across the border to Austria. Bring you home. Except there's a hitch. You only have thirteen days until we pull back to Vienna. Then all bets are off."

"Like I said, the Marine is dead. I'm sorry. I really am. I have to go." Milan opened the car door.

"Make the call, Mickey. Come home."

Milan climbed into the driver's seat, pitched the sports section onto the floor and rolled down the window. "I am happy here."

"It was good seeing you." Frank winked. "Don't worry. Your agency records were shredded years ago. There's no paper trail on you." He stepped away from the window. "By the way, I would burn the newspaper as soon as you've finished reading it. The secret police—"

"You should fall back to Vienna right away. It's not safe in Czechoslovakia. Especially for a guy like you."

Frank's eyes were heavy. "I'm not going anywhere until I confirm what happened to Johnston. The White House might not care about our boys, but I do."

"Don't ever give up, Frank. America needs more people like you."

Frank threw him a friendly wink and stepped back from the car. "I'm staying at the Grand Hotel in Ceske Krumlov for a couple of days. Should you change your mind."

"Then enjoy your little holiday." Milan cranked the ignition. "I understand the breakfast at the Grand is exceptional."

Milan pulled onto the road without looking back. He had no choice but to shun his friend. He had seen the body in the parlor. It had red hair. Even in decay, the face looked like Johnston.

He passed several cars, speeding along at 70 mph.

He didn't want to get involved in the mess. His clandestine years were behind him. He was no longer a spy. No was longer an American. He was a pediatrician. A Czech. He drove in a state of anxiety before turning at an unmarked intersection, where a broken road sign buried in the grass pointed toward Prague.

The fountain in Mersk had been a gift from the German town of Heidelberg in 1875, sculpted in memory of Elizabeth of Bohemia, nicknamed the Queen of Hearts. Before the plumbing broke, it was considered the most beautiful and possibly the most photographed fountain in the mountains. However with the sluggish economy, repairs were deemed a low priority and over the years its surface became eroded with black weather stains and its pool turned green with muck water. Dal knew the moment he first set eyes on her embracing arms and angel wings that she would make the perfect place to conduct the book burning, his little surprise for the community.

It had started at six o'clock in the morning, when people were startled in their sleep by neighbors pounding on doors——*wake up, wake up, the colonel wants to speak to us*. Whispers of Stalinism began to rush up and down the street. *What was the colonel up to? Was someone about to be arrested?*

By 7:45 a.m., Dal was ready to speak. He was in full military dress with medals adorning his uniform. He sported sunglasses and stood tall in the back of the GAZ truck. Like directing a play of inept actors and stagehands, he spoke dramatically through a megaphone, ordering the villagers to assemble in the square. "This is mandatory," he ranted. "All must comply. Workers. Mothers. Old. Young. Even the crippled must find a way to the square, be it limping, crawling, scooting, what have you. There can be no exceptions." They were lethargic in the way helplessness brings, trickling from their homes with their heads hung, their shoulders slumped, unwilling to make eye contact. Within the hour, he was preaching about the ills of Western materialism, demanding that every citizen collect items banned by the Communist Party and bring them to the fountain.

"We will conduct a search," he warned. "House to house. If we find unapproved materials hidden inside your homes, you will be punished."

By 9:00 a.m., a massive fire fueled by rock & roll records, pop culture magazines and controversial books burned inside the fountain. A long line of people had gathered with their cherished property. Anything that spoke out against communism or stoked the minds of youth with absurd Western ideas like free speech and individualism was slated for burning. While the people stepped forward one by one and pitched their items into the blaze, Dal recounted the failings of the free market system and reminded each person of the class struggle, commending those who resisted least. He understood their complaints and how they felt about having their books destroyed. Even he would privately admit that the Party had gone overboard with its official list of banned authors. Many of the writers were up-and-coming. They were the fresh voices of Czech liberalism, the so-called "flowers" of the Prague Spring. Ota Janus, knowing who these voices were, had, at the last minute, added their names to the list of banned writers.

Josef stood near the inferno, holding two novels defiantly in the air: Kundera's groundbreaking novel, *The Joke*, a satirical account of totalitarianism; and Skvorecky's sleepy novel, *The Cowards*, a sarcastic story that undermined socialism. "Kundera. Skvorecky," he was saying. "These are important writers of our times."

"Are they so important," Gurko asked, "that you would die for them?"

The days had been full of apprehension and everyone wore the scars of dread, perhaps none more than the irate baker. "These books are like good friends," Josef said. "The stories speak to us——to our souls."

"Friends?" Gurko examined him in a sort of mesmerizing craze. "What are you saying, old fool? Do you have conversations with your books? Do you drink beer with your books?"

"It's not what I meant."

"Ah, you Czechs romanticize everything."

"But our books—"

"Your books are full of lies." Gurko bullied Josef with a thump to the chest. "No wonder you have always been a conquered people. Your literature must be destroyed. There is no way around it. Skvorecky was banned years ago. I could throw you in jail."

"Banned? I didn't know these books were outlawed. What possibly—"

"Don't ask questions, fool."

The altercation intrigued Dal. Of all the citizens, the baker had shown the most resistance to the book burning. He let the argument run its course, listening to the enraged man defend his novels as being inspiring, thought-provoking, and often humorous.

"It's insanity to burn books because they represent an opposing view of one's beliefs," Josef said, saliva spitting from his lips. On arm size alone, he seemed capable of pummeling Gurko.

"Not insanity," Gurko said. "Law."

After more squabbling, Oflan, who had been standing next to Josef, touched the baker on the shoulder. "Remember what I always say about picking and choosing your battles wisely? This, my good friend, is that time."

"Yes, dear brother." Josef huffed. "But have you ever found a battle worth fighting? No. It's always 'that time' with you. Always."

"Let's go to the tavern," Oflan said. "I'll buy you a *Budvar*. No matter how much they scrutinize our new writers, we still have Kafka."

Dal took the books from Josef's hands and tossed them to the fire. "It's simple, nitwits," he said loudly. "Throw your illegal paraphernalia into the fire and walk on. Now, who is next?" He waited for Emil to approach with his progressive leaning marionette plays, one of them titled, *The Last Communist*.

Shortly after burning Emil's literature, Dal began to walk among the crowd, his shoulders broad and strong. He eavesdropped. There were conversations happening in the square: a group of women gossiped over the mayor's house arrest; the barber and several men from a nearby town exchanged news of the riots in Prague; and young people talked about Sascha's death. A mixture of ranting and conformity droned in his ears, though it was nothing to be concerned with. In fact he was feeling satisfied with the way his soldiers had conducted themselves that morning when Tad stumbled into the crowd with his violin case.

"Your war crimes have been documented," Tad shouted.

"Piss off," Gurko said.

Several bystanders, including the baker, attempted to calm Tad, until he broke away and confronted the sergeant. "What will the Writer's Union say? Your book burning reeks of Nazism."

The temperature was pushing ninety degrees and the heat was cruel and unforgiving. Gurko lost his patience and without warning punched Tad in the face.

Tad dropped to a knee, his nose gushing with blood.

"War crimes?" Gurko yelled. "You fools are misled."

Josef placed a comforting hand on Tad's back. "How could you?" he asked Gurko. "Have you no respect for humanity?"

Villagers began to break from the line and younger Czechs loitering around the shops ventured closer, anticipating a fight.

Dal had no intention of spilling blood on the street, so decided to intervene. "This is the wish of your government," he lied, speaking eagerly into his megaphone. "I have no axe to grind with you. I am merely following orders."

Josef helped Tad to his feet. "Bullies. Why hit a man for voicing his opinion?"

"Be wise . . . if you have any Western propaganda, including novels, Italian Fashion magazines or any rock & roll records such as Elvis Presley or The Beatles"——Dal waved a sheet of paper——"and if you are in possession of anything on the list of banned materials, it must be brought to the square."

Dal instructed Potapov, who had been keeping people in an orderly line with his rifle, to enter the church, to proceed to the custodial room where Bedrich lived, and confiscate the French pornographic magazine. It was no longer needed as a tool to purchase loyalty.

During the following hour, after Tad walked home a demoralized man, and Josef and Oflan went to the tavern for beer, while the books burned, the smell of fiery ink and paper smoke smothering the streets, everything remained orderly and oddly at peace.

Dal lit a cigarette and glanced toward the church. Father Sudek was sitting on the steps with his head buried in his hands. He had witnessed the book burning without saying a word. It was a sort of unspoken consent. The priest, whether he realized it or not, supported Soviet policies by maintaining his silence. And for good reason: he had come too far in recent years and wanted to maintain control of his parish. In all likelihood he feared losing his church again. Still, many questionable books filled his library shelves——books written in opposition to atheism, to censorship, to land seizure policies. For the time being, Dal considered the historic church library off limits to further search and seizure tactics.

He smoked, standing in approval of his decisions. While the book burning had brought many of them to tears, it had been for their own good. He understood his role as a defender of Marxism-Leninism principles. The citizens of Mersk were mostly uneducated farmers and shopkeepers. They lacked an understanding of real communism. They were oblivious to how the printed word could plant the seeds of anarchy in their vacuous minds. Many of their prized novels were full of anti-Moscow metaphors and cleverly written prose disguised to hide the underlying themes that spoke out against communism. True, for the most part they were naive to the divisive message spewed by the country's intellectual authors; after all, as Josef had astutely pointed out, they read mostly for entertainment, to escape the doldrums, not to learn fresh ideas. But a seed was a seed. Whether they realized it or not, the seditious words of the country's liberal writers had been planted somewhere in their cerebrum and were just waiting to blossom. Socialism with a human face? Where did it stop? He had simply intervened to save them from themselves.

Watching the downcast priest for a moment longer, he sensed the holy man was fighting with his inner demons; a lonely man invaded by a sense of guilt, perhaps contemplating a life of regret. The priest clung to the old system, the wait-it-out approach that reeked of selfishness and quiet defeat. Dal decided to remove him from his list of troublemakers. So long as Father Sudek's fight remained internal, the strength to lead his people in any meaningful revolt was unfeasible.

Next he mentally checked the baker off the list. And why not? Any man whose voice could be silenced for the price of a beer was not an anarchist worth his time.

This left only one troublemaker and she was watching from her second floor window.

"People of Mersk . . ." He spoke into the megaphone, glaring at Ayna who stood thinly veiled behind the bedroom curtains. "You are a decent people. If anything, your role in the struggle has been misdirected by your public servants. You are victims. Pure and simple. Yet some of you resist. Some of you are making it difficult for your brothers and sisters to coexist with Moscow. I warn you. Resisting the will of Brezhnev, who has the unconditional backing of your leaders in Prague, will get you nowhere. Do not make others in the community pay for your blatant disregard of the law."

"Comrade, we have burned their books." Gurko tugged on his arm. "Mission accomplished, no?"

Dal shrugged off the sergeant, glaring back at Ayna's window. She was gone. "The Azeri is pushing me," he said irately to Gurko. "And I do not like being pushed."

"I understand, but the POW. We have lost focus and——"

"Truth is, I had not anticipated a fight from the woman. She is trouble like her father. Mmm. I need a plan. Something to once and for all squash this lingering voice of dissent."

The music shop was in Liben, a poor district of Prague located across a stone bridge, famous for being the birthplace of the operatic contralto Ernestine Schumann-Heink, born in 1861. The old brick building, known for its catalog of rare sheet music, was wedged between a floral boutique and a crowded Chinese restaurant.

Milan parked next to a Soviet military motorcycle. He opened the door and intentionally struck the side of the bike, almost knocking it over. He was seething: the abductions from Vietnam, the medical experiments, Dal's lies. Standing in front of the restaurant while two Soviet soldiers walked by, he forced out a deep breath. Even knowing what he knew, what could he do about it? The government would throw him in jail if he spoke out against the crimes. As he reached for the shop's door handle, a poster in the window caught his attention:

WE ARE IN A STATE OF CRISIS. UNITE!

He stepped inside the shop and closed the door. The place stank of musty paper. A girl wearing horned-rimmed glasses was flipping through a bin of sheet music. Across the store, a young man with long hair and a mustache strummed an acoustic guitar.

Milan proceeded toward the back of the long building, past the brass band instruments, until he reached the cellos.

"Milan . . ." He heard a voice and looked over his shoulder. It was Philip Jagr, standing behind a glass counter. "How are you, my dear friend?" The overweight shop owner, gray with a single bushy eyebrow, wore a baggy tweed jacket with black trousers.

"Good to see you," Milan said. "I was in the neighborhood. I've been meaning to stop by. What's new with you, old man?"

"Another grandchild has fallen my way."

"More grandkids? How many does that make?"

"I've lost track. Ten I think."

"Well, congratulations. Whatever the number is."

Philip pulled a pipe from his mouth and circled around the counter. Instead of shaking hands, they embraced and patted each other warmly on the back. It had been nearly three years since their last visit. Too many years, Milan insisted. And yet they picked up where they last left off, reminiscing about old soldier buddies and endless drinking binges. It was as though months, not years, filled the gap between their visits.

"What are you doing here?" Philip asked.

"Music." Milan tapped his fingers on the counter. "I'm listening to Mozart these days."

"Mozart?"

"And others. Dvorak . . ."

"But you despise the classics."

"Not 'despise.' It's more that I prefer Count Basie and Duke Ellington. Lately, I've taken to quartet music."

Philip poured coffee into a stained porcelain cup. "You look stressed. What is it?"

"Nothing . . ."

"The invasion?"

"No."

"Work, eh?"

"No."

"Finances?"

"No."

"Ah, this is beginning to make sense. You've met a woman, haven't you?"

"C'mon, don't start with me."

"What then?"

"I'm taking cello lessons."

"Cello lessons?" Philip shook his head. "We fought the damn

Germans together. Who knows you better than I? You would sooner hit your thumb with a hammer than learn to play the cello. Tell me, what's her name?"

Milan sighed. There was no use lying to his buddy. "Okay, if you must know, it's a woman," he confessed. "And she happens to be an exceptional cellist." While Milan had never heard her play the instrument, he insisted Ayna was a genius. "And like many musicians living in the countryside, she longs to meet her counterparts in Prague." He had learned this last bit of information from Emil, who had stopped by the clinic with his niece for immunization shots, and then informed him about the upcoming recital and Ayna's talent for the cello.

When Philip learned she was thin, and not plump the way he preferred his women, and after further prodding discovered her breasts were smallish and not jugular, he cast his doubts upon Milan's love affair. "You shouldn't make such a rash commitment," Philip said. "The woman's thinness is an obvious sign she can neither cook nor likes to eat. Deal breakers in my book."

After marveling over the glorious size of his wife's breasts for several minutes, during which Philip compared them to everything from ripe melons to barrels of *Budvar*, Milan held up his hand, and said, "I don't need your commentary. It's actually very disturbing. You're a sick man, Philip."

"Bah."

"I only want a cello case. And something exceptional."

"Oh, you must be hard-up for this woman." Philip disappeared inside a room behind the counter. From the open door, he went on, "Honestly, I am happy for you. Small breasts or big breasts. What do I know, eh? Love is love. It's a good thing."

"That's what I wanted to hear."

"Best of all, this is your lucky day, because I so happen to have a wonderful cello case from Hamburg. It has a plush rose lining that would melt any woman's heart. Somewhat expensive, I admit. But for you . . . for a dear friend . . . I will offer you a ten percent discount."

"I had hoped for fifty percent."

Milan made sure none of the shoppers were within earshot, then with a subdued voice, he said, "So guess who I spoke to?"

"I have no idea. Comrade Dubček?"

"Try again . . ."

"Comrade Novotny?"

"You'll never guess. Not in a million years."

"I haven't any idea. But does your lady need strings? Y'know, the A string is easily over tightened. A cellist should always be prepared."

"Frank Stevens," Milan said bluntly. "And yes, throw in the strings."

Philip returned, gripping the handle of a black cello case and a pack of strings. "I misunderstood. I swear you just mentioned the name of the devil."

"Can you believe it?"

"You've gone mad."

"There's trouble in Bohemia, Philip. Trouble like you can't imagine."

"What have you done?"

"Me? Nothing. But Frank asked for my help."

"Goodness gracious. What's that sneaky bastard doing back in Czechoslovakia?"

"The KGB have kidnapped . . ." Milan sighed. "Ah, forget it. The details aren't important to you."

"What did you say to him?"

"I told him 'no.' I'm not in the game anymore."

"Good. Then you are a smart man. You had me concerned." Philip slapped the pack on the palm of Milan's hand.

"I'm surprised by your reaction. If anyone—"

"Those days of espionage are behind me." Philip spread his hands to praise his music shop. "I have all this to consider. Not to mention my wife. My children. My grandchildren. And you? You are a good doctor with a decent life. Do you want to throw it away on a decade's old promise to serve a country that left you in the cold?"

"It's confusing. I was an American." Milan looked him dead on. "And you were British."

"Nonsense."

"Our life as Czechs has been fabricated. We stayed behind after the war to be the eyes and ears of our governments. Me——for the President. You——for the King."

"To hell with them all. King. Queen. Prime Minister."

"We just stayed longer than we were supposed to."

The girl looking at sheet music sensed their heated discussion and shifted uncomfortably behind the bins. Noticing this, they lowered their tone to a murmur.

Philip said, "You. Me. We were always Czech. That's why we were singled out after the war. We fit into society. Just like pieces of a jigsaw puzzle. I can trace my roots back to the fifteenth century. My ancestors built Pilsen. I am a respected member of the Communist Party. I stand with Svoboda."

"Maybe so, but after the war, I signed up for this. I gave my word. America first."

"And what is that word worth today, eh? It will get you locked up in a prison. Or perhaps much worse, sent to a Soviet Gulag." Philip riveted his gaze on him. "Please. You must go away. Life has changed. The world has changed. I don't remember England."

When Milan reached for his wallet, Philip held up his hands to reject payment. "Consider it a farewell gift," he said with a frown, handing Milan the case. "And don't ever return or mention my name again."

"Goodbye then," Milan said, his pulse quickening.

That night a storm struck at the heart of German Bavaria, before passing over the Bohemian Forest and knocking out electricity on Milan's side of town. He lit several candles and ate cold pasta for dinner, some yams, and opened a bottle of Becherovka to drown his sorrow.

His mind, too, was a tempest, whirling with dread and second-guessing his decision to visit with Philip. Nothing good had come from their conversation. Only regret. Pulling his buddy into this mess had been a mistake. No matter how things turned out, he had lost a friend.

Milan checked the deadbolt, the chain door lock, then sat grimfaced on a recliner chair in the living room. Goddamn, he thought. He could sink or swim. Which would he do? He drank straight from the bottle, half expecting the secret police to break down his door at any second.

When thunder rattled the windows, followed by a flash of lightening, he buried his head in his hands and heaved a sigh. *Was there a way out of this mess?* His mind drifted to the boom of artillery, to the final days of the fighting. How had he survived the war? How?

Truth was, near the end of combat, when Patton's Third Army was marching into Bohemia, he held little value for his own life. The deaths of the Roma orphans had destroyed him, his spirit, his will to live. And so he had become reckless, single-handedly snuffing out a machine gun nest, skirmishing hand-to-hand with German soldiers, brazenly walking the streets when his face was plastered on wanted signs across town.

He took a quick pull from the Becherovka. He was lucky. Damn lucky. He had stayed alive like a man protected by a guardian angel. How else could he explain it? Yes, luck. But his comrades saw things differently. His acts of suicidal carelessness and stupidity came across as acts of heroism. *I'm not a hero,* he told them. *I am just an ordinary man.* The truth, which he kept hidden from them, was that he was stuck in depression and unable to escape the shrill of children's voices.

After the war, when the tales of his heroics began to spread like wildfire, he denied them, insisting they were fabrications. *Hero?* Milan felt fraudulent. But what could he have said to put an end to the showering of praise? They had patted him on the back, all of them: the ministers, top brass, his comrades, and even strangers. As the country began to put itself back together, Milan, like a national sports hero or a beloved politician, grew larger than life. Without asking for or seeking it, he somehow became a man the people could believe in. And there was nothing, nothing at all, that he could say or do to silence their kind words. It had simply gotten to the point where he finally grew numb to the adulation and withdrew into his private darkness, to that place where he felt most secure.

By 10:00 p.m., he was drunk and cursing the CIA for reentering his life. At one point, he gazed between the curtains when lightning struck and thought he saw Frank standing with an umbrella on the street below the window. Then darkness. Then nothing.

At sunrise, and still reeking of alcohol, Milan jumped in the Škoda and drove the streets until he reached the textile factories and the row of faceless concrete apartment buildings.

A convoy of Polish army trucks slowed traffic, forcing him to take a side road near the railway station where he got bogged down in road construction delays. The windswept rain was falling in sheets now as the tattered wipers sloshed water across the windshield. He stretched into the window and squinted to get a better view of the road.

He eventually passed between checkpoints and merged onto the highway. It struck him how the occupation felt orderly, with little emphasis placed on ID-ing drivers or stopping cars. While protesting, Czechs had slowly acclimated to the presence of foreign troops and returned to work as instructed by President Svoboda——*for the good of the economy*. It was an easing of tension, maybe even a reluctant acceptance of the lifestyle changes. In the meantime, people kept a watchful eye on the occupiers and carried on with their daily routines: working, shopping, sending their children to school. They trusted the government would turn back the Soviets through negotiations. What else were they to believe?

Milan rolled down the window and let the air rush into the car.

. . . he was reminiscing about America again.

There had been opportunities to defect, he realized. Though he had taken none of them seriously. Even when the communists turned life into a system of coercing neighbors, friends, and family against each other, rewarding those who reported anti-government activities, Milan never tried to flee the country. His parents were dead and his American school buddies were distant memories. Life had changed. He had planted roots in Czechoslovakia. He had developed relationships with his patients and with his colleagues. Besides, why go back to the United States when there was work to be done at the hospital——especially with children? Nevertheless, Frank's offer to get him out of Czechoslovakia did stir up old feelings.

He glanced at the *Chicago Tribune* sports section in the footwell. He had made no real effort to hide the newspaper, let alone destroy the damn thing as Frank had wisely advised. Instead, he held onto the pages like a kid with a souvenir. And why not? The newspaper brought him back to a lost time, to warm summer days when life was carefree, when he wanted to be a ballplayer——the next KiKi Cuyler. It had been years since he really remembered his youth. And flipping through the inky pages, looking at the advertisements, Coca-Cola, Chevrolet, General Electric, took him home to a cramped apartment in Chicago, to the smell of the streets, to his parents, to his childhood friends. Even in his forties, he still embraced the lost life he had left behind so many years ago. But it was nothing more than a rekindling of distant memories. Utter, stupid foolishness. He felt no real desire for the past. Just a need for a future, which he grasped at like a man sinking in mud.

The streets were deserted when Milan reached St. Nepomuk and parked next to the Soviet tank and a scatter of cars. He was hungover and his mouth tasted like crap. With the *Chicago Tribune* in his hand, he got out of the Škoda and walked to a trash can. "Idiot," he said. Idiot for having kept the newspaper. Idiot for having carried on with Frank Stevens in the first place. He stuffed the paper inside the can and brushed his hands together. At last, the question of his allegiance and flirtation with returning to America had been put to rest.

He heard the pitch of the organ and started for the doors. The morning service was underway. He entered the sanctuary and sat in a pew next to Irena. "Sorry for being late," he whispered. "Russians, y'know. Damn roadblocks."

Father Sudek stood at the pulpit. "We are being tested by this occupation. How will we survive? How will we reflect upon these troubled times? As mere mortals who walk with the Lord? Or as men tempted by the devil? I ask you, will you sink to the level of the occupation troops? Will you fight fire with fire? Or will you wear your Christianity as a badge of courage and let He who died for our sins be the strength in our hearts and the might of our resistance?"

Instead of listening to the sermon, Milan searched the room for Ayna's black hair——which was buried somewhere in a sea of blonde and gray.

DAL GAZED at the steeple and shook his head. He was a proud atheist. A believer of reason, he did not understand how anyone in good conscience could dismiss the theory of evolution in favor of creationism. "Oh you pitiful fools," he whispered. "Organized religion is purely a means for the Christian church to control the masses. Why are you people so ignorant?"

Even though it went against communist principles, he was nevertheless thankful the citizens of Mersk were devoted to their religion. He credited their faith with having helped to maintain the fragile peace of recent weeks. With Father Sudek preaching nonviolence from his pulpit, restraining even the bravest of resistors, the people had remained somewhat orderly and obedient. It was why he never publicly chastised the priest or compromised his position as a leader. He had seen this sort of thing play out in the republics of Central Asia, where local cultures had been suppressed by the Party, and Islamic leaders, devoid of social antagonisms, were strategically propped up to manage ethnic tensions. There were times—like the present—when it was advantageous to look the other way and allow citizens to carry on with their tribal traditions. The people of Mersk could have their religion. They could sit in their church. They could listen to their priest. For now, at least. Until he decided otherwise.

Dal approached the T-62 and ran his hand along the armor. Always this question of the tank. Had the iron beast fulfilled its purpose? Had the threat of losing the church scared the people to the point of submission? He believed so. As long as the tank represented a symbol of power, they would remain subservient, allowing him to pull their strings at will.

Feeling at ease, he gazed across the cobble toward Bedrich. The imbecile was picking up bits and pieces of trash from the gutters. He seemed enormously cheerful for a village idiot. Not that idiots were typically unhappy, but Dal wondered, was he ever angry? Did he cry? He felt a surge of pity for the little guy. His role in the village bordered on nuisance. He was an outcast, the dreg of society. Without religion, he was an illegitimate member of the Christian community. Then maybe he did not need their god or their communal strength. Perhaps he preferred to go it alone like a wise socialist who turned to the state for support. Either way, he was too dumb to know what he was missing in life and thrived on the routine, dwelling happily in monotony. Today the trash. Tomorrow the trash. The following day the trash. Give him a little praise, Dal thought, and Bedrich would pick up trash long past midnight.

He took a drag on his cigarette and flicked the stub into the street. He began to walk. He approached Milan's Škoda and leaned into the window. There was a cello case in the backseat adorned with a red ribbon. A present? Something romantic must be happening between the physician and the girl. He had seen Milan throw some paper into the trash can before entering the church. Strictly out of curiosity, he went to investigate.

AYNA SAW HIM sitting next to Irena and smiled. What was the doctor doing at St. Nepomuk? She glanced at her watch, a gift from Peter, and shook her foot anxiously. *How much longer until she could talk to him?*

Forty-five minutes later, Father Sudek said his final "amen," kissed the altar and strode down the long center aisle with the altar boys in their scarlet robes and other members of the procession.

While the organist played on, she rushed outside the church to search for Milan.

Where did he go?

The parishioners lingered on the steps to chat and eat free pastries served by Josef and his bakery employees. Ayna moved among them.

She heard her name, "Ayna?" Then turned to Milan, and asked, "Who, me?"

He stuck a piece of gum in his mouth. "You're a hard person to track down."

She was tongue-tied. Did she really just say, *who me?* What a dumb thing to have said. Yes, you. *Who else?* She squeezed the strap of her purse and slung it over her shoulder. "You have been looking for me?"

He nodded. "Yes. Everywhere. You would think the village was the size of Prague."

She had been avoiding him for days, slipping out of her home and taking the back way to rehearsal, walking all the way around the church and entering from a side door, just to steer clear of the clinic. Except for yesterday, stupid yesterday, when she was in a hurry and thought she could sneak past his window. Then, after he began to follow her, she had no choice but to ditch him. The last thing she wanted was to get involved with a man.

"It's rehearsal," she muttered. "Morning and night."

"Now that is what I call dedication."

"It's what I love most."

"I completely understand."

"Speaking of which, are you coming to the recital?"

"Um, not if the Russians are invited," he said with a smirk.

"Heavens, no."

"Then count me in."

"Speaking of Russians, thank you for standing up to the colonel at the clinic." Her face was serious. "Finally someone who refuses to be pushed around."

"It was nothing," he insisted.

"No one else will confront him."

"Yes, well, I suppose there is no need for anyone to get hurt."

"Were you going to punch him?"

"No. I wanted to. But sometimes biting your tongue is better in the long run. You know the old saying, 'live to fight another day.' Still, I was pissed off. The guy's a real jackass." A football rolled up and he kicked it back to Jiri and the boys standing near the fountain. "He'd love more than anything to arrest me."

"Then it was good to show some restraint," Ayna said, walking toward the square. She grew excited when his hand accidentally touched her fingers. "If you come to the recital, I'll reserve a front row seat for you."

"I'll be there. Though I am curious about something."

"Oh?"

"Emil tells me you are the best cellist in South Bohemia."

"He exaggerates."

"Is it true?"

"Hardly."

"I would take it as a compliment."

"Emil is often too generous with his opinions."

"Seriously," Milan said, "have you thought about auditioning for the orchestra in Prague?"

"Funny you should ask. It's my dream to play for the Prague Symphony Orchestra."

"What's stopping you?"

"Well, for starters, I'm not a communist."

"Good point. Except the maestro would likely overlook that technicality considering your talent."

"Plus I'm a single mother. I'd need help. Someone to watch Jiri. Not to mention the fact that I don't know anyone in the orchestra willing to open any doors for me." Ayna hated being so negative, but it was the truth. "And did I mention occupation troops?"

"Are you finished?"

"Yes."

"Those are excuses," Milan said. "I'm sure the members of the orchestra each had their own stumbling blocks along the way."

"Maybe so. However I'm told the members come from prestigious families. They have college educations in music theory."

"Keep in mind, music comes from the heart, not the text book."

"Regardless, why would they give a country girl a chance?"

"Don't give up on your dream. Let persistence lead the way." He grinned. "Which reminds me, I have a surprise for you."

She lit up. "I love surprises."

"So close your eyes. And no peeking."

"Okay, no peeking. Promise."

Standing in the square with her hands over her eyes was perfectly reasonable, wasn't it? Her affection for Milan was purely adolescent and silly, and she loved it. But why him? He was not dangerous like Peter. Or criminal like Strom. Or rebellious like Dana. Other than quarrelling with the colonel, he seemed straight as a ruler. At the same time, she sensed something. A little secret. Did he hate cats? Or steal from the alms tray? She was trying to unravel the mystery behind her crush on the doctor, when he returned and peeled the fingers away from her eyes.

"Now then," Milan said excitedly, holding the cello case. "What do you think?"

Ayna's eyes widened. "It's beautiful."

"From Hamburg."

She took the case, opened it and touched the rose interior. "It's a bit feminine, no? I mean—"

"You don't like it?"

She gave a silly laugh. "I'm only teasing you. I love it. Really. I don't know how to thank you."

"I just wanted to make things right."

"Honestly, you didn't break my cello case," she confessed. "I found it at a junk shop several years ago, broken handle and all. It was all I could afford."

Milan looked as though on the verge of telling a joke. "Doesn't surprise me. I figured the case was already broken. But it was a good excuse to become friends, eh?"

"How wicked of you."

"About tomorrow," he said. "If you're available, how about a picnic?"

IT WAS DISGUSTING, Dal thought. Repulsive even. He smoked a cigarette in the shadow of the tank and watched them flirt. They were reminiscent of little lovebirds. How quaint. How hideously quaint. Was that the romantic music of Claude Debussy stirring in the wind? He could vomit over the way they brushed against each other and stared dreamily into each other's eyes. Dear Lenin, these men today, so submissive to women, always looking to please the opposite sex, what had happened to real men like the old Bolshevik Lazar Kaganovich and Stalin's executioner Vasili Blokhin?

He finished his cigarette, flicked it onto the cobble and stepped away from the tank.

So everything——the rejection, the cold shoulder, refusing to accompany him on a picnic——everything made sense. The lovestruck physician had outmaneuvered him. Dal groaned, walking toward them. He had not seen it coming. Then again, how could he? He had no idea the man was interested in Ayna. They were an improbable match——she the artist and he the scientist. He understood why she had rejected his advances.

He approached them mid-sentence, overhearing something about a picnic. "Doctor," he said, without looking at Ayna. "I apologize for the interruption . . ."

"What is it?" Milan asked.

"We seem to be on the cusp of a minor health crisis at the villa," Dal lied.

"Crisis?"

"My men are complaining about stomach cramps." Dal's face showed deep concern. "I am worried it could be something serious."

"Yes, well, a summer virus is going around. A particularly bad one. They'll survive."

"I'm sure they will. But there is more to this."

"Oh?"

"I have an ugly feeling. That it is something else. Spoiled meat. Or maybe . . ." He gave the physician a long stare. "Intentional food poisoning."

"You can't be serious."

"I understand the nature of civil disobedience," Dal went on. "It is the duty of a population to resist the presence of a foreign army. While the Warsaw Pact troops are not here as an occupational force, as you people seem to believe, I appreciate how uncomfortable the citizens must feel given the circumstances. This said, you might mention to everyone that food poisoning is a serious crime where I come from."

Ayna gripped the cello case handle. "What about murder?" she asked sharply. "Is that a serious crime where you *come from?*"

Dal ignored the comment. The girl had justification to be angry. Even so, her hawkish body posture annoyed him and he had grown immensely irritated with her attitude over the weeks. "Your comrades might find it humorous tearing down road signs. They've managed to misdirect a few tanks. I say, good for them. It must be quite a comedy to witness confused soldiers driving in the wrong direction. I applaud them for how they have resorted to peaceful means to unleash their anger. That said, I warn you, if my men are sickened because of poisoning, it won't end on a good note for anyone."

"If the folks are tainting your food," Milan said, "I will personally make sure it stops."

"Let's hope so."

"However I highly doubt—"

"At the very least, could you check on Horbachsky? He has been stuck to the toilet since yesterday."

"He's that ill?"

"Apparently so."

Milan rubbed the back of his neck. "These viruses have a life of their own. They run their course, then go away. It's nothing worse than a common cold."

"What I am hearing," Dal said, "is that he's not worth medical attention. Why? Because he is Ukrainian?"

"I didn't say that."

"You are not racist, are you? Anti-Ukrainian, maybe?"

"No. Why do you—"

"So you will not take a moment for my own peace of mind."

"Okay." Milan was frustrated. "You win. I'll head out there this moment."

"Thank you."

"Horbachsky, you say?"

Dal nodded. "I know this request is inconvenient. I promise you, I will make up for the trouble. I will buy you a pint at the tavern one of these nights. We shall swap war stories."

"I'm too busy to socialize."

"Well then, good day," Dal said, walking away.

MILAN DROVE straight to the villa and parked on the side of the road. Something did not add up. Dal's attitude. The drama in his voice. Something. He grabbed his medical bag and approached the gate. Gurko was there. "The colonel told me," Milan said, "about Horbachsky. How sick is he?"

"There must be a mistake," Gurko said, letting him into the compound. "He's perfectly fine. See for yourself." He pointed. The Ukrainian was cleaning his rifle near the flagpole. "Not even a runny nose."

Milan suspected Dal had made a fuss over nothing. *Damn him.* "Since I'm here, I should check on the mayor."

Gurko led the way to the garden where he instructed him to sit on a slated bench and wait. This was the pattern for his visits. Ever since Milan had stumbled upon the body in the parlor, even in the rain, he was forced to conduct check-ups outside under umbrellas.

Zdenek Seifert arrived a short while later. The sun was emerging from behind a cloud and shining directly on his face. As soon as Gurko walked away, the mayor shielded his eyes, and said, "I have something important to tell you."

Milan had never seen him so worked up. "Slow down," he insisted, moving his satchel for him to sit. "Let's pretend to have a look under the hood, just in case we're being watched. Then we'll talk."

"It can't wait."

"What could be so urgent?"

"Remember the mystery man? The stranger I overheard being interrogated?"

Milan leaned back in the bench and looked at Zdenek Seifert in a lingering and deceitful manner. He had no idea who was held in the hallway near the mayor. Dal had claimed one set of circumstances concerning the man in captivity and the dead body in the parlor, Frank had presented another version of the story. Trying to explain all this to Zdenek Seifert would only confuse him. It would expose Milan as an American spy. How would the mayor respond to his deceitful past? Probably not in a positive way.

"I already asked," Milan said, sticking with Dal's explanation, which he believed was a convenient lie to hide behind. "He's Czech. From out of town."

"What has he done?"

"Shot a Russian soldier."

"It must have been in self-defense."

"I'm sure it was. Best to let it go. If we ask too many questions, it will only make things worse for you."

Zdenek Seifert sighed. "He will be sent to Siberia for this."

"The occupation has been tragic."

"Too bad this fellow in detention doesn't know his freedom is only a few steps away."

"What do you mean his freedom?"

"It's what I wanted to tell you. How we can help."

"Go on . . ."

"The room where they are keeping this poor fellow is exceptionally large, larger than my own bedroom suite. It's an artist studio. Comrade Dubček has slept in that room. The secretary loves to water paint."

"Your point being?"

"Inside the dressing room closet is a passageway. A trap door in the floor leads to a shaft inside the walls of the villa. If you follow it, the passageway takes you to a tunnel, eventually to the sewer beneath the bridge." Zdenek Seifert grinned. "A frequent and paranoid political guest of mine feared the secret police. He insisted upon having an escape route."

Milan looked doubtfully at the mayor. Was he telling the truth?

The stone bridge was down the road from the villa, beyond a snag that marked the beginning of fence and pasture and innumerable strips of tilled soil. It was originally constructed in 1535, having been rebuilt many times since then, most recently during the war when it crumbled beneath the weight of a German Panzer.

Milan parked the car on the side of the road and grabbed his flashlight. The smaller things he was willing to cast aside, the mayor complaining about the tasteless food, about the colonel's condescending tone of voice, about the soldiers' loud music in the hallway——but a secret passageway?

He climbed down the rocky embankment and walked along the creek. He had to verify for himself that Zdenek Seifert was not lying about the existence of an escape route . . . that he had not lost his mind.

He followed the shallow water, stepping from one slippery rock to another, swatting at mosquitoes. After a short walk, he stood beneath the bridge's stone arch, at the opening of a sewer duct that emptied into the creek. A horrible smell came over him. He buried his nose in his forearm and pointed the flashlight into the dark tunnel. Could someone really reach the villa from here?

He squashed a mosquito on his hand, before taking a final peek into the tunnel. Even though the mayor's story seemed plausible, Milan decided against exploring further. What difference did it make if the sewer led to a passageway beneath the villa? It wasn't like he would do anything to help the imprisoned man——whoever he was. Milan just wanted to bide his time until the Soviets left. That's all.

He drove home to Ceske Budejovice with a heavy foot. The switch from soldier to medical student to spy had transitioned like clockwork. How convenient for things to have played out this way.

Looking back, he sensed it had been planned long before the war ended. Frank and his manipulative OSS operatives had orchestrated everything from the day he first set foot on English soil. *Clever of them.* But how did they do it? How did they know he would stay in Europe after the war and not go home to his family and friends? On paper it must have added up: Czech-speaking son, plus only child, plus proud American, not to mention the sheer excitement of espionage. Did the sum of those pieces equate to Milan spying for the United States government? Likely. If anything, he knew the effort to get him to remain in Czechoslovakia was not a reaction to post-war events as initially presented to him. His recruitment had been methodical, planned well in advance of Germany's surrender and the Soviet intervention into East European affairs. The pieces were put in place with the cunning of an experienced fisherman. Hook. Line. Sinker. Medical school had simply been the bait. And Milan, spiritually wounded and looking for some sort of salvation at the time, had taken it.

Arriving at the housing estate, he climbed the stairs to the fourth floor and walked to his flat. He went inside and pulled the curtains. He needed shelter. He needed protection from the outside world. He rubbed his temples. It came to him: he had lived behind curtains his entire adult life, especially after the communists seized control of the political offices in February of 1948. At that point, concealing his American roots became an act of survival. The pro-Stalinist regime of Klement Gottwald had gone on a witch hunt, ordering the secret police to run profiles on suspicious citizens, making sure no one slipped through the cracks.

Milan poured himself a stiff drink and sat at the kitchen table.

They were looking for spies, he remembered. Political opponents. Fifth Columnists. So-called "hooligans." When the police confronted him and asked about his childhood and the days leading up to the German invasion, he charmed them, cooperating to the fullest extent. *Who did you know? What did you know? When did you know it?* He kept his answers to their questions short and to the point. With the sleight of hand, he pulled the curtains over his American past and lied with confidence, speaking of the good ol' days in Humsova, the beer festivals, the feast day, and harvesting in the land of milk, honey and wine. While many of his colleagues were sent to prison or to reeducation camps, Milan managed to deflect the questions and gained the trust of the new leadership, advancing quickly in the Soviet-style health care system. Looking back, this had surprised him the most; had they investigated his childhood, they would have discovered he was an imposter. No one would remember him in Humsova. Or maybe Frank had that covered, too?

Milan glanced at the kitchen counter. The dirty plates and stained coffee cups had piled up over the weeks. For someone who kept a messy home, how had he been so organized when it came to deceiving everyone? After all, there had been no step-by-step handbook on ways to outsmart the communists. And Frank, who in typical fashion was conveniently nowhere to be found, had offered little advice, aside from an effortless *use your best judgment——your instinct.*

Instinct, he thought. What kind of advice was that? Somehow it had worked. Milan relied on his gut feelings during the early months when he began to mold a new identity and make the choices that would ultimately change his life. Good decisions? Bad decisions? He simply rolled with it, with his intuition.

. . . and he knew right away that he had to erase his past. So he did. The reinvented Milan Husak had never been west of Paris. *Capitalism is a farce,* he told his colleagues. *Plagued by greed and corruption.* He pretended to have limited knowledge of American culture. Hollywood? Baseball? Apple pie? These iconic images were no longer part of his culture. And though it went against his moral fiber, every bit of who he was politically, he convincingly played the part of a staunch socialist, shrewdly armed with a good Marxist quote for any occasion.

Milan heard footsteps and rushed to the door. He put an eye to the peephole. *Who was it?* Just a neighbor. Just a woman walking down the corridor with a bag of groceries. Nothing to worry about.

He took a breath, then found himself gazing at a bookshelf

stacked with books lined vertically and horizontally. Not just medical books, but books on philosophy and political theory. He had been hungry for knowledge. He did not know much about government prior to the war. Then somehow he found the time to read during medical school when he joined the Communist Party of Czechoslovakia. He attended lectures and went to political rallies at the universities in Prague, where he studied the philosophies of upstarts Mao and Castro. He found an edge, even some sanity, by knowing more about Marxism than most who professed to being Marxist. In the same way that anatomy meant everything to a surgeon, words meant everything to a liar. With this in mind, he memorized communist principles and important dates in Soviet history, like the events of 22 January 1905, when unarmed demonstrators marching to present a petition to Russia's Tsar Nicholas II were fired upon by soldiers of the Imperial Guard. Historical trivia, especially the events surrounding the Bolshevik Revolution, made for convenient discussion, allowing him to divert any awkward conversations that began to border on his dubious past.

Still, some things were not explained in books. *Like how to be a spy.* Fortunately survival came naturally to him. Frank had been right to advise using his instinct. Throwing him feet first into the fire was probably the best thing Frank could have done, because it forced Milan to survive. And survival, when everything was stripped away, meant relying on his personality. Making buddies. Getting on the good side of his superiors. Sucking up to the pro-Moscow communists by going on hunting trips and skiing with the Party elite. He attended concerts and accepted invitations to events at foreign embassies, impressing everyone with his knowledge of medicine and commitment to socialized planning. He had been to Moscow several times and was well known in East Berlin. Everyone loved him, foreigner and Czech alike.

These social events were the rare times when he actually bathed in his wartime heroics, mingling with the elitists he despised most. Indeed, like his knowledge of Marxist history, his actions on the battlefield had helped to thwart any anti-communist suspicions. By the time he quietly celebrated his tenth anniversary of living as a forgotten expatriate, he had mastered the art of changing the subject and pressed on with his life. He was the definitive CIA mole. And yet, after Frank Stevens fled the country, he never had contact with American faces or figures again.

Milan sat in the recliner and closed his eyes. *Forgotten.* That was one hell of a word. He pictured the dead POW Johnston, and other POWs, and he wondered, had they been forgotten, too?

Fourth Act: Interlude

A BRIEFING FOR THE ASCENT

It is always wise to look ahead, but difficult to look further than you can see.

WINSTON CHURCHILL

A man could find almost anything in Prague: weapons, contraband prostitutes, even safe passage to the West. After working his contacts, Dal finally tracked down a hard-to-find American baseball with its tightly sewn stitches. Located at a college athletic department in Pilsen, he sent Horbachsky on an overnight mission to collect it.

In the morning, Dal brought the baseball to the café and sat at his personal table beneath a patio umbrella. After sticking the ball into the pocket of his rain jacket, he ate his toast and skimmed a few pages from the *Chicago Tribune* sports section he had found in the trash can. Someone, presumably the doctor, had circled the score for a baseball game between the Chicago Cubs and the St. Louis Cardinals. This was oddly suspicious. Baseball? Few European men understood the rules of the American game played with a bat and ball. What did Milan know?

Dal was familiar with America's favorite pastime. He had studied his capitalist adversary over the years by reading the sports sections of its newspapers. Familiarizing himself with athletic heroes offered keen insight into how the American mind worked. Babe Ruth. Mickey Mantle. Willie Mays. They worshipped these baseball players like gods.

When the doctor parked his Škoda across the street, Dal tucked the paper beneath an edition of *Rude Pravo* and waved a hand. "Excuse me. Can I have a word with you, comrade?"

The physician was dressed in khaki pants and a white button down shirt. Without his physician's white coat, he looked surprisingly fit. Perhaps he lifted weights in his spare time. After leaving a bouquet of flowers on the hood of the car, Milan crossed the street and stood defensively at the table.

"I'm running late," Milan said. "Can we make this quick?"

"Pretty flowers for the lady?"

"Yes."

"You are a romantic." Dal flashed a grin. "I had no idea."

"Well now you know."

Dal thought briefly about the relationship with his wife. Looking back, it had taken him years to fall in love with Olga, an ex-army nurse and champion backstroke swimmer. Their marriage, he would claim openly, was a union made with the sole purpose of having a family. What better mother could there be than a Soviet Army nurse? Even now, as he thought of the woman in Stalingrad, he wondered if he really loved her. Or did he mostly respect her for being the mother of his children?

After sipping his tea, Dal said, "You are not a young man, doctor. You should be careful in young love."

"What is it you want?" Milan asked impatiently.

"I am sending Zdenek Seifert to Prague."

"Oh? And when will this occur?"

"The army has already sent a shuttle for him. He leaves for the city as we speak."

"He's already gone?"

"Alas, the situation is no longer in my hands. So you are in the loop, I have relayed his diabetes condition to the Army. The Army has a crack corps of physicians. They will take care of him."

Milan became exasperated. "I should've been informed of this transfer days ago."

"The challenges of health care management are difficult for civilian and military alike." Dal folded his hands on the table. "Which reminds me. I read an interesting article in *Pravda*. It exposed the various inconsistencies of the American health care system. How some poor Americans are without access to proper care, specifically the elderly and the Negros living in the southern states."

"Oh?"

"I find it interesting how a country with so much economic wealth cannot afford to care for its citizens. It is such a tragic mismanagement of resources. I believe the communist system of health care is much better. What is your opinion? Health care for those who can afford it? Or free care for everyone——old, young, party official and proletariat alike."

"You could make the argument that each has its merits and each its shortcomings."

Dal snickered. Controlling the health care system also meant controlling the people. Such things went a long way in preventing public discontent. As long as the presidium managed the key aspects of their daily lives, confiscating guns, closing churches, providing health care, the people would remain subservient to the state. "Anyway," he went on, "I cut the article from the paper. You might find it interesting. I will drop the clipping by the clinic tomorrow."

"Sure. Feel free." Milan took a step toward his car.

"Which reminds me," Dal said inquisitively. "Have you ever been to America?"

"America? No. Why?"

He sensed Milan was lying. Visas were issued regularly to Czech doctors seeking knowledge in foreign countries. "I have been to the United States." Dal spoke matter-of-factly. "To Chicago. I have an American friend who hails from a ritzy suburb of the Windy City. Like many comrades, he is interested in bringing down the United States and moving it toward the path of socialism. He showed me around town. I remember it being a filthy place. American cities are not so beautiful. Not like they appear in the glossy pages of LIFE magazine. They reek of the financial ego on one side of town, while casting a shadow of poverty upon the other."

"I wouldn't know."

"Ah, but I am keeping you from your little lady. I will tell you more about my friend and his Marxist movement later. Maybe at the brewery over that beer I promised?"

"I expect a full report on Zdenek Seifert." Milan ignored the invitation to have a beer and walked away.

When he was halfway across the street, Dal threw the baseball and shouted, "Think. Quick."

Milan spun as the ball flew toward his head——catching it. "What's this? A reaction test?"

Had he thrown the baseball to ten Czechs, not one man would have caught the ball with such ease, let alone a single hand. Either Milan was naturally athletic, or he had played baseball at some point in his life.

"It is a silly thing called a baseball," Dal replied. He knew the doctor was right handed. Baseball players typically caught with the hand opposite their writing hand——as did Milan, who hurled the ball back to him with such high velocity that it stung the palm of his hand.

MILAN GRABBED the flowers and walked to the front door. He cleared his throat before ringing the bell. He had trouble letting go of what just happened. The colonel was up to something. But what? There had been a snarky tone to his voice. *Be careful in young love?* Had he really said that? It had not occurred to him that Dal was jealous of his relationship with Ayna. Perhaps he had deliberately lied about Horbachsky's food poisoning. Was the intent to separate them after church? Milan wondered.

After a moment, Nadezda opened the door and invited him in.

He took a deep breath and waited for Ayna to come down from her bedroom. Jiri was eating a slice of pie in the kitchen. He introduced himself to the boy, who, like a typical teenager, was detached from the conversation, but friendly nonetheless. "How's it going kid? Strong handshake you got there. You a good football player?"

Jiri was quick to answer the questions, shoveling a bite of pie into his mouth, before leaving the house with his football.

After the door slammed, Nadezda asked Milan to sit on the sofa, a coffee table between them, before pouring him a cup of tea. "Earl Grey," she said, her hand trembling. "With a drop of vodka . . . they say it helps ease anxiety."

"Are you okay?" he finally asked. From the smell on her breath, she had poured more than a drop. "Has something upset you?"

"That dreadful book burning."

"Yes, I heard. The colonel is a bully." Josef had told him about the public spectacle, how Sergeant Gurko broke Tad's nose. "He's only flexing his muscle. Trying to intimidate us."

"It brought back memories of the Nazis. The horrible things they did."

"I understand."

"Dark memories . . ." Like everyone, the woman was whipped into a frenzy over the arrival of the Soviets, comparing Dal to Hitler. She became cross, then silent, before confessing her frustration with the apathetic police chief from a nearby town. "Damn law enforcement. Never around when you need 'em."

"Things are a little murky in the government halls," Milan said. "I sense confusion and flat out incompetence from the Castle to the district police departments."

"Well, at the very least, are you on good terms with the KGB colonel?" she asked, cutting him off.

"Not particularly."

"Pity."

"There's no love lost between us."

"In Mersk, we all want to get along and do what's best for the people. You're not a country boy. Perhaps you should remember that."

"What are you getting at?" he asked politely.

"I heard what happened at the clinic."

"Oh?"

"You and the colonel were in a heated argument."

"Yes. Damn him."

"Don't you see, if he closes the clinic, he might also lock the doors to St. Nepomuk. That church means the world to us." Nadezda's eyes were bleak. "You've seen the tank parked on the street?"

"Can't miss it."

"It's a problem. Especially since the police chief doesn't care about what is happening here." She leaned forward with an empty cup.

Before Milan could respond, Ayna entered the room and smelled the flowers. She looked lovely in her bellbottom jeans, a white blouse, and a yellow headband.

"Let's go," she said, taking the picnic basket. "Russians this. Russians that. Enough already. I'm sick of talking about them."

Milan drove toward the river.

He asked questions. Lessons. The recital. What inspired Ayna the most? And she responded enthusiastically. The cello. Her favorite works. The masters who had influenced her, Franck, Handel, and, of course, Smetana.

He steered the car and looked off into the distance, trying to appear engaged. He needed a moment to rethink the morning's conversation with the colonel. Maybe Dal had found the newspaper in the trash can and was fishing for answers. If so, what did he suspect? That Milan was fascinated by American sports? Did it go deeper? Throwing the baseball was odd. Why did he have a baseball? Milan decided to play dumb with the Russians. If the subject was brought up again, he would admit to having taken the American newspaper at a conference in Prague.

He sped around a car, kids crammed in the backseat, a child waving a hand. Alone with Ayna, his mind began to sink into a murky abyss. And he wondered: what kind of man am I? Two-faced? Disingenuous? A traitor? He gripped the steering wheel, his eyes somewhere on the road and feeling hypnotized by a stretch of cracked pavement.

Ayna was talking, "My father played the violin . . ."

But he was not listening.

Instead he heard another voice hounding him: *A traitor. Yes, a traitor! But to which country?* Perhaps a traitor to both nations, he concluded. Czechoslovakia, where he had created a life, and America, his roots.

It tore at him. Then again, living with his fabricated identity had never been easy, especially early on when he struggled to make sense of everything. There had been times when depression settled in, when he missed his friends in Chicago, the sound of pine bats cracking at Wrigley Field, and, of all things, the smell of buttered popcorn. Those were the hopeless hours, when a young Milan Husak flirted with exposure and considered surrendering to the authorities. Managing his paranoia, his suspicions of the secret police, the late night sound of a car stopping near his flat or spotting a stranger standing on the curb, the unknown, always the unknown, proved challenging for his restless mind.

He asked himself: when do the lies stop?

The question had been punishing him ever since he woke up that morning to the rain pattering against the window, lying in bed watching the jagged streaks of water slicing up the windowpanes.

He let it go.

For now.

For the picnic.

By then, he had pulled off and driven to the end of a dirt road. It was quiet along the river.

Milan had brought along a 1920s Gramophone and several jazz records. He set the player on the blanket and wound the crank handle. Forcing a smile, he placed the needle on Duke Ellington's *Take the 'A' Train* and kicked off his shoes.

"My grandfather had a record player just like it," she said, interrupting his paranoid thoughts of Dal, the KGB, the CIA. "He used to tell me, 'Ayna, someday when you grow up, all of Czechoslovakia will hear you play the cello on a record machine.'"

"It can happen. Even here. Even in Czechoslovakia."

"What a dream."

He sliced an apple and offered her a piece. As they reclined on a blanket and joked about their chance meeting, it astounded him how fast things had moved between them. A week ago, he had been a contented bachelor focused on his career, sniffing out a promotion to deputy minister and an office in Prague. Today his career was the furthest thing from his mind. Instead, Ayna was all he could think about. He loved how her eyes lit up when she spoke about Jiri and when she spoke about playing in the string quartet. And yet when he looked at her joyful face, so full of life, he knew lies would destroy their relationship unless he told her the truth about what had happened after the war. But how would he tell her? And when? His clandestine past was the best kept secret in Czechoslovakia. Only Frank and Philip knew he was a spy. The truth might not go over so well with Ayna.

Nevertheless he wanted to tell her.

She would listen, wouldn't she? She would understand, wouldn't she? She would forgive him, wouldn't she?

Several times he started to say something, then stopped. The timing was bad. With Frank hounding him, it was probably best to keep a lid on things until they simmered down.

He leaned closer and touched her hand. Her fingers were long, supple, and surprisingly strong.

MILAN MADE her smile. He was charming, talking about his old record player, his love for jazz. He understood her passions, her dreams, especially her relationship with Jiri. Sometimes it was as if she had known him her entire life. She was that comfortable sitting next to him by the river. When he took her by the hand, her heart fluttered and she felt weeks of tension drain from her body. She moaned, silently begging for a kiss. She wanted more. Wanted him to touch the underside of her arm. Wanted him to slide his hand gently up her shoulder. Wanted him to . . .

Oh, but what was the right thing to do? Should she scoot away? Pull back her hand?

She stopped thinking about it.

Stopped analyzing.

Stopped trying to talk herself out of *it*.

Fact was, three years had passed since she last slept with a man. Peter, of course. Three long years of living like a nun. As they sat on the blanket, watching the water flow gently around a bend, their fingers interlocked, Ayna realized she was going to make love to him right there on the river's edge.

So what that she hardly knew him. It was probably better this way. She was not looking for a relationship, just company with the right man, someone to help get her through the stress of recent weeks. Be it a fling or a little romance, Ayna had no expectations.

She leaned her head on his shoulder and gazed dreamily at the sun sparkling off the water. Milan made her feel good about herself, about her future, about life. She wondered, had Peter ever made her feel this way? She was not sure. If she obsessed on how Milan had stolen her heart, she might begin to hate him. Because really, was it casual company she wanted? Or was she only lying to herself, trying to avoid getting hurt?

"I'm hungry, let's eat," she said, opening the wicker picnic basket. To an extent, she was telling the truth. Her stomach was rumbling. She was hungry, but deep inside she had been anticipating his hand moving on her lap and his lips touching her neck. A responsible woman, someone with Ayna's awful history of relationship troubles, of men turning up dead, would have resisted him, pushed away his hands. Because she knew better. Why then, did she sit still when he kissed her? Remain there? Because it felt too good. She closed her eyes and let go of the basket, feeling guilty but letting him have his way. Something had awakened in the pit of her stomach, the first moments of a new existence.

"You're beautiful," he said, placing a hand on the small of her back.

She turned to meet his lips. "Don't stop," she whispered. "Whatever you do . . ."

He unbuttoned her blouse, then reached behind to unclip her bra. She rolled onto her back with a nervous laugh and unzipped her bell-bottom jeans with a jerk. He grabbed the pants at the ankles and tugged. When they failed to slip off, he became embarrassed, and she helped him. After he finally pulled off the last leg, he pitched them into the grass and leaned into her, his fingers inside the edge of her underwear, waiting for the invitation to remove it.

On the way home, there was not a need to clarify what had happened or to say something ridiculous like, "I'm not that kind of girl" or whatever excuse she might have said to another man in order to maintain a respectful relationship. Girls liked sex, too. Under the right circumstances, she was that *kind of girl* and she was not ashamed of it.

She held onto his warm hand. There was silence between them for much of the drive. Every now and then, their eyes met and they exchanged affectionate smiles.

But why was she behaving like this? Out of love?

She let out a breath. The guilt had set in. She felt it briefly when he kissed her and the instant before he went inside of her. By then it was too late.

She slumped, a heavy feeling.

The curse.

The curse kills.

It had killed three times.

There was, she understood quite suddenly, no such thing as love anymore. At least not for her. Not for Ayna Sahhat.

The road took them past the paper mill, an ancient brick building with a hammer and sickle painted on the face of its four-story warehouse wall. On windy days the smoke spewing from the multiple smokestacks smothered the valley with a yellowish haze and with a rotten egg stench that watered her eyes.

Logging trucks pulled in and out of the parking lot. Milan tapped the brakes, then accelerated when the road opened up.

She looked beyond the mill, toward a green clump of trees near a hill, and felt, at that moment, very empty. The smoke. The smell.

Always reminders. That there had been a sinister time many years ago. *The first time.*

Not all of them had died.

Ayna shuddered. The memories of that day when she was alone with Mr. Janus——the last time she had gone into the woods——were unbearable. What really happened that morning of 29 September, 1954? For over a decade she had been untruthful with her version of the story. She had, in fact, led the schoolteacher on from the start. However contrary to the ugly rumors on the street, the absurd lies that persisted to this day, the whole thing had been rooted in innocence.

She was not to blame. Not *completely.*

She had been struggling with her school work. Learning about iconic philosophers——Marx, Hegel, Lenin——made her gag. Workers of the world unite? The ideological slogans bored her to no end. With the palm of a hand holding up her head, she sat in the back of the classroom and doodled, glancing through her hair to monitor the time on the classroom's wall clock, counting down the minutes to music class, to something better.

Then one day, Mr. Janus called her home to warn of a possible expulsion from school if her failing marks did not improve. Ayna's mother was irate. She told Ayna to pay better attention and blamed her for tarnishing the family name. She threatened to confiscate what mattered most——Ayna's cello.

So Ayna schemed.

She would find a way to get Mr. Janus to like her. By the time she was done with him, the schoolteacher would adore her. He would feel guilty for awarding her anything less than a passing grade. But how? After all, Mr. Janus was a jerk. He berated her in front of the classroom. He accused her mother of being unsympathetic toward the communists. *The Sahhat's are a stain,* he told his pupils, at the same time encouraging students to report on neighbors who spoke out against the Party.

. . . she would think of something.

Then Thursday came. The day of her waywardness. That day after school when she stepped into the empty classroom to say "hello" without knowing what to expect. Would it be a cold shoulder? A pat on the back? He greeted her with a cordial nod, inviting her in. They talked a little. *You want to help tidy up? That's fine. Just fine.* She came back again, performing little tasks, emptying the trash can, washing the chalkboard. He was oddly approachable——surprisingly not the complete jerk she had always known.

Then her cunning kicked in. *What's a politburo?* she asked. *Who wrote the Communist Manifesto? Where did Karl Marx go to school?*

The questions lit up his eyes. And he answered them at length, sharing his wealth of knowledge, years of scholarly lessons that flowed from his thin lips like a well-rehearsed speech. *Karl Marx was the greatest thinker of the millennium*, Mr. Janus proclaimed. He elaborated on Marx's conditions for the liberation of the proletariat and the need to eliminate capitalists and private property. He went on and on, quoting from philosophers and politicians, spewing numbers and statistics of the economy that he insisted proved Czechoslovakia was much better off under the new communist rule.

. . . and she pretended to listen, swallowing her yawns. *I want to hear more*, she insisted. *Revolution? Tell me.*

He pointed to passages in thick books and to events in newspaper clippings that showed how the revolution had reached England, France, and West Germany. And there were brothers and sisters in America, he explained, at the universities, in the town councils, working in the community, all organizing for the bloodless revolution that would ultimately put the United States on a course to socialism. *Marxism is the way forward, young Ayna. It's exciting. Embrace it.*

The lessons were intense, at times unbearable for her musically-inclined brain. She stayed focused on the goal, keeping her eyes on him while he spoke passionately of the fate of Europe and his hatred for the capitalists who stood in the way. When she discovered he had been to the Soviet Union and worked at the embassy in Moscow, she asked to see photographs of his travels.

You are someone special, he told her, the rolls of his double-chin expanding with joy. *Thank you, Ayna. Thank you for visiting me after class.*

The next day, he brought a box of photo albums to the classroom and flipped through the memories with a nostalgic glimmer in his eye. *Seems like yesterday,* he said. *Where did the time go?*

She no longer sat in the chair next to him, rather was looking over his shoulder while he pointed to photos of the Kremlin, Red Square, and Lenin's Mausoleum. Each time he started to revert to Marx, she brought the conversation back to him, to his personal life. She felt mean for being so manipulative. Then again, he had ridiculed her in front of the classroom on numerous occasions, so her dishonesty was simply a way of getting even.

And it worked. By the fourth week, she was getting good grades and feeling very comfortable with Mr. Janus, even flirting with him by placing her hand on his shoulder and letting her foot brush against his leg.

He had questions, too. The cello. Her dog. And boyfriends. *Do you have a special someone?* Ayna was embarrassed. She'd never had a boyfriend. *Have you ever been kissed?* An embarrassing question as well, but *no*. He was surprised to learn that the girls made fun of her face. *Because you are very pretty,* he told her. Now she was listening. Now she wanted him to say more. Pretty? You think so? He rarely spoke on the subject of communism again, instead the focus was on her, the young, beautiful, and talented Ayna. And she loved it. She played the cello for him. Brahms was his favorite.

What had started off as a manipulative quest to get good grades had blossomed into a special friendship. He gave her gifts: a new bow, a pretty coin purse, and, of all things, a miniature edition of the *Communist Manifesto*, which he noted was something he always carried in his pocket.

Then that morning arrived.

That dreadful morning.

Gray, with heavy rain. A day she should have stayed home and read a book, played her cello, done something, or just never left her bedroom. She was washing the chalkboard when she felt Mr. Janus breathing on her neck. *Good to get out of the rain,* he whispered. *So good.*

She froze, her eyes cast down on the floor at the worn and chipped tiles. Three words came to her: I must go. Then she abruptly left the room.

For hours that night, she lay restlessly awake in bed, eyes staring at nothing. She began to question her motives. She had been cruel——just so she could keep her cello. Was it really worth it? Being so misleading? Hurting someone? She decided to back pedal on her flirting. When she discovered his hobby was bird watching, she asked to be taken to the forest near the paper mill to see the White Falcons nesting in the trees. It was the only honest effort at friendship she had made. He agreed, saying, *Why, even President Gottwald had been a bird lover.*

He picked her up on the corner near the cemetery.

They drove to the mill, to the smell.

The fieldtrip to see the falcons, she reasoned, would vindicate her for having used him; bird watching, sharing in his passion for wildlife, would make up for all the dishonesty of recent weeks.

He parked in a far corner of the parking lot behind a row of logging trucks and put a mint in his mouth. *You are going to like this,* he said. *The falcons are breeding.*

At Mr. Janus' direction, they trekked around the lumber fence and ventured into the wilderness with their binoculars. They walked briskly along a well-trodden path, the haze burning her eyes, the rotten egg stench turning her stomach. Soon they were far from the mill, surrounded by the ancient woods. She gazed up and saw the lofty tree limbs enclosing around her like old, knotty fingers. A witch's gnarled hand, the forest turning darker, green, brown, black. When they reached an alcove, and a pond, he dropped to a knee and pointed into the treetops. *The falcons are nesting, pretty Ayna. Careful. We must keep quiet.*

But there was something odd about him that day. She began to notice his warped smile, his sweating armpits, and the perverse way he said *pretty.* The old Mr. Janus, the stern Party informant who had asked his students to report on their parents for speaking out against the communists, was back. And she smelled alcohol on his breath, not the mint.

I want to go home, she finally said.

Home? His voice grew exasperated. *Why must you go, pretty Ayna? Why must you go?*

Seized by sudden fear, she dropped the binoculars and ran for the parking lot. She knew the way. She had been here many times. In her frazzled state-of-mind, however, she turned right on the trail when she should have turned left and ended up in a swarm of evergreen shrub. There was a moment of hesitation. Which way? Forward? Backward? She decided to cut through the shrub, only to snag her foot on a tree root, and crashed to the ground, falling flat on her hands and face.

Get up, Ayna's mind told her. *You have to keep moving.*

She was close to the parking lot. Just the length of a football field, or so, she guessed. Would someone hear if she screamed for help? She was starting to stand when she heard a grumble. Someone was hovering over her. It was Mr. Janus. He was right behind her, right on top of her.

A month later, Ayna discovered she was pregnant and approached Dana, the only boy at school who had given her any attention. She flirted with him. And the flirting ultimately led to sex. Only this time the sex was on her terms, in her bedroom beneath the clean sheets, while her mother was working at the mill.

As the weeks passed, then a month, she was unable to hide her anger, and against her mother's wishes, went to the police to inform them about the rape. The investigation was brief. Mr. Janus had been rubbing elbows with the local police for years. With no regrets, he admitted to having had an affair with Ayna, though insisted he did not rape her. It had been *consensual*, he lied, methodically explaining how they had gotten to know each other after class, that the sexually awakened Ayna had led him on, teasing him. *What is a man to do?* he begged. The police chief's wife was twenty years younger than him, so there seemed to be some sort of male understanding between them. Almost everyone sided with Mr. Janus' version of the story.

So she moved on.

Trying to forget.

By avoiding him.

To replace the hurt, she made Dana love her, made him say sweet things all through the pregnancy. *Do you love me? Yes, yes, I do love you.* She easily molded Dana into the father she wanted him to be. He had a good heart. Good intentions. And he loved Jiri. At the end of the day, she supposed, she wanted to be with Dana. Maybe loving him out of a temporary need or a convenience. She remained faithful to him until that day when he drowned in the pond, in the same water near the spot where the falcons had nested.

Then the hurt came back.

The shame.

. . . though she wondered, every day she wondered: had it ever really gone away?

Milan opened the passenger door. "It was a wonderful picnic," he said. "You're a lovely woman. I enjoy being with you."

"Thank you," she said curtly, not wishing to say she felt the same way.

"How about we do something this weekend?"

"Oh?"

"Maybe a movie in Pilsen?"

"Perhaps . . ." She stepped out of the car, gripping the picnic basket. "Sorry. Can't chat right now. Let's talk later. Okay?"

"Goodbye then," he said, kissing her on the forehead.

She summoned all her strength to give him a hug, before dashing into her home, running to her bedroom, and dropping onto the bed. In her mind she was unable to erase the schoolteacher's bloodshot eyes drilling into her, his strong hands pinning her wrists to the ground, and then when he was done, zipping up his pants and stumbling through the trees.

MILAN DROVE to the hospital in Cesky Budejovice. He somehow avoided the roadblocks and arrived in time for a meeting with the rural outreach committee. The group of nine colleagues, all of them male, most of them hardened communists, were pleased at the progress he had made in Mersk.

After the meeting, he thought about canceling his appointments for the day and driving back to the village. Maybe he would have dinner with Ayna at the café? Surprise her?

He sat at his desk and stared numbly out the window, at a bird in a tree, at the parting clouds, then at an old man sitting on a bench.

Milan adored Ayna. It was the happiest he had felt in years. But the colonel and his probing questions haunted him. Dal's voice, *have you ever been to America?*

Why was he asking?

The tank had become a symbol of defeat as the muggy autumn days set in. While no one believed the Russians would blow up the church, late night chatter in the tavern fueled speculation that the KGB might soon lock the doors and turn everyone away. It would not surprise the parish. Shutting down the church was old hat for the communists. Hundreds of churches had been closed or blown up by the Party since the Iron Curtain was drawn in the late forties. Why not their place of worship? The T-62 tank, with its smoothbore cannon pointed toward the steeple, was a reminder that twenty-five years after the coup, nothing had really changed, regardless of the new breed of communist running the country. To make matters worse, someone had spray-painted a swastika on the turret.

"Vandalism," Dal said sharply. "Punishable by ten years in prison. How unfortunate. Someone in this community has made a very poor decision to destroy Soviet property."

A large crowd of about four hundred people had begrudgingly trickled from their shops and row houses to congregate around the iron beast.

"Ten years prison?" Josef asked. "Isn't that a bit harsh, even by Moscow standards?"

"Don't push me, baker."

Potapov climbed from the back of the truck, wielding an AK, while Gurko paused next to him.

The onlookers were puzzled. The street musician locked his accordion, and walking away said, "Uh-oh——someone is in serious trouble." Over the next few minutes, more and more of them crowded into the square, standing behind Father Sudek, Josef, Irena, Emil, Tad, Oflan, and Ayna.

"Who defaced my tank?" Dal asked, pointing to the flower shop roof where Bedrich watched with his binoculars. "Was it the imbecile? Does he stand against Brezhnev?"

"No," Father Sudek insisted. "He can't read or write . . ."

"He doesn't know Brezhnev from your ass," someone bellowed.

Dal shook his head scornfully. His disdain for the people was etched in stone. They could say or do nothing that would satisfy him these days. He saw the boys standing in the square and frowned. They had grown unfriendly ever since their parents discovered the football uniforms were supplied by the Soviets and then dumped them at the villa's gate.

"Is the football team guilty of vandalism?" Dal asked. "Perhaps the boys are counter-revolutionaries in the making of Zinoviev, Bukharin, and Trotsky?"

A frazzled woman broke from the crowd and took her son by the hand.

"No," Father Sudek said. "Their parents would punish them."

"Yet they accepted my generous gift of uniforms, only to turn their backs on me."

"You must understand, those uniforms—"

"With numbers on the jerseys, I will have you note."

"But—"

"Save your breath, Father. I am not upset over the decision to return the uniforms. This is not my loss. Let them run amuck," Dal ranted. "Nevertheless, one among you is a criminal. Man. Woman. Boy. Girl." There were stragglers near the shops. The most frightened citizens watched from the windows, such as Evzen and Verushka who were huddled with their great-grandchildren in their flat above the bakery. "Must I randomly decide who will be punished for this crime?" He approached Pavel the chauffeur, who hid behind his thick black glasses and unshaven face. "I don't suppose it was you. You are a gu-gu-gu-gutless aide." And to Oflan the drunk, "You are an appeaser." And Emil the puppet master, "Too idealistic." And Irena the librarian, "Too persuadable." And Tad the paternal, "Too protective." He eyed the throng, his chest bursting. "I know everything about you people. All of you."

Most of the villagers kept their heads down, stuck between wanting to flee and feeling compelled to stay.

He turned to face Josef, the only person in town as tall as him, and boldly gazed into his eyes until the burly man lowered his head.

Next he approached Ayna Sahhat, dressed in a tight-fitting black summer dress with her hair in a ponytail. She was too complex to be categorized as an artist, or a counter-revolutionary, or even cursed. She was everything mixed into Pandora's box, volatile from day-to-day, and without question the biggest threat to the afternoon's peace. Had these people any firearms, she might have risen among the rabble to become the second coming of Joan of Arc. When Ayna refused to succumb to his unblinking glare, he drew the Makarov from his chest holster and pushed the barrel of the gun into her cheek.

"Was it your cellist?" he wrapped his arm around her upper body, constraining her.

"Let go of me," she demanded. "You jerk."

"I know you are conspiring against my authority." Dal spoke coarsely into her ear. "I am onto your brainless scheming with that hard-up physician."

"I don't know what you're talking about."

"To act in love with this man, all the while holding the assassin's dagger behind your back——waiting for the moment to strike me in the way Brutus stabbed Caesar." He tightened his stranglehold. "Deceptive. Plotting. To what avail?"

"You are hurting me." She gasped, blood rushing to her cheeks.

"I am not a jealous man."

"I can't breathe . . ."

Father Sudek said, "Colonel Dal, the young woman is innocent. She's a musician, not a troublemaker."

"Oh?"

"Be reasonable."

"Reasonable?" Dal pushed the muzzle deeper into Ayna's flesh. "Remember how she came to me? Remember how she demanded that I withdraw the tank from Mersk? Does anyone question her motives?"

"But—"

"Instead of arresting her, I decided to offer your beautiful and talented musician leniency. Yes, leniency. My gift of tolerance to you people. Do you understand what this means?'" His rage-filled eyes dulled a little. "I was willing to overlook her hostility in a gesture of goodwill between our nations. Yet in the end, she betrays me. Why?"

Josef stepped forward. "Late last night after the tavern closed, I found a can of spray paint."

"You?"

"I was mad with the situation in my country. It's true. I was drinking Jägermeister."

"Hmm . . ."

"When I get mad, I drink a lot."

"Hmm . . ."

"I am responsible for this crime."

"Hmm . . ."

"You must believe me. I painted the swastika on your damn tank." Josef spat on the armor. "See, even now I disrespect Brezhnev."

Dal chuckled. "Bravo. We seem to have a fellow thespian among us. Honestly, I had no idea the baker could act. I am impressed. However other than the slick bit of improvisation concerning the Jägermeister, I have seen that spoof on the stage. It is an old peasant skit. A comedy, I believe." He turned to Gurko. "I swear. I have heard those lines in a play. You know. Where the man stands up for the woman in the face of a villain. Who was it? Chekhov?"

Gurko shrugged. "You aren't a villain, comrade. These people are at fault for what has happened today. They protect a vandal's identity."

"Nevertheless, they attempt to make a mockery of the Soviet Union." Keeping a firm grip on Ayna, Dal scanned the villagers, suspicious of those standing closest to him. "Do you simpletons think I am ignorant? That I would believe your village baker, a man whose trade thrives on measurements and precise ingredients would do something this irrational? No, this blatant act of disrespect speaks to me of youth. It speaks to me of uncontrollable anger. Of someone in the mold of your fallen comrade Sascha Boyd." He looked at Ayna. "Then again maybe, just maybe, your sweet little Jiri did this? Is he a troubled teen? Mmm. I wonder, should he pay the price for insulting Brezhnev?"

INSIDE THE CLINIC, Milan passed by the window when he caught the outpouring of folks gathered at the square. The people were swarming near the fountain, standing on their toes to get a better view of what was happening. A protest? Some slight warning bell sounded in his head. He set aside a medical file and bursting from the door, rushed across the street. *Good god, what was going on in this town?*

"Doctor, you must stop him," Tad insisted.

"My daughter." Nadezda tugged on his arm. "Please. Save her. You are the only one who can help."

Somewhere a child cried.

Milan pushed through the mob and stumbled into an open circle. He found himself standing face-to-face with the enraged KGB officer, who held Ayna in a martial arts restraint, the pistol's barrel nudged into her temple. Milan's impulse was to rush the man. Instead, he caught his breath. "Is this what your liberation is all about, colonel?"

"Stay out of this, doctor."

"Let her go."

"Don't push me."

"You are making a mistake . . ." Milan's voice quivered. "Put down the gun before you create an incident."

"Incident?" Sweat dripped from the tip of Dal's nose. "You are sounding more and more like a member of the renegade Czech politburo."

"You won't gain anything by committing a murder."

"I am feeling edgy today. Bad headache, you see. Don't make me pull the trigger."

"I warn you. Should a single drop of blood spill."

People backed away, making room for a fight.

"You have an uncanny way of sticking your nose into another man's business," Dal said. "Like Trotsky, who was a real pain in the ass for Comrade Stalin, you will not go away, will you?"

Milan ignored the comment, his eyes drawn to the bandage on the colonel's neck. He suspected dengue, primarily because of an ugly rash that had developed on Dal's skin. He said, "That mosquito bite looks infected. If you would let me have a look. I can help."

Dal snickered. "If I wanted your medical advice, I would have visited the clinic days ago. I know the address. I am fully aware of your credentials."

"This infection should be taken seriously. I am sure you're familiar with the dengue virus?"

"Dengue?" Dal stiffened. "I am a world traveler. Five continents, comrade. In Sri Lanka, I once observed a man die from dengue. It was a slow, intolerable death."

Father Sudek stepped forward. "It was wrong for someone to paint on your tank. But Ayna? No. She wouldn't do such a thing."

"If not the girl, who?"

"We will get to the bottom of this." The priest clasped his hands. "You have my word."

Dal loosened his grip on Ayna. She was no longer struggling to get away. "Tell me, Father, when is this Smetana recital?"

"Friday."

"How very exciting. You people must be on the edge of your seats with anticipation." The sweat was beading on Dal's brow. "I have overheard the quartet rehearsing in the church. The strings are sweet sounding. Lovely. But can I ask you something? At the end of the day, is there talent in Mersk? I mean, a realistic chance you will be awarded a spot at the festival in Prague?"

"We have come together . . ." Father Sudek lowered his head. "To honor Sascha."

"Pity." The lines of tension had gathered on Dal's face. "I am fond of Bedrich Smetana. In particular his opera, *The Bartered Bride*. Unfortunately, I do not recall being offered an invitation to your little gathering."

Father Sudek said, "That is certainly an oversight. Of course, we are expecting you. And your men."

Milan sensed an easing of tension. "Then it is agreed," he injected. "We will celebrate together. Russian and Czech."

"Amen," Father Sudek said eagerly.

"In honor of Smetana," Milan added, "we can work through this trouble without spilling blood. So, please. Let Ayna go."

Dal pushed Ayna into Milan's arms. "Fair enough. I shall consider the invitation to the recital. In the meantime, you people think about what has happened today. Think long and hard. Vandalism is a serious crime. As such, I will return to this very spot in the morning. I expect the guilty person to show his or her face. If not, I will be forced to cancel your Smetana gala. Then you will have nothing. And there will be no hope whatsoever."

Milan kept his arm around Ayna and walked her toward the clinic. She was crying. When he went to wipe a tear from her cheek, she brushed away his hand.

"I am okay," she insisted.

But he had his doubts. She seemed emotionally distraught and desensitized to life. There was something about the harsh tone in her voice and her provoking body posture. As they walked, he felt Dal's glare pressing against his back and he could only repeat himself, what he had been saying for days, even though it felt like a lie, "The colonel won't dare hurt you. Or Jiri. The Russians can't do that. They just can't."

THE PLAN had backfired. Dal had only put the gun to the woman's head for a show of strength. He had no intention of shooting her. Milan arriving at the last minute undermined his authority. Now the doctor appeared to be the hero of the day. "I have never met anyone so fortunate," he told Gurko. "First, there was his chance discovery of Sascha Boyd's body, followed by today's opportune heroism."

"He concerns you?"

"Doctor Husak appears to be a man of destiny," Dal said. "From my experience, this is the most dangerous type of man."

"Maybe we should shut down the clinic."

"No. It would attract the attention of the ministry." Dal popped several aspirin into his mouth straight from a bottle and crunched on them. He was feeling sicker as the day wore on and needed a nap. "Something is odd about this physician."

"What do you mean?"

"They say he's a war hero."

"The people turn to anyone these days for heroes."

"Does he look like a hero to you?"

"I haven't given it much consideration," Gurko said. "In my eyes, he seems like a typical physician. He wants to help people. Even you."

"Help?"

"That is what he said."

"I do not trust him."

"It's less than a week until we hand over the American POW and deliver the dossier to our counterparts in Prague. You appear spellbound by this woman, comrade. I know she is attractive, but she is nothing in the bigger picture. Why do you—"

Dal held up his hand to silence the sergeant. Driven by his demons, he walked down the street. Voices came to him from across the village, from behind closed doors, inside attic spaces, and other hiding spots. He knew what they were talking about: Dr. Husak had stood up to him. If the doctor could do it, why not them? Even now, he sensed, they were plotting against his authority. Anarchists. He must move quickly to make an example of someone for vandalizing the tank.

"Seems that doctor was right about your health," Gurko said. "Why not visit a hospital?"

Dal stopped in the middle of the street. "How can you be so stupid? I cannot see a doctor. I could be quarantined. Did my story about Napoleon's hemorrhoids not register with you?"

"My apologies, comrade."

"I appear to have misjudged your skills," Dal said sternly. "You have become a useless army photographer in recent days. I have charged you with one simple task——find the farmer who claimed injustice. Tell me, what has come of your search?"

"I have been unable to locate the man. The fields in Cesky Krumlov are mostly overgrown with weeds. And the workers are uncooperative. They won't talk to Russians."

"Have you searched for him in Kamenny Ujezd?"

"Yes."

"And Strazkov."

"Yes."

"How about Kaplice?"

"Everywhere."

"There are few farms in this part of the country. You must not be looking very hard. It cannot be that difficult."

"Comrade, it is just—"

"Go. Revisit the towns along the river. Do not return until you have found him."

"Yes, comrade."

Feeling nauseated, Dal placed his hands on his knees and gagged. Was it the flu? Or worse, dengue? When Gurko started to say something, he held up his hand to silence him. After another gag, a stream of vomit spewed from his mouth, his breakfast of eggs and toast. He took a moment, wiping the spittle from his lips with the back of a hand.

"My suspicions say the farmer is trouble," Dal said. "And I am always correct about these things."

LEAVING THE SQUARE, Ayna asked to be taken to the monastery. "I hate that man," she told Milan, her complexion flushed. "I hate him. I hate all Russians for that matter."

After the short drive, they got out of the car. Her face was red and streaked with dried tears that looked like faded scars. There was a KEEP OUT sign lying in the long grass. They ignored the warning and stepped past a broken chain link fence.

"He's ill," Milan said. "Not only his piss-poor Russian attitude. But he looks feverish. That might explain his erratic behavior."

"There's no explanation for him. He's an evil man."

"I couldn't agree more."

"I want to strangle him."

"I don't blame you."

"Where are the police?"

"Sleeping through this nightmare."

"Where is the Czech army?"

"They would fight," Milan insisted. "I'm sure they would fight if not for the politicians ordering them to remain in the barracks."

"I don't stand with Svoboda," she said. "The people shout 'stand with Svoboda.' But that's heresy. He is responsible for this. He should've known better than to push Brezhnev."

"The situation is a mess."

It was pointless trying to reason with her. Everyone had become the enemy and weighing in on the conversation only exasperated her mood. "The people of Mersk are cowards," Ayna ranted. "They talk about freedom, yet aren't willing to fight for it. If anyone, I thought Josef would stand strong. What good is being the arm wrestling champion of our village if he is afraid to use those same arms to punch someone in the nose?" Ayna went on and on, Svoboda this, and Brezhnev that, until she became exhausted listening to her own voice.

"You just had a gun put to your head." Milan laid his arm over her shoulder. "So vent. Vent all you want."

"A mosquito infection you say?"

"Yes."

"Is it contagious?"

"No."

"Will it kill him?"

"Most likely no."

"Damn. How unfortunate."

"Life is precious. No matter who. Even the colonel."

"Even a Russian?"

"Even a Russian."

"Now you sound like Saint John of Nepomuk."

"I am in the business of saving lives, not taking them."

She moaned. "You win. I'm not going to talk about this for the rest of the day."

"Good idea."

Milan kissed her on the forehead, and then changing the subject, he said, "C'mon let's check this place out . . ."

The monastery consisted of a Baroque manor house and farm buildings arranged around a brick courtyard. It had been abandoned for over fifty years, crumbling for two centuries and these days reclaimed mostly by weeds. A lane of stone urns led to a winding stone stair. The stairs ended abruptly, where they sat with their legs dangling. She told him about her life as a child, how the old monastery was her favorite place to hang out, how she enjoyed walking among the buildings in the spring when the wildflowers speckled the grass. "Sometimes Bedrich follows me here," she added. "He climbs the manor house and spies from the roof."

"He's an interesting fellow. Always spying through those army binoculars."

"The binoculars are his eyeglasses to the world."

"I wonder how the world must look through his eyes."

"Scary. Anyway, I've never said anything to him. It's actually very cute. But if he were a normal man, I'd think his spying was kind of creepy."

Milan lit up. "We have to go somewhere. And get away from the harassment. Take Jiri, too. Soon, the museums and opera houses will be flourishing with cheerful people again. The restaurants will be teeming with life. Czechs want to live, not be held down by the Soviets. Despite the occupation, we must enjoy our lives. "

"Except there are roadblocks and curfews and who knows what else."

"I can get around the military restrictions." He was already planning the day in his head: the football stadium, the art museum, and that French restaurant she had spoken so fondly about the other day. He wanted to show her the best time of her life.

"It's been a couple of years since Jiri and I went away." Ayna leaned into him, a cheek on his shoulder. "We don't do much aside from what life offers in Mersk. I know, I know, boring. I do want to take him places. I really do. It's just . . . I never seem to have the time or the money."

"After the recital, we'll go to Prague. I will personally introduce you to the maestro of the symphony. His physician is a colleague of mine."

"Really?"

"Yes."

"Oh, how wonderful."

"In the meantime, I have a meeting at the ministry, then I must return to the hospital." Milan decided that he would also go to the police and file a complaint about Colonel Dal——for what it was worth.

"But the recital is Friday."

"I have it marked on my calendar."

"You'll come back for it?"

"Absolutely. I wouldn't miss the chance to see you play your cello. Not for the life of me."

Dal kept his word. The next morning, he ordered Potapov and Horbachsky into the GAZ, and with the canvass top down, headed into town. He drove at reckless speeds, not braking for pedestrians, for dogs, for anything. "Move, comrades," he yelled, steering with a hand on the horn and a cigarette dangling from his lip. "Out of the way." Near the butcher shop he nearly ran over Tad and at the marionette theatre he waved to Verushka's great-grandchildren. People were in an upheaval over his careless driving. At every intersection, they scrambled to get out of the way. The excitement was contagious. Oflan. Pavel. Irena. Emil. Evzen. People emptied from their houses, from their shops, from the narrow alleys that crisscrossed the town, and chased the truck to Ayna's house.

The mob had grown to a hundred townspeople when it reached her door. The people were asking questions, wanting to know what had become of Zdenek Seifert, when the curfew would be lifted, and why Ayna Sahhat had apparently been targeted for the act of vandalism.

"Did she really paint the swastika on the tank?" the street musician asked.

Even a curious Ota Janus, on his way to the schoolhouse, had stopped his car to observe the uproar.

"Citizens of Mersk," Dal said triumphantly, with usual flair and arrogance. "This is a day like no other. Today, as I appear before you, we sever the head of the mighty serpent. Today, your liberation takes a giant leap forward." He had been drinking to ward off a headache and there was a slight slurring of his words.

"Serpent?" the banker said. "You're not making any sense."

"He has officially go-go-gone mad," Pavel said.

An irate Josef Novak yanked off his baker's cap and pushed his way to the front of the crowd. "Of all people. Why the Sahhats?" His face was red, explosive. "What have they done to deserve this?"

Dal paused for some moments, drawing attention to the question, before glancing over his sunglasses at Josef. "Try to exercise some patience while we sort this out . . ." He pointed his baton at Josef as though pinning him with a fencing saber. "Soon everyone will get answers. I promise you, baker, the evidence, every bit of it, will be compelling."

By then, the people completely surrounded the truck. Many had their hands on the hood and were touching the doors, while some lifted on their toes to get a better view. Dal, not worried for his personal safety, sat casually in the driver's seat, feeling relaxed from a morning vodka.

"We demand answers at once," Josef said while the Ukrainian soldiers struck the door handle with their assault rifles. "We have grown impatient with your false promises of peace."

A few voices moaned their support.

At the same time, the soldiers finally broke the door handle, kicked the door and stormed inside the residence.

"This is not a proper way to enter a home," Father Sudek said, thumping his cane against the cobble. "Haven't you heard of knocking?"

Dal said, "There is no time for etiquette, Father."

"Why must you do this?"

"Disobedience. Insubordination. Treason. Need I say more?"

"The Sahhats are a decent family," the priest insisted. "I have known them all my life. They aren't criminals."

"Then it must come as a surprise, if not some disappointment, to learn that a certain individual living at this address has ties to the counter-revolutionary movement."

"Lies," Josef said, with Emil restraining him. "You're a raving lunatic. I will go to the police."

Dal looked sternly at the baker. "I would advise you to keep your mouth shut. While I have identified the potential vandal, you are still on my suspected-enemy list for lying about your role in the scandal."

The soldiers pushed Ayna out the door. She was putting up little resistance, though her messy hair and a scratch on Horbachsky's cheek suggested a struggle had taken place.

"The grandmother and the boy aren't home," Potapov said.

"Their whereabouts aren't important." Dal threw a stern look at Father Sudek. "The priest will explain to the family what has happened."

Potapov handed him an album: *Revolver*, by The Beatles. Then he shoved Ayna into the back of the truck.

"The other day," Dal went on, "I demanded that all banned materials, including Western music, be brought to the public square for burning." Dal brandished the illegal album toward Father Sudek. "It was a simple request, no? Something even a peasant could understand. However Miss Sahhat seems to have her own criteria of what should be on that list. Or perhaps she is illiterate like her mother?"

Josef threw up his hands. "A rock & roll album?"

"What harm could there possibly be in music?" Father Sudek asked. It was the first time he had raised his voice at the Russians.

"Go. Have a look at our sacred fountain," Josef said. "You will see Elizabeth of Bohemia's wings are stained with black residue from the Kremlin's list of banned books."

"You people . . ." Dal paused to give emphasis to his words. "You ungrateful people. You have backed me against a wall. You leave me with no choice but to defend myself these days. Is this Bohemian hospitality at its best?" He turned to the priest. "If not Ayna, perhaps the guilty party will finally confess to his act of vandalism, eh?"

"I have spoken to everyone," Father Sudek said. "We didn't paint the swastika on your tank."

Dal ignored the comment, his eyes scanning the crowd until he saw Bedrich standing between the butcher and Irena. There was something both soothing and dangerous about the deformed little man. He seemed perfectly harmless, yet was the only person Dal was incapable of reading. Exactly what went on inside the imbecile's head? Next, he noticed something curious: Bedrich was holding a mouse. He climbed from the truck to investigate, pushing his way past the bodies of onlookers. "What is the story," he asked, "with this rodent?"

"It's his pet mouse," Verushka said. "He found it inside the church."

"A pet mouse?" Dal's forehead wrinkled.

"It's limp," Emil said. "Bedrich is nursing the mouse back to good health. One day it will crawl like other mice and be free again."

"He loves the mouse with his whole heart," Irena said.

Dal noticed how they seemed to shout their support more for the imbecile's mouse than for Ayna. This was very, very strange. He waited for some moments longer to let their rumblings reach a point of near anarchy for Bedrich and his pet, before snatching the white rodent from his hand.

"Love?" Dal glared broodingly at the blank-faced Bedrich. "What do you know about love?"

"He is mute," Oflan reminded the colonel. "Not a single word his entire life."

"He may be dumber than a box of rocks," someone said. "However Bedrich does love."

"And he is respectful of all living things," Emil added.

Despite their insistence that he return the animal, Dal kept the creature in his hand. "This friendly mouse is your pet?" he asked Bedrich. The halfwit opened his hands and pleaded for the mouse's safe return. "And you truly do love this mouse? As Irena has claimed?"

"With his whole heart," Irena emphasized.

Making an awkward political reference that was clearly meant as a joke, a joke which drew no laughs except from Horbachsky, Dal said, "I hope this rodent is a good socialist."

"Please don't harm the creature," Father Sudek said. "I beg you for compassion. Bedrich has so few things in life to call his own."

Dal watched the mouse hobble across the palm of his hand.

"Cute little bugger," he admitted.

"It is harmless." Emil smiled. "One of God's creatures . . ."

"Speaking of which, I had a puppy when I was a child." Dal spoke in a friendly tone, as though in the tavern drinking beer and remembering good times with old army comrades. He reveled in the limelight, winking at the enraged Josef, who wanted no part in the dialogue and promptly turned away. Like a captured audience, almost everyone was glued to the colonel's words, wondering what he would say next. "It was a Wolf-hound named Anna Karenina. For those of you who are illiterate, Anna Karenina is a character in a novel by the great Leo Tolstoy, which tells the tragic story of a married socialite and her affair with the affluent Count Vronsky. My Anna . . . Anna the dog that is . . . was a smart little bitch. In secondary school, I trained her to hunt pheasant. Someday I will tell you all about what farm life was like on the Volga, and, of course, about Anna."

Verushka said, "Then you are an animal lover?"

Dal wiped the sweat from his brow. "Guilty," he said irritably. "I do admit to having a place in my heart for dogs. And why not? They are man's best friend, no? But this rodent. You do realize it spreads disease?" The tone of his voice was no longer friendly. "It is filthy like the Kurdish of the eastern Taurus mountains. Mmm . . . They are despicable people who wipe their asses with their bare hands. Did you know this?" There were blank faces. "As administrator of Mersk, I cannot allow your imbecile to jeopardize the public health by keeping a pet mouse. I apologize for this point of view, as I know it is unpopular, but it's the law . . ." Dal crushed the mouse in his hand, much like someone might crush a piece of paper before pitching it into a wastebasket. Then he dropped the bloody carcass into the palm of Bedrich's hand. "And the law is the law."

People gasped. Some wept.

Evzen, Verushka, and a few others quietly left the mob, going home, perhaps fearing more violence to come.

"Have you people never heard of the Dark Ages? The Bubonic Plague?" Dal froze with the palms of his hands turned up, his shoulders slightly shrugged. "What sort of garbage do they teach you in your history books? A thousand years ago half of your Bohemian brothers died because of rodents. Now you keep one as a pet?"

There was silence, except for a stray cough and Ayna grunting, trying to break free from Potapov.

Dal saw a tear trapped in the corner of Bedrich's eye, and raised a curious eyebrow. The glistening tear, much like fresh morning dew, reminded him of the inevitability of things to come. The village idiot was holding on to precious hope when all hope had been lost. "Your mouse is not coming back to life," he said calmly. "Take heed, from death sprouts new beginnings. A fresh start. Look to the future, young man. Be bold."

"Poor Bedrich," Irena said.

Dal gazed across the square to Ota Janus, who offered a subtle nod of approval.

And that was it.

The crowd broke apart.

People went home.

Dal climbed into the truck and drove back to the villa. Behind him, Ayna squirmed, trying to escape from Potapov's locked arms.

In late morning, Dal received word that Zdenek Seifert had been flown to Moscow along with a handful of other political opponents of the regime. He took a moment to scribble a note to his superior, reminding him about the mayor's poor health, and also requesting an update concerning the Devil Dog documents. I would like to deliver them as soon as possible, he wrote. Then he wondered, *when would the prisoner transfer take place?* The rendezvous with the East Germans had been pushed back multiple times. He was anxious, wanting to hand GySgt Johnston over to agents so he could move on with his administrative duties in South Bohemia. Each passing day felt like an unnecessary risk.

He went outside and watched Horbachsky lead the POW in his daily calisthenics. They were in a sun-filled grassy place between a flower garden and the wall. The American, who wore a smirk, was pretending to be exhausted from the exercise, pissing and moaning about having been pushed too hard, then doing his push-ups with his knees on the ground. "Comrade Whore-beef-sky, you are killing me, man," Johnston groaned mockingly. "What is your problem, eh? Don't you know? This goes against the rules of the Geneva Convention." He did his jumping jacks with little effort, sticking his middle finger up at the Ukrainian when the soldier turned his back. It was disrespectful, though somewhat humorous, Dal thought, hiding his laughter. He eventually told Potapov to take over and returned to the library.

Buried away on the top shelf, Dal found a Russian translation of Homer's epic poem, *The Iliad*. He blew dust off the cover and sat at the desk. This was one of his favorite works of literature. The story reminded him of the true heroics of war, where soldiers in battle dress entered combat in chariots and launched javelins and skirmished with sword and shield. He had always believed this was the way wars were meant to be fought; not with bombs, artillery strikes, or from the air, rather hand to hand, side by side, with brothers. He was romanticizing about the ten-year siege of the city of Troy, the most famous battle of ancient history, when a ruckus coming from outside the window distracted him. He went to the window and had a look. An angry mob had gathered at the gate to protest Ayna's internment. The locals, nearly one hundred strong, were waving Czech flags and homemade banners.

At once, his mind swept back to Budapest, 1956, to the brazen protests and desperate voices of indignant students who marched in solidarity with striking Polish workers. The KGB had moved quickly to silence the bold Hungarian dissidents; likewise, he would soon quiet these unruly Czechs, although they were proving to be more unyielding than he had initially given them credit for.

He grabbed his KGB hat, stuffed a packet of cigarettes into his pocket, and with a tremendous sense of authority, stepped outside the villa and proceeded calmly toward the gate.

He encountered Josef and several townspeople standing rigid with spade shovels and pitchforks. He noticed the boys, among them Jiri, buried in the throng of angry anarchists, yelling at the top of their lungs. Amused, he listened for a few moments to the collective cries of "Free Ayna" and "Russians are criminals" and "No Gulag in Czechoslovakia." It was all so oddly beautiful, like the sweeping Mikhail Glinka, or better yet, the powerful Peter Tchaikovsky. If only he had a cassette recorder, he would love to record the chaos and replay the tape later when things settled down, for it was the type of pandemonium that motivated him, the unsung rewards that only a political officer could truly appreciate.

He stood strong, holding his ground. All this ranting against the Soviet Union did little to persuade him; he was in control of their lives, more importantly their futures. The situation, Dal would note in his official daily report, was nettlesome. They had witnessed one of their fellow citizens killed, a tank parked in front of their church, and a book burning. He had been both methodical and iron-handed. If necessary, as was most often the case in these types of local uprisings, there was more punishment to come.

He pulled a cigarette from a pack and eyed the crowd. What did they expect? That he would surrender? He peered at Father Sudek and Nadezda who stood in the front row. Everything he had read about these people, dating back to the 1800s when Napoleon used their church as a hospital for amputees, right up to Hitler's occupation, and Stalin's modernization, pointed towards weakness; they had the blood of their poor fathers, the blood of tired farmhands. And yet he failed to remember the last time when such an insufficiently organized community had been so pesky. Remarkable, really.

He lit the cigarette and blew the smoke through his nostrils. Downplaying the obvious, he asked, "What is this uproar about?"

"We have a grievance," Father Sudek said.

"Oh? Tell me."

"Concerning Ayna."

Dal recognized the stage was set for an important afternoon

showdown. The people had rallied for the young woman's wellbeing; now their voices needed a platform. This was the final wave of hysteria. This was the moment before their bubble burst and they went home feeling defeated, yet somehow exonerated for putting up an honorable fight. Such was the life of a movement. He had seen many good-intentioned causes rise and fall during his career. This cause was no different.

"It is unfortunate," Dal said, "but I do not take grievances before noon." He reminded them to read the sign posted at the gate, which detailed Soviet procedures for making complaints.

"We aren't happy with what has transpired in recent weeks," the priest went on. "Especially since you soldiers arrived."

"Oh?" Dal said numbly. "Unhappy are we?"

Father Sudek elaborated, "It's inhumane to keep the innocent Ayna from her family. She isn't your vandal. I swear by it."

"There will be no audience right now," Dal insisted, "concerning Ayna."

"But the girl—"

"Furthermore, the girl is not taking visitors."

Dal pointed down the road to the stone bridge and told them to leave the premises or face arrest. Despite the priest's futile attempt to persuade him to release Ayna, or to speak with her, his face was firm, and he leaned menacingly into anyone who questioned his decision. When they grumbled about the Smetana recital and how much it meant to Ayna, he shunned their enthusiasm for the arts and challenged them to focus on their work, in particular those who were farmhands and laborers. He had gone over the productivity charts with the district leaders and seen firsthand that production was crumbling; the system was surviving mostly due to government subsidies. While he shared their passion for classical music, he also recognized their priorities were skewed. The time for musical gatherings was not today or tomorrow, he reminded himself. It was a privilege that needed to be earned, the result of good laboring by the workers, for the workers.

Josef stepped forward and said, "We stand united for her release."

"United?" Dal pointed his finger at the crowd of onlookers. He noticed a fair representation of women standing in the mob. "Is this true? Are you united against the Soviet Union?" When no one supported the baker's claims, Dal returned his attention to him. "Paper tigers," he said with a grin and heard the people grumble.

Father Sudek said, "Ayna has been looking forward to this musical event for nearly a year." The lines of tension had gathered around his mouth. "Without her participation tomorrow morning, well, I'm afraid there can be no recital."

"Oh, you people are sick in the head," Dal said, stepping close to the gate. "How can you think of the recital right now? Ayna is facing serious criminal charges, and you people speak to me of a recital? Are you really so selfish?"

The priest gripped the wrought-iron bars, his expression contorted with blame. For once, Father Sudek looked his age, even older. As long as he remained their leader, the fledgling anarchists would stand behind him, regardless of his inability to draw blood. Dal sensed it was only a matter of time before they crawled to him and begged for his forgiveness, accepting that the military invasion, his presence in Mersk, everything that had occurred to this point, was about their liberation from corrupt ideas.

"We celebrate and honor Smetana," Father Sudek said.

"You celebrate your own vanity," Dal snapped.

"Colonel——I want my daughter to come home." Nadezda took Jiri in her arms. "Once you admired her strength. You wanted to protect my family from the Germans."

"And your point would be?"

"She will be of no future annoyance to you or to your soldiers. You have my word."

"Perhaps you should have come to this obvious conclusion many days ago, when I first extended my hand of brotherly kindness to your family." While speaking, Dal unbuttoned his collar and picked at the adhesive bandage covering the infected mosquito bite. He was feeling a headache coming on. "If I choose to return the young woman in time for your recital, it will be out of my utmost respect for the master Czech composer Bedrich Smetana——not to be confused with your silly imbecile of the same name."

Bedrich was standing on a boulder near the road, spying over everyone's head with his army binoculars.

"It would be a kind gesture," Father Sudek responded. "Such a sentiment would go a long way in forming solidarity with us."

Turning to Horbachsky, Dal said, "Give them ten minutes to disperse. If they continue with this senseless protest, arrest them all."

"My daughter . . ." Nadezda wept. "Please, you must let her come home."

The priest stuck to the bars, unwilling to back down. Dal found his protest to be too little too late, and recited eagerly from *The Iliad*, "Hateful to me," he began with a dramatic tone, "as the gates of Hades is that man who hides one thing in his heart and speaks another." Then he brushed past Horbachsky and lumbered toward the villa.

"Colonel Dal," the priest yelled. "We demand you release the girl!"

Evening had arrived without further protests. It was six o'clock, the hour for the piano works of Petrovich Mussorgsky and a tall vodka. And Dal, who often listened to *Pictures at an Exhibition* when he drank, was feeling buzzed. He sat in the library and danced without moving his feet, penciling in the day's events in his log; he had crushed yet another uprising.

He poured the vodka with a trembling hand and shot the liquor like medicine in order to ease the painful headaches and the throbbing behind his eyes. Dear Lenin, what had that damn mosquito done to him? Even his gums were bleeding. A good Russian doctor was in order. It was delusional to think otherwise. But as he had explained to Gurko, he would tolerate the pain for another week, tough it out like an old soldier. He had no other choice.

At 8:00 p.m., Dal entered the POW's room with a briefcase under his arm. He stood beside the bed, next to a chamber-pot and a boarded-up window. He took a moment to examine the prisoner. The sleeping man was locked in his leg irons and wore Soviet fatigues and a white t-shirt.

"I feel for you," he said. "Caught up in the politics, you, a soldier, should understand that this is the way the East-West game is played. Some men are kings, some men are rooks, and some men are pawns. Expendable."

Johnston opened his eyes with a jolt and scooted against the headboard. "Jesus Christ," he said. "What now?"

"Relax, comrade. I am not here to interrogate you." Dal caught a whiff of underarm perspiration, which flared his nostrils. The uniform needed a good washing——as did Johnston. "The time for questioning has long passed. Name. Rank. Serial number. Your generals back in the states would be proud of how stubborn you have been these last few weeks. I respect your sealed lips. What is it you Americans say? 'Loose lips sink ships?'"

"Back off," Johnston said. "And tell your Gestapo sidekick that I've had enough of his crap."

"Be careful," Potapov warned, stepping next to the bed. "Even chained-up, the Yankee has a quick right hand."

Dal lit a cigarette and offered a smoke to the prisoner, who refused by turning his head. "Soon you will leave this villa. Off to a new adventure. To where, I am not authorized to say. In the meantime, tonight is cause for celebration. Tonight you will have lamb and good Russian vodka."

"Lamb?" Johnston said. "Is that supposed to excite me? Because your goons are pissing on my food."

Dal ignored the comment, though made a mental note to look into the claim. Urinating on the prisoner's food was a sign of undisciplined behavior. It was unacceptable conduct. If true, he would reprimand the Ukrainians.

He saw a book resting on the blanket: Ernest Hemingway's *The Old Man and the Sea*. "Critics say that particular novel is an American classic, penned by a war hero. It was the only novel written in English that I could find in the mayor's library. Though Hemingway has been censored by the Party, I have granted you special reading privileges."

Johnston glared into the colonel's eyes.

"He is unpredictable," Potapov warned in Russian. "Be careful."

"I have always been fascinated by your American culture," Dal went on, leaning carefully into Johnston. "In particular with the motion picture industry. It is true. Against my father's best wishes, I aspired for the stage as a youth and as an advanced student dreamed of making a silent movie with the famous actor and socialist Charlie Chaplin. However at seventeen years old, and with the onset of the Great Patriotic War, the Motherland called . . ." Dal relished the opportunity to explain himself to the American, regardless of the man's defiant I-want-to-kill-you eyes drilling into him. "She asked of me, 'Grigori, will you serve in this holy duty? Will you set aside your aspirations for the stage and answer this call to defend the Union of Soviet Socialist Republics?' I did. In all its glory, I served."

"Glory?" Johnston said doubtfully.

"You beg to differ?"

"You starve your people."

"Propaganda."

"And treat them like slaves."

"Propaganda."

"Brezhnev is a mass murderer."

"Again, propaganda. You are boring me with your false textbook accusations." Aside from spitting out insults and harassing Horbachsky, which Johnston seemed to take great pleasure in doing, he had been unwilling to have any real dialogue over the previous weeks. This unexpected spat intrigued Dal.

"We have liberty in the United States," Johnston said, rattling the heavy chain attached to the leg iron. "The people make the laws, not a dictator. Unlike in your backward country, Americans are free to govern themselves."

"And govern as they may. Unfortunately for you, your leaders have likely chosen to abandon you. Your status as missing in action will eventually be labeled killed in action to save certain politicians from the headache of having to account for your whereabouts."

"That is a lie." Johnston leaned forward. "The Corps won't stop looking for me."

"I admire your patriotism," Dal admitted. "But you should not confuse the loyalty of your comrades in the Marine Corps with the greed of the politics in Washington D.C." Johnston tightened his fists. "Ah, this Cold War between our nations is a horrendous little war."

". . . they won't stop searching for the other Marines, either."

Dal shook his head. "You Americans are an interesting bag of extremes. I have met quite a few of you over the years. Mostly my contemporaries, CIA operatives pretending to be businessmen or politicians in places like Warsaw and Berlin. Always so damn confident. Just like the Germans. Honestly, I am not unlike you, Gunnery Sergeant Johnston. I, too, am confident. And a patriot." Dal ashed his cigarette. "Now then, I am curious. Have you read Marx?"

"Marx is an idiot," Johnston said. "The things done in the name of Marxism far outstrip anything out of the Third Reich."

Dal frowned. There was no use in attempting to educate the American. "In the end, this liberty you speak about will be your country's undoing. Too much opinion, in particular students with an abundance of freedom to speak out against the government, has a way of derailing things."

"Screw you."

"You doubt me?"

"I've heard enough."

"Oh, it is happening. Look at the left-leaning American students who travel to Moscow. While soldiers die in Vietnam, they flock to the Soviet Union on a pilgrimage for answers. We, of course, welcome them. They will find truth. Truth in Marx. Then someday they will become the leaders of your country, doctors, lawyers, judges, senators. Who knows, maybe even a president, eh?"

"Do you always talk so much?"

"Their politics are the seedlings of socialism. From there communism. Then the downfall of America is only a harvest season away."

"Shut up."

"And so we wait."

"Jesus."

"The protests in your country . . . the antiwar crowd . . . most of the American people are not behind you in Vietnam. Their stomachs are weak. Why else would they call it a conflict, and not a war? It is only a matter of time before the protests turn violent. The war will end in failure."

"That is where you have it wrong. The military won't allow that to happen. We know how to win a war."

Dal reached into the briefcase and extracted a folder. "Speaking of Vietnam, there were other soldiers like you. In total, nine

American sons. Nine fighting men whisked quietly away from the soggy battlefields of Que Son, en route to the Soviet Union." He flashed Devil Dog before Johnston's disbelieving eyes. "The contents of these files could start an international upheaval, capable of regime change. Your brothers . . . snatched from rice patties and secretly transported to Siberia for medical experimentation." Dal patted him kindly on the shoulder, expressing his sympathy, even commiserating over his role in the scandal. "You should consider yourself lucky. I had orders to execute you. Instead, tonight I offer you a decent meal. How is that for a fair exchange?"

Johnston said, "First of all, idiot, I'm a Marine, not a soldier."

"My mistake . . ." Dal was amused by the American's piss-poor attitude. In some ways, Johnston reminded him of his brother Alex, killed on the German front in 1943. He missed his brother and his offbeat sarcasm.

"There were three of us. What happened to the others? Williams? Thomas?"

"I imagine you have many questions."

"Were they sent to Prague?"

"To Novosibirsk," Dal said matter-of-factly. "In Siberia. It's all here, in this file we call Devil Dog."

Johnston started to say something, then suddenly swung on him.

Dal had seen the fist coming and with the agility of a professional boxer bobbed out of the way. At the same time, Potapov grabbed and threw Johnston against the mattress, then began to pummel him with jabs to the stomach.

Dal quickly held up a hand to stop the beating. The American lacked understanding. Soviet scientists delving into the minds of their foes was crucial for the war, and ultimately for the peace. He recognized how the typical man might think it was cruel, perhaps unethical to experiment on living humans. Nevertheless he agreed with the army scientists who performed the tests on the abducted servicemen; any incidental or unintended cruelty was best for the advancement of science and for the future of the Soviet Union.

"One must understand how the enemy is wired up," he said,

lighting a cigarette with glossy, bloodshot eyes. "This is ultimately how the peace is won."

He stood motionless, without any expression on his face.

There was nothing more to say.

Again, he remembered his brother, poor, poor Alex, his life cut so tragically short.

Dal left the prisoner and returned to the library. He opened the mayor's liquor cabinet and found a bottle of Cabernet Sauvignon, a vintage from the coast of Crimea in the Ukraine.

Questions, he thought. Why had he told Johnston his life had been spared? Why had he shared the secrets of Devil Dog? Perhaps it was a sense of camaraderie from one military man to another, an unwritten soldier's code. Or maybe it was the alcohol speaking. Either way, Dal felt godlike prevailing over the POW with life and death authority. Something about the exchange of words had reminded him of the dialogue in William Shakespeare's play, *The Life and Death of King John*, where a dizzying change of alliances had prevailed, building toward the slow death of the King. Life was music, but death was poetry. Sweet, delicate poetry. If only he could find the play at the village library. He would love to read it again.

Finishing his glass of wine, Dal went to the restroom and looked in the mirror at the bloodstained bandage. With an agonizing moan, he stripped the adhesive strip from his skin and exposed the mosquito bite with its ugly infection. Repulsive, he thought with horror. He used his fingers to pinch the gruesome lump, savagely draining the puss into the sink, letting it squirt and drip on the chipped porcelain. Even with the numbing alcohol in his blood, the pain was unbearable. "Ah——I wish that your children will spit in your soup," he shouted into the mirror. "Yobany stos."

He returned to the desk and reaching into the bottom drawer, pulled out a can of white spray paint. He had asked Ota Janus to do the dirty work. The man had obeyed by painting the swastika on the tank with the cunning of the deadly assailant who had assassinated Leon Trotsky with an ice pick in Mexico City. It was the first step in an important relationship he planned to foster with the teacher. Today a vandal. Tomorrow perhaps the mayor of Mersk. For now, framing Ayna Sahhat for the tank's defacement had been brilliant——even Janus had agreed. With the doctor away, it was the perfect timing to apprehend the rebellious woman and strip her by force of any lingering hatred toward Moscow.

All this devious scheming aside, Dal had recognized the importance of the Smetana recital from the start, for local pride, in maintaining civil obedience across the valley. Keeping their attention focused on entertainment and other trivialities made them happy, ensuring complacency, and for the most part, upheld the peace. As Lenin had preached, it was important to prevent discontent from dipping to that dangerous point where a fledging anarchist blossomed into an unshakable counter-revolutionary, inciting others, family, friends, neighbors. While Ota Janus had suggested he cancel the recital, he decided otherwise. "The show must go on," he had informed the schoolteacher. "For the good of this community."

He buried the can of paint in the drawer, lit a cigarette, and sat in deep thought. Was Ayna Sahhat really cursed? Or was she simply an anarchist? A troublemaker. And if he let her go free, what then?

At midnight he left the library and walked down the hall. She was locked in Zdenek Seifert's bedroom a few doors away. While she had rejected him, Dal held on to slim hope that she might reconsider his offer to picnic; at the very least he wanted her to accept his hand of comradeship; he believed it would put an end to her rebellious ways. Seemed to him she might want to confess some regret for having challenged his authority. It was all he asked.

Entering from the dark of the hallway, Dal stood near the bed and gazed unsympathetically at the young woman. She wore a short black dress and sat on the edge of the mattress, her head down, her body bathed in dim lamplight. Even in melancholy, with her spirit broken, she was as lovely as ever. If only she had welcomed his romantic advances, things might have turned out much, much better for her and Jiri. He would have set them up with a modest flat in Prague. A better job. A life. Could she have asked for more?

"This incident was avoidable," he said. "Unfortunately you had to challenge my authority."

"I heard voices. Outside. At the gate."

"Ah, yes. The voice of anarchy in its final stage of life." He paused to reflect. "It's that tragic point in the road where passion meets disillusionment."

"Who were they?" Her eyes were hidden behind the strands of long hair that fell in her face.

"Your mother. The priest. The baker. And a hundred more."

"A hundred?"

"Quite a crowd rallied. As I might have expected, they view me as the villain, not a man in pursuit of the community's well-being."

"They were asking about me?"

"They came to demand your release."

"I wouldn't have expected it. Not in a million years."

"Don't let their unforeseen behavior be so encouraging. I sense nothing has really changed from their point of view. Sorry to say."

"Why are you so cruel?"

He sighed. "The people are ignorant. You know that. I know that. Many see you as their Dark Ages witch. Why? Because to them, you reflect everything that is bad in this forsaken village. You are their bug stuck in a web. See, it is easier to blame your Azeri roots and the curse, than to admit to their own shortcomings in life. To their own miserable existence."

"It's between me and the citizens of Mersk, not an outsider like you."

"And the episode with Janus? Rape or sex?" He rubbed his chin. He was not trying to provoke, he was speaking from the head, attempting to help make sense of her life, why and how things had come to be. "Tragic, really. Like most arguments, there are varying points of view——*he said, she said.* I guess we will never really know the truth, will we?"

"Are you totally devoid of compassion for others?"

"I am merely telling you that which you choose to ignore."

"You're a monster." She scowled at him, her hands fixing her messy hair to one side of her face, where it fell over her collarbone and onto her chest.

"Monster? That is a harsh word."

"No. Not really."

"If you set aside your resentment of me for a moment, you might see that I simply want to help you find your way through the weeds." He rubbed his chin. "As well, I am worried about Jiri. In particular, his future."

"What do you mean?"

"You cannot seem to stay out of trouble."

"So?"

"The jails are overflowing with rebellious people like you. Some of them mothers. I know you would not want to leave Jiri alone, without a parent."

"Are you threatening me?"

"Mmm."

He appraised her untamable face, her red-lidded eyes were dark and full of venom. She had pushed his buttons. Pushed them like no woman had ever pushed them before. This power she had both perplexed and aggravated him. He had never met anyone like Ayna Sahhat. He moaned, feeling himself swept up in the undertow of madness. What were his next steps? How would he keep her from becoming more of a problem? Locking her up in a prison would be the easy thing to do.

Dal would consider his options.

For now, he left the room without saying another word.

At 4:00 am, he was woken by the alarm clock. He sat up and switched it off, then got dressed. He was exhausted, but not sleepy. Within the hour, he had instructed his soldiers to send the girl home.

As she passed through the gate, where streetlamps lit the road, he stood broodingly at the library window with his black tea and watched her leave. The wind blew her black dress, which she held on to with both hands. Even with her courage to stand against his authority, Dal began to sense her spirit was slowly dwindling. The fear of losing her son had hit home. She had flinched when he mentioned the boy's name, then recoiled in terror when he threatened jail time.

Though something troubled him.

A small thing.

Not Ayna's rebelliousness, rather Bedrich's loyalty.

The imbecile had stayed outside the gate all night, keeping a vigil while the others went home to sleep. For the first time, he wondered: just how trouble free was the village idiot?

Later in the morning, after he had showered and dressed for the 9:00 a.m. recital, Dal placed a blanket over his shoulders and went for a stroll in the garden. Circling around the villa, he arrived to the driveway and stopped at the GAZ truck. The military vehicle had a new dent and a lashing scrape on the front bumper. He sneezed, and then wiped his nose. The damage was good news. It could mean only one thing: Gurko had taken care of business.

Milan was driving near the monastery when he saw the police car parked on the road, and braked. The last thing he had patience for was another delay. He had a busy morning planned: an electrician was already waiting for him at the clinic; then there was the recital.

A police officer held up a hand, forcing him to a stop. Milan rolled down his window and flashed his identification.

"There was a bad accident," the officer said.

"I am a physician. I can—"

"Have you seen any suspicious vehicles on the road, perhaps a car with body damage speeding away?"

"Nothing out of the ordinary. It has all been pretty typical of late. Tanks. Soldiers. Roadblocks. You know, considering the Soviets and company."

"Yes, damn them."

Milan caught a glimpse of the crash through the windshield. "Any serious injuries?"

Before the policeman could answer, he realized it was Frank Steven's farm truck nosed straight into a fir. The hood was shot up against the shattered windshield and the driver's door was open.

"No need for doctors," the officer said. "Poor guy skidded off the road. Head trauma. Died on impact."

"Jesus." *Frank Stevens dead?* "But the road isn't even wet."

"There were conflicting tread marks on the pavement. Plus a dent in the rear panel on the truck. We determined that maybe someone had bumped him off the road."

Milan watched Frank's body being led away on a stretcher, before thumping his hand against the dashboard. Accident? Or murder?

He waited ten or fifteen minutes for the ambulance to pull away.

Then with a firm grip on the steering wheel, he drove straight for Mersk. By the time he passed the monastery, he concluded someone had intentionally run Frank off the road.

Suspecting he was next on the hit list, Milan flashed to the phone number Frank had given him. Was help a phone call away? If so, could he escape to Austria with Ayna and her son? As he pulled into a parking space near the clinic, Oflan approached the car and knocked frantically on the window.

"Ayna," he bellowed. "Ayna was arrested . . ."

Milan shifted the car into gear and drove around the square to Ayna's house. Hearing Oflan's departing words, "The colonel is a raving lunatic," he pushed his foot against the gas pedal. *Damn him.* If the KGB tyrant had laid a finger on her, Milan was thinking, he would break the man's neck.

He parked. Nadezda grabbed his arm when he burst into the home without knocking. "I can't handle this anymore," she said. "I'm a good mother. I did my best. Why me?"

"Where is she?"

"I tried warning her. 'Don't push the Russians,' I said. But she wouldn't listen."

"Get hold of yourself," Milan said. "Tell me where she is."

"In her bedroom."

Rushing up the stairs, then into the room, he reached for Ayna's hand. "Are you okay? What happened?"

She was standoffish and cold, calling him "Dr. Husak" and avoiding eye contact. Standing near the dresser, she explained how Dal had become jealous of their relationship and blamed her for the graffiti on the tank. "To top it off, while you were away yesterday, he arrested me because I had a Beatles album in my record collection. Can you believe that? An album."

"I've had all I can take. I am going to do something."

"Don't be foolish."

"Someone must. There's no end in sight."

"You can't stop him."

"He must be stopped."

"He's a madman. There's no telling what he'll do. It's not worth it."

"I can handle myself."

"I want the fighting to end," she pleaded. "Especially where it concerns me. I am a mother."

Milan was livid. "What he did to you. What he's doing to this community. It's wrong."

"Yes, but Jiri—"

"This harassment can't persist."

"Promise me. Promise you won't do anything."

He felt the blood rush to his face. He went to the open window and looked down on the street. Children were playing near the tank. A man sold flowers from a corner. The street musician had a small audience. It was like a kind of game between them, turning the cheek the other way. He recognized that Ayna had joined the masses, the groupthink that rallied behind the unspoken joys of submission, a way of life that did not fully concede to surrender, but had a white flag poking out of its rear pocket. Was her decision voluntary? Or was she simply wanting to protect her son? He sighed. It was pointless for him to carry on like the standard-bearer. If Ayna did not care, why should he? "Okay," he said with tight lips, realizing he was just as guilty as any of them for allowing the Russians to have their way. "Promise. If that is what you want, I promise."

He went downstairs to the kitchen and returned with a pot of hot tea. He was cooling off. Following him up the stairs this time, Nadezda was concerned the recital might be canceled, and pressed for answers. "The recital. Will she play this morning?"

"I don't know."

"If she doesn't play, they will snub her for good."

Milan held up his hand and asked to be alone with Ayna. He entered the bedroom and closed the door. More than ten minutes passed as she sat quietly on the bed. He remembered how content she had been on the picnic, talking nonstop with joy about her cello. Milan missed that cheerful girl. Given what had happened the previous night, could he blame her for being so downcast?

"Do you want to talk?" he asked.

Ayna cradled herself. "You wouldn't understand."

"I do care for you."

"I suppose you do."

"It's true."

Milan fell into madness, trying to make her laugh with jokes about Mozart's five-thumbed dog, and other absurd stories. He mentioned the opera house in Prague and talked about how amazing it would be to vacation at a hotel near the park. "And take in a concert," he added. Like a fool, he pressed on, admitting his deepest feelings for her, trying to win back the love he felt slipping away from her blackened heart.

"We were doomed," she finally said. "I shouldn't have led you on. I should have known better . . ."

What was she saying? Fallen out of love——that was what Ayna finally concluded. *Because of a curse.* "My ex-boyfriends died under bizarre circumstances," she went on, sitting on the mattress with her head down, struggling with the dark memories. "Victims of an unexplained curse."

Milan was unwilling to believe she had lost all feelings for him in a matter of hours, nor that she was cursed. Three dead boyfriends? Three violent deaths? Ridiculous, he thought. "Your boyfriends mysteriously dying in freak accidents is a coincidence. You can't possibly believe you had something to do with their deaths."

"I knew you wouldn't understand."

"I'm trying. It's hard."

"You're trying to make sense of things. Some things can't be explained."

"But— "

"You're no different. You're just like everyone else in Mersk."

"C'mon, stop this nonsense."

"That's why Jiri and I need to leave this awful village and never return. We need a fresh start."

Milan sighed. It was a winless situation for a man to find himself in. She was right; he was attempting to pick apart her story. And why not? Curses? It was a medieval way of thinking. The people had wrongly put that idea into her head by repeating it over the years. If only he could switch a lever and make things better, shed some optimism into her world. If only he could do this before the dregs of misery destroyed her as it had destroyed him for the last twenty-four years.

He poured Ayna a cup of tea. She took it, deliberately looking away from him, toward the window. "I've been insensitive," he admitted. "I apologize. I want to know about this curse. I want to know everything about you. I think you're beautiful. I deeply care for you."

"The premonitions," she began, her voice somber. "They came to me in my dreams."

"Tell me . . ."

Ayna held her cup of tea with both hands. "The first occurred many years ago, just after Jiri was born. It was Dana. I saw him submerged beneath the water, tangled in the pondweed. He was attempting to free himself and swim toward the surface, but thrashed violently like a fish stuck in a net. When he reached for my hand, his only way out of the water, I was unwilling to take it."

"So he drowned in your dream. And somehow you feel responsible?"

"Three days later Dana was with a girl. He was cheating on me again. He had been drinking all night. He went to the ponds near the mill. He went under and never came up."

Milan placed a hand on her shoulder and felt her body slacken. "I know there's more. Your second boyfriend. Strom, was it?"

"He trained horses for the communists," she explained. "So it wasn't surprising when I dreamed of horses, hundreds of them, running across a grassy field. And there was Strom, poor Strom, so helpless, crucified on the ground with his hands and feet bound to wooden stakes. The ropes could easily have been untied, yet I made no effort to free him."

"Trampled in real life?"

"Kicked in the head by a horse."

"Jesus."

"This was when people first pointed their fingers at my Muslim grandfathers, labeling it an Azeri curse."

"They needed an explanation for the deaths. That's what ignorant people do."

Ayna had a sip of tea. "I went to see Father Sudek in prison. Like you, he insisted I wasn't to blame for the deaths. We held hands and prayed. That seemed to help. I began to feel much better. Eventually, I met Peter. It was the happiest I had ever been. Even the stupid whispers of 'Muslim' and 'cursed' no longer seemed to matter. You see, Peter meant everything to me. When he asked me to marry him, I didn't hesitate to say yes. We were planning a move to Prague where life would be exciting and wonderful. Unfortunately, just as things were returning to normal, when I managed to tuck away the guilt for Dana and Strom, it happened again with Peter's car accident."

"I'm sorry," he said, kissing her on the head. "I appreciate how you have opened up, telling me about your past. However I would be lying if I said I believed in superstitions. You can't scare me away like this."

"I'm not trying to scare you."

"Could've fooled me."

"I knew you'd be a skeptic."

Milan was obliged to leave it at that. If anything, he blamed himself for her situation. The colonel had been harassing Ayna for weeks. Leaving her alone in the village was a mistake. He knew that. He wiped the stress from his face with both hands. He could not stay any longer. He might regret saying something. He grabbed his satchel and took a step for the door when a photo taped to the dresser mirror caught his eye: a picture of a young man holding a violin. He leaned into the color snapshot. There was something peculiar about the guy. Not the violin or his quirky smile——the red hair.

"Who is this man?" he asked.

"That's Sascha. My best friend. Or I should say, used to be my best friend. He's dead."

"The same Sascha who was shot by the Russians?" Milan had overheard people talking about the shooting in the square, but had never asked anyone for details. From what he understood, the young man had provoked the Russians into a fight. He had assumed the police were looking into it.

"Yes. The colonel's henchmen murdered him in cold blood," she added bitterly.

"Cold blood? I heard he assaulted one of the soldiers. That the shooting was in self-defense."

"You heard wrong."

"Sorry."

Milan went white-faced when she explained how the soldiers had taken his body to the villa and shaved his head so that he looked like a soldier. Everything was starting to make sense. He had fallen into the colonel's trap. Duped. All along, Milan had believed the body found in the parlor belonged to the American prisoner of war, when it was actually Sascha. *That meant . . . oh, dear god . . . Gunnery Sergeant Russell Johnston must still be alive!*

Ayna was saying, "Milan——I haven't told you about the fourth premonition."

"You said there were three."

"I lied."

"I haven't the time for this," he stammered. He was feeling accountable for the Marine's situation. Had he only acted upon Frank's request to help. Had he simply taken a moment to investigate.

She said, "It's you."

"What are you saying now?"

"You. You're the fourth premonition."

"You're giving me a headache."

"This morning," she went on, "while I slept, I saw you standing on a bridge, in the middle of nowhere, yet somehow I sensed it was not very far from here."

"Enough. Stop talking about this asinine curse."

Her eyes were fixed on him, hard like stone. "Your hands were covered in blood. And there was a vulture soaring overhead."

Milan became paralyzed by the tone of her voice, by the way her words consumed the room, speaking without kindness or empathy. "So how will it be?" he said defensively. "Death by a pecking bird, is it?"

"It was a bullet," Ayna said. "A bullet."

Fifth Act: Rage

GOLIATH'S ARMS

Hatred is the coward's revenge for being intimidated.

GEORGE BERNARD SHAW

Without saying goodbye to Ayna or her mother, Milan left the bedroom and ran toward the clinic.

The streets were nearly deserted. Someone with an open window was listening to a speech on the radio. It was the address from the First Secretary of the newly formed Central Committee. "It's fraud," a man inside the home shouted. "Don't listen to him. The committee is a puppet of the regime in Moscow."

Milan pulled out his keys and unlocked the door to the clinic. He was haunted by a heavy voice——*your demons will destroy you.*

He was a mess.

Who was he kidding? Any relationship with Ayna would be met with self-destruction, with the shrill crying of children in his ears, and now, if he walked away from GySgt Johnston, endless recriminations for abandoning a brother.

Perhaps this was the real curse.

Even as he had spoken to her moments ago and expressed his love, he felt the sharp pangs of despair in his gut. You can't bring back those children. They're dead. But you can save the American's life.

This was his salvation.

His final salvation; he was sure of it.

Milan stepped into the clinic and pulled the blinds. Looking back, it seemed obvious to him that the dead body in the parlor belonged to Sascha. Dal would have been more careful to hide the POW, plus Sascha wore street clothes and his fingernails were manicured ——signs of a meticulous civilian.

How could he have been so clueless?

He walked to his office located in the back of the building and sat at a desk. He stared blankly at a black telephone. He recalled Zdenek

Seifert's implausible story about the secret passageway beneath the villa. Could he break in? If the tunnel led to the bedroom where they were keeping Johnston, and he was careful, with some luck, it was possible to rescue the Marine. He pulled the wallet from his pocket and found the phone number Frank had given him——*his ticket to freedom*——and dialed the number.

After the first ring, someone picked up the phone and he heard a garble of voices. Milan was impatient. "Hello? Hello?"

"Who is this?" The man had an Austrian accent.

"Milan Husak."

"I see . . ."

"I was told to call this number."

"And . . . ?"

"And I'm coming over."

There was a pause. "When?"

"Today."

With the possibility of lines being tapped, the Austrian got right to the point, instructing him to go to the frontier crossing without luggage or personal belongings. "A gentleman smoking a pipe will be waiting in a Renault with broken taillights. Look for the car two streets from the Border Guard office."

"Black Škoda. Got it."

"Five o'clock sharp," the Austrian added.

Milan decided against mentioning that Johnston was alive. What was the point? He had to rescue him first. If the day ended in disaster, the last thing he wanted was more scandal in Mersk. He owed the people that much for remaining strong in the face of a madman and his henchmen. He would simply show up with the Marine and trusted Frank's group to take custody, no questions asked.

Milan realized the line was dead and hung up the telephone.

He walked several blocks up the street and purchased flowers from a floral shop. People were talking electrically, "Good thing they released Ayna," and "Today is the recital," and "You going, doc?" Milan avoided conversation, left the shop and found Father Sudek inside the church library, a musty-smelling room that was ten degrees cooler than any building in town.

The priest was listening to Dvorak's *Symphonic Poem*. "Dr. Husak," he said with surprise, "you look like you've seen a ghost."

Milan placed the flowers on a desk next to the record player and lifted the needle. "Oh, it's much worse than a ghost, Father. Do you have a moment?" Like making a confession, Milan told him the truth about his life, of his humble beginnings in Chicago, then spilled his guts about the war years, and the tragic deaths of the Roma orphans, naming all twelve of them. "So you see," he said. "I have always been an imposter, a citizen of the United States. My name is Mickey Husak. And I'm a complete fraud. Not a Czech war hero."

"Is this a practical joke?" the priest asked, approaching him.

"No. I've been living a lie."

Father Sudek laid a consoling hand on Milan's shoulder. "CIA. Spies. Unbelievable."

Milan complicated the story by explaining how a United States Marine was imprisoned at the villa. "It's strange. He has red hair, as did Sascha. Is it a coincidence? I'm not so sure. And don't you think it's odd how they carted Sascha's body away and shaved his head."

"Strange, indeed."

"They're up to something. Can't quite put my finger on it. But something"

Father Sudek accepted his admission of post-war intrigue without showing a wrinkle of disappointment. He reassured Milan that he was a hero——no matter what his intentions had been.

"So," the priest asked. "What will you do?"

"Take matters into my own hands."

"Oh? How?"

"By rescuing the American."

When Milan mentioned the secret passageway, Father Sudek nodded his head and confirmed the tunnel led to a shaft, ultimately to a bedroom closet on the third floor. "The church helped pay for its expensive construction," the priest added. "Nevertheless, you can't just enter the tunnel, somehow find this man, and then lead him safely to Austria. It's impossible. Have you lost your mind?"

"I'm sure I have."

"There are Russians everywhere. On the ground. In the air. I don't see how this idea makes any sense."

It was good to hear Father Sudek validate Zdenek Seifert's claims of the passageway's construction, because even as he spoke, Milan remained skeptical of its existence. "I know it sounds crazy," he admitted. "But I must do something. Even after all these years away from America, as soldiers, we're brothers."

"I understand the bond between military men. You're a good man for wanting to help a comrade in need. It's just . . . have you considered the villa is heavily guarded?"

"Yes. But I have the element of surprise working for me."

"You against five armed soldiers? No. Bad idea."

"Four armed soldiers," Milan corrected him.

"How do you figure?"

"The colonel will be attending your recital this morning."

"True."

"That leaves four men at the villa."

"A valid point. Even so, you against four armed soldiers is equally suicidal."

"I'm willing to take that chance."

The bewildered priest rubbed the back of his neck. "Say you somehow pull this rescue off and reach the border, what then? Returning to the United States and starting a new life won't be easy."

"My plan is to deliver the American to agents at the frontier crossing. They'll get him safely into Austria. I'm confident of this. But so you know, I'm not fleeing the country." Milan had told the Austrians he was "coming over." In reality, he had no intention of leaving without Ayna. "In all the insanity of these last few weeks, I have somehow managed to get involved with a woman."

"I've noticed," Father Sudek said, wearing a hint of a smile. "You and Ayna make a fine couple. It's been years since I've seen her this happy."

"She'll be let down when I don't show up for the recital today."

"You make a valid point."

"I don't want to ruin her concentration."

"Don't worry. She'll be fine. The quartet is ready. Ayna is mentally prepared."

"Just in case, will you give her the flowers? Tell her I've been called to Prague. For an emergency meeting."

"You're getting me involved with your lies." Father Sudek cleared his throat and walked to the bookshelves. Milan followed. "People turn to me for the truth, doctor. Not lies."

"Forgive me. I shouldn't have asked."

"So you know . . . I'd like nothing more than to see the Russians fail." The priest stood on a short ladder and reached for a wooden box on a shelf. The box was wedged between a row of woodworking books and his *Encyclopedias of Christian Faith*. A subtle, devious expression crossed his face as he carried the dusty box to his desk and unlocked the tiny padlock. "Here, have a look at this incredible thing . . ."

Inside the box was an automatic pistol, a Steyr-Hahn, manufactured by Waffenfabrik Steyr in 1911. The Austrian weapon was wrapped in purple velvet with a ribbon and silver cross tied to its trigger.

"It's beautiful," Milan said.

"I dislike guns and weapons. It's just . . . this historic pistol is special."

"How special?"

"Decades ago," the priest went on, "after the Great War, the pistol rested on a conference table in Paris. It was during a round of heated negotiations shortly before we proclaimed our independence. The Steyr-Hahn represents our ability to stand on our own. A friend smuggled it out of France."

"Some secret you have, Father."

Father Sudek placed the gun in Milan's hands. "It was cleaned and fresh ammo purchased two years ago so it could be fired on the 50th anniversary of the Armistice."

Milan examined the pistol. The Steyr-Hahn had a reputation for dependability and felt snug in his hands. He grabbed the stripper clip from the box and loaded eight bullets.

"I promise you," Milan said, "when this is done, no more lies."

He inserted the clip into the gun, shoved another clip into his pocket, and then headed for the door.

He drove to the stone bridge and parked on the side of the road. From the trunk of the Škoda, he grabbed a can of motor oil, an empty wine bottle and a hose he had stolen from Oflan's garden. He sliced a short length from the hose and quickly siphoned gasoline from the fuel tank, filling the bottle halfway. Memories of making Molotovs, and blowing up tank treads, and destroying German outposts, rushed back to him. He poured motor oil into the bottle, jammed a stopper on top and put the homemade bomb in his backpack along with the gun.

After scrambling down the embankment, Milan footed through the creek and dashed toward the drainage tunnel beneath the bridge. When asked for details, the mayor had told him to follow the tunnel to the T. "Then turn right and walk three-hundred-and-forty-eight paces," he had said. "There is a wooden hatch in the tunnel's ceiling. The secret way in, the secret way out."

He gave himself an hour to rescue the Marine. But would Johnston even be in the room?

Milan trudged on.

The tunnel smelled like urine and excrement. It was crawling with rats living in the heaps of garbage and debris that had built up over the years.

Hunched over, he sloshed through the ankle-deep water, using the flashlight to find his way in the cold blackness. Left and right the walls were elaborately covered with graffiti, Christian symbols, anti-Hitler obscenities, and love messages dating back to 1848 when Czechs convened the first Slavic Congress.

With every step the temperature dropped and his adrenaline surged. Milan pressed on until he came to the T and counted the paces to the exact location where his flashlight illuminated the wooden hatchway.

He grabbed the handle and pushed up. But there was trouble: the damn thing was locked.

"WE'RE DOOMED," Tad said. "And with a capital D. Why? Because the judge looks like an arrogant bastard. He won't like us."

"Schell?" she asked.

"The illustrious judge Eric von Schell. The schmuck who will decide if we are worthy of a ticket to play at the national festival in Prague."

The white-bearded judge wore a 1930s-era suit with matching shoes. Sitting in the front row, he leaned into an ebony walking cane and glanced impatiently at his watch.

"Oh, concentrate, silly." Ayna waved her bow. "Mr. Schell is a genius. From Leipzig. He can hear another pianist play a complicated piece and duplicate it exactly from memory, without ever having heard or played it before."

"Ah, yet another German genius."

"How many geniuses do you know?"

"None."

"She makes a valid point," Oflan said. "Never question the wisdom of a genius."

"End of discussion," Ayna said. "You should be concerned with your solo. We're betting everything on your moment in the spotlight. Are you ready for this?"

"For goodness sake, why do you ask?" he said defensively

"Because Mr. Schell is notorious for walking out on lazy violinists."

"Lazy? You think I—"

"You're not focused," she said. "That's when you get into trouble with your violin."

With the death of Sascha, Tad's beaten face, rum on Oflan's breath, and a teenager joining them without much rehearsal, the string quartet was a lame horse destined to be put out of its misery. Who were they kidding? Were they really among the country's elite, especially with the talented Sascha gone?

Truth was, Ayna had low expectations for the recital. She would surrender everything just to have a word with Milan and thank him for the pretty flowers. Using the curse to push him away was the exact sort of medieval thinking she despised most about living in Mersk. She would apologize once he returned from his meeting at the hospital, talk to him. They could work through this.

Within minutes the final stragglers had found a seat or were standing against the stone walls. It was, by far, the hottest day of the year. Several people were fanning their faces with the recital's paper program and some of them had unbuttoned their shirts. While everyone waited patiently for the music to commence, the muggy nave had become a ripe mixture of loathsome perfumes and rancid body odors.

Ayna was glad she had chosen to wear clogs and a summer dress, rather than pants. She felt much cooler this way. She smiled at the flowers beside her music stand and took a breath. This was it, she thought. Months of rehearsal had come down to the next forty-five minutes.

The voices hushed when Father Sudek entered the nave. He was dressed in a plain black cassock with white tabs on the collar. There was sweat beading on his forehead. After lighting a candle, he joined the musicians in their semicircle.

Ayna placed her bow on the cello strings.

"Today" Father Sudek said, "the good people of St. Nepomuk welcome judge Eric von Schell to our humble church." After dedicating a moment of silence to the memory of Sascha, the priest pushed the baton into their semicircle, and Ayna launched into Smetana's *Second String Quartet in E Minor*.

SOME DAYS AGO, Dal had confiscated a yellow Škoda sedan from a car lot in Pisek. At the time, he made his intentions clear to Gurko, that he preferred to drive a civilian car rather than the more threatening GAZ military truck with its Red Star insignia on the door. "The deployment of our military in the cities across Czechoslovakia has been a raging success," he said, strapping on a boot holster and inserting the loaded Makarov pistol. "From Satrava in the East to Pilsen in the West, the Czech people have been beaten down by the mighty hand of Brezhnev. Even here, in Mersk. Now, with the fighting all but over, I must shed my soldierly persona and become more visible as a political figure——someone these people can trust."

"The upper hand is finally ours," Gurko said.

"Mmm. We have destroyed the village in order to save it."

"It was only a matter of time."

"Yet the good work of Marx and Lenin has only begun. We have important administrative work to carry out, comrade. I must find the mayor's replacement by December."

Dal had a secret. He was pushing for Ota Janus to replace the mayor. The teacher's pro-Moscow attitude and scholarly knowledge of socialism would please the presidium; additionally, Janus had proved his loyalty by tagging the tank with the swastika.

As he climbed into the automobile, an army courier arrived to deliver a message. Without opening the sealed KGB envelope, Dal folded it in half, stuck it inside his shirt pocket, then instructed Gurko to open the gate. "Cancel my appointments for the remainder of the day. Tell visitors that today is a day to celebrate Smetana. On colonel's orders."

"Yes, Comrade colonel."

Socializing with the people would go a long way in rebuilding their shaky relationship. Dal shared their passion for Smetana and planned to use it as a bridge to common ground. Together they would support Marxism-Leninism. Together they would work hard for the common good. Together they would redeem Czechoslovakia.

. . . so off he went

. . . driving into town.

He was whistling Smetana's *Fanfares for Richard III* when he sped past the doctor's Škoda parked near the bridge. And thought nothing of it.

At the church, Dal avoided a drove of pigs and parked erratically on the street.

Before opening the door, he straightened his wrinkled pant leg, then grabbed a pack of cigarettes and his sunglasses from the glove compartment. He climbed from the vehicle and stood on the cobblestones, careful of the dung near his car. The mess reminded him of a third world country, of a wretched place like Tashkent. He struck a match and lit a cigarette. There was little sophistication here in the mountains. He made a mental note to ban all livestock from the streets, including the animals at the weekly farmer's market. He would impose hefty fines on those who broke the law. He would also reopen the cinema house, thus ensuring precious art returned to their lives. Pro-Moscow films, of course.

He blew smoke and watched Bedrich kneel on the cobble to pet the pigs. He had no regrets for having destroyed the little man's mouse. The killing had been carried out in the name of public health. He threw an unreturned hand of hello to Bedrich, before rushing up the steps to the church. He greeted Irena with a smile, and said, "Good day."

"I'm sorry, colonel." Irena blocked the doors. "The recital has already begun. I've been instructed to turn away stragglers."

He heard the sound of muffled strings.

"This is an important event. Your priest is smart to eliminate distractions."

"Then you understand?"

"Of course."

He had no intention of barging in, which was the impulsive thing to do. While Dal enjoyed Smetana as much as anyone, he was mostly feeling a need to listen to Ayna play her cello. He had overheard someone mention she was a rare talent. What had they said, *Not quite a prodigy?* For someone from the mountains, she was as close as one could get to excellence without having the best instructors. He had to verify this for himself.

"You don't look well," Irena said. "What is wrong? Flu?"

"I'm feeling a little under the weather. That's all. Nothing to keep me away from today's recital."

"You should get some rest . . ."

He pulled a handkerchief from his pocket and wiped the sweat from his forehead. His headache was finally gone, thanks to a cocktail of aspirin and vodka taken every four hours. Even so, the last thing he wanted was medical advice from the bookwormish Irena.

"As the librarian and keeper of knowledge," Dal began insincerely, "I have always considered you the smartest person in town."

She brightened. "How kind of you."

"However I sense this judge might be impressed by a Soviet war hero like me in attendance. What do you think?"

"Yes. Now that you mention it. Nonetheless—"

"I happen to be a proud member of the Rimsky-Korsakov Society. Our organization is famous throughout Eastern Europe. It is an exclusive group, comprised mostly of maestros, distinguished Muscovites and important men such as myself. The judge undoubtedly has heard of us."

"I should think so."

"Seems to me, my honorable presence might provide enough leverage for your string quartet to get that invitation to play at the festival. Especially should I inform the maestro how my society admires your talented musicians."

"You would do that for us?"

"Yes."

"I suppose you have a point," she agreed. "Influence is important in high-society circles. It's not what you know. It's who you know."

"Exactly."

"And you will put in a good word?"

"I will put in many good words. An entire stanza of good will."

Irena handed him a program and slowly opened the door. Even with tender steps, his intrusion was noticed right away. First Oflan's viola waning, then the music dying off. He had not expected them to stop playing. Rather than show his embarrassment, he embraced the awkward moment. "Good day," he said, throwing Jiri a wink. "I heard music. Smetana?"

Ayna seemed to scowl before turning away.

Beaten down, yes, with the entire village beaten down, Dal could sense he was on the edge of victory. It was akin to that pivotal moment in a chess match when one eliminates his opponent's rooks and takes the queen. Total control of the end game.

"Find a seat," someone said loudly.

Dal rolled his hand arrogantly in the air. "Pardon my interruption. Do play on . . ."

He sat next to Pavel, but without recognizing the chauffeur with his newly grown and perfectly groomed Lenin beard. They had not spoken since Zdenek Seifert's arrest, even though the man had made repeated requests for a meeting to discuss, he had assumed, the circumstances surrounding the mayor's confinement. Pavel promptly rose with his paper program and stood against a far wall. A few men and women huffed and joined his silent protest, leaving the colonel seated alone in the pew. As citizens shuffled uneasily here and there, Dal suffered a spell of nausea and groaned until it went away.

Then raising his baton, the priest, who had waited patiently for the colonel to find a seat, brought the quartet back into a beautiful melody.

THE TUNNEL was nearly pitch-black. The only light came from the flashlight propped between cracks in the stones. Milan had no idea how long he had been slamming a waterlogged tree branch against the locked hatchway. Ten, fifteen minutes?

He crouched to get better leverage. Veins, swollen from the exertion, snaked above his eyes. He was close to breaking in. He could do this. He walloped furiously for another five minutes, each blow harder than the last. He had made a lot of noise, probably too much noise, but kept at it. After another thump the hinges began to split from the wood and he tightened his grip and pounded again. Furiously now. Pounding until he broke apart the hatch.

He dropped the tree branch in the water and placed the backpack through the opening above his head, onto a floor. His face was dripping with sewer water. He reached up and pulled himself into a dark shaft. As he moved, an unpleasant feeling came over him, like he was climbing into hell or crossing the River Styx. The priest had warned him, hadn't he? *There are Russians everywhere.*

He pointed the flashlight and explored the unfinished space. It was approximately the size of a bathroom, with bricks and exposed wooden beams, electrical wires, and plumbing pipes.

He kept moving.

A ladder led to another hatch located in the twenty-foot high ceiling.

Milan slipped the backpack over his shoulder and grabbed the first rung. He started up, climbing the wobbly ladder with a mixture of faith and anxiety. When he reached the last rung, he pushed against the hatch and pulled himself into a narrow crawl space.

He took a moment. There was the smell of urine and body odor. Was he smelling himself after that splash in the cold sewer? Or someone else?

He clicked off the flashlight and crawled toward a crack of light and the sound of ... what was it ... Ukrainian pop music? He moved into a closet, slipped quietly through a row of coats, some dress shoes, and edged up to a set of double doors. One of the doors was ajar. He peeked into the room and saw a man sitting on the floor. It was Johnston. The shirtless Marine sat by the unmade bed, near a boarded up window. His *Don't Tread on Me* tattoo caught Milan's eye right away. Milan watched him shuffle a deck of cards, then deal a row on the shag carpet. He had a clear path to the man. It was simply a matter of grabbing him and slipping back into the tunnel.

He took a moment. There were two soldiers on the other side of the closed bedroom door. They were talking over the music in the hallway. He recognized Mazur's husky voice. But the other? Sounded like Horbachsky.

He scanned the bedroom. The room was lit by a bare lightbulb that dangled by a cord from the ceiling. To his left, a wooden easel with an unfinished painting, a small table, and some art supplies. Against the far wall, forty feet away, the bed. To his right, near the door, an antique armoire.

He turned his attention back to Johnston. Although malnourished, he seemed physically okay. He would have to be strong enough to climb the ladder and make his way back through the tunnel, not an easy task——especially for someone who had been held captive for over a year and was likely frail and nagged by unhealed injuries.

Even though it was too late in the game for questions, Milan had them: what was Johnston's state of mind? How would he respond to a stranger emerging from the closet? Would he panic? Call for help?

There was only one way to find out.

Milan grabbed the Steyr-Hahn from the backpack, swallowed once and then slowly pushed open the closet door.

Right away, Johnston turned to him with furrowing eyebrows.

Milan put a finger to his lips and held his breath. He tried to smile but was nervous. The best face was a friendly face. Someone to trust. The stunned Marine just sat there with a playing card frozen in his hand. A second seemed like an hour. With music blasting on the other side of the door, Milan took a knee, and whispered, "I'm here for you, gunny."

"Who are you?" Johnston asked.

"An American."

"No shit?"

"United States Army. First Infantry Division. I helped kick Hitler's ass back in the day."

"Don't mess with me, sir."

"It's true."

"But you sound like a foreigner."

"I'll explain later."

"Okay."

"I've come to get you out of this mess."

"Sir. Thank you."

Milan looked at Johnston's ankles and realized he had a problem: the Marine was in leg irons. The irons were secured to the bed's footboard by a long hunk of chain. *Chained up like a damn dog!* He had not planned for this. He had to think of something. And fast.

But what? From the onset, even after Father Sudek had given him the Steyr-Hahn, he had hoped to avoid a gunfight. He wanted to avoid taking life. In his profession, and in the aftermath of what had happened on the battlefield, he had sworn to save lives. His plan was to slip into the room, grab Johnston, and then retrace his steps back through the tunnel without spilling any blood. But how stupid of him to think this way. Then again, he was plotting this rescue on the spur of the moment and was amazed he had even gotten this far undetected.

He handled the Molotov and stuffed the rag inside the bottle top. He placed it near the armoire. At this point, he had no choice but to use the pistol . . . the bomb . . . his fists . . . whatever it took to free Johnston from his captors.

He gave Johnston the Steyr-Hahn, the extra stripper clip, and asked, "Who has the key."

"Mazur, know him?"

"Yeah, the big guy."

"He keeps the key in his front pocket."

Milan quietly grabbed a stool and unscrewed the light bulb, splashing the room into darkness.

"You're serious about this," Johnston said.

"Damn right."

"Sorry I doubted you."

"No worries."

"Yes, sir."

"We're in for the fight for our lives."

"Sir."

"Know any good Russian insults?"

"Does Brezhnev look like he's got Stalin's ass hair growing on his upper lip?" Johnston held the pistol with both hands. "I studied Russian in the Corps, sir. Insults were the first words we Jarheads learned."

"Good. When I give the hand signal, give it all you got."

"Sir."

"You take the first soldier to enter the room. I'll handle the next."

Milan held the stool and positioned himself behind the door. If he struck his target square on the head, he would knock the unsuspecting soldier out. He took a breath, the blood surging through his veins. Seconds later, he waved a hand and mouthed, *go!*

. . . and Johnston was ready, finger on the trigger, unleashing several months of pent-up anguish, calling their mothers "Estonian whores" and their fathers the lowly "sons of inbred Tartars."

Milan grinned. "C'mon," he whispered, "let's see what you bastards got."

The laughter in the hallway ceased right away. It was followed by the music turning off. He heard grumblings and the harsh sound of Mazur's voice, "What the hell did the American just call us?"

The soldier's voice was replaced by a click of the door handle turning and then the door opening up.

Milan gripped the stool.

The first to stumble into the room was Horbachsky, chased by Mazur.

Milan swung the stool toward Mazur's head, but the alert soldier deflected the attack and knocked the piece of furniture from his hands.

Both men went into a defensive posture, hands up.

Milan saw the Ukrainian's grizzled face plain as day: his wide nose crooked from prior fistfights, his square jaw connected to a pillar of a neck. A neck, he sensed, that was strong like the pillars holding up the ancient Greek Acropolis.

This was bad. Really bad.

He realized how much trouble he was in after the first collision, when he landed a punch that bounced off Mazur's granite jaw.

Milan ducked and weaved, giving him a shot to the kidneys.

Mazur countered with a fist that missed wildly and with several jabs that breezed past his chin.

Milan dodged to one side, backing into the easel and knocking it to the floor.

"Where are you going?" Mazur asked, pulling a jackknife from his pocket. "Now I finish you off."

Instead of going in for the kill, Mazur toyed with the knife, swiping it back and forth with a grin. The delay allowed Milan a second to reach down and pick up the easel. With a firm grip, he swung the easel like a baseball bat against the Ukrainian's hand and then followed with a firm kick against the side of his kneecap. Mazur staggered.

Milan swung the easel again.

This time the Ukrainian soldier dropped the jackknife and fell to the floor in agony.

Milan pounced on him with a flurry of punches, each blow landing with the force of a sledgehammer, shattering Mazur's nose, cracking his jaw. He gave a cry of rage, somehow having the wherewithal to grab the fallen jackknife and attack, slicing his shoulder.

Pinned on his back, and bleeding, Mazur seized Milan's hand. "Ubit' vas," he shouted, pushing back on the knife. "It's over for you, doctor."

Milan grasped the jackknife with two hands and leaned into it, moving the tip closer to Mazur's throat. "This is for the Americans you abducted. For the lives you helped destroy."

Inches now, inches . . .

"I will kill you!"

But Milan had his way, plunging the sharp blade firmly into Mazur's neck, causing blood to squirt into his face.

He withdrew the knife and savagely jabbed again, thrusting the blade to the hilt, so deep into the soldier's neck artery that it came out the other end and stuck into the wood floor. Mazur's mouth opened to speak, emitting a gasp of breath.

Sometime during the fight, Milan had heard the bang of the Steyr-Hahn and now saw Horbachsky lying in a pool of blood. The key, he thought. *Get the damn key.* With the knife stuck firmly into Mazur, he searched his pocket, found the key, and then raced to free Johnston.

The plan was to set the hallway on fire. It would prevent anyone from following them into the tunnel. He knew there were at least two more enemy combatants——the pock-faced Gurko and the physically-cut Potapov. Were they on the premises? The gunshots were an alarm. If the soldiers were in the building, they had heard the blast.

Milan held the Molotov and flicked the cigarette lighter several times. "C'mon light . . ." he said impatiently. "Light dammit." The silver lighter was a gift from the Party on the tenth anniversary of his membership. He knew it worked. He had used the lighter last month to smoke a cigar.

Suddenly a burst of gunfire erupted from the doorway.

It was Gurko.

Milan rolled back into a safe position against the wall and set the unlit Molotov on the floor. Bullets zapped the armoire, narrowly missing his head. He grabbed the AK near Mazur's feet, pressed against the armoire, and then fired the assault rifle in the direction of the doorway. Bullets shredded the walls, forcing the Russian to retreat into the hallway.

After a second, Milan did a turkey peek toward the door and was nicked in the shoulder. He gripped the warm rifle and fired again until the trigger clicked——out of bullets.

Milan pressed against the wall and pointed to the empty magazine on the assault rifle. *No ammo*, he mouthed to Johnston. *No fucking ammo!* The Marine, who was hunkered down inside the closet, leaned out and shot cover fire.

Gurko ducked away.

Milan tugged on Mazur's body, took a magazine from his pocket and jammed it into the rifle.

After a few seconds of ear-ringing silence, Gurko appeared at the doorway and attempted to reenter the room. As he did, Milan jerked the trigger to *ack, ack, ack, ack*.

The sergeant went down.

Milan snatched the lighter and flicked it twice. He let the rag catch on the Molotov, before hurling the bomb into the hallway. There was an explosion, followed by a whoosh of sudden fire. He shielded his face from the heat. When he looked again, Gurko was flailing his arms wildly, trying to douse the flames.

Milan got to his feet and took a step.

The severely burned Gurko was on his knees, somehow holding the pistol. He made a threat in Russian before Milan fired three rounds toward his stomach. The sergeant fell forward heavily and landed on his forehead.

By then the flames were spreading across the wallpaper and lashing into the bedroom. Johnston came up beside him, shielding his face in the V of his elbow and rushing into the burning hallway.

"Let's get out of here." Milan removed his finger from the trigger.

"I need a second . . ." Johnston picked up the briefcase Gurko had dropped and returned to the room.

Milan grabbed him by the shoulder and gave him a shove toward the closet. As they made their escape into the passageway, down on their knees and crawling, he wondered: where was Potapov?

THE STRING QUARTET launched into a quirky piece, blending Franz Josef Haydn's *Emperor Quartet in C* with Bedrich Smetana's *Quartet No. 2 in D minor*. It was masterfully performed. The skilled violinists used a tremendous amount of bow, unafraid to bottom-out, while reserving their best artistry for the closing stages of the song. The brilliantly arranged piece, which Father Sudek had assembled the previous winter, put a smile on the judge and prompted a spontaneous applause from the audience.

Josef Novak was first to stand, and roar, "Bravo."

Dal was enjoying it, too. His foot dancing. His head swaying. He was hypnotized by the seamless melody, under a kind of trance. A man lost in his passion for classical music, he was no longer fixated on Ayna Sahhat or plotting for control of the village or feeling the angst of being a traitor to the Motherland. An uneasy truce had been reached. Like everyone in the church, he was riveted by the strings, rooting for the quartet's triumph. Had the KGB envelope not fallen from his lap, the magical lure of Smetana would have captivated him for the remainder of the recital.

He picked the envelope up from the floor and tapped it against his leg. Even here, seated in the nave, listening to the breathtaking works by Smetana, it was impossible to escape his administrative duties. He moaned. He had grown frustrated with the constant interruptions, the steady flow of paperwork on his desk, the round the clock phone calls from the KGB director in Prague, and the locals who visited the villa daily to complain about their lives. Had he reached a point in his career where a post like this was intellectually beneath him? Most likely.

Of course, some at the Lubyanka would call him lackadaisical these last few days, maybe even a detriment to security, certainly worthy of a demotion. And there was truth to such claims. He had slipped up. He was slightly horrified to admit it. But true. However in defense of his recent behavior, the fever, the nausea, and the horrendous throbbing in his head had made it difficult to concentrate on the day-to-day work, especially the bureaucratic aspects of managing the district.

Perhaps he did have dengue.

He had spent much of the last 48 hours drinking vodka to cope with his sickness, when really, he needed medicine.

Then again, Dal could argue that ignoring medical attention and attending the recital had been the correct decision. If anything, he was certain of his good judgment. Today's recital served as a peaceful outreach, an opportunity to build upon his shaky relationship with the citizenry. There was need for peace now that he had finally broken their headstrong resistance. He deserved a break from the

Devil Dog stress. After all, the entire operation had fallen into an anxious waiting game. What more could he possibly do until next week when the prisoner transfer took place?

Dal took a silver flask from his pocket and had a sip of vodka. *Damn headaches.* At times, they were intense, much like the brain experienced after consuming a frozen drink too quickly.

It was only after Tad Kriz had seized command of the audience by slicing up his solo piece that he opened the envelope and had a read. He was expecting a routine update, word on Zdenek Seifert, or perhaps a report concerning the roadblocks. But bad news? And of this caliber? His bloodshot eyes zeroed in on the words printed below the official KGB seal:

FARMER KILLED IN AUTO ACCIDENT WAS CIA

His neck stiffened. He had suspected the man was State Security police. Not CIA. How was it even possible? How could the Americans have discovered the events in Moravia and tracked them to this tiny, insignificant village near the Austrian border so quickly? Given the turbulent state of affairs in Czechoslovakia, it was nothing short of an intelligence miracle.

The CIA agent, according to the message, was conspiring with officers in the military, possibly members of the government in Prague. Among documents found in the man's hotel room was a list of clinics located in Bohemia and a photo of Dr. Milan Husak.

Dal's hands trembled.

He recalled the *Chicago Tribune* and how easily Milan had caught the baseball. All along he had believed the Czech doctor was hiding something. Never been to the United States? He should have pursued that claim days ago. No doubt the American culture piqued the doc's interest. But was he a spy? He remembered passing the Škoda near the bridge. Why was Milan's car parked there? And why wasn't he at the recital?

Dal jolted to his feet. "Dear Lenin," he whispered, distraught Devil Dog may have been compromised. "What have I done?"

AYNA WAS the type of person who could read Kafka in the tavern on a Saturday night, amid drunken shouts and cheers and fights, never needing to reread a page.

It was no surprise that she pressed into her bow without looking up from the sheet music, unaware that the colonel was charging across the pew, that he was pushing people out of his way, and that he had sent Emil tumbling to the floor. Her ears told her the quartet was in the midst of a dazzling performance, a rare, magical moment. Sascha, she thought happily, must be looking down from heaven, proud of this day.

. . . then all at once everything changed.

She lost her timing when instrument by instrument the music fizzled away and she heard Tad whisper, "oh, fuck." Her eyes drifted from the music stand and she heard a collective gasp of shock from the audience. Dal was breaking for the door.

Her face loosened with disbelief. The dream of playing in Prague had turned into a nightmare. She might have been the last member of the quartet to stop playing, but she was the first to leave her seat. "Don't disrespect us," she shouted, charging after him with a firm grip on her bow. "This is our day . . ."

She slipped abruptly between a throng of bewildered people, including the judge, and sprinted for the doors.

She smelled smoke.

Outside, a black fire cloud billowed over the rooftops.

Someone screamed, "The villa is burning."

The street resembled a war zone. She stood for some moments longer and watched the concert goers scramble in the confusion. Had a plane dropped a bomb? Her eyes hardened like steel, searching for Jiri, before she came to her senses.

No, this was not an attack.

What then?

A second later, a sound like a swarm of killer bees grew to a deafening growl. Milan's Škoda was speeding toward the square. Oh, god, what had he done? *He promised not to get involved.* Her stomach was in knots. Her eyes flashed on the colonel. He was already on the cobble with his pistol drawn——his target Milan's Škoda. He shouted something in Russian and knocked off several rounds at the passing vehicle.

People screamed, ducked, and ran for cover.

She placed her hands over her ears.

At that point, anything might have happened, like Milan crashing or Dal turning his gun on her. She was terrified, then relieved when Milan drove safely away from the square. The bullets appeared to have missed him.

She stood motionless while Dal dashed toward his sedan.

Her impulse was to stop him.

She kicked off her clogs and ran stumbling through the crowd. He had already slipped in behind the wheel and turned the ignition when she approached the driver's side window.

A pig farmer stood next to her. The man was pounding on the windshield and his swine was blocking the vehicle. "I have a grievance," he shouted.

Dal rolled down the window and thumped the farmer on the chest. "Idiot," he said. "Move your pigs."

She wanted to get in a word.

"Soldiers came to my farm," the farmer yelled above the revving engine. "They shot five of my livestock."

"Shut up."

"What are you going to do about this crime?"

"Go away."

"I demand compensation."

"Stand back."

"But my pigs?"

Ayna thrust the point of the bow toward Dal's face, but the irked KGB colonel put the car in gear and backed away.

She missed, stumbling.

The sedan bumped into a parked Renault. Dal shifted into drive and crept forward, scattering the remaining farm animals.

This time she reached into the window and grabbed him by the throat. "You bully," she yelled. "Leave Milan alone. He has done nothing to you." Her nails dug into his skin and she tried to punch him, but he pushed her out the window and accelerated away.

Ayna stayed on her feet. She wasn't done. She refused to give up and darted across the square in lightning speed, chasing the car for a block until she was out of breath.

At an intersection, Dal's sedan sideswiped a van, then struck a startled Ota Janus, who flipped over the hood and dropped a worn pamphlet of the *Communist Manifesto* on the street.

She collapsed on the cobblestones while the car sped off. Maybe she should have gone for the key in the ignition switch. Maybe she should have found a way to hang on to his arm for a second longer. Something. Anything.

She heard footsteps, people approaching and calling her name. Someone asked, "Are you okay?"

She went numb.

Did it matter if she was okay?

The bell had stopped ringing and Bedrich was standing next to her. He was wheezing, out of breath. His normally pleasant face was rigid and unrecognizable. He, too, was no longer smiling. He, too.

"WE CAN DO this," Milan shouted. The Škoda was marked with bullet holes and had a cracked windshield. "We just have to drive to the border. That's it. Simple." It felt like the top of the 9th inning and his team was up 9-2. He was thinking about baseball, of all things. Maybe it was his competitive nature, the memories of yesteryear flooding back to him. Knowing Johnston was from Houston, he was about to ask about his favorite team, the Astros, or maybe the Yankees, or the Dodgers, when he crossed paths with Potapov, who apparently had not been at the villa, rather was milling about town. Two words flashed in front of his mind: bad luck. They were at an intersection near the hardware store. The Ukrainian soldier was sitting behind the wheel of the GAZ truck, about to stuff a cake into his mouth, when their eyes met——Potapov, Milan, and Johnston.

There had been a hesitation, a moment of disbelief, Milan kicking himself for not having instructed Johnston to hide his face below the dashboard and perhaps Potapov wondering what the POW was doing in the doctor's car.

Milan jammed the gas pedal to the floor and accelerated into high speed, passing fields, several farms, and a feed store. He snaked in and out of oncoming traffic, passing cars ahead of him, a flatbed Praga truck, a Volkswagen Beetle, finally a tractor that was slowing everyone down. A half-mile beyond the monastery, he steered sharply into a series of s-curves.

"You're a crazy son of a bitch," Johnston said with a grimace. A bullet had pierced his leg. At the time, it seemed more of a nick, though was oozing heavily.

The car roared through another curve. After the wet road straightened out, Milan flashed a nervous smile, doing his best to remain poised. "We have got to find a place to pull over," he said. "And take care of that wound."

"No problem here, sir. I'm fine."

"The goal is to save your butt, not let you bleed to death."

"But the documents . . ."

Milan looked into the rearview mirror: Potapov was some distance behind, maybe a quarter mile. Should he stop to take care of Johnston's injury? Or drive on? Johnston had accidently lost the Steyr-Han in the tunnel and the AK was low on ammo. They could not win a gunfight without bullets. Pulling over, he decided, was too risky.

. . . so he drove.

To help stem the flow of blood, he grabbed a towel from the backseat and placed it over Johnston's wounded thigh. "Apply some pressure," he said, feeling a sharp pain in his shoulder where Gurko's bullet had nicked him. He grabbed his satchel from the backseat and instructed the Marine to take a needle, the morphine, and inject himself. Always, as he spoke, he was positive and reassuring. One way or the other, they would eventually ditch the Soviets and reach the border.

"I have to tell you what happened," Johnston said. Rain was pounding hard against the windshield. "About my abduction from 'Nam . . . why they brought me here . . ." He attempted to explain what had happened since his kidnapping, but it was difficult for Milan to grasp the complexity of the Soviet scheme. Even with Johnston as living proof of KGB crimes, the trafficking network that stretched from Hanoi to Vientiane to Prague to Moscow seemed unthinkable, more like something from a farfetched spy novel. "Rats," Johnston kept saying. "Giant rats everywhere they locked me up . . ." His words were mostly unclear as he spoke of the Viet Cong, the bamboo cages, the beatings, and the flesh-eating rodents. He leaned his head back, stared up at the ripped interior, and whispered, "motherfucking rats, sir." The morphine had set in.

To keep him alert, Milan told Johnston how he had served in the U.S. Army during the war and for several minutes, with the cool air rushing into the vehicle, he talked about the resistance forces and fighting the Nazis. "We socked it to them," he said, before becoming aware of the briefcase sitting in the footwell. "Hey——I don't get it. That briefcase. Why retrieve it? What could be so important that you'd risk getting burned in the fire?"

"Proof," Johnston said deliriously. "There is more to my story, sir. You won't believe it."

"What do you mean?"

Johnston snapped opened the case and grabbed the documents. "Me. Williams. Thomas. The list of Marines doesn't stop there."

"More abductions?" Milan said. Clearly Frank had not told him everything. Horrific visions of soldiers and airmen bound by chains and wasting away in a damp cell flashed across his mind.

"By my count, eight more, sir."

The photos, the faces of Americans attached to the documents, spoke to the horror and the secrets bureaucrats in Washington D.C. were trying to keep from the American people. Milan's shoulders flexed. How could the United States government let this happen? They sent American sons to the hellhole known as Vietnam to fight for freedom. Yet according to Frank, a shadowy figure close to the president had made the decision to abandon the search for POWs in Czechoslovakia.

In some ways, this was the part he had the most difficulty with. The Washington cover-up and a possible understanding with the Soviets stank to high heaven. How could the cowards in the White House, in Congress, perhaps even at the Pentagon, sleep at night knowing servicemen like Johnston were living a hellish nightmare on foreign soil? Did the president know anything about abducted servicemen? What about previous administrations?

His foot pressed harder on the gas pedal.

If anything, the search for prisoners and missing military personnel should never end. Every damn stone must be overturned.

"I am going to bust this conspiracy open," Milan said. "Expose KGB crimes. Then help identify the lowlife scum in Washington D.C. who left you behind."

At the river, where a fence was partially collapsed, Milan slowed and turned onto a service road, one of several roads that were not on any maps.

Here, the country road was overrun with weeds and botched with potholes. It had been shoddily paved by the Germans in the late 1930s, and neglected ever since. There was good fishing out that way, Josef Novak had told him days ago, and if he drove long enough he would eventually reach Strazkov, a lumber town, where the baker made regular deliveries. Milan was trying to decide if he should perform roadside surgery on the man's leg, wait until they reached a clinic, or risk driving straight for the border, when from nowhere the GAZ truck slammed against the rear bumper.

Milan jolted into the steering column. Recovering quickly, he cut the wheel sharply and drove onto the side of the road, smashing through a dilapidated fruit stand. Pieces of wood dinged off the vehicle's hood and roof. Without braking, he sliced back onto the cracked pavement. Mud tore beneath the spinning wheels.

"We've got problems," Milan said, detecting a knocking from the engine. "I think we took a bullet in the radiator. And maybe in the motor." He had pushed the Škoda to its limits, the speedometer touching 120, and sensed the car was in trouble. Multiple fender collisions had destroyed the alignment and the wheels wanted to veer into the other lane.

"How far to the border?"

"Not sure. Can't be far."

Milan locked his grip on the wheel and kept the car steady when from nowhere the GAZ truck rammed against the bumper, shooting Milan and Johnston forward. Milan kept the wheels centered in the lane and floored the accelerator. He was glancing over his shoulder and cursing. Then found some breathing room after Potapov swerved onto the side of the road.

. . . moving.

. . . in the downpour.

The Škoda charged over a single lane bridge and entered a bend in the road near the river.

Up ahead——*was that a large pothole in the pavement?*

Milan leaned into the windshield, trying to see through the slashing rainwater. At the last second, he jerked the steering wheel and avoided the hole . . . and a spinout.

Right on his butt, the GAZ dropped a wheel into the pothole and bounced on the road. Potapov lost control of the truck and drove off the pavement, steamrolling through a cattle fence where the vehicle flipped onto its side.

Milan looked into the rearview mirror and pumped a fist. "Dasveedanja," he shouted.

He could already smell the Austrian air.

There was a kind of inevitability to the day. What had begun with optimism in the warm sun of 1945 would soon finish in the heavy rain of 1968. Milan knew this. He had been running for nearly a quarter century and was tired of the deception. He felt guilty for leading Ayna on, when all along he had unfinished personal business to deal with, like his own personal tragedies, and now saving the

Marine.

With Potapov out of the picture, he could ease up on the gas and concentrate on the next steps of evading the Soviets, avoiding the police, crossing the border. But ignoring his thoughts of Ayna was impossible.

For a split-second, prior to the colonel's gunfire at the church, he had seen her shocked face and felt like a schmuck for all the secrets of recent weeks. What he imagined must have been one of the most exciting days of her life——taking center stage with her cello——had ended disastrously. Was using the recital as cover to save the Marine selfish? Yes. If she had any sympathy for him, she would pray for his escape. Hopefully she would understand why he had to rescue the Marine and expose KGB crimes to the world.

The cracked pavement ended at the remains of a World War II German garrison. He pulled over and opened his satchel. Johnston was reclined in the seat, his eyes partially closed and a hand on the bloody towel. Milan found a gauze bandage and tied a tourniquet around the Marine's wound. It would have to do. "Hang in there, buddy," he said. "You're going home."

He cranked the ignition. In all, less than fifteen minutes had passed before they were back on the muddy lane.

NEAR THE MONESTARY, Dal had had a decision to make after the road crossed the river: proceed or take one of the service roads into the forest. At the time, staying on the main road seemed the logical choice, the most direct route out of the valley, where the doctor's Škoda could outrace the more sluggish military truck. However the road eventually led to a roadblock. He knew Milan was aware of the roadblock and that he would have no problem finding refuge at a farm with conspirators eager to help plot his next move. What was his final destination, anyway? The only sensible choice was Austria. Yet time was of the essence. Sure, he could make a phone call and shut down the frontier crossing within the hour. It would bring the daring escape to a halt. Except that sort of kneejerk reaction would only implicate him. Questions would surface: an American Marine in Mersk? Devil Dog? Sascha Boyd? If there was any hope for his future, he had to finish this messy business himself.

When Dal failed to see any skid marks on the road, he second-guessed his decision to head east. The doctor, he reconsidered, had no intention of risking a day or two hiding at a farm, looking for ways to smuggle the POW to safety——after all, twenty-three Soviet Army divisions occupied the country. Milan was the sort of man to make a sprint for the victory line, not fall back and consider other options. If this were a chess match, it would be the type of match to end in less than ten moves. Milan was bold enough to enter the guarded villa; he would be brazen enough to drive straight for the border in broad daylight. Dal's heart raged. There had been another road, a narrow country lane with potholes that split between a farm and the river. He had explored that road the previous week and knew it meandered south, eventually arriving at Strazkov. From Strazkov, one could easily reach the border. It was a feeling. After another minute he slammed on the brakes and turned the car around.

THE RAIN had stopped.

By then, the Škoda had a flat tire and its exhaust pipe was clanking against the muddy road. With the last of the motor oil pouring from the engine, the car had driven longer than Milan expected. He spoke to the sputtering vehicle, encouraging it to get past one more row of trees or some shrubbery or the next creek. He would take whatever the car would give. Another mile? Maybe two? It was wishful thinking. Within minutes, he felt a loss of acceleration when the car seized up and rolled to a halt.

Milan leaned back in the seat. "Dammit."

He got out of the car and looked at a map: they were in the foothills of the Bohemian Forest. The middle of nowhere, he realized. Then maybe that was a good thing. There were fewer Russians to worry about out here——if any. He had a sweep of the landscape: they were surrounded by a meadow with tall grass and a patch of woods on either side of the road. If he could get the car hidden in the trees, the underbrush and limbs might provide camouflage from anyone in pursuit, time for the Marine to regain his flagging energy.

"You need to keep moving, sir." Johnston was slumped against the passenger door with the briefcase.

"Let me think."

"You're wasting time."

"We're both getting out of this alive. Give me a second. I'll come up with something." Hopefully Johnston wasn't as weak as he feared. But a wounded man . . . under the numbness of morphine . . . persisting off of adrenalin . . . there was no telling what might happen. He could go into shock.

"There's a lot at stake," Johnston said. "I'll only slow you down with this bum leg. I'm dead weight."

"Stop with this quitter's mentality."

"I'm only being realistic, sir."

"It's the morphine talking." Milan folded the map. "I'm taking you to Austria."

"They'll eventually find us. We'll both be dead by sundown. Take the briefcase. You know what's on the line. Go."

The decision to stay or leave weighed on him. Milan looked down the desolate road. It stretched for five miles until it met the river, then veered south toward a bridge. Beyond the bridge the road led to Strazkov. He could find help there.

"Strazkov isn't far from here," Milan said. "I will get a car. I'll come back." He considered pulling the Marine from the Škoda and carrying him into the woods. Good idea? Bad idea? Moving him could initiate new hemorrhaging, so he decided against it.

"Just go to the border," Johnston pleaded. "And don't come back for me, sir."

"Hang in there, gunny. There's a cold beer waiting for you in Vienna."

Milan placed the assault rifle in Johnston's arms, the barrel pointing out the window. Already he had second thoughts about leaving him alone as he walked vigorously away with the briefcase. How much time did he have? He was unsure. Dal was likely on the hunt. With luck, maybe he had gotten lost or turned back at the garrison.

The road curved slightly along a creek.

It was sprinkling again.

He felt a chill from the wind.

RETURNING TO the county road, Dal pressed on with a sense of urgency. He scanned up ahead for the escapees, the muddy side roads, the overgrown fields. Where were they? A lesser man would have panicked. Not Dal. There was a gleam in his eye. He had come across skid marks on the road. Someone had driven through a vendor's fruit stand.

He slowed to drive around the scattered debris.

A minute later, he passed the overturned GAZ and saw Potapov's body lying face down by the front wheel.

He could smell victory, just as the sun was breaking through a mishmash of black and gray clouds——sweet victory. He no longer questioned the sequence of events leading up to this catastrophic day, rather remained observant, looking for signs of auto damage on the road, such as the broken tail light and the oil leakage he was following on the cracked pavement.

Like a predator, he was moving in for the kill.

MILAN HAD BEEN walking for fifteen minutes when he came upon a large standing snag and a rock wall separating the road from an open field. An elderly man wearing a raincoat was fishing at a pond, near the crumbling remains of an ancient stone house.

"You there," the man said, "hello."

"Good day," Milan responded.

"Out for a hike?"

"Not exactly." Milan wiped the rainwater from his eyes. "How is the fishing?"

"Not bad. Care to give the rod a try?"

"I haven't the time." He was looking for the man's automobile, instead he found a bicycle leaning against the wall. It would do. "I don't have time to explain," Milan said. "I need your bicycle. I'm sorry."

"What on earth are you saying, young man?"

Even as he tossed the briefcase into the wire basket on the handlebars and peddled away in the mud, Milan wondered why he had bothered to apologize. Stealing an old man's bicycle was about as low as it got.

DAL BRAKED. Up ahead, beyond a row of spruce trees, was the broken down Škoda. The POW sat in the car with an AK jutting out the window. Where was the doctor? He flicked his cigarette onto the road and pulled in behind the car's crushed rear fender.

Was Milan hiding?

He stuffed a smashed pack of cigarettes into his pocket and climbed from the sedan. He was acutely aware of his surroundings: the meadow with its speckled yellow flowers, the tufts of trees and an outcropping of rocks. He slipped the Makarov out from the boot holster and cautiously walked to the Škoda's passenger door.

This could be a trap

Johnston was leaned back against the seat, staring into the upholstery. He seemed to be in a drugged-induced state of mind. There was a bloody hand towel on his thigh and a hypodermic needle in the footwell.

"You don't look good, comrade." Dal nudged the barrel of the rifle away from his face. "If you do not mind me saying so, you look like hell."

Dal's hard eyes scanned the muddy road, which curved around a distant hill. He sensed Milan had marched on, seeking help in the next village.

". . . scumbag." Johnston was speaking to him. "In the end you lose. Taken down. A failure." He closed his eyes, breathing slow and even.

Dal lit a cigarette, the last in the pack. "To think. I had spared your life. And this is how you thank me? By calling me names?"

"Get lost."

Dal placed a hand on the roof of the car and leaned into the window. "Russell Johnston . . . all along, you have reminded me of my sarcastic brother. He was a good-humored man with an unusual outlook on life. However I am starting to rethink things. You are actually more like my old army comrade named Yuri. Yuri was a man whom I admired for his loyalty to the Soviet Union. After the war, he was captured while taking photographs of B-52s at the Royal Air Force Station in Warrington. He was strong when it came time to face his interrogators in London. He never opened his mouth to make a confession to British intelligence. I understand he died a very painful and gruesome death keeping secrets for Stalin. Lucky you, I do not have time for torture."

"You're too late," Johnston said. "He has already reached the border. With proof of your crimes."

"Proof?"

"The doctor has the documents."

"Lies."

"You showed them to me, remember? You're fucked. It's all in that briefcase . . ."

"You are lying to me."

"Fucked," Johnston said again, this time with a grin.

PEDDLING IN the mud and up a hill, most men would have succumbed to exhaustion. Not Milan. He leaned into the handlebars and breathed in short gasps. Focused. Determined. Driven. His legs burned as they propelled the bicycle onward. He was fortunate to have made it this far. And yet he cursed his survival. It was torturous to go on. If anyone deserved to die, it was him, not the Marine.

In the army he had been trained to understand the bigger picture:

that on the way to winning a war many battles might be lost, including the loss of good men. This sort of thinking was a page right out of Sun-Tzu's treatise on the *Art of War*. He understood the logic. That the war was more important than the battle. But leaving the Marine to die was an option he refused to accept. Johnston's life was a battle worth winning. He could save him, plus deliver the documents to the Austrians. He would have it no other way.

He kept his eyes on the front tire spinning on the road and peddled vigorously. *You. Can. Do. This.* Moments later he heard a gunshot blast in the distance and told himself it was the sudden backfiring of a car or perhaps a hunter's rifle. He wanted to believe anything but the cold truth: that GySgt Russell E. Johnston was dead.

DAL SPREAD his bloody hands over the Škoda's hood and felt the engine heat. The car, he estimated, had broken down less than an hour ago. There was still time to find the physician. He could not have gotten far on foot. He placed the automatic rifle in the back seat of the sedan and sped off down the road.

Having left the concert-goers in a frenzy, with black smoke on the streets, he was relieved the documents had not burned in the fire. After all, recovering them had been a state priority. Failure to return the secrets to Moscow would destroy his reputation; worse, it would launch an investigation.

Thing was, he could survive the death of the POW. There had been an exit plan, orders from his fellow conspirators to execute the prisoner at the first sign of trouble. This was just done. But the Devil Dog dossier? No. He must find it. The KGB investigators were fierce. They would become suspicious and ask questions about its unexpected disappearance. With little effort, they would learn about the plot to smuggle Johnston to Cuba, and arrest everyone involved. Such things were not easy to hide once there was smoke.

He groaned. His demise would come quickly, regardless of his many personal triumphs in the Balkans, in Czechoslovakia, and the numerous medals earned over his career. In all likelihood government agents would move quickly to close the loop and murder him before the first question was even asked——poisoned, shot in his sleep, hung from a belt. They would make it look like a suicide.

He shuddered. For the first time since he had put on his KGB uniform some decades ago he felt the dread of impending failure.

The road lifted, cut through a mat of forest, and then flattened onto a barren shoulder of a hill. Dal was beginning to think the doctor was no longer fleeing on foot. Had he hitched a ride with someone?

Soon he came upon a pasture and a series of hedgerows. Feeling hopeless, his thoughts turned to Olga and his children, how much he would miss them: the picnics in the country, the hunting trips with the boys, telling embellished, larger-than-life stories about the many adventures he had had during the course of his career. He flashed to his young mistress in the Georgian SSR. Delicate. Beautiful. Exciting. He felt responsible for her wellbeing and worried she would return to a life of prostitution. So much human tragedy. And all because of him. For greed. For selfishness. For ego. Many lives would pay the price for his decision to turn against the Motherland. Too many lives.

He looked into the rearview mirror without pride, shaken by his own downfall. What had happened to the man who once stood unquestionably loyal to the Soviet Union? He did not have an answer. That face, tense, anxious. Who was he now? A stranger. A fallen comrade. Someone he no longer recognized. He knew only one thing: that he would surrender to KGB authorities with dignity, rather than seek political asylum or attempt to claw his way out of trouble. Dal had made his bed, he would lie down in it. Being forthcoming with his crimes——telling the truth exactly as he knew it——might save his family from a life of humiliation and harassment. The Dal's were patriotic citizens. His oldest son, Marc, was enlisting in the army that winter.

He slumped into the steering wheel. He had heard the heartbreaking stories of other officers who had fallen from grace, their careers torn apart, their families ostracized from society. He never believed it could happen to him. Until now.

He was looking for a place to turn the car around when in the distance a bicyclist appeared on the road.

. . . his last chance?

. . . maybe.

With luck, the cyclist had seen Dr. Husak wandering along the road. It was a long shot, and desperate of him to think this way, but entirely possible. Would the cyclist cooperate? Would he answer questions truthfully? He realized the man would likely be unhelpful, lying for the sake of pride. Czechs did not rat on their brothers and sisters. They were loyal to each other. He was considering how best to ask the questions, when he realized it was unnecessary. The man on the bicycle was Milan. He was a full hedgerow ahead of the sedan, hunched over the handlebars like a cyclist on the final leg of a race.

Dal braced himself, his mind devoid of all rational thought, of the past, the present, for the future. He was simply reacting: he had identified his target and was moving in.

He pressed his foot on the accelerator.

Faster.

Closing the gap.

In his haste to run Milan down, he did not recognize the T in the road and hit the brake at the last second.

Milan bolted right, onto a paved road that led toward a wooden bridge.

With the skill of a racecar driver, Dal downshifted into the turn, the tires screeching on the asphalt while he accelerated the nose of the sedan toward the bicycle. Trouble was, he had not seen the cow standing in the road.

. . . the collision was equal to that of a head-on impact with a small car.

MILAN HAD no idea a car was roaring down on him. When he heard the crash, he shot a glance over his shoulder and watched the yellow sedan flip onto its hood, sparks shooting up against the pavement. He could not believe his eyes. Of all times. Of all places. Of all things. Why an accident now?

The car slid to a stop in the long grass at the edge of the road. His immediate feeling was that of inner conflict. What was the right thing to do? He felt tugged between moving on to find medical assistance for Johnston or helping the injured driver. He had an obligation, he thought rapidly. To Johnston——a victim of his own government's cowardice to live up to a promise to bring him home. And to the servicemen who had been abducted from Indochina. Their horrible fate in Vietnam, Laos, the Soviet Union, wherever they ended up, must be exposed. Yet leaving someone in pain, possibly to die in the overturned car, was not an option either. He finally made up his mind and spun the bike around to help.

Somehow he would have to make this quick.

Somehow.

Halfway to the wreckage, his back stiffened and his hands locked onto the handlebars. He had made a mistake. The man crawling from the car was Colonel Dal.

Milan took another half-peddle forward and stopped.

DAL UNBUCKLED his seatbelt and pulled himself through the window of the overturned vehicle. Damn cow, he was thinking. There were shards of glass stuck in his arm and a small piece of glass embedded in the skin near his eye.

He stood on the pavement. Everything was occurring in slow motion. Gasoline spilling onto the road. The fallen cow moaning with a broken leg.

. . . and the physician peddling toward the bridge.

"Going somewhere?" he whispered. "Not so fast, doc. I want my fucking documents."

He reached into the car and grabbed the AK.

Milan was already halfway across the bridge when he put the rifle to his shoulder and pulled the trigger——but missed.

Dal took a step. There was gasoline spilling onto the pavement. It had reached the lit cigarette he had been smoking prior to the collision and the overturned car burst into flames. He moved away from the burning sedan, taking up position in the middle of the road. Everything about him was executed in a methodical, overtly professional manner. The way he flexed his shoulders. How he drew in a deep breath prior to pulling the trigger again.

This time the *ack* of bullets struck Milan and sent him headfirst over the front tire.

. . . the bicycle tumbling.

. . . the briefcase toppling onto the bridge's deck.

Dal lowered the rifle and watched Milan struggle to his feet.

The physician's will to survive was impressive. Then again, likely it was the body reacting to fear, pushing him on, in the way a headless chicken runs amuck in the moments after decapitation. He felt no empathy and fired off another burst of gunfire, 7, 8, 9 bullets. The projectiles hit their mark and Milan fell face down onto the wood planks.

"Spokoinoi nochi," he said in Russian. *It is over for you, comrade.*

He shouldered the rifle and started walking toward the bridge, into a freshening breeze. He felt his wet shirt, probably blood in the area of his ribcage. There was a memory that came to him, that week of hunting in the Siberian mountains with the boys, the day they had shot a Bull Moose, and afterward when he had given them instructions on how to field dress the animal.

He walked under a line of trees, unaware the side of his face was bloodied. With the death of the physician, he would save Brezhnev from global humiliation. Earn another medal? Absolutely. However medals meant little to him these days. Medals were for the young and those seeking validation.

He approached the bridge.

. . . there was a gust of wind.

. . . and another.

At first, the cool air was a welcome gift on his burning face. He needed this. It momentarily soothed his headache and the stinging in his eye sockets. But the briefcase, he discovered with sudden horror, had landed next to the bicycle tire and broken open——the dossier papers spilled.

He mumbled something in disbelief when the wind kicked up and the papers began to flutter across the planks.

Was he seeing things?

He dropped the rifle and broke into a sprint, his knees kicking up high, his arms pumping. If the papers blew over the bridge, it would be impossible to recover them. He ran, showing no emotion. He ran, reaching for a lifeline. He ran, feeling like the slowest human being on earth.

. . . but he was too late.

A flurry of wind blew most of the documents between the horizontal rails, hundreds of pages, one by one, gone. When he arrived out of breath, he leaned over the rail and saw the papers floating on the river beneath the bridge, swept away in the gentle rapids.

He stood motionless with the wind shrieking in his ears and with his eye swelled up and his lungs heaving. A document or two was stuck to the wet planks near his shoes. He bent over and picked them up, then stared numbly at the secrets printed on the papers, before crumbling them into a fist.

He hung his head.

He was no longer angry, rather was flooded with guilt and shame.

Several minutes passed before Dal turned his attention on Milan, who was lying face down on the bridge, his glasses fallen from his face. "I have heard of many incredible prison breaks in my lifetime," Dal said, finding a kind of consolation in speaking to the bleeding man. "Prisoners escaping barefoot across the frozen tundra. East Germans tunneling to the West. But this escape? Even in failure, it must be the most impressive of all. Mmm. How did you do it?"

There was not any sunshine now, only overcast skies and steady wind.

Dal huffed, stepped away from the rail, and then crushed Milan's glasses with his boot.

"Listen . . ." Dal's voice was gloomy and downcast. "I want to tell you what happened. About that moment in my life when I first recognized the disparity between the people with power and those who are powerless." He searched his pockets unsuccessfully for cigarettes. "During the war," he began with a sigh, "my unit had been reassigned to the assault on Berlin. It was during the final weeks of the fighting, in what had become Germany's darkest hour. There, in the heat of battle, we came upon German troops embedded in the city's rubble. They weren't real soldiers, of course. The typical German man of fighting age had already been killed or taken prisoner. What was left to defend Berlin was nothing more than a ragtag citizen army. Teenagers. Grandfathers. The wounded. Nevertheless they had weapons. And their intent was to kill us.

"After a brief gunfight, white flags were raised, one after the other, rising from the shattered brick and mortar debris of a once spectacular city. 'Nicht schiessen,' the Germans shouted, their arms high above their heads in surrender, 'don't shoot.' It was odd, for we had not expected them to give up so easily.

"I remember thinking, where is the honor? You have come this far, why not fight to the death? Oh, looking back, I suppose they were too exhausted to fight on; like most soldiers, they were eager to return to their loved ones and rebuild their lives. And why not? Europe had been decimated. Enough was enough.

"But it was an accounting problem for us. I have often wondered the exact number of men who surrendered that day. One hundred? Could there have been more? Possibly. On the other hand, there were only ten men standing in my squad. And with shellfire screaming overhead, we were pissing our pants as they streamed forth from the rubble."

A thick, purple blood oozed from the corner of Milan's mouth.

Dal was certain the physician was listening, and pressed on, his words bringing the past to life. "A few blocks away there was a burst of machine gun fire and the crushing steel sound of tank treads rolling along the ruined cobble. Our comrades were caught up in a bad crossfire and needed reinforcing. In some ways, this mass surrender was an act of aggression——a diversion. Because while we amassed the Germans at gunpoint, good Russian soldiers were being shot at on nearby streets. No doubt some of them were killed.

"And yet I sensed it was a test for me. As a result of bravery in battle, I had recently been promoted to the rank of non-commissioned officer——leader of my squad. And so I asked myself, what next? What must be done? We could not possibly take these Germans prisoner. At the same time we could not let them go free."

Dal looked into the sky and closed his eyes. It felt good to speak of the fighting in Berlin. He had never spoken so intimately of the final days of the war.

"I made the decision to have them lined up in single-file rows against the remnants of a library wall," Dal pressed on. "I ordered them to keep their hands high above their heads. 'Eyes closed,' I yelled above the shellfire.

"Now before I say more, you must understand, my men, including myself, we were frightened out of our wits. Any soldier, as I am sure you are fully aware, who tells you he is brave in battle is lying to you. Really, we were just men. Ordinary men. Like the Germans. Wanting nothing more than for the war to end and go home to our families. But there was no cease fire in effect and my soldiers looked to me for strength in a time of bloodshed.

I gave the orders.

It was clear what had to be done.

'Fire,' I shouted.

And they fell.

"We quickly pulled together a new line of them. And shot them, too. We repeated this over and over again. I had not expected them to be so submissive, without raising a voice in protest. Had we attempted to shoot them as an entire group, which was the impulsive thing to do, chaos would have ensued. Human instinct, the need to breathe air, would have pushed them to fight for their lives. In sheer numbers alone they had the advantage and could have easily overwhelmed us with their bare hands. But it was the order, the systematic way in which I carried out the executions before their downcast eyes, in concert with how I instilled terror into their exhausted minds, which enabled ten Russian soldiers to overcome more than one hundred Germans."

Dal pushed Milan over with his boot so that he was lying on his back and they were looking into each other's eyes. "This *thin wall* that separates the strong from the weak? If the truth be known, it is only as strong as the fear that cements it together."

He pointed his Makarov calmly at the physician——in the same sympathetic way a rancher might put a horse out of its misery——and then he shot a bullet into his head.

And he was not afraid.

For Bedrich had mounted many roofs in the village, including the library, the marionette theatre and the rows upon rows of houses, all connected by a single red roof. Today, however, was the first time he had ever climbed to the top of the church. That was what made it different and why Bedrich believed he had accomplished something significant. Even his hero Josef Novak, big, muscular, strong, Josef, had never climbed so high.

He leaned against the slanted roof and scooted along tile by tile. In places the stucco, red baked against the warm sun, flaked off and stained the palm of his hands. There was a cadence in how he moved, left hand, right foot, right hand, left foot. Always leaning just so, and careful now of the wind. He identified loose tiles based on their weather stains and avoided them. Only once, when a pelican landed nearby, and he paused to marvel over the beautiful white-winged creature, did he lose his concentration and accidently kick a wedge of stucco, sending it crashing to the cobble below.

And people were there; a crowd gazing up with their hands over their mouths. Men and women shouting, "come down" and hollering "be careful." And some, he thought, calling him a "fool."

But Bedrich knew what he was doing. He was not a fool. He was a skilled roof climber. With his experience, he safely inched his way toward the steeple and sat with his chin to his knees. He had never felt such a thrill. Here, he was taller than the trees and gazing across the rooftops he saw the sparkling river and the road stretching for miles. Endless, it seemed to him.

He had many questions and counted them on his stubby fingers: why did Father Sudek allow the Russians to harass the citizens? Why did Father Sudek allow the Russians to shoot Sascha Boyd? Why did Father Sudek allow the Russians to burn their favorite books? Why did Father Sudek allow the Russians to arrest Ayna?

He dug into his pocket and found the decomposing remains of his mouse. He missed the creature's appetite for food and how it hobbled along on three legs. The mouse, his tiny, dear companion, had been a good comrade, a loving comrade. He dangled the carcass by the tail and looked into its dried-out eyes. Why, of all things, did Father Sudek allow the Russians to kill his mouse?

With a tear in his eye, Bedrich pried up a tile and solemnly buried the rodent beneath it.

HOURS AFTER the recital's disastrous ending, with long shadows stretching across the square, Ayna was feeling sick with worry about Milan. She stood on the cobblestones with Father Sudek, Josef, Oflan, and Evzen, and listened to the townspeople gossip about what had happened that day.

"Who was in the Škoda with the doctor?"

"Had he set the villa on fire?"

"Will the colonel arrest him?"

Bedrich's antics were an additional distraction. How the clumsy halfwit managed to clamber atop the church baffled everyone. For several minutes, they stopped talking about the shooting, the car chase, the judge fleeing town, and gazed bewilderedly toward the red roof.

How did Bedrich do it?

There were no ladders leading to the roof. And the stairwell inside the bell tower was rotting and had been in disrepair for many years, making it completely inaccessible.

Josef's best guess was that Bedrich, even with his portly body and short legs, had somehow climbed the bell's thick-knotted rope, before making his way onto the bell and out a window——a feat previously accomplished by a handful of delinquent teenagers.

"I've seen him climb many walls," Ayna said, doing her best to ignore Evzen, who was smiling grimly to himself. "The walls at the old monastery are no challenge for him. These walls, even higher, must be easy, too."

Oflan started to theorize, then stopped, and said, "Oh forget it. What difference does it make how he got up there? The simple fact is, he must come down."

"He knows what he's doing," Ayna insisted. The urge to call him down was strong. She fought it off. "We shouldn't scare him."

"I agree." Josef nodded. "Let him be."

Father Sudek thought it over. "We don't need more people hurt today. There has been enough violence on our streets. Look at Ota Janus, dead in the street. And Emil's broken wrist. Enough is enough."

Evzen said, "Bah. Bedrich has lost his mind."

Before she could defend the halfwit's risky behavior, Ayna heard someone whistle and screech, "KGB!"

She glanced over her shoulder. People were scattering, men, women and children running for their homes, toward alleys, jumping into cars. As they cleared the street, she saw him. Dal. He was standing on the cobble.

"This isn't good," Josef said. "The colonel has that crazed look."

"He must be stopped," she said. "Finally. Right now." She regretted raising her white flag that morning. Whatever Milan had done, she supported his actions.

"Mmm," the priest muttered.

". . . that same crazed look," Josef elaborated. "That look we saw in 1945 when the Nazis killed Ayna's father."

EARLIER, AFTER commandeering a station wagon from a newlywed couple who had unsuspectingly stopped at the bridge to help, Dal took a spade shovel and buried Milan and Johnston in a shallow grave. He was unremorseful for the slayings, and offered no eulogy or even a moment of silence for the dead. He just needed to bury them, hide the evidence and return to Mersk. Working mechanically, he scooped dirt over their bodies, then covered the ground with leaves and fallen oak tree branches.

He walked to his car, then drove to a store near the farm collective. His eye was black and swollen. There was blood on his clothes and hands. People dropped their items and fled the store.

"I want no trouble," the clerk begged. "Take what you want."

Dal grabbed a bottle of vodka, some aspirin, a carton of cigarettes, and left without paying. While he drank, his feelings of denial slowly gave way to bewilderment and anger for the loss of the Devil Dog dossier in the river. He really was fucked, exactly as the POW had warned.

Dal had swigged a third of the bottle by the time he parked in front of the hardware store and stumbled drunkenly from the driver's seat with a crowbar.

THE PANDEMONIUM on the cobble went on. Total mayhem. Like someone had yelled fire in the cinema house. *He's got a crowbar. Blood on his shirt. Run for your lives.* In the rampage to get off the street, people shoved each other and cursed at friends, forgetting for a moment they were neighbors.

Ayna was running, too. It felt cowardly. She was unafraid of him. Why was she running? Someone gave her a violent push and she stumbled into Oflan. Jiri scampered ahead, before falling behind. She quickly lost sight of his red-striped shirt in the stampede, passing through the bakery's narrow door and stopping behind the pastry counter. After the last person stuffed inside the store, Josef quickly shut the door and rammed home the bolt.

"We're out of harm's way," Josef said. "The colonel can't knock down this door. It's too strong."

"Why does he have a crowbar?" someone asked.

"Get control of yourselves," Josef insisted.

"What if he has a pistol," another said, "or a machine gun?"

"I will think of something." Josef raised his hands, hushing their voices. "This isn't the time to panic."

Ayna was skeptical. She knew the colonel was unrelenting, but tried to remain calm and cleared her mind. Just breathe, she told herself. Everything will be okay. She brought herself under control and began to search for Jiri. "Where are you?" she shouted, her eyes darting between the bodies, people taller, people shorter, all stuffed together inside the bakery like cattle waiting to be slaughtered. He must be in the room somewhere. Ayna felt herself start to tremble, a cold sweat forming on her forehead.

AFTER MAKING an attempt to look somewhat presentable by tucking in his blood and dirt-stained shirt, Dal lit a cigarette. There was an arrest to be made. *Maybe multiple arrests.* He staggered along the row of shops and houses with the crowbar in one hand and the vodka in the other.

As the streets cleared, he tried to imagine how the doctor had pulled this damn thing off. Dal had put procedures in place to prevent intrusions. It tore at him, the breakdown in security. At the end of the day, the Ukrainians were experienced prison guards and Gurko was as dependable as any soldier in the Soviet Army. That a civilian could somehow enter the secured villa and free the prisoner from captivity boggled his mind. There must be a logical explanation. Culprits. Yes. Culprits. *Who were they?* Ayna Sahhat was the only citizen capable of leading any kind of treachery. She was cunning. She was unafraid. She had tested him time and time again.

"If I can catch her once upon the hip," Dal said in slurred words, reciting from Shakespeare. "I will feed fat the ancient grudge I bear her."

He recalled the play *King Lear*, Scene seven of Act three, when Cornwall hastily plucks out the eyes of Gloucester as his servants watch in horror. That bloody scene was similar to what was taking place in Mersk. The people running from him, scurrying for the protection of locked doors, they were much like the fearful servants in that play. Instead of a fictional king, they had rejected the will of a high-ranking KGB political officer, having served Dal and his policies with prejudice. *Whom among them could he trust?* He put the fiery vodka to his lips and drank. He remembered now, yes, he had convincingly played the part of Cornwall in the army theatre, and recalled his sense of empathy for the character, against the feelings of those in the audience who saw him as a monster.

"Where is the anarchist Ayna Sahhat?" he asked Irena. The woman kept her head down, rushed inside the library and locked the door.

He moved into the street and stumbled toward the tavern. It seemed only fitting that his vengeance began at the local watering hole, the hornet's nest of Bohemian treachery, where the late hour plotting of evildoers went unchecked like hungry mice in the night.

He placed the vodka bottle on a slatted bench and peered through the windowpane. Tad Kriz and his children, the reclusive Pavel, and the viper-like Verushka cowered behind tables. He delivered lines from *King Lear*, words rolling from his tongue with grandiose flair, phrases he had not recited in years. "What confederacy have you with the traitors?" he asked spectacularly. He became exasperated when they failed to respond to the question and thumped the palm of his hand against the door. The onlookers backed away from the window. He gripped the crowbar and began thrashing everything in sight: a welcome sign, the door handle, a pot of flowers. He heard women screaming and children crying and swung the crowbar more furiously.

As he shattered the tavern's window, Pavel appeared at the doorway and said, "ge-ge-get a hold of yourself."

Without difficulty, Dal overpowered the lanky chauffeur and shoved him to the ground. People hiding behind tables and chairs urged Pavel to run. He put up his hands and attempted to protect his head, but Dal gripped the crowbar and bashed his skull with a spray of blood.

"Ayna," he shouted, grabbing the vodka and proceeding on. "I know you hear me. Surrender."

Moving into the square, pooled here and there with black puddles from the afternoon downpour, he returned his attention to the last of the fleeing citizens, a window shutting, a car driving away, a dachshund slinking into a side street. Even the street musician had dropped his accordion and ran for his life. They had vanished from the cobble, scurried away like roaches caught in sudden house light.

Now Dal had center stage.

This was his moment.

Feel their mesmerized souls, he was thinking.

He scanned the square. Where was she? What was she thinking? What was her next move? With the cigarette dangling from his lip, he began to speculate over which home harbored his pretty anarchist. "Aiding and abetting the enemy is a crime," he warned, fumbling with the bottle, which slipped from his hand and shattered on the cobblestones. "Do you people understand the penalty? You will be imprisoned for conspiring against my authority. And yet, I suspect there are heroes among you. The librarian? The jeweler? The banker? Who has the courage to bring the girl to me?" Again he scanned the upstairs windows, the closed doors. "Citizens of Mersk. Consider this proposition wisely. Bring her to the square. There will be immunity for the whistleblower. And a handsome reward."

But no one stepped forward with the Azeri woman.

Dal fumed.

He could take them one by one and put them to the gun, interrogate them. Eventually everyone talked. "Ayna Sahhat," he said. "Do not defy me. The punishment will only become more severe the longer you hide." He fell in and out of character. One minute he was clearheaded, the career political advisor wondering what had gone wrong in Bohemia, the next he was Cornwall, wicked, vengeful, Cornwall.

Dal wiped his forehead with the back of a hand. The situation was ugly. There were no winners in today's mess. Both he and the young woman had suffered a great deal——she from a lonesome desire to be loved and he from his sworn duty to uphold the laws of socialism. Yet he did not pity the girl or her wicked curse. She had rebelled. She had disrespected him. In her secret plotting she would fail. He alone would decide when the final curtain fell.

With a firm hand on the crowbar, he bashed the windshields of parked cars and plodded toward the charred fountain. There were pigeons. And breadcrumbs. And trash. Annoyingly there was also pig excrement in his path, which he blindly stepped in. "These uncultured peasants," he said to himself, scraping his left boot against the cobblestones. "How can they live like this?" The smell turned his stomach. He would arrest that pig farmer. He would fine him triple the penalty for not cleaning up after his animals.

Slowly he calmed down, catching his breath.

He noticed Jiri sitting crossed-legged at the fountain, with his back against the parapet. The boy was reading a magazine, in all likelihood unaware that he was alone in the square.

Dal approached, his shadow overcoming the magazine's glossy pages. Jiri looked up with a faint nod of hello and removed his headphones. "What's wrong?" the boy asked. "You have blood on your shirt. And what happened to your eye? It's swollen. You look like a Cyclops."

Dal towered over him, intoxicated, though broad and strong. As Jiri had pointed out, the shard of windshield glass had completely swelled shut his eye.

"We had a little accident today. That's all . . ."

AYNA WALKED to the bakery's paned window. "The colonel can't bully each and every one of us," she said, attempting to rally the people. "We outnumber him. We are hundreds. He is one." And yet the sound of his voice——*do not defy me*——sent shivers up her spine.

Someone said, "Hey, he's going after Jiri."

Her eyes darted in desperation. She could not find her son in the bakery, though was certain he was somewhere. Wasn't he? Oh, my god, she thought. Had she confused him with another boy who was wearing a similar shirt? "What are you saying? Where's Jiri?" she asked. "Where's my son?"

"He's outside," a boy said. "With that freaked out colonel."

"IT'S BEEN A bad day," Dal said to Jiri. He set the crowbar at his feet, and then shook a cigarette from a pack. "It's true. A bad day for the ages. Some day when you take on more responsibility in life you will have disastrous days like this."

"Uh, if you say so."

"Days like this are best defined not by how they start, rather how they finish."

Jiri looked suitably confused. "The people are mad at you."

"Oh?"

"For ruining the recital."

"Yes, yes. The quartet performed like a well-oiled machine."

"Yeah, until the ending . . ."

"Ah well, there were two dangerous criminals on the loose. I had to apprehend them. To protect you. And to protect everyone in this village. That's my duty as a KGB officer. Mmm. I cannot expect you to understand, but my actions were in your best interest." He paused, rubbing his forehead. "Really. I had every hope for your mother's success this afternoon. I was rooting for the quartet. I had even planned to declare today Bedrich Smetana Day."

"What's the deal with you? You look irritated. Are you mad at us guys for giving back the uniforms? Our parents made us do it."

"No. Not mad."

"What do you want then?"

"Do you smoke?"

THE COLONEL was leaning into Jiri with a cigarette when she arrived. "Leave him alone," she barked, smacking it from his hand. "Don't you dare touch my son."

Dal tossed up his hands in mock surrender. "I've been calling your name . . ."

She stood in front of Jiri, her body a shield. "You've caused enough trouble."

"You seem confused by the facts. Your friend. The doctor. He is someone who stirred up some very serious trouble."

"Where is he? Where is Milan?"

"Ah . . ." He grinned. "I've piqued your interest, eh?"

"What have you done with him?"

Dal made his hand into the shape of a pistol and stuck it to his temple. "The hottest love, so it goes, always has the coldest end." He pretended to pull the trigger and said, "Socrates. Though I do not think the tragic fate of your lover is actually what the Greek Athenian philosopher had in mind when he wrote these famous words."

Milan shot? Was he dead? Her heart sank, though she remained strong for Jiri. Had to. "Go find Josef," she said, pushing her son toward the bakery. "Stay with him until I come get you."

"It wasn't my intent to harm the boy." Dal watched Jiri scramble away. "I'm a father, too. I am only interested in your role in today's scandal." He picked the cigarette up from the old stones, where it had fallen next to the crowbar, stuck it between his lips and struck a match.

"Why are you doing this?"

"Because the doctor couldn't possibly have rescued the prisoner from the villa by himself." He blew smoke through his nostrils. "He must've had help. Who?"

"I wouldn't know."

"Tell me. Who are the conspirators? Who helped the doctor rescue the prisoner?"

"What prisoner?"

"Don't play games with me."

"I'm not."

"Names," Dal persisted, slurring his words. "Was it the baker?"

"I have no idea."

"The priest?"

"I don't know."

"Why protect them? You will spend the rest of your life in prison for lying."

"I told you," she insisted. "I don't know anything about a prisoner."

"And the fire at the villa?"

· "Or the fire." She stared at his puffy black eye. It reminded her of a burnt cake.

Dal grumbled. "You have this way. Always pushing back like a door that refuses to close."

"You're not wanted here."

"Ah, Czech hospitality has left a bad taste in my mouth." He shook his head and gazed across the square. "Do we really need to go down this road again? Most of your comrades understand what is at stake. They have fallen in line."

"You may confiscate our guns," she said, taking a moment to choose her words. "Control our printing press. Close our church. All in our 'best' interest. However you and your Moscow thugs won't take my soul."

"Ah, that language makes for good theatre," he said. "But in reality?"

"It's true."

"You say that now. But have you already forgotten? Will you still be thinking this way in prison? Away from your son? When you are not around to watch him grow up? No. You won't. Trust me. You won't."

Ayna squeezed her fists. She had been holding herself together by willpower alone and now nothing else mattered. Not her life. Not Jiri. Nothing. When the colonel glanced over his shoulder, again reminding her that she stood alone in her crusade against his legal authority, her anger had reached a boiling point and she flailed madly at his swollen eye, jolting his head. She punched again, surprised he dropped to a knee so quickly, without swinging back.

She caught her breath. Her tremors produced in her a state of shock. *What next?* Dal had his hands over his face and was moaning and grunting like a dying animal. His defenseless posture seemed like surrender. Had he given up the fight? No. It was wishful thinking on her part.

She inhaled through flared nostrils and took a step. Instead of running for the bakery, where Josef stood at the door calling her name, she picked up the crowbar and thumped the colonel on the shoulder, and a second blow, until he fell flat on the stones.

"Kill him," the butcher shouted from a window.

She heaved a lungful of air. Now was her last chance to act. Are you going to slay him? His head was exposed and she had a clean shot to crack his skull, but froze, unable to finish him off.

"Damn," he mumbled. "That hurt like hell."

More and more people yelled from their windows and doorways, "Do it" and "Bash his skull" and "Don't let him get away."

Dal did not seem to mind that the people were inciting a murder——his murder. He was wholly focused on his injury. While she stood there, he carefully squeezed the gash on his cheek, forcing the shard of windshield glass through the bloody flesh until he held the pebble size object between his fingers, and was inspecting it with childlike curiosity.

"Amazing," he said, flicking away the glass. "Amazing something so fricking small can hurt so badly."

Verushka screamed, "What are you waiting for, stupid girl?"

When she came at him with the crowbar, he grabbed the bar with a hand, rose to his feet, and shoved her to the ground.

Ayna landed hard, then scooted away.

"Too late," he sneered, hurling the crowbar into the street. "You hesitated. It's best to strike while the iron is hot."

She crawled toward the fountain, aware that her wrist, the hand she had used to punch him, was painfully limp. Was it sprained? Broken? How was she going to hit him now? She bumped against the parapet. There was no escape. This was it. *The end.* Turning toward him, she feared he was about to shoot.

. . . . instead he was taking off his leather belt.

And he whipped her. "Fear it," Dal said with bloody gums, reciting from *Hamlet*. "Ophelia, fear it, my dear sister."

"Leave me alone," she shouted, slapping away the belt.

Dal grew stronger with his theatrics while she crumbled at his feet. With a sturdy voice, he said, "And keep you in the rear of your affection."

"Stop," she said. "Please stop." She was curled up against the concrete parapet, in the shadow of Elizabeth of Bohemia's wings.

"When the blood burns," he went on dramatically, "how prodigal the soul lends the tongue vows." His Shakespearean rhythm was near perfect, even with an intoxicated slurring. "From this time be somewhat scanter of your maiden presence."

"Don't hit me," she pleaded. "Whatever you want. You can have it. I promise. Just leave us alone." He struck again, the belt wrapping around her bruised forearm like a snake. She attempted to stand, her knees cut and bleeding, but he nudged her with his boot and pulled away the belt.

"So speaketh Polonius," he concluded.

A stream of blood made an inverted Y down Ayna's neck. Her breath was rattled, her ears ringing. "You're insane," she whimpered, her body shrinking away.

Pinching the cigarette between his fingers, Dal paused, his eye vacant and blinking several times. "This sickness has interfered with my ability to remember the dialogue from the play. Tss. It's embarrassing. I am quite sure I missed a line or two."

He raised the belt above his head, like a master about to discipline his slave, when suddenly a rock crashed on the cobble and landed near his boot.

He lowered the belt.

Ayna brushed the hair from her eyes: it was Bedrich. He had tossed the stone. He stood at the edge of the square, beneath the shade of a birch tree, with his shoulders pulled back.

"Bedrich?" Dal said in disbelief.

Ayna leaned forward——awestruck. Bedrich was clutching another chunk of cobble. She thought he looked like someone else, a stranger, the stronger man hiding inside his deformed body all these years.

"Go away," she finally shouted to Bedrich, terror in her voice. "I can take care of myself."

"Of all people. Him? The village idiot?" Dal scratched his head. "Your Knight in Shining Armor?"

Bedrich set his lips tightly together. Not in anger, but in wanting to form a word. She had never seen him do this. Was he attempting to speak? She felt mesmerized, forgetting for a moment that she had been whipped, that her wrist was sprained, and that Dal was hovering with a belt.

Bedrich? What is it?

The halfwit stood there, his mouth open, the tip of his tongue moving between his rotten teeth like a man stuttering in silence until he uttered a simple, but clearly understood word, "No."

Ayna went numb. Hearing his voice made her jaw drop. He sounded Slovakian. She had always wondered what he might sound like. Now a thrill came over her. Bedrich had blossomed before her eyes. At long last, he was someone to be reckoned with. She could not help smiling, even with the danger he had put himself in.

"Well, well, what do you know?" Dal said. His eyebrow shot up quizzically. "The village idiot speaks."

"Bedrich, go away," she said again.

Instead of leaving, the halfwit reared back and pitched the other cobblestone, which landed near a trash can, nowhere close to the bemused colonel.

"How futile," Dal said. "Ah, to be expected from such an inept man." With a firm hand he reached down and picked Ayna up by the neck. His hands were large, his fingers wrapping around her skin like five squeezing pythons. "This is your last opportunity. Tell me. Who are the conspirators?"

She showed her teeth and attempted to bite his hand. Desperate, she made a fist, though never landed a punch. His hand was firm, beginning to compress, a reflex away from crushing her throat.

. . . losing consciousness.

. . . her world turning black.

When a rock struck Dal in the kidney and he released his grip.

Ayna rolled on a shoulder.

Josef stood next to Bedrich, and said, "Keep your hands off the girl."

Suddenly heels were clacking against the cobble. People were showing their faces, more and more of them stepping out from their shops and homes. Ayna saw them standing with rocks and other blunt objects taken from their homes——anything that could be thrown. An eerie calm swept over the square, like the somber quiet at a funeral service.

Dal whipped out the Makarov and pointed it at Josef, Bedrich, Oflan, Nadezda, and Pavel. He seemed confused, unsure who to shoot first, when an ashtray pelted him in the knee. He buckled, stammered back to a standing position. "I will arrest whoever threw that object," he said, pointing the pistol from person to person. "I order you. Stand down. Or else, you will be charged with a crime."

Next, a rock struck his hand and he dropped the gun.

Dal made no effort to pick up the weapon——he just stood there, tugging his wallet from a pocket and then flashing his KGB identification badge.

As he did, Ayna rose to her feet and ran toward Bedrich, her eyes jolting back and forth between Dal and the circling crowd.

Finally, Tad stepped forward with a piece of cobble. Amid a round of hissing and shouting, he heaved the stone and struck the colonel squarely in the forehead. The thud of Dal's skull cracking was grotesque, sounding like the dull knock of wood being chopped.

Dal faltered on his heels, flashing the badge. He had been hit by a wave of delayed shock and there was blood oozing from a laceration above his good eye.

She had no idea who threw the next stone. Or the stones thereafter. But the onslaught had begun, debris hurling from all corners of the square, striking the colonel's arms, legs, stomach, head. The objects knocked him backward into the fountain's ash-stained pool, where he landed spread-eagle like a fallen heavyweight boxer.

After the last stone skidded across the cobble, she heard Irena say, "The evil brute is dead."

Someone else said, "In the Lord's name."

Father Sudek stood on the church steps, hunched over his cane. His consenting eyes were beaming with the same sort of masterful expression he often wore when conducting the quartet.

Now she heard distant sirens, maybe an ambulance, maybe the police.

When she looked again the priest was gone.

She broke from Bedrich's sleeve and stepped cautiously toward the fountain. There was a man and a woman, not far off, embracing their children. Other people returned quietly to their homes and shops. A few like Tad and Emil, gathered behind her without celebration, in a sort of disbelieving curiosity. *Dead?* Dal looked pathetic sprawled out in the dry pool with blood on his face, his arms at his side with the palms facing up.

. . . still.

. . . any moment.

She leaned into him, her heart beating more violently than ever. The Russian monster was too strong. He could not be dead. *Impossible.* She listened to his sluggish breathing, what sounded like a slowing freight train, just one more burst of steam, one more rotation of the side rod, a final turn of the wheels. The impassive Josef looked on, a hand on her shoulder. From the corner of her eye, she saw Bedrich pick up the colonel's gun and stick it between his belt and pants, before hobbling away.

She stood there and observed Dal in his dismal state. There was blood trickling down his cheek. She was undaunted by his gory half-grin and slowly blinking eye. He was staring at her and no one else. He knew something, maybe a secret. Would he tell?

Battling for his last lungful of air, he faintly uttered a line from what Evzen said was Homer's *The Iliad.* "Once harm has been done," he gasped. "Even a fool understands it." There were some who swore these were not the words Dal had spoken, rather, they insisted he had recited a famous quote from the Roman poet Horace. "It is a sweet and seemly thing to die for one's country."

It did not matter. She had heard something entirely different. She was standing the closest to him and knew exactly what he said and what he had meant by it. A kind of guilty suffering rushed up and down her spine. She had been pulled into every despicable word that left his mouth and in silent confession she lamented how it made her feel.

At least it was done.

Ayna took a deep breath, taking in the enormity of what had just happened. The sirens had reached the square. The police. All these weeks later, the police. She felt her shoulders slacken and glanced across the cobble. The people were lingering, some were gazing at the colonel's dead body and others were picking up the debris, making little mounds of stones.

She saw a peacock, and the blind veteran, and then she went home to be with her son.

THE END

HISTORICAL NOTES

In late 1989, a flowering of peaceful demonstrations spread across Czechoslovakia. Known as "The Velvet Revolution," the protests led to the collapse of the Communist Party's control over the country and the subsequent conversion to a parliamentary republic. Decades of oppression had finally ended for Czechs. They rejoiced on the streets, at the Old Town Square, in the countryside, free once again to live their lives without government intervention.

The Soviet occupation of Czechoslovakia lasted for another year and a half. The last occupation troops left the country on June 27, 1991, just six months before the collapse of the Soviet Union.

On New Year's Day 1993, Czechoslovakia peacefully dissolved into its constituent states, the Czech Republic and the Slovak Republic.

In the 1980s and 1990s, Jan Sejna, a former major general in the Czechoslovak Army, who defected to the United States in 1968, claimed the Soviet Union had abducted U.S. servicemen from Korea and Vietnam and routed them through Czechoslovakia to the Soviet Union, where they were used in medical experiments.

In 1992, Dmitri Volkogonov, a military adviser to Russian President Boris Yeltsin, told a U.S. Senate committee that more than 22,000 U.S. soldiers had been taken to the Soviet Union from German prisoner of war camps.

That same year Boris Yeltsin told NBC news, "Our archives have shown that it is true—some of them (POWs) were transferred to the territory of the former U.S.S.R. and were kept in labor camps. We don't have complete data and can only surmise that some of them may still be alive."

From August 2, 1991 to January 2, 1993 a special congressional committee convened to investigate the fate of United States service personnel listed as missing in action during the Vietnam War.

At the end of the investigation, the Senate Select Committee on POW/MIA Affairs issued the following statement, "While the Committee has some evidence suggesting the possibility a POW may have survived to the present, and while some information remains yet to be investigated, there is, at this time, no compelling evidence that proves that any American remains alive in captivity in Southeast Asia."

To this day, the Russian GRU refuses to make public certain documents that could prove or disprove assertions that U.S. servicemen were sent to the Soviet Union.

We may never know the truth . . .

R. Cyril West
1 January 2014

ABOUT THE AUTHOR

R. Cyril West studied Arabic and International Relations at the University of Arizona. One of his earliest memories of the Vietnam War was in 1973, when he sat with other school children at an elementary school near Hickam Air Force Base and watched American Prisoners of War held by the North Vietnamese return home during Operation Homecoming. He hopes this novel will spread awareness about America's heroes, the 83,000 U.S. servicemen still missing from foreign wars. He lives in Portland, Oregon.

R. Cyril West
Email: author@rcyrilwest.com
Author web: www.rcyrilwest.com
Facebook: www.facebook.com/rcyrilwest

ACKNOWLEDGEMENTS

I am indebted to Chip Beck for writing the foreword to my novel, as well, for keeping me focused during times when the POW/MIA aspect of the plot felt very dark and I briefly considered abandoning the project. I am also indebted to my editor, Rachel Glenn, for her numerous readings and crucial edits that brought clarity to the story. I am grateful to the author and mentor Ron Terpening for his excellent criticism and advice, and the author Ron Argo for his encouragement. I would like to thank George Voorhes Jr. for his amazing art; Marty Pay, Al Guevara, Lou Colabella, Kenny Rohaly, Marcelle Heath, Danielle Workman, Jackie Booe, Danny Glenn, and my parents, for their incisive and helpful comments; and above all my wife, Kristina West, for believing in me during the endless hours it took to research and write this novel. And finally, though certainly not least, I would like to thank the people on my Facebook page for offering their support, and *likes*; and at the end of the day for honoring our POW/MIA heroes.